I0713042

What reviewers are saying about *Experiments At 3 Billion A.M.*

The tales in *Experiments at 3 Billion A.M.* are masterpieces of subtlety and suggestion, electric with emotional power, brimming with inventiveness, enigmatic, inconclusive and delicately drawn, touching, without being sentimental, evocative and often deeply unsettling and shocking. This then is that rare achievement, great writing and great story telling.

- The Future Fire: Social Political &
Speculative Cyber-Fiction

It is difficult to pigeonhole the stories' genres as Zelenyj is able to draw from a very extensive palette, enabling his prose to create a wide variety of colors and moods; this is some of the best slipstream fiction I have read for a while. Unconstrained by genre or convention he lets his imagination roam across an impressive variety of environments – from horror, science fiction and poignant stories of everyday sadness, but always with an innate sense of wonder and a deep humanity running like a gossamer thread throughout. He mixes his genres with the hand of an expert producing some really emotive pieces, sometimes melancholy, sometimes hopeful but always interesting.

- Sci-Fi Online

Zelenyj is an incredibly talented writer who works the full spectrum of speculative fiction with ease and the ability to blur out any genre lines you may care to draw. Science fiction, fantasy, horror, slipstream and relentless re-combination, Zelenyj does it all with a narrative clarity that makes for fast, enjoyable reading.

– The Agony Column

Mr. Zelenyj has an eloquent style of writing that gives each story a unique dark flavour and his vivid imagination brings the characters to life for the reader and takes them places they would never expect to go. Some of the stories pull on the heartstrings as they bring the reader close to the characters, but each story has its own dark place - some with brutal toothy malevolence while others are shadows full of emotional pain.

- Monster Librarian

For the record, Alexander Zelenyj's brilliant and bizarre *Experiments at 3 Billion A.M.* is a must-read. Zelenyj's fiction is both startling and a genuine comfort; his poetic tales accomplish the seemingly impossible by granting his reader the opportunity to experience the world through eyes wholly new. The slipstream stories contained herein, ranging from playful to outright apocalyptic, are unique and simply extraordinary. Captivating, charming, and a challenge to our preconceived understandings of life, love, and all things both worldly and otherworldly, the weighty *Experiments at 3 Billion A.M.* is a tome to be treasured.

- Brian A. Dixon, Editor,
Fourth Horseman Press

Gripping and enjoyable… a good collection of tales to keep on your bedside table…

- British Fantasy Society Journal

Experiments At 3 Billion A.M. surprised me from beginning to end…this fine collection is quite impressive, especially coming from an author I knew nothing about. Recommended.

- Horror Fiction Review

SONGS FOR THE LOST

ALEXANDER ZELENYJ

Songs For The Lost
Publication Date: 20 October 2014
Copyright Alexander Zelenyj

Cover and Interior Art copyright David Rix
Cover Photography and Exploration by Elizabeth Walker

ISBN: 978-1-908125-32-3

The following short stories originally appeared in a variety of publications:

The Fire That We Deserve – published in Terminal Earth anthology, Pound Lit Press, 2010; reprinted in Revelation: Volume IV anthology, Fourth Horseman Press, 2013

Your Bone Spider Will Find You – published in Rotten Leaves, 2011

Dying Days Of Treasure Spiders Everywhere – published in Structo, Issue 6, 2011

Through Fogs Deep And Fires Long – published in Sex And Murder, Issue 20, 2011

A Roman Plague – published in Revelation 4:4, Fourth Horseman Press, 2014

God-Eater – published in Technicolor Tentacles anthology, Library Of The Living Dead Press, 2011

Thank You, Baby-Stabber – published in Shotgun Honey, One Eye Press, 2014

On Tour With The Deathray Bradburys – portions of this story published in Ballads To The Burning Twins: The Complete Song Lyrics Of The Deathray Bradburys, Eibonvale Press, 2014

But One Day All Of This Will Be Gone – published in Writings On The Wall anthology, Seven Archons Press, 2012

An Angela Named Vengeance – published in Sex And Murder, Issue 17, 2011

Two Blue Eggs In A Silver Dream – published in The Medulla Review, 2011

Far Beneath Incomplete Constellations – published in Blind Swimmer anthology, Eibonvale Press, 2010

Come On, Night! – published in Pulp Empire, 2011

Black Lash Of Lucifer – published in Ballads To The Burning Twins: The Complete Song Lyrics Of The Deathray Bradburys, Eibonvale Press, 2014

Songs For The Lost – published in Way Out West anthology, Fourth Horseman Press, 2009

www.eibonvalepress.co.uk

Everywhere was green   *but no more.*

ACKNOWLEDGMENTS:

A lot of wonderful people offered their support, inspiration, friendship and wisdoms throughout the writing of this collection. They know why their names are here, and I hope they know how grateful I am for them:

My mom, of course; my dad; Dan and Cindy Zelenyj; Tom and Laurie Zelenyj; Lindsay McNiff; Kevin Durda; Rachel Blok; Claudio and Catherine-Mary Sossi; Nik and Leisa Pieczonka; Rachel Eagen; John Ditsky; Liam and Mara O'Donnell; Nick Angelini; Chris Piccolo; James Karlsen; Andrew Murphy; Ben Denes; Jeff Rogers; David Owen; Ian McIntosh; Dennis Hunkler; Mary Kaye Lucier and Luciana Rosu; Tania Amine Esquivel; Shannon Duench; Joy Donaldson; Sarah Sinasac; Lucyfur; Brian A. Dixon and Adam Chamberlain of Fourth Horseman Press; David Rix and Douglas Thompson of Eibonvale Press; and Elizabeth Walker.

...as well as any spectres I may have forgotten.

For Nik Pieczonka, mad scientist, mighty friend, and reliable keeper of the Vault.

CONTENTS:

Hide deep.

Three Billion And Six

An Introduction by David Rix

Emotions are there to sing about . . .

It is now the best part of six years since the clock first struck 3 Billion A.M. That seems a long time, for a writer, for a publisher and purely for human beings living their lives. For myself, my own 3 Billion A.M. ghosting of the roads still continues but it is the far stranger London streets that I am ghosting, not the Thanet Way. The press has developed from 5 titles to 25, yet still remains what it has always been – the delicate art of sitting at a computer trying to coax the world to leave me alone sufficiently to make a few books. Out there, many many more of you will have learned just what a ghosted road at 3 Billion A.M. is – and many many more of you will have learned to sing, whatever your singing language.

So at 3 Billion + 5.5 years (to be precise), plenty has changed – yet plenty more also remains the same. Perhaps indeed, the most crucial things. The pain and chaos of the world never seems to fade – the shattered glass that is the human soul never seems to heal – and just may be our companion for eternity. That's the depressing thought with which I shall launch this entire massive volume.

But bear with me . . .

If you have read Alexander Zelenyj's previous book, *Experiments At 3 Billion A.M.,* then you will have some idea what to expect. In terms of styles and affiliation, this new collection if anything only spreads wider. The list of genres that *Songs For The Lost* touches upon is a large one:

<table>
<tr><td>•</td><td>surrealism</td><td>•</td><td>fabulism</td></tr>
<tr><td>•</td><td>magical realism</td><td>•</td><td>weird erotica</td></tr>
<tr><td>•</td><td>literary</td><td>•</td><td>Bizarro</td></tr>
<tr><td>•</td><td>gritty realism</td><td>•</td><td>psychedelia</td></tr>
<tr><td>•</td><td>subtle to extreme horror</td><td>•</td><td>modern fairy tale/fable</td></tr>
<tr><td>•</td><td>science fiction</td><td>•</td><td>pulp</td></tr>
<tr><td>•</td><td>weird western</td><td>•</td><td>noir</td></tr>
<tr><td>•</td><td>weird war fiction</td><td>•</td><td>superhero fiction</td></tr>
<tr><td>•</td><td>children's fiction</td><td>•</td><td>poetry</td></tr>
<tr><td>•</td><td>urban fantasy</td><td>•</td><td>as well as other less defined things</td></tr>
</table>

This suggests a diverse range of styles, which is true, but you will find more here that is common than different, I think. The author is using these familiar genre trappings to perform a seduction – to give you a comforting wash of something familiar while at the same time acting as a guide beyond that familiarity to somewhere else. To a literary area that fits very well with the 'genre' that Eibonvale Press has embraced – slipstream. The literary writing that exists between the cracks, the parasitic fiction that draws on all yet is enslaved to none.

The result is that, as you read these stories, you will find them unexpectedly profound, challenging, harsh, painful and thought-provoking. Indeed, more than once you might find yourself shaken to the core – summoned to think and feel, or deal with events on levels that are rare for this or any kind of writing. And the reason for this is simple: the true main theme of these stories is not any kind of alien or apocalypse, god or phantasm, the main theme is very distinctly human emotion and human nature at its most extreme. Human pain on a level that is very real.

In many books, films and TV, the approach to pain and emotion are something that might be called casual and theatrical – a puppet show or pantomime, a spectacle rather than an immersive or actual experience. The action hero punched in the face, the tormented heroine wandering dreamily through the stage of a story, the ironic and jaded horrors of the slasher or torture porn genres . . . Often it is dismissed, and at the very least understated and unreal – even in much horror writing, where the basic mandate is to explore extreme experience. Meanwhile though, back in reality, pains and fears and horrors of all types tend to be squashed and smothered, censored and veiled, politely kept out of the way or hidden under a cloth. It suddenly turns out that fears are something we are frightened of, horrors are horrifying, and pains are painful. Who knew? And so we try to sanitize them from this world. But the result of that is a weird dichotomy, with the fake and fantasy world more immediate to many than the reality. This is something that may prove problematic since one can assume that such horrors, so deeply involved in reality, our natural instincts and what we are as a species, are something that need to be faced not forgotten. One cannot hide from horror without leaving oneself open to horror.

And the questions come . . .

How different are we at heart from a bloody and cruel nature? How do our capacities for nurturing and aggression fit together? What exactly is our role in the world? Are we then an entity seeking to rise above our natural roots or an animal with delusions of morality? Why is it that both of those options feel like a betrayal?

I am not sure that there are any answers to these questions yet – at least ones that attempt to acknowledge the inherent contradictions within us and the fuzzy non-absolute nature of all reality. However, by writing straight from the heart and with unflinching honesty, Zelenyj manages to do what many writers fail at and really takes some deep wading steps into the pains and despairs of reality and humanity, far far removed from the fantasy land of action heroes or space operas. It was this that made the stories stand out 6 years ago when the clock struck 3 Billion A.M. – and this only slightly smaller yet considerably more focussed volume certainly follows down that same ghosted road.

It's not that the 'message' of *Songs For The Lost* is one of universal despair though, by any means. This needs to be clarified. Just as in reality, our own darkest emotions and experiences rarely come with total blackness. The dark emotions – desperation, despair, regret, repression, pain, fury – engender a parallel need for escape, and with it a kind hope. In a way, one could even see this as the formation of a bizarre form of spirituality, though not in a particularly religious sense – and it is this rather desperate and illuminating hint of spirituality that forms the singing heart of the book. In spite of the hardship and horror and maddening, soul-destroying sense of futility that sometimes seem to fill the world, people still persevere, still go on living and hoping – even if that hope may be transmuted into a craving for some kind of paradise or redemption from without. And just as the concept of Utopia never really exists, so the concepts of paradise or redemption can shift and change – they may be positive, negative or illusory. And as with many quests for either escape or illusion, the costs can sometimes be high.

Beyond even this though is the effect it has on the reader, which is also far more complicated than mere black and white. My own first encounter with this kind of deeply emotional horror was the very complex film Suicide Circle (*Jisatsu Sākuru*) by Sion Sono – a film many regard as impenetrably murky, dark and even dangerous. But the first and greatest impression that film left was astonishment that having been dragged through such a wasteland, the end result was so life-affirming. After you pass through those valleys, it only leaves you with a realisation of just how beautiful beauty can be – how incredibly warm the human can be – and how precious and powerful life itself actually is.

Like *Experiments*, this is a big book – a big container full of a very strong and heady wine, intended to be dipped into and savoured. It will be a companion for a long time, maybe on those nights when you need a fix of human emotion in your quiet bed . . . or need to sing a song again, for the world or yourself to make sense.

Even one without either words or music, for the language of songs is infinite . . .

Foreword

by Brian A. Dixon

Ray Bradbury once offered advice to all those daring enough to take up a pen or challenge the typewriter: "You must stay drunk on writing so reality cannot destroy you." The threat, Bradbury knew, is real. His writings are a gift to all those fortunate enough to have ever become drunk off his prose. Alexander Zelenyj is just such a man. He has been drunk on Bradbury ever since he first picked up a copy of *The Martian Chronicles*. He discovered the battered paperback in the back of a classroom and, enchanted by the cover artwork, immersed himself in the novel, ignoring the day's lessons at school. *Songs For The Lost* is a testament to the fact that Mr. Bradbury proved himself to be a far more inspiring teacher. Zelenyj would go on to write intoxicating prose of the sort that proves none are more impervious to the brutal offensive waged by so-called reality.

When Alex refers to the author as Sir Ray Bradbury, he isn't being flip. His debt and devotion are transcribed in every line of his poetic stories, as evident as his debts to H. P. Lovecraft, China Mieville, Richard Matheson, and Gabriel Garcia Marquez. Bradbury's is a world that exists between genres, a place of signs and wonders in which the inhuman is introduced only as means of demonstrating who we really are. In even his most startling or unsettling tales there is something that charms us. Ask him about these stories and Alex will speak of the "romance" of Bradbury, that bewitching sense of comfort and beauty that accompanies those tales that deliver us beyond the boundaries of recognized reality. It is an uncommon quality in fiction. Once its influence is observed in this collection's tales of dark roads and higher powers, it signals what you will find in the literature from this remarkable author from Ontario, Canada.

The first short story I read by Alexander Zelenyj—my *Martian Chronicles*, so to speak—was "The Demon Takeover of Windsor, Ontario." As the editor of *Revelation* magazine, dedicated exclusively to publishing apocalyptic fiction, I was sifting through a slush pile of narrative doom and brimstone more brutal than anything described in the magazine's biblical namesake. Here was a story that piqued my interest with the title. Eyebrow raised, I began to read: "The voice in the plastic receiver at my ear had died along with the lights in the small convenience store." That's how it began. A tale as fleeting and mesmerizing as a kiss in the dark, this was a story of fear, of perseverance, of the collapse of our culture and the enduring dominance of nature. It was a tale that captured the human spirit and served it up raw, without any hint of condescension or glamour. I found myself immersed in a weird and wondrous universe that I was utterly unprepared for. I've been drinking up his words ever since.

As an editor and as a reader, Alex is continually surprising me. Like the best of bizarro geniuses, he stands as a talent who defies definition. Just when I think that I know what to expect from him, he'll unleash a work both experimental and astounding. Throughout the years he has proven himself to be a captivating storyteller, an accomplished scholar, and a dedicated professional. Alex is as comfortable composing song lyrics for the meta-fictional Deathray Bradburys as he is examining the mythological influences evident in modern cinema. In eagerly taking on alternate history and slipstream anthology projects alike he has risen to artistic challenges that would have left lesser writers retreating to more comfortable corners of their creativity. Through it all, his imagination and his boundless enthusiasm remain undiminished. There is an infectious quality about the words that he weaves. Believe me when I tell you that it is the essence of the man himself, the product of a personality both captivating and inspirational.

Those within earshot at the end of my day know that after more than ten years of editing *Revelation* magazine I have grown weary of the apocalypse. The undead are insatiable, that dusty road through a post-apocalyptic wilderness is never-ending, and the judgment of mankind is as inevitable as it is epic. The end of the world takes its toll. Truly great storytelling in this vein calls for an inspired approach, as in any genre, and no author is better suited to confidently guiding us beyond our limits than Zelenyj. There is something of the apocalypse in each and every one of his stories. Indeed, though we have published strange tales by talents from all over the world, he has graced the pages of *Revelation* more often than any other author. He has left his mark on the magazine and on each and every one of its readers.

Stories written by Zelenyj are inherently apocalyptic, imbued with a palpable sense of spiraling chaos and mounting unease, but after sampling the short stories presented in this collection you will learn that for him the end faced by mankind is only the beginning. Here is an author who eagerly deconstructs familiar literary genres before reassembling the jigsaw pieces into something astonishing and new. The title story offers a standout example. "Songs For The Lost" is a novella like no other. It is neither space opera nor fairy tale, though there are moments when it seems to be both. Though it bears the hallmarks of the American Western it is not beholden to the heritage of any one time and place. It is a breathtakingly beautiful story of solace and redemption. The longings and laments of its cast of misfit characters are familiar to us at once, even if those characters are alien to us all.

Songs For The Lost cannot be categorized, raising a worthy question. Why do we reach for books such as this? We read so that we may experience the world through eyes that are new, and the experience is never more satisfying than when we are in the hands of a storyteller as inventive as Alexander Zelenyj. From "The Demon Takeover of Windsor, Ontario" to "Songs For The Lost", his stories have quickened my pulse and set fire to my imagination. They delight even as they dizzy. Perhaps the experience is stimulating because this is not mere psychedelic fantasy. Dipping into the bizarro universe woven by his inebriating narratives is like peering beneath the cracked and peeling veneer of reality. Zelenyj is a mad yet marvelous seeker, an eccentric impresario, a conductor of dreams as charming and hypnotic as Rod Serling himself. Follow him and you will find yourself among lost souls touring abandoned hopes and forbidden dreams at the edge of an impossible paradise. Each story concludes with a wink signaling that he knows what you have always felt, deep down—that there is more to this life than meets the eye.

And therein lies the power of Alexander Zelenyj. We fill up our lives with the familiar, with mundane routines and ridiculous consumer products, laments and trifles and limitations. Through it all there is an ache deep inside of us. It is the ache of an unspoken truth, the key to surviving the destruction wrought by reality. Stories such as these share that truth, the promise that keeps us going. Life in this universe is more strange and dangerous and wonderful than you have ever been led to believe.

Two heroes gone,
but never gone
The ancient stars they burn strong.

THE FIRE
THAT WE DESERVE

And he woke. And he'd taken the fire from his dream and brought it with him into the world. And the world was on fire.

- Unknown

The rustle of the surf soothes. It's an old voice. It's been friendly to us two beach children for a very long time. It's offered solace to the world since the beginning, I think wondrously, as if this is the first time I've considered this idea. We're beyond reach of its foamy spray in our place on the concrete promontory overlooking the deserted beach but I yearn for its touch. We've been here for hours, watched dusk submerge the sun into the lake and the moon materialize as if from nothing overhead and colour the beach in winter light.

The lonesome sound of a loose chain knocking gently in the breeze against the boarded-up concession stand drifts to us. The stone fountains marking the length of the beach at regular intervals look like small sculpted shrines from our vantage. The wooden lifeguards' lookouts spike from the sand like miniature Wickermen, looking dismal and lonely devoid of watchful human occupants. Sand particles dance across our bare feet like the delicate touch of spiders. It's been too long since last we've visited this childhood haunt. In its care, I feel nearly safe, as it used to make us feel similarly hidden from the world during our youth.

"Let's get down closer to it," I say, nodding beyond the guardrail and towards the foamy shallows.

"Okay," she says, distantly. It's hesitance making her voice this way, removed. She makes no move to vacate her place adjacent to the monolithic totem pole rearing skywards. I examine her. It's the quintessential her. Shoulders bowed earthwards as if in obeisance to something divine; face round and pale and like the moon; eyes pensive and lost-looking; too thin, her simple garb of plain white t-shirt hanging raggedly over her bare legs, the dull green suggestion of the bikini she wears beneath peering through in the moonlight. I look beyond her: the totem pole at her side is stout, and dwarfs her small frame beneath its shadow. Its rolling basalt plain of carven visages seems to glare hungrily at her. Men have looked at her this way in her life. She's usually only looked away, and wisely, but the world's gaze has occasionally been as tenacious as the colossal carven eyes watching her now; distended and grotesquely immense, black wooden lips curling into malign leering mockery while she fidgets helplessly before them.

I urge her once more, "Please? Let's get closer."

"Okay."

We place our bare feet onto the peeling metal railing separating observation platform from beach – making certain to avoid disturbing any of the myriad corpulent spiders suspended in their sticky beds among the metal bars – and leap lightly up and over and into the sand. Its soft touch is welcoming. I feel young again leaping like this. We've discussed the simple and nostalgic joy of this very act and motion in this selfsame place too many times to comment on it now but I feel the need to do so besides. Still I resist, though, and only face silently the surf surging before us.

She takes my hand. It feels good. We're wholly transformed now, young again in this place, holding hands like child siblings do before this simple act of companionship grows awkward to the eyes of observers. We drift across the sand until the sun-stored warmth of its caress turns wet and cool beneath our feet – soon the tide is licking languidly about our ankles.

"Are you upset that I've made us come here tonight?" she asks in a subtly imploring tone.

"I've learned to trust your dreams," I tell her simply.

"I'm sorry about that."

"Don't be," I'm quick to say. "It's...It's amazing. I'm lucky to have seen it so many times." Fear tickles me along my spine, though; a feathery ghost-presence along the nape of my neck; a gusting breath over my heart.

We walk along the tide line. The languor of the day has been refreshed by the chill of post-dusk. A splashing sounds nearby and we look but find nothing in the white foam or murky depths beyond, and walk on.

We pause a moment later, at her behest. She faces the lake. I stare out, too. Its immensity makes us as motes, another pair of sand granules. It's the sea and the ocean and all the space of the world. I can't distinguish its conclusion and the darkening sky's beginning.

"The lake," she says, dreamily. "It's beautiful tonight."

"Very," I agree. "It's where we came from." I hear the immensity of the words, feel foolish and melodramatic until she responds.

"It is. I guess it's fitting, somehow, that…"

We haven't spoken of it since the day before, when she'd come to my house; taken my hand; cried; spoken with difficulty through her tears; explained her new dreams; reminded me of her old dreams, although I'd of course needed no reminding; explained that they've come together at last, old and new merged as she'd always known that they would.

I believed her, of course. As I always have. She's my sister, and she's shown me her queer truths countless times. I felt unprepared. She understood. I cried, too. She held my hand through it.

Then, today, near dusk, we'd come here to watch the spectacle, together in this place of old sanctuary for us; among the ancient rusted steel tangles of the jungle gym; the observation platform with its concessions and wooden benches overlooking the sand; and the beach itself, which took us into its sandy folds on many nights when we'd felt utterly abandoned in a bitter-tasting world but for each other. Drifting onto the property earlier, we'd felt like ghosts arriving at the time when the main body of beachgoers had been departing, bundles of blankets and baskets in tow, skin bronzed from their tenure beneath the sun. We'd watched the stragglers dissipate, too, like occasional sand specks blown at a zephyr's behest onto the abutting grassy sward to the rear of the beach and the adjacent lawns and sleepy neighbourhood streets beyond.

I feel calmer now, in our solitude, though only just. I murmur, "Do you think? I mean, do you *really* think…Tonight? That it's *tonight*?"

"…Yes." The old certainty infuses her voice. There is no more doubting: tonight is the time.

A pair of gulls appear from the darkness over the water and pass low over our heads. Their cries are unnerving. They remind me of children in pain, but of course I don't say this to her. A moment later and several more follow, imitating the wails of their predecessors. When yet a dozen more materialize from the air, she comments simply, "Look."

I nod. "Where are they coming from?" Where they're coming from isn't really the thought which troubles me, of course. They come from some innocent place: a distant beach; a strand of sandy knolls to the north; a copse of thin trees; nests; speckled eggs. But what urges their frantic and headlong flight? The unspoken question rides the air between us like a spirit presence.

She makes no answer to what I've said or left unsaid and when I look to her I see her staring fixedly along the tide line in the direction we're following. I pursue her line of vision – the long line of crabs scuttling from the spume astounds the eye; like medieval siege engines they roll forth in frantic waves towards the haven of dry beach country, while some of their prodigious number float lifelessly on all sides; armoured husks painted black with what appears some unknown fiery touch and bobbing heavily in the rolling shallows.

We watch together a while, bewitched by the spectacle. Eventually she says, "Because I wanted us to see it together. If I'm right and it's the end. I want us to see it. Like this. Together. Who else would I want to be with now?" She looks to me. Her eyes are haunted, desperate.

"Okay," I tell her, and add, "Me too...And you're always right."

She doesn't need to offer explanation, of course but, as is her nature, she seeks to besides. "You were the only one who helped during that time... You know. A sister couldn't ask for a better brother. It was a dark time. I felt so alone. But I had you. And I got through...I wanted us to be here together..."

She drifts off, and I'm crying and I know that she is, too. This mutual faltering disheartens me. I need her strength if I'm to stand and face this gathering wind and the squall it heralds. A younger brother learns to depend on his elder sister in these ways. I wait, and allow my ragged breathing to subside accordingly in the gradual mellowing of my hysteria. The tears dry on my face in the subtly energized air.

We stop walking without speaking of doing so. We scan the horizon in silence. Something stirs there. From the far west to the remotest east as far as can be seen. A black flickering in the lingering torchlight of daytime which limns the plane where water meets sky.

"Do you see?" My voice is soft, scared. I cringe at the weakness in it, so un-brotherly.

"Yes. I've seen this before." Her words drop firmly into the rising wind, as charged as the newly sizzling air.

I'm shaking my head. Somehow it feels as though I must make the gesture in accompaniment of the words, "I'm sorry your dreams have been this way. I'm so sorry."

"It's not your fault."

"Still I'm sorry. My God. Look at it. You were a little girl when you first..."

"It's okay. It's okay." The elder sister once again comforting and offering strength to the faltering younger brother. I resign myself to her greater courage, and ask:

"Will it...Will it hurt? Will it hurt very much?"

"...No."

"You're lying."

"I'm sorry."

The horizon surges blackly. A violent claret burns there.

"What did we do that...What did we ever do? To have this come for us like this? I mean, it's not...fair." I'm speaking louder now, in accordance with the rising wind, the sand lifting from earth and tapping at our faces.

"We must have done something," she says stonily, assuredly. "For something like this to come...Something like this can't be random. This... There has to be a reason for this."

It makes sense. I think of the wrongs that I've committed in my life, and those done to me and to my poor, sweet sister. There have been many when I consider closely. My heart clenches when I think of her as a child burdened beyond her years. I shiver in the wind. I blink in the sandstorm pelting my cheeks. We stand resolutely in our places in the face of it. There is a battering of our calves then: we look and see that the lake is spitting up its denizens. Carp and salmon pelt us, slipping in the current rushing between our legs, piling into each other where our legs bar their passage. Their silvery scales are blackened, as if burnt by some extremely powerful incendiary source. Several gulls and sparrows litter in the lake detritus about our bare feet, too, shrivelled and curled into themselves, feathers likewise scorched.

"My God," I mutter. A nausea is rising from my belly. I anticipate its arrival in my throat and wince, seek to swallow in an ineffectual attempt to sway its imminent presence.

She says, "I'm happy that mom and dad are gone. And spared this."

"Me, too," I say, watching the surging waters in the distance. "My God, me too." I add, "Despite what they were," and hope that I haven't said too much.

"We've all done something," she says. "Everyone's done something wrong. In an entire life, who doesn't? Collectively, taken together...We deserve this."

Pride fills me: she's my sister. This wise woman and predictor of inclement horizons. So mature and brave-eyed. She's not finished delivering her wisdoms, though.

"I'm glad we're here. I...I always feel young when we're here."

I smile at the words, somehow. Somehow they've urged this impossible reaction from me in this tremendous moment. "Me, too. Always."

We watch the horizon. It seethes. It moves in so startlingly vast a manner that it spellbinds the eye. It indicates the scale if not the enigmatic nature of the calamity stirring there.

It's been on my mind all day. I let the words out into the rising gale wind. "I never forgot, did you know? I always remembered and I always believed you. That day when we were kids, and playing in the backyard. You'd seen...this. You'd seen *this*. You'd fallen asleep on the lawn chair with a comic book across your lap. I was reading in a chair beside you. You woke up screaming. You tore the comic in half. Two pieces. Completely in half. You screamed so much. You flailed around on the patio. Mother ran out from indoors, losing her mind, thinking you'd been bitten by a snake. She never believed anything you told us, of course. About that. Like she never believed everything else, too." I gesture waterwards, and say, "You screamed this picture out loud. I was so scared, because I believed you. I always did. From that afternoon onwards especially. You were only six years old. And so many times since then, too. You saw this."

She's nodding. Emotions are vying for ownership of her features. She succeeds in maintaining a stoic gaze trained towards the brewing horizon. She's so grateful for me but she's always been the stronger of us.

We've remained on the same course during our walk, parallel to the tide line, but the water level's risen substantially within the past several minutes, as has its temperature: gone is the lake's cool touch, replaced with a monstrously amiss warmth that burns the skin. Something thuds into my calf. I look and see the stiff gull, its soaked and charred feathers imbuing it with an appallingly pathetic appearance. It's been blasphemed – I notice then that its head is missing. A thick layer of ashen black surrounds the wound. We're examining it wordlessly when a human arm bobs between us: long and burly, it had once belonged to a robust man. It, also, is charcoal black, and crumbling in long strips in the pitching current.

She gasps a moment later. Her hands fly to her mouth as she seeks to stifle a cry which she doesn't completely succeed in doing. I look away, too, but likewise not before witnessing the collection of blackened limbs roll in with the perverted tide; legs and arms of varying sizes, several torsos and loose heads like black coconuts bobbing in the scalding waves. Meat pieces which once formed whole men and women; flesh components of sailors and fishermen and families enjoying their final midnight sail. Three-quarters of a child drifts towards us, severed roughly from the knees downwards; face absent in the wake of a great ash countenance flaking apart in long sheets of black. An amorphous lump, festooned with seaweed clumps and which holds some lingering indefinable semblance to a dog or other large animal rolls past us, slapping the packed sand as it's hurled beachwards.

An enormous wooden plank rears from the surf nearby, remnants of a boat carcass; turns about wildly; disappears in the spume like a giant ladle into a violent cauldron. An ashen buoy rises from the depths, too, and is likewise interred beneath the weight of roiling water immediately after appearing.

The moonlight illuminates the scene bleakly. I loathe its wan light for the things it shows us even as I understand my own misplaced conceit.

We teeter in the gale wind. Water laps at our knees. Soon our thighs are submerged. We falter in the watery wake but make our stand where we are. The beach behind will give us no shelter, of course. There can be no shelter from this. Her dreams told this and we have evidence of their veracity before us. Hands raised as paltry shield against the sand whipping at our eyes, we only continue to scan the distance.

It's near to us where we stand huddled close, rocking in the mighty squall. The small hairs on my forearms are reaching anxiously to meet it. It's nearly upon us. A light burns profoundly on the water. It burns the very lake away. It's bearing down upon our tiny shred of beach. In its embrace individual wrongs are razed. I think of our parents interred in cemetery silence and feel no joy in knowing that this will be my final thought of them.

"It's here. It's finally here."

Her voice in the raging air is soft but certain. Its sound reflects her as I've always known her to be, perfectly. Its sound is strong, its timbre courageous if faltering: she faces this thing as she can. She doesn't turn and seek to escape its wrath. There is no reason to attempt this and she refuses besides. I love her. I communicate this love through a vigorous clenching of her hand in mine. When she returns this embrace, I feel as though I may be prepared for what is coming.

"Thank you for always believing me." She's shouting her words now. The courage in her voice remains. "You were the only one."

The reliable rustle of the surf is no more – our old friend is gone. In its place a tempest roars such as has never roared on this beach or any other sandy strand before. In its cacophony we continue to clasp each other's hands and this, as ever, is the strongest we can be.

Peace.

Paradise.

YOUR BONE SPIDER

WILL FIND YOU

She fingered the keen blade extending from the finger-smudged plastic base of the pocketknife. Its edge, caught in the moon's light, flashed a silvery smear through her tears. She pressed the blade against the throat of the snow-white kitten pinioned between her knees, wincing as she did this but resolute in her action. She paused there, though, unable to go on. The animal's plaintive, mournful meowing shook her. Its soft emerald gaze seemed to implore her. She closed her eyes on the moon-coloured picture of her great cowardice and fury. A moment passed. A wind from off the river gusted through the great desolate yard, chilling her in her denim jacket. She shivered against its insistence, her bangs annoying her eyes and her cheap plastic earrings jangling loudly as she trembled. With as steady a hand and determined a mind as she could muster she pressed the blade into the kitten's scrawny throat.

Her wrist was then caught in an unyielding grip. She tried turning about to confront her assailant but, thrown off-balance, only toppled onto her side amid the tufts of wild grass spiking into her face, momentarily blinding her where they shot up through the time-shattered cement. She felt the knife pried from her fingers, discerned through the pounding rush of blood like a river in her ears the heavy breathing of the man behind her, and the renewed frightened yipping clamour of the kitten from somewhere near at hand.

She ceased her futile struggles, allowing her arm to grow limp in his grasp. She waited, heart hammering, until the kitten's saviour released her. Cowering, she peered over her shoulder. Gradually, her vision cleared, and the man coalesced from the star field against which he stood silhouetted. His eyes were hard but solemn. They burned in their appraisal of her. She couldn't help but look away from them, to examine her hands in her lap, the frayed cuffs of her jeans, her fingernails bitten down low and the grime wedged behind them. She took her first impression of him with her, though, and saw his dishevelled hair, unshaven features, wan skin, filthy sweatshirt and jeans as if he lived in the streets, or perhaps in this very lot behind the derelict warehouse.

She looked to him after a prolonged moment had passed in silence, found him looking into the middle of the vacant lot with his intense stare. She peered there, too, saw the snowy kitten padding there, away from her and her knife. When next she looked to the man his eyes were beholding her, accusatory but still curiously sympathetic, impelling her against her will to look to her hands again. They looked small, she thought distantly, thin-fingered and too weak to wield knives effectually.

She saw from the corner of her eye as he raised an arm. She followed his hand gesturing in the direction of the river somewhere in the night. More specifically, she understood, he pointed towards the skeleton of the warehouse before them. Its belly had long ago been eaten by fire. Its roof, she saw, had collapsed inwards. Long fire-blackened wooden and steel support beams spiked outwards from the rubble like an enormous splintered ribcage. The structure's aura of death and abandonment had called to her when she'd wandered through the lot thirty minutes earlier, and found the kitten pawing at a spot in the grass, looking startled at her presence, shaken in the crisp wind, utterly lost in the night.

Suddenly the man's hand was beside her face, palm out as if offering her to take hold and be guided from the lot by him. He turned his gaze to the warehouse and then again to her, beckoning still with his hand.

A ball of fear unfurled itself in her stomach at this invitation. "I'm not going with you," she said indignantly. "Fuck you, man."

The man's voice was younger-sounding than his weathered features appeared, his tone firm but its timbre un-coarse, un-ravaged by time. "Oh yes, you will."

The man's striking incongruity startled her, his unremittingly calm demeanour and grave gaze unsettling. She watched him with a hard, angry stare. She considered her proximity to the street beyond the empty warehouse towering between her and freedom. She considered her small voice in this large unfrequented lot near to the river past midnight on an icy Fall night when most sensible, untroubled people were indoors and sleeping and wandering in their good or bad dreams. She watched his tranquil but uncompromising eyes a moment longer without words and then finally she spat at him, audaciousness in her voice and a seething look of disdain in her gaze, "I'm not scared of you. Fuck you. Let's go then. Come on." She stood and led the way towards the shell of the warehouse hulking at the periphery of the weed-choked lot.

The man eyed her curiously, then followed in her fuming wake like a thunderstorm blowing across the cement and into the black mouth of the derelict building.

The place smelled of rotten wood and old fire. The floor was filmed in ash and dust and debris. Shadows ruled the immense room despite the moonlight pouring through the hole where the roof had once been and illuminating the central portion of the space.

She walked brazenly into this moonlit area, feeling immediately as though the shadows surrounding her had begun to encroach into the lunar light. Once there she turned about, extending her arms defiantly. "I'm here. Okay. Now what, man?" Her eyes, the man saw, were angry and dark. He looked into them. He watched her without words, and then only nodded sympathetically, a gesture which infuriated the girl further. "Well, what the fuck, man? What do you want? Eh? What do you want from me? Have I got something you want, man?"

His voice was soft following hers, a caress from the shadows pooled before her. "This is a lesson for you. To not do things like you tried tonight. To not add to the darkness and foulness in the world, when it's not in you to do. How...How old are you?"

She grew silent at this. Dark suspicion returned into her appraisal of his indistinct form. Her mouth moved as if to speak but no words came. Emotions played across her features, naked in the lunar light for the man to examine as closely as he wished: her telltale emotions, with the added weakness of her general unattractiveness: speckled around her mouth with tenacious acne whose presence haunted her no matter how diligently she scrubbed her face with soap-lathered washcloth each night before bed and upon waking every morning; the hint of purple lingering among her brown chin-length hair from when she'd dyed it herself several days before, the only way she could afford, with grape-flavoured Kool-Aid, so that teachers would look at her disapprovingly and certain boys with interest; her thin lips and makeup-less cheeks and eyes as un-feminine as a boy's. Grown discomfited by this unexpected turn in their strange exchange, the girl fidgeted in her place, but remained standing helplessly beneath the man's scrutiny.

Then, as if he'd extracted something from her that he'd wished to learn, the man said with a solemn, teacherly tone, "There." His hand stabbed from the shadows and was pointing with a grubby finger into the darkness beyond her. He stepped forward a step and she saw his feral eyes devouring her, as if he gained strength from her great unease. "Look!" he seethed with greater vehemence, until she turned in her place and followed his gesturing hand.

When it became evident that she discerned nothing in the shadows he placed his hands on her small shoulders and edged her forward step by incremental step. Her instinctual resistance to his pushing her forward ceased, and she allowed him to move her easily. Then, when they were bathed in the shadows beyond the perimeter of the moon-washed central space, his whisper guided her: "There, in the heap of rock and wood. In with the bones, those pale sticks rising from the debris in the centre. It moves there."

She wondered if the wan timbers rising from the heap were indeed bones, felt an instant queer thrill and revulsion at the thought. They watched silently. Then, there, amid the blackened wood and soot-smudged bricks and bones, she saw long, slender skeletal legs unfolding.

She held her breath reflexively. She placed a hand across her mouth as if she might cry out though no sound issued from her. She looked with incredulity at the great pale spider and the bones over which it traveled. She sought to fathom the weird spectacle of it floating in the dilapidated warehouse remains like some malign spirit or scavenger. Its size was staggering – both her hands placed beside one another would be dwarfed by it. It wove a strange pattern with its nimble legs, making a soft but clear percussion in the huge quiet, a sound of sticks rattling across the rubble. She remained standing in her place though her revulsion of the thing urged her to hasten away. She shuddered, no longer discerning the man's hands where they remained resting – gently now – on her narrow shoulders.

"I first found it ten or more years ago," his foul-breath whisper came in her ear. "Crawling on a homeless man laying dead in a room of rubble. The man's skin was like ash, grey, powdery. He looked like his life had been drained from him. His neck, though, was dark, black with bruises. Like he'd been choked to death. It was perched on his chest. It seemed to be... watching me walk towards them through the room. It didn't move, just sat there on the hobo like it owned him. I guess it did."

She heard his words as if in some peculiar time-delayed manner and murmured, feeling as if too-long after he'd fallen into silence, "What... What is it? I've never seen a spider so big. Not even in books."

He eyed her curiously. A tender look entered his gaze, as if he suddenly realized the age of the girl he was observing. "A spider? Is that what you see?"

She nodded, noting absently the strange nature of the man's question. Turning to him, feeling suddenly greatly afraid, she whispered, "What do *you* see? I mean – what is it?"

But he only watched her with his new eyes of unsettling sympathy, and then turned to observe the gargantuan thing once more.

They watched it a while, and then he told her, "I see a great...hand. I see a large, strong hand. Masculine and muscular. Fingers long, hard. With long, dirty nails. That's what I see. It's...It belongs to the homeless man, the hand. It's the hobo's hand I see." He paused, and she heard him swallow deep in his throat, and the pause before he next spoke seemed to her to be one wherein he gathered himself. Then, "It's the hobo who stole me when I was around your age, with a knife at my throat in the lot behind the convenience store behind the house where I lived with my parents in the neighbourhood just beyond this lot. He was younger then. Quick and strong. His *hands* were quick and strong. And awful. When I saw him next, he was dead, in this warehouse. I come here to...to see it. I come here to see it and give my thanks. It's always here. Here and elsewhere, too. I've seen it throughout the city. In overgrown fields, on the hoods of cars in driveways after dark. Once inside a locker in the change room at the downtown gym, stuffed into the bottom of the locker like a grey baseball mitt. Once it was on the porch of a well-to-do house on the south side, a giant hand spread open in the middle of one of the two chairs sitting there, facing each other at midnight." He paused, and swallowed audibly again, and making his voice gentle, said, "I see it often hanging from bars in jungle gyms, in schoolyards around the city. In sandboxes and the steel-and-wood skeletons of bleachers, and in school parking lots. I've looked inside dusty old school buses parked there, and found it on the leather seats, waiting.

For me, though, it's always here, in this place. This place is the place I see it without fail. I know this place. I know this place well. It's good that...It's good that you see it, too."

Her breath had been stolen by his revelation. She felt tendrils of cold snake all along her body beneath her denim jacket and t-shirt and jeans. Her heart crashed behind her chest. She turned to the spider, saw its hackle-like forest of pale fur spiking from its rotund body, its baleful grey eyes beholding them coldly, its long, needle-like legs perched delicately in its place atop the mountain of rubble. She felt the words rising up from her like vomit, unbidden and unwanted, bitter and shameful.

She said, in the quietest of whispers, though it sounded like thunder in her ears, "I woke up yesterday. In the middle of the morning. He...He was...He was *raping* me. *Raping* me. Oh God..." And she wept softly, and shook violently.

In the bated silence they felt acutely the thing watching them with its cold avid gaze, unmoving in its perch, as if estimating their intent, weighing their sin or innocence.

After a moment, the man spoke, softly, too. "Then it'll find him, too. It finds everyone, I think. They wake up one day, they look up one day, and they're face to face with themselves, like they've never been before. I hope it finds him soon. I'm...I'm sorry I frightened you."

She nodded. She wept harder, hugging her thin arms about herself.

The man whispered, "I mean that. I am sorry, but I saw you, young and angry and foolish with a knife in your hand. I saw your future, of regret, and, and...I wanted you to know. I saw your eyes, and I wanted you to know about...this."

He let her have another moment of silence and grief. Into it she eventually murmured, "I didn't mean to want to hurt the kitten. I've never done anything like that before...", trailing off, dismal and small.

"I know," the man said to her. "I know."

He let her cry. He wept, too, as he did on nights such as this. And all the while the pale thing remained there with them, unmoving but watching, silvered in moonlight and kingly in its throne of debris and dilapidation, like a protector of the place and perhaps them convened within it, too.

When the girl's crying ceased several minutes later, the man murmured, "Here." She looked to his hand proffered her. In the centre of his palm lay her pocketknife, its blade folded into its rounded plastic shell. She stared at it. She shook her head, denying the idea of it. He dropped it among the dust and stones at their feet.

Eyeing the thing on the summit of ruins, she said, "Are there...Are there really bones there in all that rock and wood?"

"There are bones everywhere," he told her softly, watching the rubble with her. "The city's filled with them." Then he turned to her. "Goodbye," he said. "I have to go home now."

She eyed him curiously. She wondered, for the first time, about the man's home, his life outside of the night and this place of shadows and moonlight and memories. She wondered about those things which interested the man, his hobbies and passions, the everyday activities in which he engaged, and the people – the friends or family – with whom he shared his days. He eyed her with a peaceful gaze over his shoulder as he trudged through the toppled warehouse.

He left her like this, in the dust and ashes. A great fear stabbed its way into her heart in her new aloneness. She shivered and cast huge eyes around the chaos of shadows surrounding her. Her nostrils seemed wholly filled with the aftermath of fire and death. She considered the thing before her, like an amputated appendage belonging somehow always to the city. She wondered of its other forms, in the lost, weeping eyes of others like herself and the haunted man who brought her here to this place. She wondered what other awful aspects of human beings ghosted the streets and alleys and lots and fields, and she shuddered. She shuddered a long deep shudder, and her hands ached from the chill air, or else from a deeper cold awakened in her at the new knowledge she had about the world and the things happening in its secret folds.

She stooped and retrieved the pocketknife from the floor. She eyed the crooked landscape of wood and stone and bone. To the spider she said, in a clear voice, "His name's Frank. Just so you know. His name's Frank and he stinks like sweat, and his breath stinks like vinegar. He's hairy all over. Thick hair all on his back and arms and chest like a big tarantula. I hate him more than anything in the world."

The spider, watching her, placed two of its long legs together before itself as if in prayer.

She turned from it and its kingdom of rubble and bones. She hurled the pocketknife she'd been savagely clutching – conscious even as she did so of her girlish throw, weak and crooked and nowhere near the middle of the wall she'd been targeting – and fled the shadowed place.

Moonlight drenched her anew when she arrived in the vacant lot. The air tasted cleaner somehow than before as she sucked it into herself despite it being the same city-air of smog and foundry fumes she knew every day. She relished its faintly acrid tinge but with the subtle suggestion of the nearby river permeating it, too, icy and aquatic, the perennial smell of the docks, where old boats lay tethered bobbing in the current, where dirty ducks occasionally were to be found, too, misplaced in the chemical waters with their pretty emerald plumage and innocent passage.

And to the night, quite like a fervently-uttered prayer, she seethed, "Just you wait. Just you wait." And she felt relieved, expelling that fury from herself with the words, and the great burden of it like all the concrete and stink and badness of the city filling her up and blown out like smoke into the air.

She turned eastwards and began her fearful and brave walk home. And, strangely, the longer she walked the cleaner the air tasted, the cleaner her thoughts seemed to become, unsullied with dreams of blood and vengeance that had never really been like her to dream at all.

Twins burning.

DYING DAYS OF
TREASURE SPIDERS
EVERYWHERE

The projects burned before them: children hung like listless simians from the rusted skeleton of the decrepit jungle gym; the black and white trash tenants of the townhouses haunted their porches languorously, drinking bottled beer and smoking cigarettes while watching the street with despondent eyes; the occasional car rattled past trailing exhaust and adding a chemical stink to the already pungent reek of late-staying June bugs that stippled the house fronts and streets and sidewalks.

The familiar scene filled the boy's chest with a thick kind of anxiety. He inhaled the awful air hungrily but felt as if something blocked its passage inside him.

His grandfather's voice was husky, as if from disuse, but the boy knew that this was only the natural sound of his old-man voice, the sound of sand granules crunching deep down in the moist darkness of his throat. "How is your collection of spiders these torrid days of August, my boy? They're well, I imagine? They're used to the sultry weather, I'd say." His grandfather always sounded as if he were reciting poetry from books, which always calmed the boy when he was upset about something in the same way that reading books made him feel better, too.

Now, though, the boy only nodded mechanically. Eager to obey his grandfather's wishes, though feeling physically depleted and as though any movement was beyond his capabilities just then, he leaned from the porch overlooking the dirt garden abutting the left side of the cement. He retrieved the large, sun-warmed glass marmalade jar embedded in the soil and held it aloft between his small hands for the old man to see.

Squinting into the sun-flashing jar, his grandfather examined the creatures within. "Oh my, what colourful friends you keep, my boy. Vivid! Bright as flowers! What is *his* name?" and he cocked a trembling crooked finger towards the immense yellow banana spider owning the upper portion of the jar, its prodigious leg-span covering completely the breadth of the lid's underside.

"Sunny," the boy answered. "Like the *sun* sunny."

"Ah," and his grandfather was nodding, the hint of a smile playing at the corners of his mouth. "A fitting name, surely. He is a splendid specimen, that's clear. Just look at him! The size of him! His grace hanging in his jar sky! His pride, evident in how he overlooks his glass kingdom." And, turning to his grandson, he added, "You, my boy, are a daring child, to brave such a king and transplant him to this kingdom of your own making. I can't imagine where you found friends such as these, in what high tree-places you had to climb, and into what dense green brambles and bushes you had to crawl and search."

The boy, with some effort, succeeded in smiling for his grandfather. The old man, seated beside him with a glass of lemonade in his liver-spotted hand, saw clearly the strained nature suffusing the gesture, as well as his grandson's overall discomfiture. He sipped from his lemonade, savouring the tang of its aftertaste on his lips, and murmured, "Remember this lesson, son, and for your sake remember it well: there will never be days like these again, no matter their good or bad ingredients. Live them like there's no tomorrow and you'll be making the most of what you have."

Of course, the boy, despite trying hard to take his grandfather's wisdoms to heart (as he sought to take all of his advices to heart) was unable for his huge grief and only stood nodding his head falsely where he stood before him like a quietly respectful knight before his king. The porch was coloured with sunset's burnt orange fire, though a murky tinge hung in the air, too, as if heralding the arrival of inclement weather. The boy toed the concrete at the foot of his grandfather's tattered lawn chair, making sure to avoid crushing the lone ant winding its way across the burning concrete square.

"I know, I know, my boy," the old man murmured, wincing in the glare and scrutinizing the boy. "It's a harsh lesson, in its way, and disheartening. But take heart in this, son: know that the lesson is also filled with huge joy, once you've grown to fully appreciate it, that is."

The boy cradled the jar in his arms. He examined each of his spiders carefully. The two small specimens skittering among the loose grass blades along the glass bottom like revellers among fallen confetti; a larger arachnid perched on the tip of the narrow oak branch, his body black with bright emerald markings; its twin hiding among the grass beneath, its design the same but its colour scheme one of black paired with blood-red;

and of course the massive banana spider suspended over the rest like a ruler overseeing his subjects.

After a time, the boy, frowning, said, "They must be too hot in there. I put holes in the lid but still I bet it's too hot in there for them."

The old man said nothing, only continued watching his grandson carefully.

The boy removed the jar's lid and placed the container delicately on its side in the stubby lawn grass. He and the old man watched as the spiders within made their collective way cautiously to the jar's rim, and convened briefly on the grass before its mouth as if jointly plotting their next move before making off in all directions, the sun finding their brilliant skins like reflections from a collection of marbles dropped into the grass.

"The day thanks you, my boy," the boy's grandfather said, a proud glimmer in his eyes. "You've enriched its fabric plentifully."

A moment passed in silence between them. The old man sipped his lemonade, offered his glass to the boy who only shook his head and stared into the street or sky while pacing the small expanse of the concrete patio. Eventually, he sat down upon the brick stoop protruding beneath the front door, not so much relishing (as he usually relished) the sun scalding his bare arms and legs but bearing its relentless touch. He wanted to shun this too-bright smoggy world and retreat indoors, to the safe blue shadows of his curtained bedroom, where he might immerse himself in comic books and the colourful tales they held. But he remained with his grandfather, because this is what they did each night after supper while the boy's parents cleaned up inside, and to abandon the old man felt wrong, and in a world where incredibly wrongful things happened too often the thought of committing another such deed made the boy feel sick. So he shared the hot silence with his grandfather, following the determined progress of red and black ants wending their ways across the cement or among the grass, laden with leaf bits like backpackers on the march. He sent flashes of lambent sunlight reflecting from the glass watch-face around his wrist out across the street, to dance erratic patterns along the siding of the townhouses there. He picked at the scabs owning each of his knees with a cautious hand, relishing the stinging pain he awoke with his probing fingers. Finally, he sought interesting and wondrous pictures among the cumulus, but clouds were few and far between in the pure blue sky, and those that did float there were wispy and small and difficult to imagine with, which only left the boy with his own troubled reflections. The sun hung relentlessly overhead but its light seemed dimmed to the boy's eyes, a waning circle, as if partially obscured by clouds or swallowed by an eclipse; or else simply sinking in the near-dusk hour towards its temporary death beneath the horizon.

The boy and his grandfather sat and sat in the baking silence.

A nearly imperceptible cracking disturbed the gargantuan stillness. The distant song of cicadas buzzing from the trees ceased, as if grown hushed at the small but great noise, too. The jungle gym children ceased their chattering in the hazy distance, possibly likewise awed by the startling, somehow unearthly disturbance. The boy and his grandfather, startled from their pensive somnolence, followed the direction of the noise, looking to the concrete floor of the porch. Directly between them, a small fissure had appeared, and peeking forth from the aperture was a narrow green stalk, as of a flower. Peering closer they saw its bulbous tip, where fragile petals grew upwards and came together into a tear drop-shaped bud holding ensconced within its embrace some hidden beauty – its flower, of course – with the potential to brighten the milky-aired, dusking day.

"Perhaps the world of old is at last come to reclaim itself from us," said the old man, sounding especially wise to the boy. "Perhaps our little green friend is repayment for your gift to the day." And here he nodded out towards the lawn before them, with its hidden arachnid jewels, and concluded, "Perhaps there's a lesson in this, too."

The boy looked to his grandfather, awed, and again to the fragile-looking but mighty green stalk. He stared at it for a minute, imagining or actually perceiving its subtle perfume of peaches on the muggy air.

He returned his gaze to his grandfather when the old man grew suddenly rigid in his chair. He'd left the lemonade glass lifted midway towards his waiting mouth, his eyes straining into the distance. A moment passed and he lowered the glass to his bony knee and exhaled deeply, sounding to the boy's ears as if he'd just returned from a very long and wearying journey. Then, his voice hushed, "Look, son. Over there and up there. In the trees in the park, past the projects shimmering in the haze of the east. There's something there. Something strange and special. I can sense it but I can no longer see it. That's your special gift, while you have your good and young age, and eyes less clouded than mine. For now, for these lucky days of your huge fortune, you're able to see it among those sun-fired branches, while some of us can only feel it. Look, look."

The boy looked. He stood from the stoop and drifted to the edge of the patio, the tips of his grass-stained sneakers hanging past its concrete lip and making him feel distantly as if he was a sailor, a captain of a ship and standing in its prow while searching the water horizon stretching endlessly before him. He cocked his head one side to another, squinting in the burnt air. He sought to conjure something wondrous and happy among the sun-limned trees but saw only his grandmother as he'd last seen her: heaped like a collection of bones in the hospital bed underneath the stark sterile lights, more a skeleton than the plump woman she'd been, the roses vanished from her cheeks, gaunt and deflated from their former roundness like shrivelled apples gone bad; her bald head gleaming alarmingly through her remaining wisps of snowy hair; cloudy yellow eyes staring at the ceiling, utterly vacant of the person once living there; while the transparent plastic nebuliser mask suctioned to her mouth and nose added a fantastically horrific aspect to the scene, as if she were the unwitting subject in some mad surgeon's experiment gone terribly, terribly awry. It had been weeks since that haunting and endless morning in the cemetery – the sad look of everyone dressed in black, making their faces appear more pale than he knew them to be; the charged air, as if the day itself was in mourning like everyone gathered among the headstones beneath the milky sky; the dull, hollow clamour of dirt clods being shovelled overtop the casket embedded inside the gaping earth following him into his dreams that night and most subsequent nights, too, a terrible percussion that awakened him with heart thundering and breathing ragged and tears never very far behind the well of his wakening eyes.

"I know, son," the grandfather said, crumpling further into his raggedy chair and soothing the boy a little merely with his reliable ability to read his murky thoughts. "I know it, too: it's hard. A very hard thing, to truly, truly bury those things passed away from us."

And he wept, long agonized sobs that made the boy fidget and scan the house fronts on the opposite side of the streets with increased determination, as if he were seeking some very particular thing among the blank tarnished facades; only to find dejected-looking project denizens like himself, unmoving in the meagre shade of their porches, sleepy from the heat or weary from the strange, indefinable darkness hidden among the deceiving bright air.

The old man stabbed the sky with his quivering finger. "I feel it now, son, more than ever. Oh, it's a strong feeling, and one worth investigating for a boy with the eyes for it." Following the gesture, heart thumping, the boy looked from the house fronts and with renewed determination to the trees of the park abutting the nearby parking lot.

Something took form from the oven air. A vague shape coalesced among the emerald leaves and tiny crab apples like sapphires decorating the trees like a holiday celebration of the summer. He watched it materialize, details embellishing themselves and growing more pronounced with each passing second that he held it within his steadfast gaze.

The boy smiled. He laughed a moment later, laughter free and hearty, the laughter his grandfather had once owned before he'd grown old and confined to creaking thrones unfit to bear his bent but regal frame. The boy looked avidly now among the leaves of the trees. He turned his attention then with an earnest enthusiasm into the air over the trees. He looked where the dropping sun – bright and blazing now and freed suddenly from its stifling eclipse – limned the crumbling projects in fire.

And he saw.

He *saw*.

"Do you see?" his grandfather asked the boy, eagerness infusing his voice, desperate and brimming with a hopeful joy. "Do you see her? You do, don't you? You do."

The boy nodded. His grandfather smiled, and wiped at the tears suddenly returned in his eyes. "Good, my boy," he murmured. "Very, very good. The young colt hasn't grown into a new skin and run away on me just yet." And his large weathered hand patted a gentle melody of camaraderie and thanks on his grandson's back.

From the lawn before them a jewel flashed, and then another and then another: brilliant yellow and emerald lights reflecting the sun's final moments of that day as it sank and sank beyond the houses, freed monarchs reclaiming their kingdom among the grass and trees. In the distance, laughter sounded, free and joyous and drifting like a song on the humid air. A car horn barked somewhere like a cry of celebration or fanfare documenting the scene.

The boy continued nodding, seeing all of these things, examining the world as he knew it – faltering, tenuous, yet filled with the potential for secret worlds gathering their strength beneath the streets and of familiar floating faces among the summer leaves – through his stinging, clearing eyes.

The same shall drink of the wine of the wrath of God, which is poured out without mixture into the cup of His indignation; and he shall be tormented with fire and brimstone in the presence of the holy angels, and in the presence of the Lamb: And the smoke of their torment ascendeth up for ever and ever: and they have no rest day nor night, who worship the Beast and His image, and whosoever receiveth the mark of His name.

- Revelation 14:10-11

MARIA, HERE COME
THE DEATH ANGELS!

The jungle reeked. Its pungent stench, a miasmic brew of competing flora species and rotting vegetation, reached the outskirts of the village.

The weary men were gathered in a loose circle there. This, their makeshift camp of two days wait, baked in the torturous air. The weeks behind them – of slinking like animals through the wilderness, and fighting there, too, and fighting there and fighting there – weighed on them. They were the ragtag remnants of Rogue Angel Company. Tired, weak from hunger and malarial fever, most of them wounded. They each of them owned lost eyes.

In the distance the village children stood huddled, watching the men curiously, whispering among themselves.

A man, turning onto his side where he lay in the grass, groaned. The bandage encasing his thigh was stained red with blood and brown with dirt. Then drowsy quiet returned while each of the men drifted between the place they were and those places they yearned to be.

Into the dead silence, Private McCall's voice carried like an unexpected beacon of light. "You know, I've seen angels here. I mean it. You boys lookin' at me like I'm nuts but it's true. The real McCoy, with my own eyes."

The men were indeed looking up from where they finished their meagre rations or habitually cleaned their weapons or lay with eyes closed against the angry molten glare of the sun. Their murky eyes cleared as they examined their companion but still they eyed him with suspicion. Still, their weary expressions haunted them.

McCall finished, a song in his voice. "And here they come to save me again."

The men followed the Private's gaze staring over their heads. There in the bloody dusking west hung a murder of great mechanical birds. Choppers! Rescue! Salvation!

Everyone erupted into joyous laughter at the Private's words, ecstatic at the sight of their deliverance so close at hand, the deathly pall of their dark mood lifted. The village children, following the direction of the men's gesticulations, pointed and cried out excitedly, too.

"Angels! Yeah, McCall you got it, brother!"

"We're saved, boys!"

"Fuck yeah we are!"

"Dustoff!"

"From up high, here they come!"

They leapt from their rocks and logs and finished their duties with renewed energy, as if their bones and muscles and hearts knew no ache. Some threw their dirty helmets skywards in celebration.

"You boys want to join me in Heaven?" McCall went on in a mighty voice rising over their clamour, fuelling everyone's relief and joy at the sight of the machines and the transient escape they represented. The captain eyed him approvingly and clapped a hand on his back.

Private Dobbs, though – off to the side of the group and thumbing once again through the handful of photographs he kept stashed inside his shirt pocket – caught something in his companion's eyes which seemed to betray a deeper knowledge or meaning that the rest of the platoon hadn't noticed.

"Thank you, Lord," McCall muttered under his breath, to himself and no one else but for Dobbs, who heard, and would wonder about it for the rest of the day. "Thank you for my time on this ripe Earth." And then he'd slung his Ithaca 37 across his shoulder and was on his feet, eyes in the sky.

Soon, the host arrived, and with it a great wind that whipped about the men like a storm.

Night-time Pattaya was awake and in the throes of living. The bar was tiny and congested with smoke and the sweat of the humanity filling it to its corners. Soldiers crammed the room, rejoicing in their shore leave with prostitutes riding their knees while waitresses wove among the throngs carrying glasses to and from tables.

Dobbs watched his pals, Lambton and Calling and Cartier, stagger off with a girl apiece. He smiled, genuinely happy for them. Placing a hand over his pocket, he smiled and sipped his tepid beer.

He felt his eyes on him. Looking from his drink he found McCall leaning backwards on his stool, his empty glass on the table before him filled with cigarette ashes. Dobbs smiled at him, and winced when he saw McCall's eyes lower to where his hand hovered lovingly over his breast pocket.

"What you always hidin' in there, pal?" His raspy voice came through the music and conversation like a knife. "Huh, pal? I bet she's a pretty thing, whoever she is. Am I right? I'm right, ain't I?" He was smiling, and Dobbs laughed sheepishly.

"You got me figured, McCall. Yeah you do. She's a beauty if I ever seen one. Makes me the lucky man I am."

McCall nodded approvingly. Turning his attention to the smoky air he reached a hand out, closed his fingers. Dobbs watched, impressed, as he opened his fingers and the giant black fly flew from his hand.

"You're a magician, brother," Dobbs laughed, swallowing his beer and waving at a passing waitress to bring him another.

McCall only shook his head. He cut the air with his voice: "She got a name? You got a picture you can show me?"

Dobbs put his glass down and retrieved the pictures. Pride filled him. He loved showing her picture, and did so whenever he could. She made him better in the eyes of others, he'd always thought. She made him a man when he usually only felt like a boy playing soldier alongside men. Passing the pictures across the table he said, "Her name's Maria." Watching McCall scan the photographs, seeing his appreciative appraisal of each in turn, cajoled him into revealing his greatest desires to his fellow platoon member, though they didn't know each other very well at all. "I'll be done here in six months, God willing. Shit, I can't wait to see her. It feels like forever. I just can't wait, brother."

McCall whistled, holding a picture towards the overhead light for clearer inspection. "I *bet* you can't wait. Boy, I ever had a girl like that I'd be counting the days till' I got to fuck her brains out the minute I was back, too."

They laughed together. They knocked their glasses together in a toast to Dobb's Maria and to beautiful girls everywhere. They watched soldiers dancing with whores to 'My Boyfriend's Back' spinning on the jukebox and crackling the old tinny speakers. They finished their beers and ordered again. The night was long and easy. Dobbs thought that he could live with nights like this if he had to, where he didn't have to worry over shadows in the grass that might snipe him homebound in a bag. Nights like this would do until he was home again with his friends and his girl and the food he liked to eat and the things he liked to do.

His reveries urged him to call across the table, "Hey, McCall. You like baseball? You a baseball man? Who's your team? Who's your best player?"

McCall eyed him strangely. He laughed, shaking his head. "Nah, brother, I don't know baseball worth a dime. I never could play. Never wanted to, neither."

Dobbs nodded. Drunk and less inhibited than he would have been otherwise, he ventured, "You know, I don't even know your home town, brother. You look like a county fella somehow. Don't ask me why. Just a feelin' I got."

McCall, wearing the same pensive expression, said, "Come on, brother. I need some air. This place stinks to high fuckin' Heaven of sweat and smoke. Sneak your beer, though. No one's lookin'."

They slipped from their stools and out the tavern's back door, surreptitiously toting their glasses. The voices they left behind sounded ecstatic.

The late evening air was cooler but humid still. Mosquitoes annoyed their eyes but they were drunk and didn't care. They were used to hungrier mosquitoes besides, and bullets hungrier than any creature.

They wandered a meandering line out back of the tavern and beyond its small gravel lot into the thick elephant grass. Beyond the trees they could glimpse the morose lights of the ghetto district. Following the gurgle of the water they found the river a minute later, dark and spotted with reflected stars. They stood there, looking into its depths, drinking their drinks.

"What did you say was her name?"

"Hmm?" Dobbs shook his head, chuckling, wondering at the languorous mood come over him, as though the water enchanted him, or else he'd only just caught up with the fact that he'd drank one too many.

"Your girl?"

"Maria." Maria. Even her name he cherished. The way it conjured to mind everything about her. Her voice her smell her ways, how she looked as pretty with short hair as with long. Maria.

"Maria," McCall said in a protracted way, sounding as though he was savouring her name just as Dobbs was savouring it. "It's a nice name she's got, for sure."

They lit cigarettes and smoked in silence, enjoying the moonlight. The hum of the nearby bush was there with them, too, like some great electrical thing.

Into the nocturnal calm: "She ain't never gonna see you again, Private."

It took a moment for the words to seep through Dobbs' muddled thoughts. When they did it was in conjunction with the burst of sensation which tore through his stupor. His eyes cleared and he stared with mute horror at the dagger hilt protruding from his stomach. He examined it until he understood the fact of it piercing him. He felt its blade ruining him inside. A growing pain emanated from the spot. The sight of his blood pouring from the wound and running the length of his pants stunned him. It seemed queerly as though he was divorced from this happening, as if he were watching a film of this violent act committed not upon himself but upon another person, but for the pain. He'd never smell her smell again. This great loss was his.

McCall's breath was rank as sewage as he leaned close to his ashen face. "Maybe they are angels, Private. And maybe I'm the strongest of them all. Maybe I'm the great deceiver now, and I can't wait to get back into the jungle to do what I do best in the world. I love the jungle, Private. It's where I met the Master, okay? I fuckin' *love* the jungle. With all my wrathchild's heart."

McCall curled his fingers over the dagger hilt. He wrenched it from side to side. Dobbs fell to his knees from the pain. He felt the blade slicing through his insides, the obscene collision of this razor-sharp intruder with his delicate unguarded veins, muscles, organs, his crumbling architecture. His agonized cry was swallowed behind McCall's hand as it clamped over his mouth. He extricated the blade slowly and then plunged it into the Private again and again and again. The blows opened Dobbs' neck wide, and his belly, too, to reveal his tangle of intestines coiling in the mud near the river's edge like a grotesque orgy of serpents.

The moon moved across the sky. The forest grew loud, violent in its animal clamour, and then, after a time, became somnolent-sounding. McCall stabbed and stabbed. A while later, McCall sheathed the dagger in the scabbard he wore beneath his shirt, without wiping it clean. He examined the body gleaming in the lunar light. Minutes passed and he proceeded to drag it to the edge of the river and roll it into the water like one would a log. Dobbs' devastated corpse bobbed briefly before submerging beneath its black surface.

McCall looked into the waves. The stars shook frantically there. He was still watching when the water grew calm and the stars had fallen into stillness, to haunt the river with their frosty, otherworldly light.

A subtle tremor on the air gave the spy away. McCall spun and found the Thai boy huddled behind a skeletal berry bush nearby. Realizing he'd been discovered the child stepped out from behind his meagre cover and hovered anxiously in his place, looking as if he were steeling himself to flee but was unable due to his fear. The wooden fishing line he held quivered on the air in his small trembling fist as though in the throes of a frenzied invisible fish.

McCall sized him up with hard eyes. He undid his pants and pissed into the mud, watching the boy unwaveringly. "You know who I am, don't you, boy?"

The boy nodded, his eyes moons of terror in the darkness.

McCall nodded in return, as though satisfied with the honesty of the child's response. He finished his piss. He gobbed into the mud. He murmured, "Off with you now. Maybe we'll meet again one night, in the forest, in the city. Beware of me, boy."

The boy scampered mouse-like into the shadows.

The soldier turned and strode into the night.

The boy, having nearly reached the relative safety of the scraggly tree-line abutting the lot – and his village not far beyond – dared to slow and look the way he'd come. With fearful eyes he searched for the soldier but nowhere did he see him, despite the wide open space of the lot with the river flowing on one side and the squat, ramshackle tavern a ways in the distance. A chill crawled the length of the child's spine. He understood then that he would have to be strong in the world. In his peripheral vision he discerned a shadow pass across the stars and blight their glow but when he looked there was nothing, only the night sky, dark and immense.

Where worry has no home.

ALWAYS AN
ANGELWITCH
OVER SUICIDE HILL

I:

There's one thing in this world that I know for sure my dad loves. It's a photograph, grainy and yellowed and warped around its edges with time. It isn't of my mom, or me, or my kid sister who died when a Trans-Am hit her on her sixth birthday and put the permanent shadow in my mom's eyes that everyone notices but never talks about. Mom accepts dad for what he's become but plays dumb to it, too, like she doesn't notice his ghosts looking out from his eyes every day he looks right through us.

Of course, his beloved picture is a picture from back then, because when else: him and his pals draped like wet clothes all over a hovercraft sitting in a Cambodian river. Everything's green in the picture: the river, the sky, the tree-line, their uniforms and helmets, with only the red or brown of their skin shining through it all. One thing he said about the picture always got me thinking and puzzling as a kid, and romancing every inch of what that picture held and might hold, hoping to see what he saw but never quite finding it there in all the green.

"Blind luck we caught her in this snapshot, boy. Blind luck. There she is. An angel. Me and the boys, and an *angel* there with us. Everyone in this picture made it out, son. All of us. I know why, and so do my pals. We had ourselves an *angel* watching over our steps through that shit. Angel Company: she thought we were special and I doubt we'll ever learn why, but I'm grateful she did."

As a kid I'd always ask him, eager and excited: "Where, pop? Where is she? Do you mean the boat? Is that what you mean? Is she the angel you mean? Where is she then?" all while imagining fairy-like ghost-shapes in the sunlight speckling the water or searching for but never finding some secret design in the hovercraft's sleek but battered hull. But he'd only smile for me in his aggravatingly kind and patient way, like a teacher waiting for his lesson to sink in to the mind of a daydreaming student. But I wasn't distracted. I wanted to see her. I wanted to believe in her. But where was she, right? Where the hell was she and what was wrong with me that I couldn't see her?

II:

We were simple kids with simple desires: passive stoners on the hunt for pot and booze and secret outdoors places for sex, and the occasional myth to give a bigger meaning to our otherwise hazy boring shitty lives. Escape artists, creative enough to find pathways away from the day-to-day boredom and frequent catastrophes that kept us humbled and afraid of what the future might have in store for us.

We invented the Witch of Suicide Hill one long drug-fucked midnight, and we embellished her on future nights and wee mornings, but never expected her to be born through our story-telling, not really. But her manifestation came later, a hazy while after her invention between tokes on the joint the five of us were sharing and swigs from the bottles of cough syrup we were passing around, the woods around us dark and foreboding and hiding every terrible and thrilling ghost we dreamed into being.

The hill was local legend: every grade schooler feared it, every high schooler got drunk and stoned and fucked on it at some point, or dreamed of doing all of the above there. It also frightened us all, though not all of us kids admitted to being under that part of its weird spell: maybe it was the hulking look of it etched against the backdrop of fields stretching for miles and miles to the south, with the trees surrounding it like giants worshipping at an immense altar; or maybe it was the strange aura that surrounded the place, that seemed to come from the hill itself, like it was a colossal sleeping animal, hibernating, a leviathan biding its time until the right gang of teenagers chanted the right spell to wake it from its ancient dreams. It got its name after a girl – nobody really remembers her name because she was before our time, though everyone pretends to have known her, and to know her story, like it was their own – who killed herself there. Some say she used pills and that her vomit had made the grass crunchy and yellow when a grandpa and grandma found her asphyxiated corpse the next morning while walking their dog; others say she opened her wrists with razors and swear her blood still soaks the grass on certain weird midnights when the moon's bright and the Devil's wandering the nearby woods and influencing the local wildlife and ghosts in dark ways.

We told it this way: the girl, a teenager around our age, crawled up the hill one stormy night after her parents drove her out of the house with their fighting (why she crawled I can't recall but that's how we'd told it and it always seemed the right way to tell it). Once gaining the top of the hill, she looked skywards and opened her mouth wide, drinking the rain down until it drowned her. When they found her, whoever they were, the girl was hard to recognize, she was so water-bloated and blue-skinned. We imagined her resurrected shell like this, a monstrous mermaid, lost-eyed and haunted by her past that had sent her crawling uphill in search of a drowning by the sky; and this became our witch who haunted Suicide Hill, giving it its bleak name and wandering the woods and swimming in the deep dark dangerous river cutting through the oaks and willow trees, casting her weird magic over the forest and fields and animals and teenagers dumb or drunk enough to hide out there, too. We named her Maria – Blue-Face Maria – after a missing Woodslee girl we'd heard about, and spooked each other by pointing out the shadow of her scampering way out in the thick of the trees or floating in the water or crawling up the hill after midnight.

It's a big hill, grassy and steep. Nearly sheer along its southern face, and treacherous in bad weather. It was a weird summer weather-wise, setting records for rainfall and twister touchdowns, and the river flooded enough times that it turned the fields and wilderness surrounding the Hill into constant swampland. Deep, misty, mysterious. And dangerous. A perfect home for troubled spirits, real or invented, to roam.

III:

My dad was miles-deep into crazy country with the bridge burned long behind him, and my mom drank more than any of us did by way of coping with his madman antics. Jenny understood: her parents were white trash through and through, and noticed her only on the last day of every month when rent was due and her part-time gig at the bowling alley saved them, and saved a place for the two of them in the liquor store checkout where the welfare cheque was cashed like clockwork. Mainly it was me and Jenny versus the world, but our friends were close ones, and all fucked in the same kind of ways, too: always broke, hungry, pissed off and bored: Robert, king stoner and happy drunk, always looking for the joke in good or bad situations because if you can't laugh, he liked to say, well, the other option isn't so good; Paula, older than the rest of us by one year and shunned by her classmates because she wasn't the prettiest girl around, not by a long shot, happy to hang out with the only small band of loserdom that would take her in; and Trevor, big reader of horror magazines and worshipper of the midnight hour, the best of our gang at spinning the tallest tales to get us thinking away from the usual shit.

No wonder smoking and drinking were such good friends of our gang. We never talked about the mirror-people we were becoming to our families who embarrassed us so much, but I'm pretty sure we all thought about it, at least when we were sober.

My dad served. He wants everyone to know it, or maybe he just wants people to know there was a time when he was needed to serve and he did. When someone refers to him as being a veteran he's quick to set them straight: "I was a soldier..." Like 'veteran' doesn't quite define him adequately enough. Like the war isn't done with him yet. He'd been a sniper, specifically, God-gifted with a sure shot and cherished by the military, but he doesn't like to tell people these details for some reason. Sometimes, when his pride's wild and strong, he tells the world that the soldier's still serving: "Once a soldier always a soldier." This is why 'veteran' doesn't hold water: it implies deeds done, past and buried. My dad's tour hasn't ended just yet. A tour never does, he taught me once.

At least I had Jenny: we'd started dating at the beginning of the summer, and it went good from the start. She was great: mellow and sexy, angry but quiet, and she thought about things, too, like me. Plus I've always loved blondes in general, and dirty blondes in particular. Yeah, she was so cool. Us versus them, that was our motto from the start, whoever and whatever they were.

*

I found my mom crying once that summer, but she never found out about it. I was on my way out, to meet up with Jenny at the pool hall, and saw mom standing at the kitchen window with tears running down her cheeks. She was smoking, and her cigarette was shaking between her trembling lips. The ashtray was on the counter beside her, and I could see all of the lipstick-smudged butts piled there in the ashes, looking bloody and hurt. I thought maybe she was seeing Allie again, dead and crumpled all over the curb, her tricycle twisted and broken beside her. I watched her for a while, though, and knew it wasn't Allie in her head. I could see him through the window, too: dad taking a break from it all in the rickety old rocking chair we kept on the backyard patio, looking like any other dad or husband relaxing in the late afternoon sunlight, smoking a cigarette and watching the sky. But I knew better, and found it right away: his trusty M-16, laid across his lap, rocking along with him, like the extension of the man he'd become all those years ago.

I don't know why I didn't say anything, try to comfort her in some way. Maybe I felt embarrassed because I was crying by then, too. Maybe I just felt that everyone's alone with their sadness in the end anyways, so why bother trying to bring her a peace that wouldn't stay with her.

Later that night me and Jenny left the pool hall and split a bottle of DM in the woods near the Hill. Laying there in the old sleeping bag we always shared, watching the stars coloured cough syrup-purple through the trees, imagining the shuffling sounds of Maria crawling through the leaves nearby, she whispered in my ear. Her whisper was anxious, her lips hot and moist and sexy on my earlobe, "Are you scared? Like, of tomorrow?"

I kissed her. It was the only answer I had. It was a good one. It was the strongest one I had to give. It got us through the night, leading first to sex and then to spooning warm against the cold air and finally to sleep and dreams as purple and thick as the potion inside us.

IV:

So we called on her soon after, near August's sweaty end. Like a summoning without the black candles or sacrificial beasts, just our belief. Because we did believe in her. We'd given birth to her and she felt real to us. More real than most things we saw and felt every day. We needed proof of the magic we could summon. We needed to be saved. It was a weird and uncertain time. Summer was almost over, and a dying season was coming on strong. It was a call we had to make.

We were standing in a circle in the dark heart of the woods. A little stoned and plenty drunk, the mossy ground at our feet littered with empties: beer cans and cough syrup bottles. Pot smoke merged with the mist in the air and made everything uncertain and eerie. We said things like "We summon thee, Witch" and "Rise Witch, rise" and "Come home to your hill, Witch, and show yourself to us". We meant every word, too. Being smoke- and drink-fucked had nothing to do with it. We'd have said the same things – less creatively, but with the same sentiment, heartfelt and desperate – if we'd been sober. Jenny held my hand through it, clammy with excitement. Our friends were a comfort there in the dark and wet, too: Trevor, eyes closed in concentration as he led us through our summoning chants, the expression on his face telling us that we'd be wise to follow his example because a look that desperate meant he needed our Witch to rise, maybe to help him forget his dad run off with a girl half his mom's age; Paula, looking happy to just be there at all, quiet and timid as always but with eyes clenched tight in her concentration, lost in the world of our ritual; Robert with his torn jeans and long hair and pot-lazy smile, relishing the spectacle of us gathered in the woods like cult members on the brink of exiting the world for a better place.

I sensed Jenny saying something, and watched her mouth the words: *Please Witch, please.* Yeah, Jenny needed her bad that night. We all did.

The river flooded that night, the twenty-fourth of a weirdly windswept August and the most severe flooding of the whole summer. The water rose quick. It's where she lived and slept when not haunting the hill, our strange and powerful Witch: in the river. In its deep green scummy water, in the muddy river bottom tangled in the underwater weeds and submerged garbage, in the dangerous undertows that had pulled more than a few swimmers under for good throughout the years. The sky pissed hard and the river she rose fast and washed out the distant cement trails before we could find them on the outskirts of the woods; the mud paths we were on turned into quicksand sewage and sent us sliding and slipping through the underbrush. Thorns snagged our clothes and scratched our skin, burrs stuck to our clothes like hungry parasites, rain blinded us, thunder shook us, the night strangled us in its thickness, black and black all the way through.

We found our way by instinct: we knew those woods like we knew each other: intimately. Finally we crashed through the tangles near the base of the Hill. The deluge hit us hardest then, outside the cover of trees, in the open with the fields stretching dark and huge to the south and the slope rising like a mountain face in front of us. One of us – I think it was Robert – gave an inhuman cry, garbled and scared. We followed his pointing hand, thrilling at the movement above us on the slippery, rain-washed slope. Squinting through the downpour and windblown foliage, we saw.

It was my dad owning the bald summit of Suicide Hill past midnight, with rain lashing down from the sky. He was naked, with eyes so lost to the moment he didn't seem to see us gathered at the base of the hill; or he didn't see us for who we were, jaded teenagers out looking for fun and escape but getting washed out by stormy weather and the mighty magic of the Witch we'd foolishly raised; his son looking for a dad who'd gotten lost in a jungle in another decade on another continent. He called down to us in a mighty roar of a voice, like he was a prophet or god and we His disciples: "Killing a man means nothing, don't you know, boys? Killing a man don't mean a thing because the only thing that matters is the death of a soul, and man he has none. Man he has none, for the deeds he's capable of! Naw, God squashed what soul he had with the first stone arrowhead knocked and let off! That's why his angels left Him at his throne and walketh among us upon this scarred earth!" I don't know how we heard him through all the racket and roar, but his voice was a bugle's song cutting the night and I've never forgotten a dark wise word of its message.

We watched as he hefted the M-16 to his shoulder and aimed at something in the sky. We recoiled at the salvo he fired out into the night.

I wondered whether he found his target up there. His voice, reaching us through the roar of the storm, told us he had: "Blood! Blood! Oh, it's raining tonight, boys!"

I saw her first: deathly blue-skinned like we'd dreamed her, hair caked with mud and leaf bits and grass, crawling uphill at a good fast clip just like we told her story. Our mossy-cheeked rotting Blue-Face Maria, river-weed clumps around her shoulders like a disgusting shawl, making a bee-line for my dad feeding the sky bullets. He was oblivious to the danger he was in. We screamed at the sight of her, terrified at our conjuring powers. We waved our hands for him but he was caught by his bloodlust and kept pumping ammo upstairs. I was just starting uphill, too, to save my dad from our horrible creation, but the Witch was already on top of him. He kept firing his gun. Blue-Face Maria paused directly alongside my dad, looking up at him, watching him with weird eyes, like he was her saviour, from the sky and whatever it held. She sat this way for a few seconds and then crawled past him and out of sight over the hilltop. Another minute of him shooting up the night and then he lowered his weapon and scanned the sky from north to south. Then, nodding to his left as if towards someone invisible to us, he made his voice roar its bugle-roar again: "Thank you, darling! Oh, thank you for watching over me all these long hard years, darling!" The fury was gone from his voice then, though. Instead it was filled with something else. Joy. *Joy* would be the best way to describe it, although it doesn't quite say enough.

The last we saw of him that night was a strong picture, etched in lightning and shadow: hand to temple in a rigid respectful salute to the wilderness of the fenland and flooded trails, then slinging the M-16 across his bare back, turning and marching with his practiced step over the summit and disappearing down the opposite slope, in the wake of the Witch.

With his retreat came a shocking peace from the storm: the rain let up in its viciousness straight away. Soon it stopped completely. Lightning flashed its goodbye in the far west, without its constant brother thunder's soul-shaking voice.

V:

Me and my friends were getting stoned in the garage the next afternoon when the ghost arrived. Just like that he was with us: my dad, or the shell of him, back from the dead and whatever Hell witches and wraiths and warlocks and soldiers go to, with whatever trace of the man he'd once been loitering inside his body like a squatter in a condemned building. He snagged the joint right from between my fingers, crossed the room with it between his lips with a thoughtful expression on his face, came back to us and collapsed between Jenny and me on the ratty couch. He took a long good toke, eyes narrowed, a smile on his lips. Turning to Jenny, checking out her tits in her tight tank top with a careful eye, and then saying to us all: "Man, these are the days, boys. A break from the shit, all the thunder quietened down for a blessed bit, just smoking with your buddies. Stolen moments, like finding gold nuggets dropped in a landmine field." He didn't always talk this way, not always, but when he was lost in it he was lost in it deep and good.

"What shit, sir?" whispered Robert, stoned to a mellow playfulness, grinning good-naturedly through the smoke. He was wearing his old green army jacket, even though the humidity was bad enough to keep all of us hidden in the shade of the garage that whole afternoon. I think the memory of the night before had inspired to him to dig the jacket out of his closet and brave the angry August heat with it sticking to his back like a second skin.

My dad only slipped deeper and deeper into it that afternoon. He leaned back on the couch with a squealing of its springs and said, "Oh, I guess you ain't seen the papers yet, pal? Eh? You ain't read 'em yet? Well, good for you, but I best tell you now. Best you hear this latest shit from me than anyone else ain't your pal. Just over breakfast I read about all this: a girl was raped on the flipside of town, and butchered and left in the river, what was left of her; and a fire got set and burned down a portable schoolhouse, with one old man janitor stuck napping inside, poor, poor man; and the highway gunman got another one, near Kingston this one, and what's that make, just over a dozen and he's only been at it since the beginning of summer?" And he looked appreciatively at the cloudless blue sky framed in the window, and he said wistfully, "Such black news – *black* news! – on a perfect-looking day. The Devil truly is the great deceiver, ain't he? Dropping his apocalypses on us all the time and we can't sometimes hear it over the bees buzzin' and the children playin'. Shit, man, what year is it anyways? They say the mess and shit's over but we know, *we* know…"

We listened to the bees droning through the backyard, and the children whooping from over the rooftops. A tranquil stoned daze fell over us all. We baked in the stillness and heat. At some point we realized he wasn't with us anymore: my dad, stealthy soldier as ever, had crept off without any one of us noticing, melting into the bushes and flowers.

We said nothing, just enjoyed the peace.

Yeah, my dad was still back in the jungle. He still is. We keep him like a secret, like the broken family member nobody wants or dares to talk about for fear of making someone in the family upset. Luckily for us, all our families are fucked-up families, so dad fits right in among the greater tribe of us. If there's a tribal chief, he's it, watching the trees for suspicious green shadows and dreaming napalm dreams. He kind of turned into that role he'd dreamed up for himself on top of Suicide Hill on the storm-night, when the world of his dream got mixed with the world of ours. Or maybe there were no dreams at all that night. Maybe everything that happened that long weird summer was no dream at all but all the realest this weird world can get. Maybe us and him are just the exact same kind of crazy or sane, only from two different generations.

I thought then of dad's picture, and the invisible angel it held, and I knew I'd never see her, no matter how hard I looked. But that was okay: she was there besides. I know that now.

The weeks they'd passed too quickly – September was right on top of us, and the uncertainty of a school-less law-less time loomed like another storm front bent on demolition of the highest order. Yeah, fear was in the air then. It was there with us all that summer, with the heat and haze and humidity and sunlight and fish flies and mosquitoes and weirdness.

VI:

Me and Jenny were still listening to records in the garage later that afternoon after our friends had crawled home, when my dad dropped back in. He came like a spider, in through the broken window opening onto the backyard: no shirt this time, his big chest smeared with mud, caked through his hair and making his grey crew-cut brown, his camouflage pants and boots covered, too. A dirty bandage, spotted with deep red, was wound around his hand. Pieces of foliage clung to him, too, green strips of different sizes with serrated edges like nothing I'd ever seen growing in the garden or neighbourhood. I wondered what firefights he'd seen, what blood. He made no sound. None at all. Not even a jingle or jangle of dog-tags disturbing the yellow stillness. A professional or a natural or both. He acknowledged us with a quick nod of his head, a look of friendship in his glaring eyes before spinning around and making his nest in the window frame. He un-slung the rifle from across his back and took careful aim along its nose, guarding the garden and sunlight outside.

Jenny smiled at me. I held her real close and we lay together, watching my dad in the sun-washed window.

He was a sniper. We were friends in this dark world.

The curse is finally broken.

Walls too mighty for enemies to breach.

OR THE LONELINESS
OF ANOTHER
MILLION YEARS

He eases the jalopy from the lot and into the street. Its engine labours, sputtering and coughing like the decrepit elderly man who'd lived one floor below his before pneumonia had taken him to a better place. Dawn's broken over the tenements. Bloody sunlight blinds him as he rolls into the east. His neck aches, and his lower back, too. Spending nights in the car is making an old man out of him, too. He considers his fortieth birthday passing two weeks before and decides he's getting there besides.

The streets are empty everywhere. Curbed cars, rust-flecked and like relics from another age; garbage overflowing from steel receptacles on street corners, spreading like dirty water into the gutters in all directions; the gutted houses, boarded up with simple wooden planks as if the squatters within sought to keep invaders at bay; the old synagogue that dominates one street corner looking much the same, its heavy wooden doors unwelcoming, impregnable; newspapers stirring forlornly in the intermittent breeze, and he wonders what stories they tell. He wonders what stories they tell and whether any of them would mean much to him today.

I'm the only person left: this he tells himself, relishing the fantasy even as it's shattered – a skeleton swathed in rags snags him in his daydream and pulls him into the reality of the day. It waves a bony hand on the too-bright air as he rolls the car to a halt at the stop sign before which he has no need to stop, given the nearly deserted nature of the streets about him. He waves in return to the urchin he passes every morning in exactly this intersection, always feeling as though the man represents a gatekeeper of sorts, waving travellers through from the ghetto to what lies beyond. He idles a moment at the corner, leaving his hand raised, in this way communicating to the grubby skeletal man floating inside of his filthy clothes the honesty of his morning greeting. The old man smiles his toothless smile at him, a rare gift of sincerity and one the man accepts gratefully these days.

He gives the vagabond a smile, too, as difficult as it is to muster. Once he achieves this feat, he urges the car eastbound still. He feels very much as though he's surpassed a great obstacle in forcing the smile from his weary and desolate mood. With this hollow sense of victory filling him he plows right for the sun ascending over the bloodlight-drenched city.

With the ghetto behind him the comforting illusion of post-apocalypse lifts like the haze and stink from the concrete surrounding him.

People abound. Everywhere he looks he finds them, behaving as they do, engaged in all their inconsequential activities and duties; an attractive woman, middle-aged, dark-haired, bespectacled, rushing agilely in her high heels with briefcase in hand (he once yearned for women like this but had long since decided they belonged in the dreams of men different from himself); a dapper suit-clad man, forty-ish, prematurely snowy-haired and with skin burned pink from weekends spent poolside in the sun (he could have been this man, if he was a wholly different man to begin with); a pair of teenagers drifting listlessly along the sidewalk, a couple sporting identical black jeans and t-shirts and jet-dyed hair, members of the same high school clique and seemingly so immersed in the escape or reassurance of each other that they don't notice the scornful look delivered them by the trio of road workers standing in the partitioned-off construction area overlooking the sidewalk (he remembers these children, as he was once them, too, and he remembers also the men leering at them for he hated them during his youth as he does now). Perhaps these men will erect a skyscraper between them, he muses, with the help of many other workers like themselves, adding to the vast hive-like and inhuman character of the city.

The man considers these things while observing the sidewalk scene from the driver's seat of his parked car. The sun burns him through the windshield. He cracks the window but it isn't enough. Soon he must catch the breeze, such as it is, or risk growing irascible, which happens with him when the temperature becomes uncomfortable, and also when he's been too long in an enclosed space (perhaps this is why the claustrophobic nature of living in the city repels him, while bucolic dreams of meadowland and forests and valleys watered by rivers and streams consume him). He's a man of winter besides, and loathes all things summer in the city — the congestion of buildings magnifying the humidity like a mallet smacking his chest unremittingly; the early-rising sun stealing the lengthy delicious nights of the season before, hanging in the west long into the evenings like a punishment; the pervasive stink as the seasonal temperatures cook the garbage in the cans and dumpsters across the city, and simmer the sweat from the bodies of the humanity milling in every nook and inch of all the streets and buildings and parks and bus stations and among the buses themselves, teeming with riders and their multitude of stenches and germs and callous words.

He considers the ghetto as it must be at this time of the morning, and decides he won't even return there today at all. The sight of the homeless wandering like resurrected cadavers along the sidewalks; the rummies passing in and out of sweaty, miserable consciousness in the useless shade of stoops and porches of the tenements and shabby house fronts; the emaciated prostitutes strutting up and down the sidewalks, watching passing cars with feral, desperate stares; hordes of gangly children emerged like cockroaches from their ramshackle homes to become scorched browner by their time spent outdoors beneath the tenacious sun, lost in their games of hopscotch or army tag or road hockey and seemingly oblivious to their fates as determined by growing up in the heart of poverty and hopelessness — these are a species of dispossessed humanity he can't bear to witness today, the man decides, being that he's steadily becoming one of them and doesn't feel strong enough to loathe himself anymore than he does already.

He leans into the car and, fiddling with the controls, tries tuning into the radio but, unsurprisingly, finds nothing to suit his deeply melancholy mood. Only happy music, sad music, excited and energetic songs and those angry over something, all doing nothing in the way of moving him, or the weight from within him. A moment passes when a peculiar electronic squeal erupts from the tinny speakers, a mechanical shriek overwrought with white noise and static before the frequency realigns itself to deliver a smoothly crooning country song's voice which the man quickly silences altogether. The droning of that short electric cry lingers in his ears, though, as if in its chaos he'd discerned a familiar note, an old voice.

He leans from the car once more. He looks around himself. Of course — standing outside of his unreliable car, sunlight illuminating the streets before him and the tides of humanity rolling over them — he feels true despair prickle him inside.

"Where am I going?" the man asks aloud. The burning air gives no answer. The city, surrounding him with its infinite edifices and maze of streets and alleys and the outlying traffic-clogged arteries of the highways and cloverleafs, only continues its deep humming breathing, indifferent to insects like him crawling along its labyrinth of concrete lanes. The three road workers, near at hand, as one, turn at his words, eye him curiously, maybe a little contemptuously, before returning their attention to the tools laid out in the dust of the yard before them.

Go build your building, the man thinks, hating them and the things they might fashion from the bricks and steel and dust gathered in the construction space. He swallows, finds that his throat is a desert of rawness. He turns one way and then another, an inexplicable desperation seizing him. He finds the small sidewalk confectionary. Its dirty red-and-white striped awning beckons him, or rather some thing in him; the youth from which he'd sprung reluctantly over the years, eager to revisit just such a place of brief sanctuary and leave with a bag of penny candies in his fist, or an ice cream cone for his summer-dry throat, or a comic book to take him away, or in his teenage years a dirty magazine tucked inside of his jacket, to be leafed through in the security of night, after his parents had went to bed and no one anywhere – except for God Himself, if his parents' faith in such matters was to be believed – was able to see and judge him.

He moves his heavy feet. They take him across the sidewalk and through the shop's rattling door. He arrives inside the sweaty room, the delicate jingle of door chimes announcing his entrance. The Vietnamese proprietor looks from the magazine spread across the counter, eyes him warily, returns his eyes to the pages. The man drifts to the back of the store, where the refrigerators make a line across the entirety of the wall. He eyes the bread loaves lining the nearby shelves, his belly growling, but decides his thirst is undeniable. He pulls open a sliding door and retrieves a bottle of cola. He feels it sweating in his hand as he takes it to the counter. He looks to the magazine on the counter while the proprietor rings through his drink. Naked airbrushed breasts, a triangular bushel of pubic hair, a look of agonized ecstasy contorting the young Asian girl's features as the man fills her from behind. The corner of one of the pages is warped, as though from the hot sweaty thumb of the man leafing through the magazine, lingering on the images to which the issue is now opened. The shop owner tells him how much his drink will cost him and the man hands over the change, not bothering to count it. He keeps his eyes in the magazine. Its nakedness entrances him. Once, seemingly long ago but really not very long ago at all, these images would have awakened desire in him. Now, only a faint something stirs between his legs. A reflexive reaction, a lingering tick like a memory recalled bitter-sweetly and which he seeks to forget but that lingers a little still. And the man thinks, of course, of his wife of years before: the smell of her, the look of her, the sound of her in his arms in the bed they'd shared for a decade before she was swallowed inside one of the city's countless insatiable mouths, never to be released again.

He's shaken from his reverie by the shop owner's vehement voice. Seeing his glaring eyes, the man tunes in to the situation at hand. "You are short one dollar – I cannot give it to you." The man's vulture-like hand covers the bottle guardedly, in a manner which suggests he is accustomed to customers trying to cheat him or barter with him unfairly.

The man nods, seeks the required change in his pockets. He's relieved to find it (his meagre remaining funds are quickly depleting themselves with just such frivolous purchases as this) and, handing the proprietor the coins, takes his perspiring bottle and goes again into the burning day. Standing on the sidewalk, he spots a forlorn pigeon pecking at nothing in the gutter, a low warbling murmur escaping its throat and sounding utterly despondent in the air. Depressed by the bird's tuneless song, he turns away from it and trudges westwards.

He ventures there as if compelled by some strange, unknowable impulse within him. Leaving the car in the street, he walks the half hour's walk to the old neighbourhood. It smells the same as he remembers from those bygone days: greener than elsewhere in the city for its lush elms, but carrying the tinge of the city's cloyingly inescapable stench of exhaust and foundry fumes. It's no verdant valley or deep shadowed forest but it's the closest he can have.

He takes his time. He dawdles on memorable street corners, recalling street hockey tournaments when he scored winning goals for his team; the porch where he kissed a girl for the first time (moon-coloured, the porch then, and surrounded with curling fern's tendrils whose heady smell mingled with Carolin's girlish flowery perfume to create a too-rare scent

which from that moment on he would associate with things carefree and paradisiacal); the stretch of sidewalk from where he'd watched in horror as the rickety Dodge van had crushed his beloved Chihuahua into the street, fuelling his nightmares for the rest of his twelfth summer.

He wends his way through the maze of townhouse streets, sucking in the green but tainted air hungrily, as if seeking something in it to savour more than he is likely to achieve. He reaches the crescent where he lived as a boy with his parents, cozy and disconnected from the wildness of the streets beyond, and now as then offering the illusion of disconnection from the rest of the city, the world, all people everywhere except the tribe dwelling within the fortressed cul-de-sac.

He finds the boy sitting on the curb, immersed in the world of his solitude. His eyes are clutched tightly against the glare of the sun, while his head is cocked fixedly skywards, mouth held rigidly wide in a snarl. The sun flashes from the braces that cover his teeth. But for this odd expression, the man considers that the immobile child looks as if he might be immersed in meditation or prayer. His shorts and runners are dusty and grass-stained, his once-vivid red t-shirt faded, unwashed. His skin is bronzed by the sun, his hair messy, knees emblazoned with old and fresh scabs from his summer adventures, a round pink hillock of scar tissue running across his forearm evidencing just such a long-distant exploit.

When the man's shadow falls over him, the boy stirs instinctually from whatever it is that absorbs his attention. He clutches something to himself which the man can't see from his position on the sidewalk behind him. He eyes the man with a hand shading his features, unspeaking, sizing up his visitor with a guarded look as city children all learn to do early on.

"Hey there," says the man in a gentle voice, seeking to show his peaceful intent. As he predicted, the boy only continues observing him cagily.

Leaning closer over the child and making his voice cheerful (and an effort this proves to be) the man says with curiosity, "What do you have there? Does that thing work?" Knowing, of course, that the cheap- and weathered-looking toy radio in his grimy hands couldn't possibly.

The boy nods, a little enthusiastically, or so the man believes. When he ventures, "So, what are you listening to? Radio station? Baseball game?" the boy turns bashful again, and only shrugs his bony shoulders.

Something in the gesture, and in the boy generally, speaks to the man. Perhaps it's that the child reminds him of himself as a boy, gangly and shy and quiet and alone with his guarded expression and imaginary company.

"I grew up here, too," the man says, hoping to calm the boy's wary demeanour. "We lived in that apartment right there. Third floor, corner, facing west." He watches the sun-washed windows through squinting eyes, a million images and scenes and emotions taking their turn with him.

"I live right over there on the first floor," the boy points out for the man.

He nods, pleased to have elicited words from the taciturn boy. Because he's feeling nostalgic and morose, he's prepared to offer an anecdote or two, spin the boy a few tales from his days serving duty in this lacklustre townhouse neighbourhood. But: "They're talking about it again," the boy says with equal parts caution and poorly-veiled excitement, changing the subject of their conversation with a hurry the man understands all too well. He nods, eyeing the boy quizzically. The boy, cradling the radio in his hands, explains, "About the *door*. They've been talking about it a lot the past few days. I've been able to catch the signal, when I'm lucky. Usually it's only baseball games and oldies and stuff but sometimes..."

He drifts off, eyes wide, intent as he listens for the toy radio's voice.

"The door?" the man asks, intrigued by the nature of the boy's diversion.

The boy nods, his features taking turns changing from distrustful to bashful to eager, as if he were indecisive about letting the man in on his secret afternoon game. When the man urges, "Which door? To where? Who's opening it?" he wins the child over.

"A door to away from here. I...I been hearing them – I'm not sure who *they* are – talk about it all summer, on and off when I could catch the signal. This past week, though," and here he turns a cautious and eager eye skywards as if seeking to pierce the smog- and exhaust-teeming air beyond the serenity of the crescent, "I've been catching it lots of times. Anyways, they're opening the door today, just before supper-time. And anyone who wants to go through, can go through."

The man is amused. He enjoys the idea of this boy's game taking him away on a day like this. Perhaps the child has noticed this amusement registering in his expression, because he suddenly mutters, a little petulantly, "Anyways, where do you live now, mister? How come you came back to your old neighbourhood?"

"I don't really know, about either," he tells him honestly. "I live nowhere, really. I slept in my car last night. And I just walked and walked, following my feet, and here I was."

"Where's your car?"

Suddenly the man is overcome with a sense of detachment from the old vehicle. He doesn't want to ever drive it anywhere again, he decides. The curb by which it rests will be its burial place, he decides, until a towing company marks its perennial presence and drags it to another fate elsewhere. He will let it slip away from him, as he's allowed other ingredients of his life to slip away, too: home, employment, friends. Distantly, he murmurs, "That-away," gesturing absently over his shoulder while the boy turns his eyes in his sweaty face to scan the empty street behind them.

A vicious duelling of voices drifts from a window. Cursing one another, the husky female smoker's voice and the equally caustic male bellowing. Amid the perceptible hatred of the heated exchange comes the clatter of something metallic, a pot or pan striking against a countertop, a wall, the floor, a person's skull. The man can tell by the way the boy huddles into himself, the way he eyes more fervently the radio in his hands as if willing it to return to life, that the voices of the din belong to his parents.

He tells the boy, "I remember fighting like that. It makes you want to just go outside and lose yourself in the day."

The boy seems to digest these words a moment before nodding his head slowly. Turning to the man he says, "Yeah. There's better places to be than inside there." Into the queer stillness he adds a moment later, in a more subdued voice, "They hate me. Both of them. Her boyfriend especially. He gives me black eyes sometimes. And burns." Then, he adds, as if grown accustomed to pondering the anomalous nature of the fact, "I only got my braces because my grandma paid for them so I could have a nice smile for her. She's...She's great, my grandma. But really old."

The man nods. "Well, that's very nice of her. I noticed your braces when I found you today. They're as bright as the sun. You'll have a handsome smile one day. You'll get all the girls."

But the boy only fingers the lump of scar on his arm with a pensive look in his eyes.

They share silence, the man standing a little awkwardly before the boy seated on the curb with the radio in his hands. He considers the child's dark – though, somehow, not quite unexpected – revelation regarding his familial life. He contemplates leaving the child to his game of needful escape, and reluctantly re-entering his day himself, of ghosting the city's usual places: loitering in the handful of schoolyards where he once attended school; passing the mall where he used to fritter weekend afternoons away with friends back in the days when he had friends; the bars and theatres he used to frequent; the Laundromat where he'd chanced to help out a pretty woman who'd forgotten change for the machine at her apartment several blocks east, paying for her laundry and a dinner at a small Thai restaurant afterwards, once they'd gotten to know each other more than seemed possible during the span of a 23-minute-long laundry cycle while the world passed by outside as it always did while leaving them wholly untouched within their shared bubble. The man would pass by the tenement where he and the woman shared their first apartment in the months following their Laundromat meeting, and he would feel likewise compelled to visit their second apartment – in which they'd spent the entirety of their honeymoon – located in a marginally better neighbourhood than their first; until the dark day of her disappearance, and the reality of his situation seized him, repainting his former vision of the world and him in it: he was utterly alone without her, and he would forever be this way.

And following these difficult ruminations, eventually, against his better judgment and dissatisfied as ever, the man would wind his way back into the ghetto nest from which he crawls every morning to begin anew his meandering, agonizing Sisyphus-like circuit of the unchanging city.

The man is startled from his reverie at a small, sharp electronic clamour from between him and the boy. He looks to the old plastic radio in the boy's hands. He wonders at the empty battery compartment he spies along one side of the plastic frame, the unequivocally inoperative appearance of the ancient toy device.

When the noise ceases the silence of the street seems immense, hateful almost, as if it seeks to reassert its dominion over the scene as forcefully as possible. The man's breathing is laboured, though he senses the humidity is no longer the culprit. He eyes the radio in the child's hands rabidly.

"May I?" the man asks, surprising himself as he reaches a hand towards the boy.

He hands him the radio wordlessly, wearing a curiously patient expression, as if waiting for the man to learn some lesson.

The man fiddles with the plastic radio – turning knobs with a strained creaking of its plastic frame, adjusting the angle of the long silver antennae so that it points first away from the sun and then towards it, and taking turns placing an ear to the radio's speaker – all to no avail. He eyes the toy with a disheartened expression, feeling distantly foolish.

A quiet crackling comes again. The man's heart awakens, thumping a din inside him. He nearly drops the radio onto the concrete. He places it to his ear and silence greets him inside the little speakers. Looking to the boy, he sees him gazing into the sky, mouth open wide, a finger raised at a curious angle across the side of his lips as if communicating via sign language with the clouds, eyes closed in rapt attention as he interprets the noise miraculously exiting his mouth. The child's braces reflect sun-flashes from the sky, further mesmerizing the man. He notices, distantly, a small wedge of something – a sliver of bread or oatmeal, a pastry crumb – wedged between a silver wire and an incisor, a commonplace ingredient from the world which somehow reasserts the startling nature of what he's witnessing.

He listens, awed, unmoving from his scrap of burning street.

Amid the fizzing white noise and sputtering signal, the man thinks he discerns a voice, perhaps multiple voices, the language they speak strange, outlandish, yet familiar. Buried within the electrical clamour, rising intermittently through it before quickly submerging into the hubbub.

The man waits, unaccountably anxious, exceedingly eager. He wants to reveal to the boy that he's heard this voice before, somewhere, sometime, in some part of him to which he hasn't had access for a very long time. He looks dazedly to the radio in his hands, a mere children's toy once again. He turns again to the boy, face aimed sunwards, steel-enmeshed teeth bared in an excited-looking snarl, lips quivering with the strain of maintaining the unyielding posture. He peers skywards too, into the impenetrable blue, crisscrossed everywhere with vapour trail lines like demarcations on a map of the sky. On a nearby rooftop an ancient weather vane glints dully in the sunlight.

After a moment, the noise subsides; queerly, as if an invisible hand had gradually decreased the volume of the communication until it was no more. Silence returns between them, heavier than ever in the stillness and baking air, in the aftermath of the event.

The boy eyes him more openly then before. His whisper is conspiratorial, and excited: "Did you hear it, mister? I told my mom, and tried to let her hear it, but she just shook her head at me. But you heard, right? They'll be opening it up today! It's for sure now! This afternoon! But only for a really short time before closing it up for another million years."

The boy's eyes of eagerness harbour a desperation plain for the man to see. It mirrors his own desperate eyes, he knows. The child is a revelation, a miraculous occurrence slipped through the languor and painful sameness of the day. He feels something, unfamiliar but familiar, seep its way into him: his own youth, long-dormant but startlingly alive once again, an old and dear friend returned from a long and difficult voyage. And with it, the man senses a hope for the day's secret worth, as if in his new clothing of youthful infatuation he gleans the inherent potential secreted amid the day's regular and disheartening fabric; as if, somewhere within the hazy maze of its sun-kissed streets and burning buildings, he might find the great miracle awaiting him: an unexpected chance for deliverance during this very final effort of his waning will.

"A million years is a long time," the man says thoughtfully, distantly, ruminating on the import of the words even as he speaks them. His wife's eyes – long-ago disappeared from his days but the sanctuary of their peaceful expression never forgotten – stare out at him from the years, stoking the old consuming ache to which he's never grown accustomed.

The boy nods, looking humbled and awed by this wisdom, too. From within the apartment's ajar window, the fighting voices rise and rage anew: "I hope you die, you bastard!" "Well, maybe I'll kill you first, you ugly goddamn whore!"

The man turns and gazes over the sun-drenched crescent spread before them. As he looks he perceives a low humming, seemingly rising from the concrete beneath their feet or from the steaming air itself, and existing in range somewhere between the electric voice of the cicadas and the distant hungry murmur of the city. "Right over there?" he asks, hearing how an edge of excitement has crept into his voice, sensing his heart palpitating a faster pattern than before.

The child is quick to speak up. "Right there! In the middle of the crescent! 4:45 sharp, I heard, just before supper-time!" Then he adds, in a hushed voice and with an unconcealed hopefulness which endears him to the man very much, "Do you wanna come, too?"

Yes, I'll be your father, yes, we can start over, the man thinks suddenly, strangely but not so strangely. He nods without hesitation or thought. He says, "Yes. I want to go, too. Very much, I want to go, too." He eyes his watch, and then the dusty sunny cul-de-sac burning in the still air. The smile he gives the boy weighs nothing on him. Like water it falls from him easily, to cool the anguished heat of the day from his skin, his throat, the concrete world around them. Seeing this, the boy smiles freely, too.

They idle in their places, kicking stones and surveying the crescent and speaking in low somnolent voices when the inclination seizes them. In this way – through their quiet conversation, with the ease of their shared silences, and with the comforting intermittent accompaniment of static and excited buzzing chatter and uncanny yet familiar language from the boy's electric mouth – they drown out the fighting voices drifting on the air, the sapping heat of the day, the tumult of the city waiting like an insatiable malevolence beyond the shelter of the cul-de-sac. The sun falls and falls across the sky, turning the street the deep red of blood and charging the air with anticipation, an invigorating hopefulness the man hasn't known for a very long time. He thinks of his wife, swallowed by another day, long past. He'll always think of her. In this day and in the next and in any day that comes for him.

He smiles at the boy. For now, the day is theirs, belonging to them more than to anyone else the entire city through and through.

Who dies first?

- REH

FOREVERMORE YOURS,
THE HATRED CHORD

The tiny wooden stage squeezed into the room's corner was unimpressive: lit morosely in feeble luminescence from the ancient lighting rack; a pair of battered amplifiers like time-weary guards adorning either side of the wooden platform; and a dusty tattered black velvet curtain hanging behind with kitschy speckles meant to represent stars dusted into its fabric.

Then her arrival, and the ragged backdrop was disappeared, and only the woman and her songs were with him in the cramped dingy tavern. No more drinkers lining the bar like dirty pigeons; no more stink of smoke and sweat and urine in the air; no more thoughts circling in his skull, banging from each other and hurting him with their thorny touches.

Her dress on Mondays was always pale in colour. This he'd noticed, like he'd noticed other details of her wardrobe over the Winter months during which he'd become a fixture of the bar: her mannerisms while standing before the microphone, regal-looking when singing, or waiting discomfited during the scant applause and ribald catcalls between numbers. This Monday she wore a powder blue dress, with matching shoes and a pale blue stone hanging between her collarbones from a silver chain so thin it was nearly invisible from where he sat huddled in his regular booth to one side of the stage.

He watched her, enthralled with her every move as she drifted across the stage to her place before the microphone stand. He squinted in the uncertain light, and found it: she wore also a small slim emerald grasshopper broach. Every night of the week she wore a specific insect on her person – Tuesdays were ruby ladybugs and Wednesdays sea-green praying mantises and Thursdays rhinestone dragonflies; Fridays a vivid orange Monarch butterfly fluttered from her dress and Saturdays a bumblebee clung there like bright sunlight, while Sundays the mellow snow-white glimmer of moths shone from her bosom.

Her Monday grasshopper, adorning her left breast, caught and reflected the dim stage lights in a tiny but brilliant radiance that mesmerized the eye. Her shoulder-length hair, a straight platinum cut encircling her narrow features, was made silver by the lights. Her skin was pale, too, and with her dainty wrists and thin legs and eyes watching the floor of the stage before her or the air over the heads of the audience – but always avoiding the eyes of those gathered in the little room – everything about her defined fragility.

The man, as he always did, drank his drink and waited for some occurrence that might prove his notions of the woman true – gossamer wings to unfurl from her narrow shoulders and carry her through the smoke and stink to some heavenly place, or for him to look about him and find that he'd been in such a place all along and only been unable to see it for the deceiving perpetual fog of cigarette smoke. And, as ever, she only stepped two small steps to the microphone, placed her ruby lips to its round silver head, and in a subdued, reticent murmur announced herself into the sordid room.

"Good evening, gentleman and ladies. I am Maria Santo. I will sing for you now."

Her delicate voice cut the smoke like a gently-wielded scythe, violently soft among the vulgar clamour of bar patrons, and far too lovely to occupy the same room. In its aftermath the man couldn't help himself: he smiled a grave sympathetic smile, in his eyes only, and waved to a passing waitress to bring him another drink, though he wasn't yet finished with the glass of rum sweating in his hand; and then he settled himself into the comforting red faux-leather seat of his secluded booth, and waited.

He was anxious, as he was always while watching and listening to Maria Santo. He was apprehensive while in her presence, and felt as though he stood on the cusp of some great or tragic happening.

From the ancient speakers came the delicate tinkle and pipes of a calliope – its player, and her musical partner, hidden as always somewhere behind the curtain, in the dim dusty backstage depths of the tavern – and her evening of songs was begun.

*

Scant applause and half-hearted cheers throughout the gloomy room. The man, stunned and shaken inside his booth, wiped the beer froth from his lips and the tears from where they bothered his eyes, making the singer a wash of powder blue and silver. He wondered, distantly through the fog of drink and his great weariness, whether she noticed his tears, or whether she noticed them every night while she sang her songs. He wondered whether she saw his tears when on occasion she chanced to find him crying in his booth and whether she might be curious about those places from which his sorrow came; and whether perhaps seeing his tears there each night like a reliable rainfall she might wonder if they came from the selfsame place from which her own mournful voice sang.

Her final number, as every night, was preceded by the identical introduction, the only words she uttered into the microphone throughout her entire performance outside of her curt introduction at the beginning of the set.

"I dedicate this song to William."

No one seemed to discern her voice from among the weary din of the tavern; glasses clinking, the droning murmur of midnight conversation, the occasional crisp crack of pool balls ricocheting on the pool table in the opposite corner of the room.

The man noticed the words, though. His breathing grew more ragged than it had been during her penultimate song. His heart quickened, and a tugging grew up in it, too, as if his blood were the tide and she the moon to which it was eternally committed. The man wondered about those words. He yearned to know the mysteries of the woman standing on stage beneath the feeble lights, for he sensed somehow that the paths that had led them both to the tavern each night might have been similar ones.

She stood in her place, still and radiant. The strummed, open strings of what sounded like an acoustic guitar or sitar came suddenly crashing through the speakers, a braying, discordant sound that spiked into the recesses of the small room. Without beauty, a chord-less collection of open notes struck by a savage hand. In their fading echo, a deep silence descended, marked merely with an occasional gruff inebriated voice cursing the aural intrusion. Into the relative silence, her breathy, pained voice —

unaccompanied now by music of any kind – appeared like a foghorn's light in the night, though its message, which the man knew well, guided into uncertain places.

> *Momma, the world is bright and kind*
> *You are all I have ever known*
> *Then in a great darkness a man was born*
> *And inside a night he brought it to me, too*
> *Momma, I cannot jump away*
> *Momma, this dark is spun too tight*
> *O you, you are the one I hate*
> *O you, you are the one I hate*

This verse she sang in succession, again and again in a courageous and melancholy and plangent acappella, while the tavern patrons smoked and drank and grumbled among themselves, and while the lone man witnessing the spectacle of Maria Santo wept inside his lonesome booth.

A final tumult shaking the speaker cabinets and the glasses and bottles behind the bar – the weird indefinable un-chord returned – and the coda was complete. As it faded, so too did Maria Santo – her voice evanescing into the smoke-congested rafters, she herself drifting without goodbye towards the velvet stage curtain and disappearing spectrally among its starry folds.

The stage, without her, looked barren and distressing.

The smoke hung in a thin layer of cumulus over it, looking threatening, and bringing to the man's mind the look of a battlefield in the aftermath of carnage.

In the wake of her passage – in the wake of her haunting voice and message – the man continued to weep in his booth. Huddled into himself, too distraught to try to conceal his sorrow from the wary-eyed waitress when she brought him his drink. He only gulped it quickly and waved for another a moment afterwards. Its taste was bitter, though, and only made heavier the sadness which crushed him.

He was midway through another glass of rum when a miraculous occurrence drove away the fog of his drinking. Staring through it he saw her like an angel descended in the gloom of the tavern. She'd forgotten something, he guessed, watching her scan the stage with wide fretful eyes. Maria Santo stooped and, a moment later, stood straight and with something claimed from the stage in her fingers, drew her hand to her chest. He watched spellbound as she turned and the bauble glimmered from her dress – her grasshopper, detached from her during her music, or awakened from lifelessness and leaping forth in the sombre, aching dirge of her closing number to lay unnoticed upon the stage, was reclaimed by her.

He found himself smiling widely. A great joy awakened in the man while observing the insect jewel adorning the singer once more. She drifted again towards the curtain of stars. Desperation awoke in him then. Terror, too, at the thought of her leaving him once again that night.

Without thought, his voice called her name.

"Maria. Maria Santo."

No one heard his trembling voice from among the tavern denizens – all remained immersed in their conversation and drinks.

Maria Santo heard him.

Stopping before the gently undulating velvet curtain, she turned, cocking a delicate ear towards him, her grasshopper's prismatic glow splitting the murk of the room once more. The man knew then that this was the first time her eyes had looked directly into his own, and that when she sang her eyes remained unwavering in the air before her while she looked into much, much more distant places. He shuddered beneath their light: blue and pale like her dress, but piercing, as though she was both startled by and intensely curious of the single person who'd taken notice of her from the throngs of perpetually indifferent bar patrons. He was transfixed. More miraculously still, she came to him, across the stage and stepping onto the parquet floor and gliding to his very booth.

She stared down at him with an impenetrable gaze. He shrank from her but basked beneath her scrutiny, too. He smiled, he trembled, he sought for words but in the end could only continue his dazzled and sheepish way of staring at her. Perhaps a nervous laugh escaped him. Perhaps he eventually offered her a seat at his little table.

A moment passed and, as if waking from a deep sleep, the man stared and there she sat across from him, bathed in a light that seemed to radiate from herself: Maria Santo, watching him with strange, inscrutable eyes.

A very uncanny thing happened: the conversation with Maria Santo was one he was never to recall. He felt distinctly that a great deal of time had passed – indeed the bar had grown louder and quieter and then louder and quieter again, with several fights breaking out and broken up throughout – but still the man would be able to recall nothing of what they spoke, except for the very final moments of the conversation. Those final moments he would never forget, for he was to regret his part in what was said through every sober and drunken moment of his remaining life.

Made bellicose by drink, too-loud and churlish, he heard his helpless fool's voice and the fool's question with which it dared to sully the night: "Miss Santo, could you answer me the question that's been plaguing me for these months and months? Who is *William*? Eh? Would you share the secret of William with an avid admirer? What did he do to deserve that final song of yours this night and every other, I wonder?" Perhaps he'd meant for his remarks to seem jocular, or possibly to appear as a roundabout road to a conceited sweet-talking of this striking, exotic and enigmatic woman whom he knew, deep inside, was exceedingly beyond his hopes of attaining. Perhaps it was only the voice of the rum asking the question, for its voice was a strong one, and difficult to quiet in even the most blatantly shameful and inappropriate situations. Or perhaps it was simply his desperate need to understand her mystery and to equate himself to her through this knowledge that urged his impetuous tongue.

He watched her face fracture. Full ruby lips grimace in anticipation of the tears that welled immediately from her eyes. Her mascara grew smudged and grotesque in a moment's time. Her shoulders shuddered and her dainty hands trembled as she sought to pull a tissue from the tricky recess of the wooden dispenser on the table. Soon, her whole body bowed forwards, until her head she placed on the sticky scratched tabletop, weeping silently.

The man gaped. He downed his remaining rum in a frantic gulp but the liquor gave him no answers on how to remedy the situation he'd created. He lit a cigarette with shaking hands and sucked on it hungrily, anxiously. Still the beautiful woman lay collapsed before him, no matter his paltry attempts to make her sadness disappear.

"Hey, I'm sorry, miss," he stammered, hands raised in the air in indecision as to whether he should touch her, seek to calm her through his platonic embrace. Her eyes when she raised her head, though, stayed his hand. In their distress he saw that she wanted nothing less than to be touched. He murmured, voice humbled and genuinely regretful, eyes in his glass, "Miss Santo…I'm really, truly, *deeply* sorry to have upset you and… and for your sadness. I'm so sorry for your sadness."

She answered him. She spoke to his question, to his immense curiosity, and to his sympathy, though her answer would only haunt the man forevermore with its tantalizing mystery.

"I will sing this song until I die." Her eyes grew wider, more desperate still, and with an unsettling pleading tone infusing the words, she gasped, "And maybe then I will not have to sing anymore?"

With these words she left him alone in the booth. He watched her drift hastily and silently through the room, ascend the wooden stairs onto the tiny stage and then disappear once more into the starry curtain.

Goodbye, Maria. Maria, goodbye. This the man thought helplessly watching her glide like a spirit across the dimly-lit room, her powder blue dress spectral and uncertain. He opened his mouth, but was too drunk and too weary with his years to call the words after her as he wished he could. They echoed in his thoughts, though, and with them rose a bitter taste of regret he knew well, and loathed greatly:

I think I know how you feel, Maria. Oh, I really do. I know your big hate. I know the place from which it comes. Maybe we're the same. Maybe we could be close, if only.

The man ordered another drink, and then another before last call was announced by the barkeep in his raspy smoker's voice; and then he begged for a very, very final drink that the barkeep allowed because the man was his most regular customer, but mostly because he saw the man's eyes peering at him from the dim lamp glow in his darkened booth: lost, fractured, and desperate for the power to hold a woman who – for reasons that only she knew – could never again be held.

*

His final drink lay half-drunk in his hands. Its warm brown colour now saddened him, for the man felt the liquor's power diminishing.

It was then that an elderly man limped past his booth. He paused there, and turned a cloudy eye upon the man licking the inside of his glass, savouring its liquor. This old man was short, and bent, and a thin crop of white hair encircled his otherwise shining bald head.

The man in his booth knew instinctually who this stranger was. He was the musician who, backstage and hidden behind the star-beaded curtain, played the piano and organ and calliope upon which Maria Santo floated her ethereal voice.

"You are the cloud, my friend," the man slurred from his booth, "Upon which she floats." He heard the poet in his words, and chuckled with undisguised pride.

The elderly gentleman – and he was a gentleman, dressed as he was for his invisible performance in a striking black tuxedo, cummerbund and bright crimson bowtie, with a top hat held formally beneath an arm – called through the murmuring noise of the wee morning tavern, "Thank you, friend. The honour is mine that my humble efforts are discerned at all from the rare beauty which floats upon it."

The man, though drunk, smiled appreciatively at the words. He admitted, with a resigned and theatrical nodding of his head and a raising of his glass on the air, "She sings beautifully."

The elderly man, as if sympathizing with the look of the man drunk and lost-eyed in the booth, answered solemnly. "She sings for herself, and no other."

He nodded, and made as if to continue on his way. The man stopped him, urgency in his voice and defining his great distress as he jolted upright in his booth. "Wait, sir. Please. I was only wondering, could you please tell me – her last song, her last song – what was that you played? You were in it for a moment only, but what *was* that sound? Was your instrument a sitar? A guitar, un-tuned? It wails like a Theremin but it crashes like a drum. I – I've never heard a thing like that, except for here in this tavern, every midnight on the nose."

The little man seemed to bow a ways closer to the wooden floorboards. His eyes grew murkier still. They now echoed those of the man staring expectantly – helplessly – from his booth.

His voice grew hushed and in a conspiratorial murmur he said, "I…I don't know what to tell you. It…It is a note I have never played, in all our nights playing here on this little stage, though it haunts this place every midnight. Where it comes from…" He drifted into silence, putting his smoky eyes into the smoky air. And he finished, stunning the man into a silence from which he would find it difficult to climb: "I swear I have seen it, friend. Sometimes, on some midnights when her final song is sung – if you look closely, through the smoke and shadows and throngs of bar-goers gathered here – if you look upon the walls of this little tavern, you will see that they cry, too, like you cry, and like I cry, too, secret and hidden behind the stage curtain. Tears pour down their dark wood and gather in puddles in the corners of this room. I've put a finger in these puddles and tasted the salt they carry. And during those times – through the babble of voices drunk and talking and arguing and seducing each other into regrettable beds – during those times of sorrow one might hear a soft crying, too, from some place I can't exactly tell you where."

They looked at one another in silence a moment. Then the old man bowed his little head to the man in his booth and said, "Have a good and safe passage through the night, friend. Goodbye." And he limped on his way, towards the rear door which led into the small gravel lot behind the tavern.

The man watched after him.

A brief moment of brightness came. A fluttering at his left eye caused the man to look askance. Through his weird vision of drink and stinging eyes it materialized: the moth, pale as snow and fragile as powder, and wholly misplaced in the barbaric atmosphere of the tavern. He watched entranced as its delicate wings beat an erratic but mighty rhythm among the smoke. They took it higher and higher. He craned his neck towards the shadowy ceiling. He blinked and it was no more, gone into the ether.

He reached a hand ceilingwards. He felt pathetic. He felt foolish when the waitress brought him his final-final drink of the night, eyebrows raised in the patient questionable way with which many people looked on him those days. He put his hand onto the gummy tabletop and stared into the frothing glass before him. Once again he found no answer floating in the rum. He peered surreptitiously about him but no secret glimmer of snow could he see through the dirty haze anywhere.

He knew then with a painful certainty that he would never truly know the mystery of Maria Santo, though he would always feel as if he knew it with all of his aching heart. And he knew too that he would return to his booth the following night, and the nights after that and after that, and there he would sprawl and drink and weep through the concerts of the mysterious woman with whom he shared the unknowable mystery.

The man, as happened every night and would continue to happen every forthcoming night, grew glad of the smoke grown thick in the air of the tavern near closing-time. It hid him from the other stragglers, and them from him, and made it easier to pretend that behind the clouds there were good and bright and peaceful days waiting for him, and for everyone else with a song of furious woe playing in their hearts.

Rogues in the House.

Was it a dream the nighted lotus brought?

- from The Song Of Bêlit

- REH

A ROMAN PLAGUE

"Dura-Europos has fallen, brothers. The Persians own the city."

The Legionnaires of the colonia, Italcus, listened raptly and with grave features to their fellow soldiers standing before them, weary and wounded from the bloodshed they'd left behind. These three men were survivors of the sacking, defeat defining their postures, shame in their eyes.

"The Sassanids are desert devils," said the man beside the first, shaking his head in astonishment. "Mining 'neath the city, filling the tunnels with poison gas, choking our brothers. The Euphrates, she runs red..." He drifted off, a stunned look in his eyes.

"We've come to spread word of the defeat," said the third man, a desperate look seeped into his sallow features, as if seeking to prove the wisdom in their retreat, the courage in their hearts. "Those who survived have been taken to Ctesiphon. Slavery awaits them."

"*Barbaricum* filth," spat Aquilinus, captain of the colonia, grimacing with disdain, eyes smouldering. The raised smooth-skinned scar running a crooked line from left cheek to chin shone white amid his livid, burning features. "News of this will see the Gauls calling along the border, and the Huns and Visigoths, and others, all while Rome answers this affront. Hadrian's Wall, I fear, is not so strong to repel them all."

"My lord, we must make haste and bring word of this massacre – Rome must know!" Marianus was ashen-faced beside his old friend, clutching the sword hilt in the scabbard at his waist. He was a veteran of countless campaigns, many won and some lost, and the gravity of this defeat shook even him.

Aquilinus' eyes were hard as he surveyed his men. "We remain here this night, and ride at dawn."

In the west, thunder sounded, like a bugle calling for battle.

Moonlight paled the grey stone walls of the garrison, the wild grassland beyond.

The Legionnaire Valentinus stiffened at his station along the wall, an inexplicable chill of dread snaking along his spine and making his nape hairs rise. Something was amiss; something in the night that had been as it should be was now wrong. He gripped his javelin tightly, looking to east and west from his post but he found no sign of enemy, no shadow of Sassanid or Gaul slinking low to the ground, moonlight glinting from drawn blades; only the shadow-drenched land of grass and granite stretching away in all directions, the forest hulking in the east like a great and impregnable wall.

When next he looked up he found her silhouetted against the red gibbous moon, standing within the nearby parapet. Utterly naked, her skin white as snow, her long hair wild, windblown and blood-red. Valentinus stifled a cry and staggered back a step, aghast, when the phantom figure stepped from its perch on the edifice and descended like a moth upon the air toward him.

She drifted down and down until her small feet alighted upon the stone floor without sound. He saw then her eyes: feral and hungry. Her tongue lolled from between her succulent lips, a corpulent grotesque muscle the deep blood-colour of raw meat. Her erect nipples were sharp black darts stabbing through the queerly charged air at the Legionnaire even as she opened her arms to him.

"Halt!" he commanded her, tearing himself from the bewitching paralysis that had overcome him and raising his pilum towards the woman's chest. But the glimmering in her eyes mesmerized the soldier, taking fast hold of him once more as she approached soundlessly to stand before him, the barbed iron tip of the pilum pricking her between her breasts, letting loose a thin line of blood, jet-black and viscous as oil.

She opened her mouth wide and the voice of a hundred wolves bayed at the soldier, freezing the blood in his veins, loosing his bowels. Among the feral cacophony came another, human voice, masculine and deep, coarse and guttural:

"A storm is come, to mock and make mud of the towers of men, so that you may better see the greater paths before you."

Thick clouds rolled across the moon, deepening the night's dark.

A red rain awoke the troubled Legionnaires of Italcus.

It beat with great violence upon the roof of the barracks and pounded the dirt of the open courtyard, making of it an immense pool of crimson-slicked mud. The deluge lasted but moments but the force of it awakened the fort, its uncanny aura sending rattled sentries scrambling to sound an alarum of bugles.

The soldiers emerged wary from their barracks, pulling on tunics and scale armour and fastening sword-belts around their waists; while the sentries, holding torches high, stared stunned from their posts along the stone walls surrounding the outpost, all seeking to fathom the ghastly nature of the precipitation; until slowly, through a fog of incredulity, understanding came over them all: for among the great crimson pool owning the courtyard they discerned one of their own, recognizable only by the shreds of his tunic, his crushed bronze cuirass and shield scattered among the ragged remnants of the man's body torn asunder into a million pieces:

limbs and organs and naked bones and a sickening brew of unrecognizable, pulped remains. His pulverized helmet lay in the blood-puddle's centre, its once-imperial crimson plume sullied with his gore.

Men cried out, unsheathing shortswords and seeking to look in every direction at once — among the dense shadows beyond reach of the torches' glow, into the crooked towers and ramparts, even to the sky itself — but could not find the unimaginable enemy in their midst.

And then she was in the centre of the blood-filled courtyard, among them all. Her red lips smiled. Her wild eyes blazed, appraising the soldiers hemming her in. Her hands were dripping crimson. Blood clung to her arms to her elbows, too, and splashed her breasts, and made a thick circle around her leering mouth. A long shredded strip of flesh lay tangled in her red locks. The glistening necklace she wore was the Legionnaire's intestines.

The captain, Aquilinus, glowered at her. "I woke from a dream of you, witch, and saw you crawl forth from a black hole gaping in the earth!" he swore, tearing his shortsword from its scabbard at his hip. Beside him, Marianus cried, "Nay, my lord, I swear to you I saw the witch with mine own eyes, when a black star fell from the sky only minutes ago! And then the screams of our brother, not long after, and the dark rain!"

A soldier stabbed his sword towards the intruder, exclaiming, "Look! It is Cacus, the fire-spitter!"

At mention of the demon's name the men shuddered; they shuddered as they saw the woman's hands raised upon the air, palms towards them, a plume of fire smouldering in each; they shook with dread when she opened her mouth to show them the fire glowing within.

She mocked them with vile laughter — the voice of a cackling hyena pack, a brood of screeching gypsies casting dark magics in night woods — silencing them all. Into the great bestial clamour the woman's hoarse voice sliced like an assassin's dagger. "Your paltry empire, your frail walls, your weak skeleton army of brittle bones and trembling hearts and small hungers: a greater fire shall sweep you all away, for there is always and always a mightier flame. Far mightier even than that wielded by little brothers Cacus and Vulcan."

The Legionnaires raised their weapons threateningly.

She tittered at the gesture, and crooned grotesquely, "Soldiers, I only want us all to be together, for together we *could be* the army of fire to burn away weak veils of peace the lands over. We could rule the Earth, forever, and forever, forever, and forever."

Aquilinus stepped forward. He beat a fist upon his iron cuirass and aimed his shortsword at the woman. "Rome rules the world, witch, and you would do well to know it. We know not whence you came, but swear that you shall pay for this vile blasphemy of magick."

At this she spat blood and embers into the dirt. A serpent slithered forth from the black tangle of hair at her groin. The fires in her hands flared higher, excited. She took a step forward, menacingly, and they saw her left foot, cloven now, and black-furred.

Aquilinus gave the command: "Cut this whore to pieces."

The Legionnaires rushed the pale woman, bristling steel.

Their swords whirled about her but she moved faster still, an impossibly fleet blur that bewitched the eyes of the hardened soldiers, slowing their muscles and blunting their weapons' kiss. Among the clash of their arms the woman's weird imploring litany sounded in their ears and hearts, over and over and over:

"I only want us all to be together. We could rule the Earth."

After a time many of the Legionnaires' swords had found a comrade's flesh, slashing a throat wide in a torrent of blood, lopping off an arm at the elbow in a geyser of crimson; for weird visions materialized in the heart of the chaotic fray, causing confusion and panic and fear the likes of which were unknown among those disciplined men of war: one soldier, Albus, screamed shrilly as the gigantic black scorpion scuttled upon him to spear him clean through his torso with its tail like a colossal scythe slicing crops; his comrade beside him, Longinus, stood helpless and transfixed by the poison-eyed stare of the basilisk that descended from out of the star-studded sky to snap his legs in half with its gargantuan serpent's fangs; the young brash soldier, Thracius, flailed in the dust, screaming shrilly as two long rusty nails impaled his eyes, though none had witnessed where they had flown from; a spearman's head was decimated by the jaws of the great black bear that strode like a king into their midst upon its hind legs, bold and proud and fifteen feet high its countenance of fury roaring into the darkness; this beast dispatched another Legionnaire as well, crushing him like kindling beneath its long-clawed foot, scattering his throwing-darts in the red mud; and even brave Aquilinus, in the end, was held spellbound, shortsword hanging low towards the earth, by the spectacle of the hulking horned blasphemy blanketing him beneath its shadow, its awful demonic visage glaring down upon him with immense molten eyes, its smouldering volcanic maw opened to sneer at him like all the rabid hunger in the world.

Among the carnage she danced a lithe dance, pirouetting easily on the air, slipping and feinting and turning fluidly, unkissed by sword or dagger or javelin. Her engorged crimson lips smiled all the while, rapturous as she rejoiced in the screams rising moonwards.

Blood flowed like a river un-dammed; fire rose high enough to lick and scald the stars trembling in the early morning sky.

A day of great celebration arrived in the Sassanid village, Al-Salihiyah, near Dura-Europos, only several miles from the final Roman colonia, Italcus, along the frontier between Rome and Persia; minstrels plucked their harps and sang with jubilation while the people danced and cheered, for news carried swiftly among that long-harried people, of a plague that had befallen the Legionnaires who guarded this neighbouring symbol of draconian Roman rule, Italcus, as too their fellow soldiers at once-proud Dura-Europos had been destroyed; the irony did not escape the Persians, who had long referred to their would-be oppressors as the pestilence that had decimated their numbers over the centuries, seeking always to squash their culture, their dignity, their history, their own right to rule the world. Over time this great vanquisher was likewise named Justice; and Retribution; while some named her more simply, Fire, and she would grow to become that whispered ghost, those dusty lines joining history and myth.

Some villagers of Al-Salihiyah, who had been awakened by the sounds of fighting, claimed strange visions that long night of mysterious slaughter: a child watching from its bedroom window saw a pack of hyenas loping through the village streets long after midnight, each with a human infant gripped between its slavering jaws; a woman filling a ewer from a well swore to have watched an immense bat, pig-sized, flitting helter-skelter low over the rooftops, chattering madly and spitting fat blood droplets onto the houses like the wickedest of curses; an elderly farmer wept with hands clasped together and a prayer of thanks upon his lips as the woman glided through the thoroughfare, her naked breasts gleaming in the moonlight, her fingers aflame, her serpentine torso undulating in the dust, leaving a wet trail in the wake of which followed a phantasmagorical mirage:

The troupe of Legionnaires, marching wearily, heads bowed earthwards: bloody; charred; chained.

Dreams un-plagued.

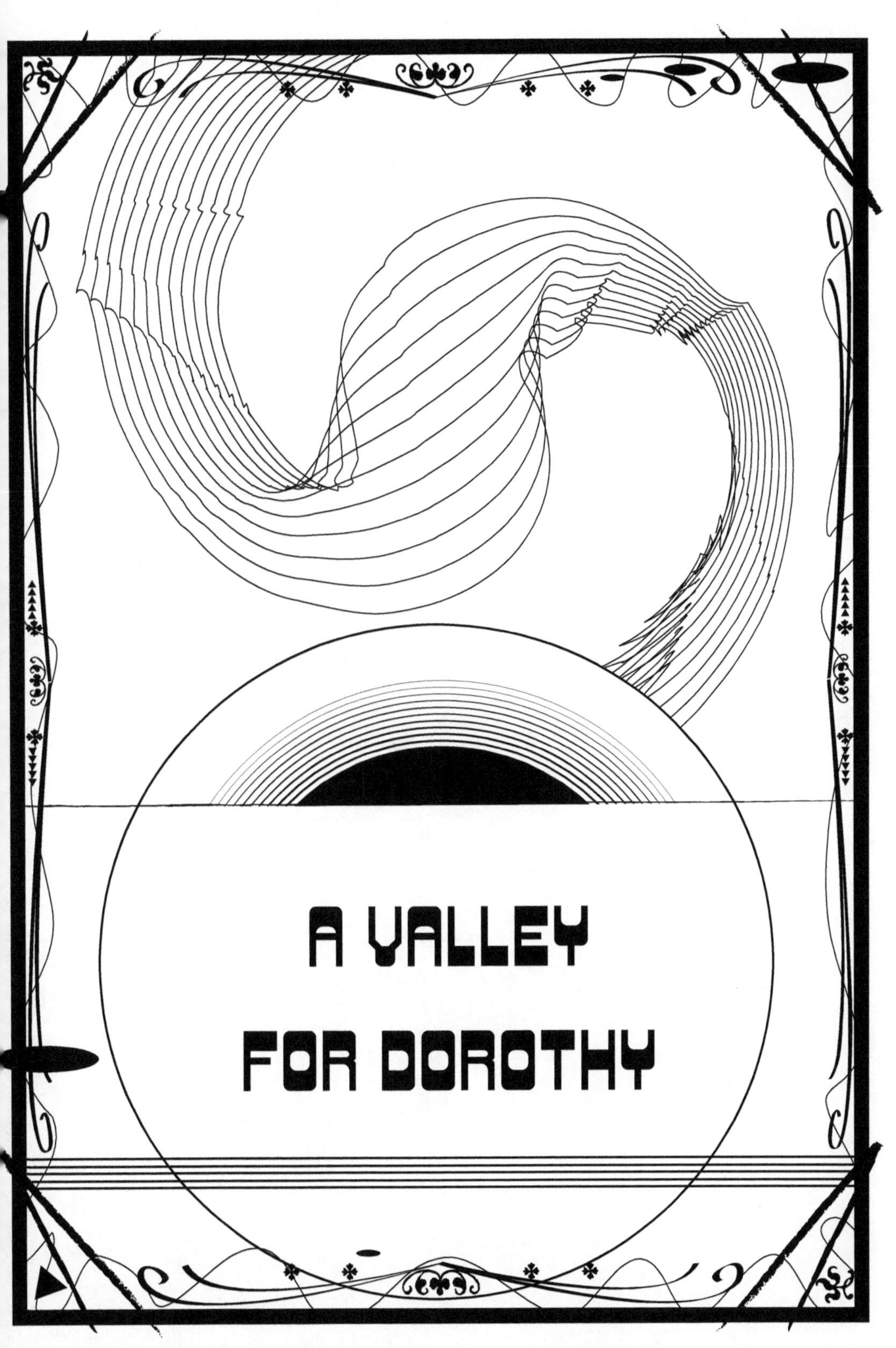
A VALLEY
FOR DOROTHY

The days were long for the toil filling them, but the nights, oh, the nights: an eternity growing up each dusk and stretching long and long until the dawn sun scalded the mountains of the east like a great malefic fire to cleanse the world of all the sorrow it carried within its endless miles and eternal hours; though of course the sun, great deceiver that it was, gave no such mercy. For the nights always returned to hound Henry Barber, who hadn't slept a good sleep in forty years and more. They stretched the same wicked length and depth, laden with all of the pain he'd known in his days, and pain he'd known much of.

And so it was that another eternal night had set upon Henry Barber: he put his hands on the air to examine them by the young lunar light. All of the old scars and the stories they told, and the new scars and their stories, too, those mounds of flesh paled by the years or raw and red and new, criss-crossing his hands and arms; and the dirt, as well, always dirt like a perpetual second layer of skin cloaking him, and working with the scars to make his hands unsightly; always the dirt dusting his skin, caked beneath his cracked fingernails like a permanent part of the battered man he was. Though he could not see inside himself he knew his heart was similarly battered where it hung lightless within the shell of him, for it ached and burned beyond measure then as it had every night since the days of his youth, days he only ever recalled as if through the densest of fogs; a vague golden-aired time, a half-remembered oasis before the light was put out of the world and all of the darkness he came to know so well was ushered in.

He stared down into the hole he'd dug in the earth. It gaped at him like an immense black toothless mouth. He shuddered, despite having faced countless such mouths. "Sleep forever," he said to the blue-skinned bloated woman he'd dropped into the earth-mouth minutes earlier. Her crime unknown, her violent demise known intimately to Henry Barber, the sound of her corpulent corpse thudding its way along the rough-hewn grave into the darkness like a feed-laden sack still haunting the nocturnal air.

And Henry Barber slammed his spade into the earth, and hefted the first mound of the woman's burial dirt over her in the tomb darkness below.

The milky semi-light of pre-dawn filtered through the grime-encrusted window to illuminate the small work shack. Henry Barber's employer, a portly, apple-jowled, greasy-haired scumbag named Huxtable Crocker, eyed him shrewdly with a beady black gaze from where he sat squeezed behind the small wooden desk and looking to Henry's eyes like some fat fish beached and doomed outside of its water hole.

"Barber," he growled through a mouthful of tobacco bulging his shiny red cheek like a balloon. "I got a job for you, but a job the kind you ain't gonna want to have no part in digging. I need you to dig me a hole, but not like any of the usual holes. This hole's gotta be deep and deep, and deeper than any hole ever dug, by you or any other gravedigger this world ever seen."

Henry Barber nodded. A job was a job. He'd dug holes for hundreds of dead men and dead women, and plenty for men and women not dead yet but with their fates preordained for them by vengeful minds and the dark and bad mediums of their doom: bullets and daggers, cups of poison and suffocating piano wire and choking hands. He'd dig this hole and fill it and buy himself supper and some beers with its depth. He'd dig any hole he had to if it would keep him alive, though he wasn't very much content to be alive – the only thought more distressing to him was his death, and what might lie waiting for him then. His employer could stress the importance of this latest of countless holes for digging and he'd treat it like any other: a job to work to help get from this day to the next. A job he'd do well, because he owed his employer for the many jobs he'd given him in the past, and he owed him for more besides.

The boss lowered his gravely voice and, with chary sidewise glances to left and right, grated, "You gonna dig me a hole for to bury a demon."

Henry Barber thought on this a moment. He nodded, still pondering the words and their possible meaning. A shivering began its creeping along his spine and among the hairs along his forearms, and this uncanny shiver he didn't like at all.

As if seeing this invisible reaction in him, Huxtable Crocker narrowed his vulpine eyes more shrewdly still, and whispered, "She'll try to deceive you, for she's a deceiver through and through."

Henry Barber thought the boss was referring to his wife – possibly he'd caught her with another roughneck and this roughneck proved to be the final straw for her; maybe he'd just grown weary of her dark eyes flashing at every cock and balls strutting the muddy streets of their oil town.

"Yeah, I'll bury your demon."

The boss smiled a vicious smile. He laughed grimly. "Barber, you a strange fella. And you got courage in you. But don't you for a second be believing this special hole's waiting for my wife, or some tart with my bastard child growing in her belly, or some roughneck I caught deceiving me in secret. This demon is the genuine article, Barber. Maybe you got trouble understanding it. Maybe you don't care much for the Holy Book and the things it say – maybe that Book's some kind of bane of your days like it is for some kinds of us men – but I ain't lying to you one word."

Barber matched the boss's narrowed eyes with his own. His voice was frosty: "I don't know no banes, Crock, and I ain't much for reading. But I'm gonna dig for you again, like I told you."

Huxtable Crocker's sardonic, grotesque grin creased his features. "You a man with honour in you, Henry. That's why I'm asking you. I'd never give this job to no one else. I'd rather try it myself and have it murder me, what with my age eating my bones. Some say a man can't ever bury no demon, but I got faith in your skills and your grit. How much you think I'm offering you for it?"

Henry Barber sucked on his cigar. Its burning sounded in the A.M. stillness like the crisping of autumn leaves. He said calmly, "I'm thinking it's a lot heftier than the measly nothing I get paid for busting my balls in your fields, and keeping quiet about all the holes you need dug in this world."

The boss chuckled again. "I appreciate your candour, man. I always did, did you know? I got respect for you, and that's saying something because there ain't many I respect in this shit world of wicked and gormless men."

He spit brown stringy phlegm onto the mud-caked wooden floorboards, and finished: "I'm giving you retirement money, Henry. Money enough to keep you fed and without worry for the rest of your years. You been my steadiest hand for how many years I can't recall no more. You always clock the most hours in the fields. The best digger I ever saw, and by digger you of course know my meaning. You work the shittiest of shit jobs and work them better than the rest. You never bitched a word about none of it. You deserve this."

Henry Barber ruminated on this a minute before answering. "Alright. Maybe I do. So okay: I'm gonna dig your hole."

The deal with Henry Barber's job as hole-digger was that he dug the holes, filled them with their occupants, and most importantly took those occupants out of the waking living world, in the complete opposite order.

"Henry," Huxtable Crocker said, leaning towards him, his belly rolling onto the desktop like a hideous toadstool. "Are you a believer?"

"I believe in some things."

"Well, whether you believe or no, what you're gonna see might bend you. It might bend you near to breaking, and might do just that. You need to know this, so you ready for it, even though ready ain't something a man can be in a bad situation like this."

Henry Barber wasn't in the habit of asking his employer unnecessary questions pertaining to his jobs. Now though, something compelled him. "I got one question: where did you find your demon?"

"Oh no, Barber. It ain't that way at all. My demon found *me*, though my resources found me its nesting place." He smiled a smile tainted with regret. "I ain't lived a saintly life, like you might know. This cursed thing was heading my way for years on end. Maybe you can be like my guardian angel, Barber. Or my angel of vengeance. Stranger sights this world's seen, maybe."

Henry Barber thought on this. It made sense to him. He nodded, watching Huxtable Crocker unfurl the creased and time-yellowed scroll of parchment and spread it across the desk. Pinning it open with a pair of rocks, he leaned back in his wooden chair, screeching its frame with his weight. His voice was grim: "You gotta look and look good, and put it all in your memory, Henry. In case you don't make this one, I got to have these directions to show the next brave or mad man."

Henry Barber leaned over the map, examining its faded lines etched into the ancient, flaking paper. A rough black circle marked a place among the tangle of crags several miles south of town, beyond the county line among the baddest of the badlands – difficult country, barren and lifeless but for roaming coyote packs with the hunt on their mind. He knew the area, having buried many a man and woman thereabouts – he could find the thing's nest easily enough.

Henry Barber glanced up at the slippery sound as Huxtable Crocker slid the leather satchel across the desktop towards him. He took it from the desk. Untying it, he glanced within. He sought to betray no emotion or reaction but wasn't certain if he'd succeeded. His toad-like employer, sinner and scumbag and wicked man deserving of his hauntings, had made good on his word.

Henry Barber touched thumb and finger to his hat's brim and tipped his head to the ashen, fear-eyed man behind the desk. Turning, he strode from the work shack and stepped into the day.

The sun was lost to the badness of the day. The tenebrous sky glowered, oppressive clouds devouring the daylight as the wind lashed the clothes against him like a punishment. The muted caliginous light upon his face as he trudged across the mud-puddled fields felt angry, spiteful, burning him with an uncanny touch he'd only ever known the moon to scald him with during its eternal vigils. This was different: this was a different day than he was accustomed to, and it made him wonder how long and deep a wicked night lay waiting for him.

The way was long, and so he traveled by horseback from the outskirts of the town, across the county's fields of waving wild grass and marigold while the sun crept the sky from far east to bleeding west; until the path became too perilous for the beast, all jagged granite crags and tricky, un-navigable slopes and arroyos rising and plunging from the plains like ancient monolithic citadels. There he tied his mount to a small gimp of a tree bending in the gusting breeze, seeking to calm its braying whinnies with a palmful of sugar cubes.

The moon was risen and red when he entered the maze of the crags, winding his way upwards with cautious steps, rising steadily to a dizzying height above the plain far, far below.

A stench of offal on the wind told him: it was near.

He grew faint, his stomach sought to revolt, though he succeeded in steadying his reeling senses and keeping his breakfast in his belly. Another quarter hour of crawling a precarious path through the brambles and thorn-bush dotting the jagged slopes, and, peering through the skeletal arms of a massive blackened and leafless bush, he saw the great maw of the cave. It was black, its granite lips scalded and scorched with an ashen dusting.

The hairs on his neck stirred looking upon it. His balls shrivelled up inside of his sack as if bitterest winter blew its breath upon him. His heart grew cold and cold. What felt like a great sickness clutched at him, constricting the breathing in his windpipe and stabbing daggers into his temples.

Still, though, Henry Barber stepped one and another steps forward, determined to see his job through to its grisly end. He un-slung his rifle from where it hung across his back and clutched it in a fist; in his other he held the looped rope, wound through with the stout chain of iron which he'd felt compelled to reinforce it with before setting out at dawn that day. The daggers hanging on either hip were heavy with the ghost-blood of countless men and women, but somehow offered little reassurance. Still, crouching low to the ground, a hunter's gait, Henry Barber slinked his brave way into the stinking stygian mouth opened before him.

The queer thought arrived and nipped at his courage as he slipped into the blackness: he knew this blackness. He knew its taste, its kiss and bite and touch. And it knew him, too, he sensed, like no other knew his mystery.

As he edged forth Henry Barber held his small lantern high, though he wasn't very grateful for its illumination: the wavering orange light crawled over the granite walls with their design of deep gauges and scratches, as if the claws of some great rabid bear razed them regularly; and he was forced to sidestep the mounds of bones littering the passage at irregular intervals, soaked in something like yellow bile or vomit, for fear of sending their rattling din echoing into the heart of this mountain-bound kingdom. He grimaced as he stooped to examine a cache of such bones: a frail skeleton sleeping upon the muck-heavy ground, its small skull cracked in twain. Henry Barber wondered how old the boy or girl had been when their doom had arrived to steal their life. He stood a moment later and, scowling into the darkness, continued on his hunterly way.

Yes, he was near to its vile nest.

He crept forth, descending step after descending step, for the ground began a deep sloping downwards. He walked for so long that he grew to wonder whether his progress had taken him beneath the floor of the plain, and if so, exactly how far below. He sweat in the infernal heat emanating from below. It felt like a great hot breath on his skin. It burned his skin and sizzled his hair, and the stench of carrion grew more potent as he crept on his wary way.

Without warning, Henry Barber stepped from the passage and into a room. This room was furnished, and furnished in a familiar way: a small wooden bureau he knew, and a window he knew holding a gibbous moon he knew, too, and with a bed he knew well owning a familiar shadowy corner, too. And there, beside the bed, a series of absent floorboards revealing the black mouths of a pair of holes: the first holes he'd ever dug in a long life of digging. This familiarity bewildered him, shocking him into immobility while his dazed senses sought to give a name to his surroundings or reject them from the dank deceiving underworld into which his job had taken him.

Henry Barber's heart shook, for he realized that even then he faced the thing. It lay upon the tiny bed, creaking its wooden frame with its great bulk overflowing the small confines, bulging the wool blankets, soaking the wooden floorboards with the mucus and urine dripping from its orifices, drenching the mattress. As if sensing his awareness of it, it clambered from the bed in a spasming of its many limbs, splintering the frame and rearing to its full height, scraping the ceiling with plate, horn, tentacle and spine. Its diseased shadow blanketed him like night putting out day, its bedlam of voices howling and barking and growling and bleating and lowing and screeching and gibbering at him all at once.

Peering closer among the gigantic ruin of the thing, he saw her: a swarm of distended rotting cocks undulated about the young girl's head like an abominable Medusa's headdress, caressing her neck and cheeks with a moist clamour. A hissing escaped their holes among squirts of jizzum and piss and blood. Their fetid stench reeled the senses, and beneath their reek Henry Barber felt his knees buckle. Shafts of hair-covered appendages – a grotesque orgy of bruised and bloodied and tumoured arms and legs and canine and lupine paws and tails – shot upwards and flailed towards the gibbous moon orbiting in the bedroom window as if in rapt worship of its numinous silver light; while random groups of immense nictitating eyes watched him hungrily from among the tangles of limbs, bloody and bulging.

Acting instinctually he brought the rifle to his shoulder and fired into the seething mass before him. Its huge weight buckled beneath the blast. A great and perverse shudder rippled through its swollen festering body, a prolonged groaning issued from it. A colony of pustules convened upon one of its immense sagging dirigible-like bosoms burst, and their acidic effluvium squirted like semen over Henry Barber's shaking hands, burning his skin. He remained resolutely in his place, aimed carefully, and let fire another bullet. The blast was greeted with another sexual spasming, and a high-pitched crying like the excited laughter of a blood-maddened hyena pack cornering a kill.

Henry Barber, having succeeded in crippling the demon, lay his rifle beside him and looped the rope-chain in his hand, whirling it about his head. He let it fly expertly despite the terror gnawing at his insides, the open noose of it finding purchase among the undulating cocks and swollen sacs, and finally slipping and tightening about the narrow neck of the girl nearly hidden among the saturnalia of appendages.

The abomination spoke then, in a condemning rasp of voices curdled with blood and phlegm and semen bubbling in the corners of its million cock-mouths and from the blasphemed mouth of the girl, too:

"Here I am, daddy. Here I am, daddy. Here I am, daddy. Here I am, your wicked love."

Henry Barber tasted a sea of salt. It flooded from his eyes at the words. It couldn't be helped. He was a tough one, but a man still, with a beating heart within himself. Through the monstrous bedlam of the many-voices he discerned her former voice, angelic and pristine and unsullied.

Through the torrent of his emotions and through the stinking gale wind of the girl-demon's condemning diatribe, he grated his answer like a judge likewise delivering his own sentence while tightening his grip on the chain-rope.

"I'm burying you now. Darling, sweetheart, I been trying to bury you for years, Dorothy, but tonight the night is finally come for it. Every hole I ever dug I dug for you but never none of them took you away from my mind. But I got to finally bury the big pain of it all. I got to, darling. This is my one and only shot at it, maybe. Maybe this is my one shot at burying the Devil that got inside me and owned me for one night. Forgive me for my terrible sin…In you go."

He accepted then that it was his daughter whom he faced, upon the stage of her bedroom on the night she last lived in the awful shit world that was awful and shit enough to birth a man as wicked as himself: the first hole Henry Barber had ever dug, after waking from the blasphemous frenzy that had gripped him one deep Winter's night while the world outside was banked in rolling snow-hills and the world indoors burned with a malevolent heat, and seeing her lying upon the wooden floorboards of their home: bedraggled and bleeding and shrieking a weeping lament that would forever haunt him; her agonized caterwauling litany that needed to be silenced there and then for if it wasn't his sanity would splinter in the tidal roar of it; and reaching for her again but this time with a different violence burning in his desperate hands as he squeezed and squeezed and squeezed and choked the life from her little pale throat before reaching for the rifle leaning against the wall and likewise silencing the howling woman with flailing hands seeking to halt his madness – his wife, whom he'd cherished before his transient madness stole his reason – and blowing a hole clean through her stomach with a single close-range blast from the gun's angry mouth.

Two holes dug in the deep hours of the first eternal night Henry Barber had lived.

And with these visions replaying themselves before his eyes yet again, in the deep dank hell-nest beneath the crags and inside the earth, Henry Barber pulled tremendously on the fraying-rusted rope-chain encircling the thing's brawny swollen shoulders and diminutive vulnerable neck. It fought hard to remain in the world. Their struggle was vicious, and long. They grunted, and sweat, and clawed, and scratched, and bled, and howled in their efforts.

In the end, though, the long-tormented man won this battle, and succeeded in dragging the bloody, maimed demon into the hole he'd made for it many and many years before. Its masculine hands and lupine paws scrabbled for purchase on the floorboards but Henry Barber beat the thing downwards into its hole with the butt of his rifle, splintering its wood so that he was made to resort to bashing the thing with his iron fists, bruising and bloodying and cracking them, too. Stomping upon its jagged fingertips and slithering frenzied cocks with his boots, he watched it plummet into the darkness.

Up from the heart of it, the perverted child-beast's voice echoed its judgement of him: "I'm with you always, your wicked love..."

To the echoes he said, "Sleep forever."

He felt it in that moment of burial, too: the black seed within him, ever breathing with an eternal life, never to be interred deeply enough, the Devil's rape-seed left to fester forever; or else one man's own inherent wickedness grown up from his dark poisoned heart.

And with this perpetual weight crushing his heart, Henry Barber left the room and descended the black granite corridors, down and down and down towards the mewling, agonized din echoing from below, to finish the final job of his too-long career.

He sang as he worked, which was strange for Henry Barber, who'd never been good at carrying a tune and who'd never had an ear for melody. A wordless tune but with an increasingly purposeful, mournful melody, as though the song's words were close to becoming birthed within the blood and relief of the funereal moment. It echoed its way through the dark labyrinthine tunnels and into the dark fields above to hush the nocturnal birds and field mice in their foraging and to stir county dwellers from their slumbers to scratch their heads and wonder, uneasily, as to the haunted quality of their dreams.

And all through the night and morning Henry Barber dug, and he dug, and then Henry Barber dug deeper into the earth still; guiding his spade's tip until its steel grew twisted and bent and brittle with the tenacity of his work; and when the battered tip was sundered from its wooden shaft Henry Barber dug with the wooden pole alone, until it too splintered in his fists and stabbed his flesh in a dozen places; and then he clawed away at the earth with his bare scarred hands, bloodying them and adding a new story to the countless tales of blood and murder and vengeance already collected there. And all throughout this endless digging into the earth Henry Barber hauled the chained, captive, brokenly-wounded but undying horror he'd tracked in the dark pathways scratched into the earth and that he'd felled in the dream-room above, drawing it ever closer to the molten land where it belonged.

He wept, of course, while he worked, long into those morning hours, salting the earth upon which the burial tunnel ran, and then finally upon the very grave site itself in the deep bowels inside the world, upon a spot where the rock was impregnable and the fiery heat had grown too great for even a man such as he, gritty, driven, possessed in his mission. There he left the chained thing, in this way burying the child who'd owned his heart from the moment he'd beheld her infant's eyes like blue jewels watching him openly and unafraid, and too innocent to exist in a world which owned men such as him.

And then Henry Barber, humming his unexpected, wordless song, began his long, slow climb upwards towards the light, heaping armfuls of soil and bone and jagged stone over his shoulders as he went, filling in the deepest and final hole he would ever dig.

In the years following, an anomaly of the county's geography was discovered. A group of farmers seeking to locate tillable land in the little-explored southern-most miles were amazed when they stumbled upon a cave which opened onto an expansive underground cave system and ravine which cut beneath the flat county landscape. Of prodigious depth, and several miles wide, geographers and cartographers at the time defined it as an underground valley, and named it thusly after the leader of the party of farmers who discovered it and mapped the vast majority of its labyrinthine trails and corridors: Barber's Valley, after Henry Barber.

To this day, nearly thirty years after the discovery of the site, Barber remains one of the few locals to inhabit the land upon which the hidden valley exists. A retiree, his property consists of a lovely house with accompanying garage and barn, and more than fifteen acres of verdant land, as well as a variety of farm animals. His home is located within sight of the original cave, marking the boundary between the county and the increasingly inhospitable terrain of the southern badlands. Barber has grown over the years into something of a local legend, and is known as much for his predilection for song as he is for his saturnine temperament and preferred life of solitude. It is said by those who visit the area around Barber's Valley that an old guitar's sombre chords haunt the air there, and a grizzled old man croaks his song – copied many times and sung now by younger voices the county over – in his distinctive bullfrog's croon:

> *O little darling, the world is bright and kind*
> *You are all I ever knew*
> *Then in a great darkness a man was born*
> *And inside a night-time it was brought to me, too*
> *O little baby, it wasn't Richard Bane cut you with his knife*
> *The papers was wrong about him through and through*
> *He hung and he swung un-guilty*
> *And the demon he slithered free*
> *O sweet girl, I seen me choke you all night*
> *Darling, I can't jump away*
> *Darling, this dark is spun too tight*
> *O me, you are the one I hate*
> *O me, you are the one I hate*
> *I'm so weary from all the days*
> *But I had me just one more hole to dig*
> *But I had me just one more hole to dig*
> *Now there's a fire in the valley that no wind ever quiets*
> *For I had me one final hole I dug*
> *And now I live only to tend the hole I dug*
> *I deserve this fire*
> *I deserve this fire*
> *It's my lover, forever*

And the children of the county bordering the badlands – and the roughnecks and farmers, too, though they laugh it off to flaunt their manhood and hide their fear – tremble at the words, and recall them in some deep and primal place within them while laying sleepless in their beds after midnight.

Another popular story concerning the old man Henry Barber speaks of the ghastly clamour arising from his home or thereabouts in the nights and bottomless mornings; a banshee's caterwauling that silences the coyotes in the fields and shakes the people in their homes fringing the area of the secret valley. A tortured song, of deepest anguish and suffering that some say contributes to keeping the land a mostly uninhabited place, despite its lovely wildflowers and picturesque woods and sweeping vistas, making it very much like a tainted Paradise known to few.

Darling, we have only to live through the cold years
At the end of them, a Summer night

THROUGH FOGS DEEP
AND FIRES LONG

They'd met at an outdoors music festival in the sweaty heart of summer, noticing one another standing alone at the parking lot's periphery while the throngs of people watched the stage and the band on it. She looked small and shy and cute, her summer dress clutching at her body in the humid night air. He was looking tall and gangly and more than a little drunk staggering a weaving line towards her observing him with her small dark eyes.

Their initial conversation easy, as if they'd known each other many years. Tipsy and wishing to impress her with his intelligence and quirky sense of romance, he'd told her, "Let's hang out tonight – maybe we'll stumble on an empyrean." Explaining to her his definition of empyrean while she'd smiled at him with an amused patience: a good place for them to be together without anyone else there to intrude on their conversation and peace.

They'd spent the night together, killing the long hours in late night coffee shops and on parking blocks overlooking vacant, moon-washed lots long after the shops had closed for the morning and the loud drunken bar-goers had stumbled homewards.

With the sun rising they'd retreated indoors, to his nearby apartment and a platonic sleep holding one another gently while the day breathed at the tightly shuttered windows.

It was on their second night together, while seated in her van in a lonely lot overlooking the Detroit River shimmering with the moon in its current, that they'd first kissed. He'd been gentlemanly about it, and simply asked her permission: "I want to kiss you right now. May I do that?"

He'd never been kissed like it before: desperation lived in the gesture, her lips clutched to his own as if they were long-lost lovers reunited after many years apart. Again they'd returned to his apartment, beating the dawn and spending the hours before noon making love in his darkened bedroom.

A week later she cut him.

She'd drawn the knife from beneath the pillow where she'd slipped it while waiting anxiously for him to enter the bedroom, surprising him not long after he'd slipped inside her. Blood trickled over its keen edge. His throat bled more and more. It was an epiphany. Something in them awoke in the blood and heat of the moment. It made him fuck her harder. Sex had been good throughout their few days together but this was something entirely new. Nearing climax she lunged forward and bit into the wound she'd opened. She tore at it with her teeth. Blood spurted. The taste of iron filled her mouth. They screamed together, revelling in their inhuman harmony. They came at the same time.

Soon afterwards she was driving him to the hospital, the towel he clutched to his neck heavy with his blood.

In this way, through a cut and a bite, began Daniel and Ellen's ascent to better places.

"It doesn't look so bad," he called from the bathroom where he examined his neck wound in the mirror over the sink. Its raw edges had scabbed over in the week following, and the surrounding purpled bruising had faded to a sickly blue and lighter green-ish tinge beyond this.

He saw her reflection appear in the doorway behind him, earnest-eyed. She said, "It looks beautiful."

They watched each other's reflection. Wordlessly they retreated to the bedroom to stretch the night hours.

*

Their relationship deepened. Their secret nights stretched interminably and within their eternal folds the things they did grew in number and extremity. Often she led the way and, emboldened by her courageous madness, he would follow her into new places.

She beat him. He beat her. Open-handed and fisted. He dislocated her jaw once, and she broke his aquiline nose on several particularly primal occasions. They took to using tools with which to pleasure each other, initially ordinary household implements because they were too sheepish to enter a sex shop let alone purchase any of its products. She liked being whipped across the back and shoulders (first they used leather belts and electrical cables, later an actual tasselled leather whip); and he relished when she burned his neck and chest and genitals (eventually substituting the run-of-the-mill butane lighter for candle wax, which she thought added significantly more romance to the act). Knives for cutting and stabbing and pliers for pinching and twisting and rope for binding: all these implements and others played their roles in fairly equal measures, too. More often than not they returned to the simplicity of using their hands: choking each other, pinching, scratching zigzag patterns into each other's flesh; and biting until blood was drawn into the bed with them, their perennial partner in the night. Every so often they would need to rush to the emergency in the middle of the wee morning, making creative excuses for spurting neck injuries or gaping stab wounds in thigh or ribcage or her left nipple cloven in two.

They grew to admire the scars they gave each other. Like art, they considered them pieces worthy of scrutiny, to revisit and reinterpret often. She'd given words to themselves in this way, one night while watching him towel off after a shower:

"You're like an art gallery."

Smiling, he told her that she was one, too.

*

Their evening escapes grew to invade their daytime duties to work and academia. Distraction plagued her while seated behind her desk, the computer screen all but forgotten before her and the payroll spreadsheets unfinished as visions of her and Daniel's previous night together haunted her.

Likewise, it became increasingly difficult for Daniel to concentrate in class, his professors' lecture voices dwindling into inconsequential background noise as startlingly vivid scenes of Ellen distracted him: her lips wrapped around his cock; her welt-lined buttocks quivering as he attacked them with the belt in his fist; her plaintive, primal cries bouncing from the bedroom walls as he fucked her from behind while gauging her back with the thumbtack gripped between his fingers. Then, stirring as if from a profoundly deep dream to find himself back in the lecture hall, the students around him oblivious of his most recent journey as well as the erection sprouting and throbbing between his thighs.

The manifestations began making their appearances soon after.

She'd see them over Daniel's shoulder while he was fucking her, floating above the bed. He'd see them coalesce from the dark wet tangle of her pubic hair while he gave her cunnilingus.

Vague half-formed, hallucinatory spectres born during the long hours of their fucking. Amorphous and ethereal, obeying a sensual sentient choreography as they mimicked the writhing figures entangled beneath them. Silently moving through the air, something in their fluid movements beckoning to Daniel and Ellen; as if they were meant to follow the lights to whichever place they disappeared each night.

In the aftermath of the sex-visitations neither Daniel nor Ellen questioned what they'd witnessed. Neither did they rationalize the experience, chalking it up to imaginations running wild with frenzied lust. They knew: their love was mightier than a definition so small. They knew: there was a reason they'd been shown this gateway. And they knew: they were meant to understand this mystery, somehow, to fathom it and embrace it, somehow.

Once, while laying sweaty and weary and bruised beside each other after sex, they watched a pair of the spectral presences drift along the ceiling over their heads. They coiled about each other, their pale luminescence glowing a sexually-charged crimson wherever they touched. The lights disappeared within the ceiling, trailing tapering appendages, as if urging them to follow.

"I want to go," she whispered, fighting tears that had risen from her without warning. "So badly, Daniel, I want us to go, too."

He said, watching the amorphous lights disappear and leave them in blackness, "We weren't built for this world, darling. We have to do something, darling."

In the wake of his confirmation of her own despair, she allowed herself to cry. He did, too. Together Daniel and Ellen remade the nature of their tears, as was their way. They clutched one another tightly until they were ready to fuck again.

Occasionally – very, very occasionally – the outside world trickled into their shared bubble of escape.

Something stopped her hand and the knife it gripped, its moon-glimmering blade ghosting his cheek. Concern and a lucidity entirely removed from her earlier mania shone in her eyes when she whispered, pleadingly, "Why do we like to…why do we *need* to do these things?"

His answer was simple and so brazen with revelatory truth that it elicited a startled cry from her and pulled her headlong into her frenzied passion once again: "Something awful happened to me, too, and I've been living with it every day since it happened. I…I was really young when it happened."

She kissed-bit his lips. He bit her back harder. She wept through it while slicing patterns across his back with the butcher knife in her trembling fist. Above them the spectral lights mirrored their fucking, wrapped about each other in a hungry intimate air-dance. Feral and violent, Daniel and Ellen stayed entwined until the sun rose, stealing the moon and the silver ghosts it had painted across the bedroom walls.

*

As the months passed they began exchanging letters via postal mail, a romantic mode of communication in a fast-paced virtual world in which they too often felt misplaced.

Having used the key Daniel had given her to enter his apartment, Ellen made her way directly to the bedroom closet. There she retrieved the extra-large bubble envelope from where it lay resting conspicuously on the top shelf. It was marked with a single word, in her neat cursive: *Daniellen*. She spread its contents across the bed: their collected correspondence, letters dog-eared from much rereading, some stuffed in envelopes, others loose and folded neatly. She liked that they'd decided to keep them together in one place: one day they planned on making an album of them, each letter framed behind cellophane like the pieces of art they were, like documented proof of the places they came from and the place they'd found in each other.

She placed a hand among them, drew a handful randomly from the pile of them. Opening the first of these, she read:

Daniel,

You said you thought about me a lot when you arrived home last night!

So, let me ask you: what do you think about, specifically, when you think about me?

Am I taking this in a very naughty direction? I think I am! You know *I am…*

I blame Cosmo.

Love,

Ellen

Smiling at her playfulness and boldness she replaced her initial letter in its tattered envelope and retrieved the next, remembering from the red paper on which he'd written it that it was his answering letter. Always more like prose than mere personal communication, always brimming with a fiery kinetic energy she relished, his letters never failed to arouse her.

Ellen,
Don't blame Cosmo: the culprit is you…
…I think of kissing you, and how your lips and tongue taste. I think of all the incredible wild sounds you make when I'm touching you, and putting my fingers inside you, and moving my tongue inside you. I think of how your voice changes when I'm doing these things to you, and takes on a primal high timbre that makes me crazy. I think of how you smile sometimes when I'm touching you, a very specific smile of ecstasy and release that I've only ever seen from you while we're in bed together. I think of how amazing you feel when I'm doing these things, and how amazing you taste and smell when my tongue is moving around inside you in search of the secret madness I always want to awake. I think of how wet I make you. I think of how much I love squeezing and licking and kissing and pinching and scratching and biting and burning and sucking on your nipples. I think of how much I love gently running my fingers across your inner thighs, and then squeezing them as roughly as I can, and then kissing them and biting them and leaving the scars of my bites deep inside your skin. I think of how much I love it when I'm in your mouth, and of how the anticipation of exploding in your mouth while you're sucking me builds and builds until I think I'm going to lose myself in the moment and never return. I think of your tongue and what it does to me. I think of how much I worship the sweaty burning little temple of your body, and how much I love turning you around on my bed and filling your cunt from behind and just fucking you forever, until the sun replaces the moon in the sky and still I can't stop fucking you. I think of how amazing it is when I'm standing behind you and filling you up completely while you're bent over our bed, as if we're worshipping the bed for the holy place it is. I think of you on top of me, riding me hard and fast while I bite your swollen bleeding nipples and bite your neck and wrap my fingers around your throat and squeeze and squeeze and tell you how much I want to put my tongue inside you again and climb on top of you and hold you by your ankles while I fuck you until you've lost your mind in the fucking. I think of scratching you with my nails and carving messages into you with my knife and leaving a new belt of welts across your hips from candle wax dripped across your skin. I think of your spit hot on my face and your blood burning on my hands and your hair tangled in my mouth while I'm making you scream like an animal. I think of you telling me you're coming while I'm fucking you and fingering you, moving your hips and legs around in my bed like you're possessed by a demon, and how incredible this serpentine writhing

is to behold — frantic and helpless with head thrown back and toes splayed and eyes crying and fingers clutching your perfect scarred breasts — and so madness-inducing that I'll never be able to properly articulate to you. I think of the cigarette between your fingers burning circles into my chest and the smell of my charred skin mixing with the smell of our sex on the air. I think of the knife in your trembling little fist threatening my jugular while I'm growing harder and longer inside you, and your feral eyes watching me and waiting for what will happen next. I think of becoming so enraptured in the moment and each other that we feel as if we're close to losing what shred of control we have remaining and just devouring each other with the most incredible lust we've ever known, so that when we're finished and laying beside each other, sweaty and weary and bloody and scalded and spent, it feels as though we just returned from the longest and most mind-alteringly miraculous trip with each other, from a place far and far and so far away. I think of how amazing it is that I'm able to elicit a reaction from you like crying while we're in bed together, and how that in our rare case it's a positive and purging and desirable emotion, and you feel incredibly good while experiencing it. And I think about how I want to make you feel this good, and much, much better, every time we're together, in bed and out.

I promise you, Ellen: I will take the tears from inside you, from whichever deep well they exist, and drink them all away until that well is dry and you have nothing but happiness filling you. I will drink away all the badness of memories and fill you with new memories: us, together through all the darkness the world hurls at us, together through it and stronger than it by far. And we'll pity the darkness its weakness when faced by the burning light of us fucking and loving and loving and fucking forever…

…Thank you, Ellen, for always being there when I come back from bad days, and reminding me how lucky I am to have found you.

Daniel

Ellen stared at the words covering the paper, remembering her initial reaction to it. Heart hammering, lust reawakened in her, she let the paper drift onto the bed and hurriedly opened the next letter.

Daniel,
Last night was the only good crying I've ever done in my life.
Thank you.
Yours,
El

Looking among the chaos of letters strewn on the bed she knew exactly which answered the one she'd just read, recognizing it for the mark of semen like a series of continents etched into its crumpled, battered surface. She recalled how he'd fucked her on that particular night, clutching her calves while thrusting into her, pausing from time to time to glide the knife blade across her stomach while she dug her nails into his forearms; and later filling her mouth; and the prodigious amount of his ejaculate she'd swallowed. She recalled this night and this letter with them in bed, crushed beneath their entangled bodies, sodden with their sweat and come and blood, marked with their bodily fluids like a signature of their passion and loving violence.

El,
All day long, I kept remembering in the most uncannily vivid way how it felt when we were sitting up in my bed last night, kissing and biting and licking each other for that prolonged period of time before fucking. I've been experiencing the amazing ghost-sensation of your breath on my face, and your lips brushing mine, and your tongue in my mouth, and the feel of your neck and shoulders and nipples between my teeth as I'm biting you and making you gasp and cry out and shiver and writhe in the incredibly entrancing way you do. I want to bite you and kiss you and ravage and scar every inch of your perfect body right now. I want to sign my name in your skin with the knife in my hand. I want to trace your new scars with my tongue, exploring the intricate map of you again, and again, and again.

You open a gate for me, to a place beyond definition. Its ingredients are fire and blood and come and sweat and more love than the world could ever contain.
Tonight:
I am going to devour every part of you: hands, arms, neck, mouth, tongue, breasts, thighs, calves, feet, and then finish by devoting myself to consuming the amazing and transporting portal of your cunt until the light that burns inside of you lies revealed for me to swallow.

*I will cannibalize and drink every inch of you, and then breathe you
out like fire to burn away this sad, desolate, angry world.*
Yours,
Daniel

In her eagerness to read more she neglected to replace the letter in
its envelope. Instead she dropped it beside her and snatched another from
the pile.

Daniel,
*I was thinking about you today. The day after we spend the night
together I always find myself zoning out and thinking about the night before.*
*You have no idea how much you mean to me, and I wish that there
were some way that I could show you, and you would believe me, but I don't
know that there is.*
All I can say is that I'm yours, always.
Love,
El

Finally, she reached among the papers fanned open before her and
came away with a single sheet of paper which she recognized for its bent
corners, its tattered evidence of having been read and read time and again.
Unfolding it she read his words to her, written following the night that,
wholly devoted to their shared moment of fucklust and bloodlust, she'd
given him the gift of a first cut, and then drowned his chest with candle
wax and touched him with naked fire:

Momma, the world was bright and kind
You were all I ever knew
Then in a great darkness a man was born
And inside a night he brought it to me, too
Momma, I cannot jump away
Momma, this dark is spun too tight
O you, you are the one I hate
O you, you are the one I hate
But you don't have to worry, momma

> *You don't have to worry about your boy:*
> *I found a girl*
> *I found a girl and with her we make a new world*

The letters inspired her to masturbate. She removed all of her clothes, laid in his bed amid the letters, on her stomach with her pelvis raised, touching herself. When she was nearing climax the thought occurred to her: snatching the telephone from its cradle on the night table beside the bed, she called him at school.

She could tell by the officious way he answered that he had someone in his office with him, an undergraduate student disputing a poor mark on a term paper, a professor meeting with him about this or that. In a playful but firm voice she told him:

"Daniel, I'd like for you to come home to me right now, and cut me, and burn me, and shock me, and hit me, and fuck me, and punish me for making you feel uncomfortable right now. I need you to be the demon possessing me. I need to be consumed by you. I need to be completely *consumed* by you right now. I'll be waiting." She clicked off the phone and lay with it pressed to her breast. She was waiting for him like this when, thirty minutes later and his office hours cut short and forgotten behind him, Daniel burst through the door, pulling at his clothes as he came to her.

Their city was mid-sized and considered a blue-collar lunch-bucket town for its many automobile factories and trash bars. Daniel and Ellen were drinking at such a bar, only because of its close proximity to his apartment. As always, they felt out of place there, on this night especially, being that the long holiday weekend just passed had seen them indulge in their secret deeds with even greater fervour than usual: without co-workers and classmates from whom to conceal the various evidences of their nights together they'd felt even less inhibited than usual. But their scars were on the mend, and they wore their coat collars up around their necks, and they huddled closely together over the little wooden table, and so they remained invisible to the other bar patrons and content within the usually impregnable bubble they created between themselves. They were talking quietly about their respective days, discussing with excitement their forthcoming anniversary and the ways they would celebrate. There were nights, though, when against all odds the outside world succeeded in invading their fortress.

A couple entered the small dingy room. It was clear from the way they loitered in the entrance and examined their surroundings – furtively but with eyes looking into every corner at once, as if they didn't wish to appear as the newcomers they were – that it was their first time in the bar. It took Daniel and Ellen a moment to recognize them as Daniel's neighbours, who from time to time would bang on the bedroom wall in condemnation of the sex noises keeping them awake. The woman's gaze passed over Daniel and Ellen huddled at the small table alongside one wall, did a quick double-take and found them again. Her eyes widened with something like horror, drawing her partner's attention. They looked Daniel and Ellen up and down with a blatantly critical and disdainful eye, examining openly the scar-mottled flesh of their arms, the purple and black bruises and welts like tattoos adorning their necks, the fine blading-scratches etched across their faces. The couple whispered something between themselves and appeared ready to leave, when the man turned back and called out over his shoulder towards Daniel: "So, when can we get our turn with her? You'd both like that, right? You sick fucks." Shaking his head, he spat with theatrical disdain onto the tiles. Together they exited the now-hushed venue, indignant, contemptuous, and with no small amount of discomfiture showing in their faces, in the telling manner with which they hurried on their way.

"Maybe we should bolt the doors and shoot up the whole damn stupid place." She was genuinely angry, resenting this unwarranted derision from people who neither knew her nor wished to know her. She felt exposed and ostracized, too, suffering ambush in the middle of an otherwise tranquil night. A shuddering grew up in her, encompassing all of these emotions vying for ownership of her – in its wake she felt depleted, defeated.

His wisdom came in a gentle voice, though his eyes were troubled. "Every inch of the world is so covered in fog that no one can see anything but the tiny space of their own life around them. Let people live there. We're like fogcutters, you and I. Right? We sail through the thick of it. We chart open waters."

Daniel and Ellen took solace in each other, clinking bottled beer in a toast to themselves. "To navigating the misty streets together," he said, and they smiled at the romantic flavour of the words.

They looked through the window after the departing couple walking down the sidewalk: they might go elsewhere for a drink, this man and woman, and then home, possibly have sex later that night – good or bad but non-transporting in any case. They might split up before long, or continue plodding through their same-old lives, wholly content or wholly dissatisfied, but either way with their vision of the world dimmed by what they deemed aberrant and forbidden. Daniel and Ellen, though, bonded by blood and love and a secret cache of shared memories, would endure. They'd beaten much with an initial cut, bite, and revelatory bloodletting. Friends, if they'd had any besides each other, and family, if any knew what it was their children had discovered in each other, would have envied them their finding. He was right, Ellen mused: in a world of loneliness and wickedness, they'd found a solace known to few, a feat all the more miraculous given their misanthropic ways.

And yet something in her continued its persistent gnawing, and it was the selfsame ache she saw in his eyes every so often, once the rabidity of their lust had went to sleep in conjunction with the ghost-lights disappearing into the ceiling and walls and he lay beside her staring at nothing with distance in his eyes. She witnessed this transformation overtake him then, while he sipped his beer and stared off into the smoky air of the bar with eyes miles and miles away, making her wonder, making her anxious, making her fearful: without him anchoring her she could feel herself drifting into old and deadly places. She clutched his hand, and though he squeezed her tightly in return, still the fear continued to constrict her, a forbidding touch the likes of which she knew she couldn't endure alone.

Much later on, in the deepness of the A.M. long after they'd made love and fallen asleep to the swirling tangle of phantom-figures weaving patterns in the air over the bed, Daniel woke to find Ellen missing from beside him. He followed the faint illumination in the hall to the bathroom door and listened to the sound of her crying within. Among her weeping he discerned the words, muffled through the door:

I hate you. I hate you so much. Why won't you finally fuck off and die?

His heart ached: it was the sound of her old despair, a world removed from the good crying.

*

The day had arrived – their true anniversary, marking a full year from the night they'd discovered their true nature and bond – and Daniel vowed to make good on his promise to Ellen.

"My gift to you…you'll love it. It's the most I could ever give you. I've been waiting for this night to give it to you." He said this while helping her from her clothes and handcuffing her to the bed; both wrists to the sturdy oak headboard and her ankles to either side of the footboard so that her legs were held parted wide. He repeated the words while running fingers between her breasts, down her belly, among the curls of her pubic hair and across her cunt, along her inner thighs and tracing a path the length of her scarred calves to her small feet.

She trembled. A shiver snaked its way the length of her spine. She exhaled a wavering breath. She smiled. "I can't wait for it," she told him.

He smiled at her spread before him, his own gift that special night. He pinched her disfigured nipple. He leaned to her. They kissed. He ran his tongue from her lips to her small round chin, down her quivering bruised and blood-blistered throat to her collarbone where he bit her gently but not so gently.

Standing from her, still smiling a feral smile, he said, "One moment, my darling."

When he returned to the room several minutes later he was naked and stroking a massive erection. She smiled when she saw him, her Adonis, her beautiful and mighty conqueror.

He climbed expertly on top of her. She was wet. He slipped his cock into her. She groaned, tingling with the expectation of what was to come. He shook, too. He told her he loved her cunt. He explained how much he loved her but admitted he could never define his love with mere words, only through the medium of his cock filling her, his tongue filling her, his fingers filling her, his lust filling her up until it swallowed the outside world and pulled her into ecstasy with him again. This was the poetry she deserved from him. She wondered excitedly what pleasure-pain he was going to give her on this, their special celebratory night, and watched entranced as he revealed two more pairs of handcuffs encircling his wrists and with which he bound himself to the headboard alongside her own bonds.

She watched with a start as he reached as far upwards as he could with his handcuffed hand and dropped the key to their bonds through the ajar window and into the night. Her eyes widened with alarm. She smiled then, whispered in a voice tinged with excitement and fear, "Oh my. Now what are we going to do? We'll be trapped here forever." Knowing, of course, that she was safe in the throes of his mad plans.

He shared the secret with her, in a whisper like a scream into her ear that reached her heart with a vicious and beautiful stabbing of epiphany:

"Do you smell it, El? I've always loved the smell of gasoline. I drenched the apartment with it. A sea of gasoline everywhere. I dropped a match into it before joining you here. I've set the place on fire. We're burning down right now, as we speak. The door is locked and bolted. The building alarms will go off anytime and warn everyone but no one will get to us in time. Happy anniversary, darling."

Her eyes widened further. Her jaw dropped. She breathed, "We'll never get out." He felt her heartbeat against his chest pressed tight against her: mighty and frantically fast.

He nodded, smiling as he leaned to her and clenched her upper lip between his teeth, biting her hard enough to draw blood. He grew harder inside her. Her nipples, crushed against his scar-mottled chest, grew harder, too. He began moving around inside her. Her wetness had grown, an ocean of warmth for his cock to move through.

Minutes stretched past languidly. The fire's glow seeped into the bedroom from the apartment beyond, red and wavering like some living agitated thing. The temperature had risen sometime during their fucking. The bedroom had grown hot. Sweat beaded their faces and bodies. They shone with it like melting wax figures. The excited crackle of flames devouring wood and wallpaper came to their ears and, a moment later, the distant wailing of the building's main fire alarm. In the air over the bed they appeared: the orgy of phantasmagorical figures, a dozen or more of them tangled in an elegant but excited air-dance, sending red tendrils of their light towards Daniel and Ellen entwined in the bed and other appendages ceilingwards, once again as if urging the lovers to follow in their wake.

She gasped the words into his ear, the epiphany like a sun exploding inside her: "Oh, sweetheart…they'll never hurt us again…No one will ever hurt us again…"

He whispered into her face: "Oh, darling, now – finally – I'm going to fuck you *forever*…"

She smiled. He did, too. He thrust into her with greater violence. She moaned. She screamed. He did, too. The fury of the fire grew, devouring the door and eating its fill of the room. Wallpaper curled away in strips and plaster fell away in charred jagged pieces that clung sizzling to their naked flesh. The heat rose and rose and scalded their bodies while smoke darkened the air. In the great conflagration she screamed; he screamed; and the flames themselves roared with a voice like all the agony in the world pushed to its threshold and – breaking through the difficult barriers of sin and death – became something else entirely.

Through the suffocating, scalding fireful of pain:

Happiness.

Ecstasy.

Peace.

They woke, as if from the longest of lives and into the gentlest, most cradling of dreams. They struggled to see but the strength of the light blinded them. It seemed to flow all about them in a saturnalia of perpetual movement, caressing them gently everywhere. Tears flowed from their eyes as they thought back to the night behind them, of fire and fucking. It seemed distant and like a dream, too. It had been no dream, they understood, sensing the potency of the alien atmosphere surrounding them. The light touching them was warm, and stirred against their skin, like a million burning kisses, like the kiss of a naked flame, like a tropical sun. The scent of flowers was heavy on the air – heliotropes, roses, magnolias, and countless others merged into a heady brew – dizzying them further. A sound of music around them, too: the song of a million birds nesting and rejoicing among the trees. The thousand gentle ghost-touches continued to caress them, coddle them, soothe them.

They sat up, the ground beneath them soft and thick: the lushness of grass, the velvety touch of flower petals. They clutched each other, anchors, as ever, for one another. Their eyes cleared. They made certain that they were the first thing they saw. From the brightness they materialized. Their scars were vivid against their pale complexions, blatant and regal like insignias of honour, marks of valour from a time when they'd needed to be courageous. Light seemed to shimmer in wavering prismatic lines from these scars, as it encircled, halo-like, their bodies, too. They smiled. Together they'd reached their empyrean.

They stood on trembling legs, still staring into each other's watering eyes. Inside, they felt a great missing thing. They understood then that they were unburdened.

Then, as one, they turned and faced their Paradise.

Follow the ships that come not back.

- REH

GOD-EATER

The day was idyllic:

The late-day sun in a cloudless sky, colouring the backyard golden. Air scented with flowers, the garden brilliant, handsomely manicured. Gathered with their friends on the lawn, seated beneath the balmy shade of the umbrella awning overhanging the round patio table.

At the centre of their attention was the crib, with its special cargo.

"It's a *caul*," she was quick to explain as she pulled the sun-warmed wool blanket back with a gentle hand for their friends to see. "It's called a *caul* but don't worry: he's a normal little baby, through and through. Some babies are born with them, and they disappear not long after. Our doctor explained it. It's rare, but nothing very unusual. He's absolutely normal."

"No, of course not, Barb. It never even occurred to me. Don't be silly. He's beautiful. Absolutely gorgeous." Jennifer, tactful if transparent, watched the child with enormous eyes and a wide, stupefied smile.

Her husband, Jerry, was equally obsequious and stunned. "Really, he is. An Adonis in bloom, I'd say."

Neither Barbara nor Howard cared whether their friends were overcompensating in how they fawned over their unusual baby. He was a gift. He was perfect. He was theirs. This they'd grown to understand once their own initial shock had subsided, and was replaced with the potency of unconditional parental love. They would nurture him and raise him into a great man.

They all examined the drowsing infant with astonished eyes: beautiful, truly, with his immaculate features, cherub-cheeked and ruddy, his golden curls and tiny pink puckering mouth, as if he was searching absently in his sleep for the sustenance of his mother's teat. These details readily apparent, once one's fixation on the gruesome abnormality of his physiognomy was overcome, the translucent purple flesh-strip like a thick bandage of bruised scarred skin sewn across the child's eyes, blighting his vision of the world and the people in it gawking and owning unsettled expressions.

In this much-anticipated moment of revelation of their baby's strange beauty, Barbara felt relief fill her, and warmth, and she smiled. They were content, she and her husband. Howard called what they had being "set". *We're set now,* he would say, when standing with hands on hips in examination of an afternoon's diligent work in the garden, once weeds had been pulled and hedges trimmed and seeds planted in newly-turned soil. *We're set,* whispered with a quiet exultation following sex, laying sweaty and entwined in the darkness of their bed, their new house humming its gentle, soothing house-murmur as sleep luxuriously came over them.

Howard smiled to himself, too, examining the scene as if from a bird's eye perspective: he and Barbara, hosting an afternoon gathering with their closest friends, surrounded by their verdant garden on one side and their beautiful home on the other, bathed in the August sunlight. The geraniums and roses redolent in the gentle air, and the long weekend of leisure and festivity unfolding exactly as they'd hoped. And at the centre of the day, the focus of the celebratory mood: their little Joseph, newborn, pristine, like a jewel freshly-sculpted from the mortar of their love and commitment to each other.

A sharp little pain stabbed in Sarah's chest. Something clouded the brightness of the afternoon for her. She continued smiling, replacing her hand in her husband's, feigning immersion in the conversation he held with everyone; though she cast a wary eye to the sky, to the vibrant flowers nodding in the occasional zephyric breeze.

"Oh Jesus, Barb," exclaimed Jennifer a moment later, a hand across her mouth, drawing Sarah from her strange reveries and into the moment again.

Beside Sarah, Stanley, her burly husband, recoiled with a girlish cry stopped short in his throat.

They turned as one, putting their eyes into the crib.

The caul lay in shreds – long raw strips of skin unfurled and fallen to either side of the child's face like the opened petals of some gruesome meat-flower – and Joseph's eyes lay revealed. They were filled with blood.

From the infant's small soft mouth, words, in the deepest of voices:

160

"I see."

As one, as if in predetermined response, their friends spoke and froze Barbara and Howard in their chairs, their single voice a drugged murmur drifting in the late afternoon stillness:

"He is God-eater. The great burning is come."

Also as one, they all four of them made talons of their fingers, and gripped their own throats, and tore the jugulars from their necks in explosions of blood and vein and cartilage that drenched the grass. The wine glasses slipped from their hands and onto the lawn. They toppled over in their chairs like poisoned monarchs.

Near to them, upon the lawn, a plume of flame appeared. It smouldered angrily in the mellow air. A breeze blew, and brought foul air, feces- and smoke-tainted. In the distance, a great baying began, as if a pack of feral dogs were closing in on its prey.

Howard and Barbara continued to stare without words, immobilized by the spectacle of blood and death invading the peaceful daytime. The warm putrid wind sagged over everything.

A moment later and Barbara gasped anew, clutching at her husband's arm. He followed her gaze into the crib again, and a cry tore from him, too.

A great grey worm lay curled within the crib. Its skin glistening within a sheath of glutinous matter, mottled with black tumours and stray spiking hairs like cactus needles.

Their baby curled and coiled among its blankets, and closed the single bloody eye in the centre of its head to the daylight. It squirmed beneath the brilliance, a violent rebellious shuddering that creaked the frame of its crib. A moist slippery sound accompanied its frantic movements, alien and revolting.

Their friends' soliloquy played over and over in their heads. It would be the song they heard in the darkness before sleep came for them, if it ever came again. Unbeknownst to his wife, Howard thought suddenly of the secrets he kept, dark and vile things he'd done and which he'd strove his best to ensure remained buried beneath the years. Barbara, too, thought then of a secret she'd kept from her husband, with whom she shared everything but this single thing that she'd sworn from the beginning to keep locked in its own clandestine room within her memory, untouched, untouched, powerless to harm him or anyone else.

They watched with revulsion, awed, as the stout grey worm crawled forth from its crib. It clambered over the rounded plastic lip of the crib, and slipped down its length to settle with a great and grotesque flatulence onto the grass. Once there it turned its immense bloody eye upon them, a ripple coursing through its body, before crawling sluggishly in the direction of the garden. They watched it disappear there, sullying the flowers with its swollen, wet body, its stench of offal. It left in its wake a vast trail of gelatinous effluvium, bubbling as if at boiling point, while islands of feces drifted along its winding, diseased course.

The crib lay between them, immense in its new emptiness.

Nothing else was changed:

The blue jays sang from the spruces. Grasshoppers leapt in the grass. The fetid breeze and flame expired and the perfume of flowers slowly returned and owned the air once more. The ghost of their baby's former gentle, sleepy burbling among its warm nest of blankets haunted the air, too – they longed for this innocence, now lost to them among the sullied soil of the world. They were still a mother and father. In the distance, over the rooftops, children sang, displacing the wild song of predators.

Somewhere, as ever, they knew, evil walked, too.

The sun seemed suddenly too-bright, a false brightness presiding over everything like the golden smile of Heaven touching the world before a great storm's arrival. They wrapped their fingers around their throats beneath it, and with their free hands clutched each other, as strong and good in the gesture as they could be.

Why can no one ever hold a Fire Spirit?
- Jeffrey Lee Pierce

I've held a Fire Spirit
and still she licks in me

THANK YOU,
BABY-STABBER

The tiny austere interrogation room was congested, its air rife with tension. It mimicked in this way the stricken city outdoors, burning in its sixth straight week of a record-breaking heat wave, in its season of great disquiet.

"We don't have all day, Daniel," said the grizzled detective in a calculatedly even tone, the refined product of a lifetime of experience in exactly such encounters. "You haven't answered my questions yet and we've been here hours, talking in circles about this and that." The smell of sweat hung in the air, giving him reason to consider the putrid stench permeating the streets: in ill-fated conjunction with the record temperatures had come the city worker's garbage strike. Streets the city through were teeming with refuse, bags and cans and dumpsters overflowing with it and the rats feasting in droves.

Seated beside him, Daniel Olander struggled, brow furrowed in thought, skin clammy with sweat, hands miming patterns in the air as he sought the words by which he might explain himself; until a queer look of peace came into his eyes, replacing the agitation that had characterized him throughout the entirety of the interrogation until then. He murmured, "I just…I don't know how to say it except to just say it outright, but…"

"That's okay, Daniel. Say it any way you want to say it. I'm listening." The detective had softened his voice. He could be a friend and confidante, too, if the man beside him required it to spill his dark tale.

"I just…I simply really enjoyed doing what I…I relished and felt good doing what I did…because it was *right* to do."

At this the detective stirred in his chair, though he sought to hide his excitement. "Did what, Daniel? What are you trying to tell me?"

"I mean that I feel good about breaking into all those homes, all of the houses and apartments, and stabbing them all… stabbing them all and cutting them all to death."

The detective could sense the collective relief and celebratory cheer which erupted throughout the police headquarters at this long-sought admission from the man long suspected in connection to the heinous crimes. "Why is that, Daniel?" he asked calmly, watching the gaunt-faced man closely where he sat beside the small table. "What about it makes you feel good?"

Daniel Olander looked into his eyes when he answered, "Some babies grow to become murderers. Rapists and monsters."

"And what does that make you, Daniel? If you've committed these crimes?" The detective sought to keep his voice level, to quell the fury and outrage and disgust from owning him, though he feared his eyes brimmed with it all. He was envisioning the sixteen infants he'd witnessed firsthand, their tiny throats slit from ear to ear, their chests riddled with great gaping wounds, drowned in pools of their young blood drenching the cribs in which they'd been discovered by horrified mothers and fathers and siblings.

Daniel Olander replied with a voice of wonder, as if providing a very obvious answer. "That's exactly it, sir. I'm protecting you all…from *me*. I'm the baby grown old, you see? Better one black angel than many. Stop the children, stop the blackness. A cleansing, and then a new beginning. This is my gift to you all. Do you understand this?"

The detective grew livid, but hid his emotion well; and then frightened, and made sure to hide this weakness even better; and then, a brief moment of bewilderment stole over him as he sought to understand his great confusion of emotions; and then, unexpectedly, a great gratitude had swept over him, and he allowed it to show with a small sympathetic nodding of his head.

Because he did understand. His had been a long career and the things he'd seen throughout the years, oh, the things he'd seen: he truly understood the good in this.

"Thank you," he found himself telling the notorious Baby-Stabber, the bane and nemesis of the city throughout that entire heat wave-haunted, scorched and wicked summer, a moment later turning a stunned and apologetic glance to the video camera recording their revelatory conversation in the interrogation room.

168

He had an overwhelming feeling in that moment that a wind blew through the city from a place far and far away, relieving the people of the terrible and oppressive heat and stink like the first sign of winter heralding a respite from the long season of fire.

CHUX AND BUX
AND THE QUEST FOR
BRUSSELS SPROUTS
Coauthored by Rachel Blok

Chux and Bux first became friends during snack-time. They discovered each other at the top of the bazim tree while searching for delicious mee-mee fruit.

"Hello," said Chux, in surprise.

"Hello," responded Bux lazily.

Chux, like all Boombaxans, was very short, with soft magenta skin, six fingers and one antenna which helps to locate food. Chux had bright red hair and blue freckles. His arms were long and perfect for climbing, but his feet were the size of dinner rolls. Chux would have liked dinner rolls too, if he knew what they were, but on Planet Boombaxo, there was no such thing as dinner rolls. In fact, there was no such thing as dinner: Boombaxans eat all the time. During school time, the young Boombaxans take fifteen recesses in order to eat their food: zox-mox bars (which are like spaghetti, but sweet and purple), fooomoool roll-ups (which are like pancakes, but very very thick and have orange and blue polka dots), and banana chips (which are nothing at all like bananas or chips). Boombaxans sleep very little and when they do sleep, they dream about food. In fact, Chux had just woken up from a nap in which he'd been dreaming about delicious mee-mee fruit.

There was a tall bazim tree outside his village. He'd never been brave enough to venture there before, but he was so hungry and there was nothing to eat in his xobo hut. When he got there he didn't realize there was another Boombaxan up in the tree.

That was Bux. Chux liked the look of Bux right away. He liked his hair, which was crimson, and his freckles, which were aqua-marine. Chux had never seen a Boombaxan with such bright hair and freckles. Bux, unlike Chux, did not seem nervous in the bazim tree at all; he seemed right at home.

In fact, Bux had been there all afternoon. He'd eaten almost all of the fruit – all of it, except for the last delicious mee-mee fruit. Because he, like most other Boombaxans, tended to eat everything in sight, he was planning on eating that last delicious fruit too. But when he saw the hunger in Chux's eyes, he thought to himself: *I like the looks of this Boombaxan. I'm going to give him this last delicious mee-mee fruit.*

And so their friendship began.

One day, while outside during their fourteenth recess in zood-xood school (which, in case you are wondering, is like grade school, except Boombaxans use their antennae to write instead of pencils), Chux and Bux were talking about food. Bux's teachers always thought that he was their most inquisitive student. Chux, a year younger, was also very smart for his age, which was three boom-billion years old. (Boombaxans age very slowly. Scientists believe this has to do with the huge amounts of banana chips they eat, which are nothing at all like Earth banana chips.) In their discussion of food, Chux and Bux wondered aloud about different kinds of food from different kinds of places, maybe places far away from Boombax.

Bux joked, "Maybe there's a planet where they have banana chips that are yellow!" And they both laughed.

Then Chux said: "Maybe there's a village where their mee-mee fruit is red and round!" Bux thought that idea was very funny.

They joked and laughed like this for almost the whole recess, little noticing the bright light that had soared across the sky and landed near the zood-xood school playground. During their fifteenth recess, which was five minutes later, Bux, who had very keen eyesight, detected something shiny at the edge of the playground.

They went to investigate, although Chux was a little nervous. The shiny object was quite large, big enough for at least ten Boombaxans, round, with windows and lots of coloured devices inside. Bux, who was very brave, led the way inside. There they nosed around, poking their antennae this way and that way. Chux was very hungry, and his antenna came to the rescue again: there was food onboard somewhere! They nosed around some more. "What's this black box?" wondered Bux. "I don't know," answered Chux, "but it smells good." They had a bit of a hard time opening this strange box, but they were very smart Boombaxans, and soon enough (although recess was now over) they were successful.

"What are these?!" cried Chux, and rummaged through the remains of someone's lunch (although he didn't know what lunch was). There were breadcrumbs and a nearly empty bag of chips. Chux tasted these, but was not impressed. "Blazoo!" exclaimed Chux. "That tastes awful. I don't even think that's food."

"Oh, but this is," said Bux who, always adventurous, was chomping on some delicious small round green plants (which were in fact brussel sprouts). "Here, try some." After a first hesitant nibble, Chux's eyes lit up and he began munching with abandon. "Wooz, Bux, you're right! These are delicious! I wonder where they come from."

Bux, being very smart and inquisitive, started nosing around among the colourful gadgets. His six fingers did this and that, his antenna poked in here and in there, and after fiddling with these buttons and those devices, a screen lit up. The words written there were different than Boombaxan (which is made up of many, many *z*'s and *x*'s), but Bux was very smart and somehow figured out how to fix the shiny object.

In no time they had the object (which was in fact a space probe) twirling and whirling and whizzing in the sky, doing spins and other tricks. After a while of this fun, Bux had an idea. "We have about four hours till our night time snack. I think my Mox and Dax would really like these small round green plants before they go to sleep. We should try to find more of these delicious plants to share with everyone!" Although Chux was at first unsure about this plan, he also wanted more of these delicious brussel sprouts. So off they went.

There are many, many planets between Boombaxo and anywhere a space traveller can get brussel sprouts, and Chux and Bux stopped on many different worlds. There was a planet called Thoralite with a sky coloured like rainbows and no water and tall skinny creatures who seemed to eat nothing at all, least of all small round green plants. On the planet Baltow 28, there was no ground, only sky, and all the children there had long wings and tails and beaks, and they ate small silver insects that lived in the clouds. Next came the world called Bo-Po-Po-Bo, whose many creatures, great and small, spoke to each other through song, and all the words of all the songs they sang seemed only to be "Bo-Po-Po-Bo". Chux and Bux had quite an adventure on Sessalg-O, when they disturbed the lair of an ancient monster shaped like a beach ball with stripes all across his big belly, and a very long polka-dot tongue. It seemed that this monster wanted only to eat

Boombaxans. While escaping this monster's lair, Bux knocked into a big red button inside the ship. It made a bleeping noise, and the ship began heading in a different direction. Bux and Chux, very smart Boombaxans, realized that the ship was now headed homewards, wherever that was. Chux was now very frightened but then Bux reassured him: "Now we'll find more of these delicious small round green plants for sure!"

He was right.

They zipped through space, passing comets and moons and meteors and the occasional flying saucer, until they came to a bright blue and green planet (which was, in case you are wondering, Earth). They whizzed through the clouds and soon found themselves landing gently. They waited a moment, then ventured outside.

"Chux!" said Bux.

"Bux!" said Chux.

They were standing in the middle of a gigantic field of brussel sprouts, stretching out as far as their Boombaxan eyes could see.

"It's the world of the delicious small round green plants!" exclaimed Chux.

"We made it! Let's eat." Bux was hungry.

They dove into the rows of delicious brussel sprouts, their antennae whirling madly. They ate and ate, and then ate some more. They were about to eat more for their dessert when Chux suddenly cried: "Bux! I feel like we're being watched."

They were! They noticed two strange-looking creatures watching them from behind a nearby tree. Chux whispered to Bux: "They're very weird. They don't have magenta skin or antennae! And their hair is brown and yellow! Look at how short their arms are! I'm scared!"

The strange creatures Chux and Bux saw were in fact a boy and a girl named Peter and Lucy, who were also quite astonished at the sight of two Boombaxans in the middle of their father's brussel sprouts field. Peter, who liked being brave in front of his sister, inched forward and offered a chocolate bar to the visitors, who did seem to like eating. Bux, wanting to be brave in front of Chux, crept forward and accepted this gift. "I bet this is food, my antenna is sure going crazy," he whispered to Chux.

They shared the chocolate bar, but found that it tasted awful. They wanted to be polite, and likewise offered Peter and Lucy some of their brussel sprouts. Peter looked at the brussel sprouts, but he wasn't that brave, and shook his head no. Chux and Bux were surprised at these creatures who liked bad-tasting brown flat things instead of delicious small round green plants. Lucy whispered to Peter: "It seems that they like Father's brussel sprouts. If we let them have some, it'll be less for us to have to eat." Peter responded: "Good idea!"

After much motioning and pantomiming, Chux and Bux realized that Peter and Lucy were offering them as many brussel sprouts as they could take with them. In fact, the two Earth-children helped the two Boombaxans load many armfuls of brussel sprouts onto their ship. As Chux and Bux prepared to leave, Lucy said: "Come back anytime for more!" Chux and Bux could not understand this strange talk, but in good spirits, responded: "We'll come back and visit you very soon!"

They waved goodbye, and Bux started the ship. Soon they were flying through space, past the planet of beach ball monsters, past the same old flying saucers and a few new ones, past the planet with no ground, past clusters of twinkling stars, past fizzing comets and spinning meteors and deep and dangerous black holes, heading back to Boombaxo. Once they arrived back home, Chux and Bux presented their parents with the brussel sprouts. They also found them to be very delicious, and Chux and Bux were congratulated on this amazing find.

Bux's Mox and Dax were eager for their son and his new companion to bring home some more delicious small round green plants.

"Don't worry, Mox and Dax," promised Bux. "We will. We will. We have friends there!"

GLOSSARY TO THE WORLD OF CHUX AND BUX

bazim tree – a very tall fruit-bearing black tree with orange leaves which looks like Halloween

Boombaxo – a distant planet inhabited by a gentle alien race whose main concern is eating

Brussels sprouts – 1. delicious small round green plants 2. the bud-like, edible heads of a cabbage variety, *Brassica Oleracea Gemmifera*

Earth – 1. a bright blue and green planet which is the world of the delicious small round green plants 2. the planet third in order from the sun on which human beings live

fooomoool roll-ups – like pancakes but very very thick and have orange and blue polka dots

zood-xood school – the educational system for young Boombaxans up to the age of ten boom-billion years old which teaches them things like cooking, eating what you have cooked, and recess

zox-mox bars – like spaghetti, but sweet and purple

August, hedge us in your arms
Sirius, enfold us in your Summer

ON TOUR WITH THE
DEATHRAY
BRADBURYS

"Good evening!" shouted the silver-masked singer into the microphone, his gloved hands raised ceilingwards in a grand gesture of salutation. "And welcome thee to this night when the skies and Heaven above shall open wide and bleed down and down and down their light and love unto this soil, and into the red, red, red, red world below! And in this middle-country, oh, in this right-here right-now lieth you and us! And you are beautiful, and we are the Deathray Bradburys, and this world – oh, this sad, lonely, wicked, *vengeful* world – oh, she is no match for us! For tonight we are gathered here to offer you celestial salvation from your woes! The Twins are burning and the Twins are calling! Paradise awaits! Join us, brothers and sisters – *this is our night!*"

The sparse crowd milling in front of the band in the gloomy cigarette and pot smoke-congested basement bar roared their approval. Most wept openly, while others merely chugged their beers, treating the spectacle as they would any other band playing the tiny decrepit venue.

Feedback erupted from the battered amplifiers. The similarly silver-skinned bass player, his wings spread like an immense metallic curtain behind him, shouted a count-in into his own microphone: "One-two-three-four!"

And the Deathray Bradburys brought their rock and roll salvation to their disciples one final time.

*

The Deathray Bradburys:
A Brief History, An Eternal Mystery

555:

The binary star Sirius, also known as the 'dog star' or 'Big Dog' because of its place in the constellation Canis Major, is the brightest star in the sky and has therefore long been revered by peoples throughout the world. Its very name comes from the Greek word 'seirius', meaning 'scorching' or 'searing', its brilliance and prominence in the sky having earned it a long-standing place in occult symbolism and the mythologies of some of the world's most pre-eminent empires. The ancient Egyptian's entire mythology and religious system, for example, revolved around Sirius, owing largely to the fact that their ancient astronomers observed that the Nile flooded whenever the sun was aligned with the star, providing fertility to the land. Known as the Nile Star, Sirius was said to be the birthplace of their most prominent deities, including Osiris, Isis, Seth and Horus, and its rising formed the basis of the Egyptian's calendar.

The mystery of humankind's connection to Sirius deepened in the twentieth century. In 1931 French explorers and anthropologists Marcel Griaule and Germaine Dieterlen first made contact with the Dogon, a small reclusive tribe living in Mali, West Africa. The anthropologists discovered that the Dogon's folklore included a rich and elaborate mythology revolving around the star Sirius. This mythology was based on information said to have been passed down through generations as far back as 3200 B.C., and included an extensive and inexplicable knowledge of the science underlying the star. With advances in European and Western astronomy came proof that much of the Dogon people's knowledge relating to Sirius was accurate, a seemingly miraculous fact considering their Stone Age society's complete lack of scientific discipline.

How, without scientific equipment of any kind, could the Dogon have known that a smaller star, now recognized as Sirius B and invisible to the naked eye, orbits Sirius, that its orbital cycle is exactly 50 years long, and that it rotates on its own axis? It was only in the 1950s, after all, that a telescope was developed that was powerful enough to see Sirius B, and it wasn't until 1970 that it was first photographed. Further, the Dogon showed knowledge of Sirius B's immense density and classification as a white dwarf star – this primitive people named the star *Po Tolo* (Tolo in the Dogon language means 'star' while 'Po' is the smallest seed known to their society) and referred to it as the 'heaviest star', describing it as being 'white' in colour.

The Dogon also claimed knowledge of a third star orbiting behind Sirius B – they called it *Emme Ya*, and its existence was conclusively proven as recently as 1995, when French scientists Daniel Benest and J.L. Duvent detected motions in the Sirius system that they attributed to a possible third star. It is now commonly referred to as Sirius C and remains a point of intense interest for astronomers.

The Dogon said their knowledge of astronomy was long ago passed to them by the *Nommos*, an extraterrestrial race of intelligent amphibious beings sent as emissaries from Sirius. Descriptions of the *Nommos* can be equated to mermen and mermaids of ancient legend, and can also be found in Sumerian, Babylonian and Accadian myths. Most accounts of the tale describe these beings as having arrived in an ark-like craft, amid great thunder and fire. Their purpose, according to the Dogon, was to act as spiritual saviours for the human race, bestowing their metaphysical and astronomical knowledge to those who would listen. For this reason the *Nommos* were also called the 'Teachers' and the 'Monitors'. The Dogon claimed that the *Nommos* would some day return to Earth, taking control of its waters and ruling the world, in this way making the world 'clean again'. It was also said that the *Nommos* make periodic visits to the Earth, and reward followers for their devotion by bringing them back to Sirius, which the Dogon believe to be a heavenly realm or paradise.

Over the years it has become accepted that the Dogon could not have acquired their vast scientific knowledge of Sirius without contact with a technologically advanced civilization – whether this scientific knowledge was terrestrial or extraterrestrial in origin has never been conclusively determined, although there is a great deal of evidence in support of the latter. The tribe's inexplicable and astonishingly advanced scientific knowledge is given incontrovertible proof in the form of a 400-year-old Dogon artefact which bears a clear depiction of the Sirius configuration, as well as the Dogon's ceremonial celebration of Sirius A and B's cycle, a ritual dating back to the 13th century.

Sirius continues to enthral people the modern world over, as it has since before times of written record. This long and rich history has infused the unprecedented events revolving around the Deathray Bradburys and their alleged spiritual connection to the binary star with an added scope and an ever deepening mystery.

666:

The enigma of The Deathray Bradburys has endured over a decade, and could be compared to sifting through the ruins of a once thriving civilization that inexplicably vanished without a trace, leaving a proverbial ghost town for bewildered fans and researchers to examine and re-examine and speculate over in its wake.

Very little is known about the Deathray Bradburys. The seminal band's career was short-lived: the five-piece formed sometime between 1995 and 1997 and concluded their recording and touring existence in late summer 2000. Although their place of origin isn't known for certain, it's speculated to be somewhere in the greater Windsor-Essex County area of South Western Ontario, due to the fact of their playing an exorbitantly large number of performances within this geographic region (though the band did tour throughout other parts of the country in their later days, as well as into the United States). The most prominent cities frequented by the band included Windsor, Chatham, London, Hamilton, Kingston, and Toronto, and smaller towns in the vicinity of Windsor, such as Belle River, Comber, Woodslee, Harrow, Leamington and Kingsville, among others.

Stylistically, they played a raw and minimalist form of garage rock, with a heavy nod to the frenetically-paced, three-chord punk rock of the late 1970s and a melodic sensibility reminiscent of 1950s bubblegum pop and doo-wop. They precociously merged this with an overtly psychedelic guitar and keyboard influence - along with typically reverb-drenched vocals - which embellished the band with a distinctly spacey quality in keeping with their overall cosmic aesthetic. They were famed for their unabashed embracing of B-movie inspired imagery - each band member wore retro/pseudo-futuristic silver costumes and masks (complete with antennae, goggles and, occasionally, wings!) so that no one ever learned their identities. Interestingly enough, the band members never disclosed their names, either real or stage names, preferring the mystery that came with total anonymity. They likewise refused to do interviews, although admittedly any noteworthy print publications that would have been interested in giving the then little-known band coverage were few and far between; the only forums known to have written about the band were fanzine-type publications with very limited circulation, most likely passing from person to person at live performances, through small independent record shops, or via other underground channels.

Yet the Deathray Bradburys would become most famous in underground circles - and ultimately to the rest of the world - for their lyrical fixation, an obsessive focus revolving around themes of escape from a decadent, increasingly violent and racist world to a paradisiacal place of salvation. The idea of this haven, at first glance a seemingly fictitious creation, was repeatedly reinforced as authentic by the group's proselytizing on-stage banter and the recurring mini-essays and poetry-like texts found as liner notes in their recordings, describing the tenets of this belief, as well as a timeline establishing a set date for a planned exodus from Earth to this paradise. Going to a Deathray Bradburys concert was much like attending an evangelical sermon, complete with a self-proclaimed prophet - in this case the band's lead singer/front man, delivering impassioned between-song orations imploring the band's followers to embrace the higher power of which they sang - and throngs of spellbound followers in rapture of the spectacle unfolding before them.

The basic story as proposed by the Deathray Bradburys in their cryptic lyrics described a future mass exodus that they themselves were to lead (exactly how the band came about this knowledge was hinted at but never fully disclosed). Those chosen to accompany them were individuals with a deep emotional and spiritual need to escape their own personal woes, and more generally the misery inherent in life on Earth. As the story went, those who followed the band and believed in their promise of salvation would likewise be saved alongside their musical heroes, ultimately to be transported – some believed spiritually while others believed physically – from their lives and into this heavenly paradise among the stars: the 'light' of the Sirius binary star system. The group's lyrics speak of Sirius in fanatically reverential terms, and have a foundation based in the historical and mythological roots relating to the star.

The exodus was scheduled to take place, for reasons once again apparently known only to the band itself, on the final night of August in the year 2000. Debate continues concerning the means by which this 'ascension' was intended to occur – many analyses of the group's lyrics and literature speculate that mass suicide represented the medium through which the salvation promised by the group was purported to take place, as evidenced by recurring references to the drinking of 'potions' of ambiguous 'energy'. Suicide is indeed a recurring theme throughout the band's body of work, and specifically the repeated allusions to the 'freedom' it provided from unrelenting misery and sadness. The song 'Robert The Mighty', for example, seems to be an ode to pulp writer Robert E. Howard, elevating his life and subsequent suicide to divine proportions in accordance with the Deathray Bradburys' belief in the transcendence afforded those who took themselves from the mortal world.

In 'County Road 26 To Infinity', tribute is paid to 'the angels Boreal and Wood', a worshipful reference to both cult leader Michael Boreal, the founder of the Sirius Group who led his disciples in a mass suicide on the island of Magahatti; as well as James William Wood, infamous for his abduction of the fifteen women who would come to be known as the Essex Fifteen, each a victim of forced or assisted suicide (debate still rages as to which) and promised ascension to a heavenly realm: Sirius. Members of the so-called Essex Fifteen are likewise mentioned throughout the DB canon, such as in the songs 'Peace-Star For The Lost Sixteen' and 'Maria 16' – a reference to the youngest victim of the Essex Fifteen, Maria Reed; the numeral appended to the name in the latter echoing the title of the former, and signifying the band's sympathetic belief that Wood himself should be included in the group of suicide victims, bringing their number to sixteen victims rather than solely the fifteen women.

Topically, the band wove an eclectic number of subjects within the greater tapestry of the recurring and unifying themes of suicide and escape from a violent world. References to lilies recur throughout the band's lyrics, providing a link to the inexplicable phenomenon of this flower species growing in abundance at the site of the Essex Fifteen group suicide in Essex County, Ontario. The flower became symbolic of the band, and fans attending their concerts would reputedly wear them in their hair or throw them onto the stage during performances. Constant comparisons are made in the band's lyrics between the sullied and decadent modern world of the city to the purity of times long past, the beauty and splendour of bucolic environments versus the dangers of the modern world and its insistence on (often dangerous) technological advances; as well as the contrast between the innocence and wonder of childhood and its loss in adulthood. These ideas draw a neat line to the band's namesake, Ray Bradbury, much of whose work delves into these very themes.

Interestingly, given the Deathray Bradburys' quasi-cult/religious stance, their lyrics make no effort to deny the existence of God or Satan, but rather suggest that their own prophetic visions offer their disciples an alternative to both. Biblical references throughout their literature to the Devil, angels and giant figures reminiscent of the Nephilim (the Biblical giants said to be a product of the union between the sons of God and the daughters of men) suggest an acceptance of the tenets posited by a variety of organized religions, while simultaneously giving equal credence to subjects rooted firmly in scientific foundations and ancient alchemy – these include the scientific experiments and aspirations of trailblazing inventor and physicist Nikola Tesla; the age of the dinosaurs, an epoch spoken of in romantic terms for its absence of humankind, often described as a violent and ruining force; interstellar phenomena such as stars, worm-holes, and space travel; and more arcane sciences, such as ancient numerology, alchemy, and occult mysticism.

Mythological subject matter recurs in the group's lyrics as well, ranging from allusions to the Greek myth of Icarus to ancient African lore, with the story of Tombanik, an active volcano long said in the folklore of the region to be inhabited by a god fallen from the sky. Interestingly, these myths involve themes of flight and celestial phenomena, both themes seen elsewhere in the band's writing. References to the sea and ocean abound in their lyrics as well – the Greek sea-god Proteus appears in several songs, as well as direct references to the amphibious sea-dwelling *Nommos* and their promise to reclaim and purify the Earth's oceans.

Aesthetically speaking, the Deathray Bradburys evoked a unique combination of imagery in their lyrics, ranging from the cosmic to the bucolic representing the positive side of the spectrum, and the modern world/society – specifically the city – as its antithesis. This, and the need (and means) to escape from a world too often rife with emotional suffering and anguish, marked the foundation of the band's message.

Fantastic as the premise of the group's promised ascension sounds, its appeal to a contingent of the underground music community was profound: fans of the Deathray Bradburys treated the band as some religious devotees treat their faith, with absolute conviction and a dedication bordering on fanaticism. This lyrical subject matter – as well as the prayerful, angry and outraged manner with which it was often expressed – found particular appeal among disaffected youth, as it offered both a sympathetic voice while speaking very clearly to an end of suffering and a promise of rescue from a downtrodden existence. For this reason the band began drawing increasingly loyal crowds to their concerts at small bars and all-ages community centres even before the release of their debut album, sowing the seeds of their future legacy. Rather judiciously, the band omitted certain details of their invented story, lending it a deliciously cryptic and enticing air that allowed for fans to fill in gaps as they liked.

Knowledge of the Deathray Bradburys' seeming sincerity in the proclamations they made grew through word-of-mouth to define the band's agenda, setting them apart from their peers, as well as any rock and roll groups that came before them or have come since. The group's entire catalogue – comprised of a single full-length album entitled *There Is A Place* (self-released on Saucer Records in July 1998, reissued as a tenth anniversary special edition in 2008 by Ryko Records) as well as several obscure 7" singles releases and countless bootleg recordings – reflect this thematic focus, occasionally with gleeful simplicity and vulgarity appropriate to their punk rock roots, but more often with a breathtaking poeticism paralleling their literary inspirations and worthy of the grand and grave subject matter of which they sang. The Deathray Bradburys' wildly eclectic stylistic approach ran the gamut from anthemic rally calls directing their followers and praising their collective spiritual beliefs, to impassioned tributes to their literary and other influences, to poignant philosophical dissertations on the nature of living in and seeking haven from a difficult and uncompromising world.

Some have argued that this obsession and seductive rhetoric made the band as much a cult based on persuasive charismatic manipulation of its adherents as they were a group of musicians. Whatever their agenda, the band's musical prowess can't be ignored. With a variety of tightly-crafted, deceptively simple pop-inflected anthems drawing influences from a variety of genres and styles to their credit they represented something of an anomaly in the music world: a garage band of immense talent and originality whose chief objective was not only light years removed from the lofty goals of fame and fortune which so many other bands aspire to attain; but the purported fulfillment of spiritual ideals they pursued to the utter neglect of a burgeoning career. In the process they provided a source of spiritual hope for their small but madly devoted fan base.

777:

It remains unknown what became of the members of the underground band the Deathray Bradburys following their final performance at the Coach And Horses in Windsor, Ontario on Thursday, August 31st 2000. For all intents and purposes, the band – along with a reported thirty local missing persons linked to the event, and one hundred ninety-five people from throughout other areas of the province – quite literally fell off the face of the Earth, coinciding with the date set for their preordained, fictitious(?) exodus. An extensive province-wide search was undertaken throughout the months following, yielding no clues whatsoever as to the whereabouts of those missing. The case, a decade on, remains unresolved while debate continues as to whether this represents one of the most elaborately staged mass-scale hoaxes in history, or something else entirely. As a result of these unexplained circumstances the band's ever-growing cult status remains assured, as well as the legacy of mystery and romance – and grandly evocative music – they've left behind. It goes without saying that the group's body of lyrics continues to be scrutinized.

In positing theories as to the whereabouts of the Deathray Bradburys and their missing followers, perhaps it's best – if exceedingly romantic – to conclude with the enigmatic yet seemingly prophetic words of the band itself:

> *There is a place*
> *Far beyond all of this despair*
> *We promise you, friends:*
> *There is a place for us all.*

– from the song First Colony

First published in *Underground Tracks* Volume 1, Issue 252, November 2010. Author: A.B. Sossi

"*I* know," said the man to himself, closing the music magazine across his knee where he sat on the wooden bench overlooking the Detroit River. He did know. The truth, more startling than any fabrication he could concoct.

He'd had a girlfriend in those days, when he'd been young and reckless and living a life he wished he could have back. She'd followed the band with a religious zealot's devotion, and had gotten him into their music, too. He loved punk rock, loved B-movies, loved the fusion of the two to create the most purely fun music he'd ever heard. But she'd believed in the Deathray Bradburys in a way he'd thought went too far beyond their fun B-movie aesthetic. She'd believed all their goofy, tongue-in-cheek rhetoric purporting to offer salvation to their followers, and escape from their lives if escape is what they needed; even going so far as to have their symbol tattooed into her left breast: the oddly ancient-but-futuristic silver hexagon filled with a pair of darker rings. She'd never been one to fawn over her artistic heroes, either, so seeing her uncompromising devotion to the band was more than a little unsettling at times.

He recalled their argument that distant night, post-show, she begging him to accompany her onto the small tour bus, a converted school bus, along with a dozen other fans and the band members themselves. They'd argued outside of the venue for nearly thirty minutes while the band loaded their gear into the bus, and the handful of their fans boarded along with them.

"Please, Matt. *Please*? Will you just come? Just trust me, okay? This is for real! All of this is seriously *for real*."

Of course, jealous as he was of the band who'd succeeded in turning his girlfriend into an automaton groupie slave, he'd dismissed her, telling her indignantly to do whatever she wanted, but that she'd be doing it without him. He'd glanced back once as he went on his way, seeing the bus lurching from the alley behind the bar and onto the street heading east. This was the last he'd seen of it, and his girlfriend, heading into the drowsy A.M. and a lunatic's promise of much, much more. Even then, though, before the great disappearance became realized – during the final days that the Deathray Bradburys were still considered by many merely a fun good-times band with a healthy dose of theatricality mixed into their repertoire – even then he'd felt a pang of guilt, remembering the secret darkness that his girlfriend hid from the world at large, the secrets of her home life which he alone was privileged to have been told. Even then, in the throes of his disbelief, he understood her own need to believe.

"The joke was on me," he muttered, staring at the stars reflected waveringly in the scummy river. "Fuck." There was no escaping their light, so he cast his eyes resignedly skywards, dismayed at the completely cloudless view in all directions: stars everywhere, a billion remote points of light everywhere his eyes roved. It was a view he sought to spare himself as often as he was able. He murmured, "I miss you, Katie. I miss you, baby. I'm sorry I didn't hear good enough."

He was crying then, for himself, the unfulfilling day behind him, and for his great blunder over ten years before. But eventually a smile worked its way through his regret and melancholy and onto his face, as it always did when he reminisced about those long-lost times: a smile for Katie, who was at peace, somewhere.

Another dead, forever led by the dreams in his head

ELOPERS TO SIRIUS

The day was golden-aired. Its light poured into the cabin through the open windows and doors, touching them both where they stood close to one another in the baking stillness. The pungent scent of vegetation hung on the sultry air: the distant jungle's perfume, a thick and intoxicating brew of banana and elephant grass and wildflowers that seemed to have seeped into the bamboo walls surrounding them, the light silk bedding, their clothes, their pores so that even their breath exited as an exotic zephyr as they spoke in hushed voices, heads bowed together.

"Are you scared?" His voice was electric with his own fear, and excitement at the imminence of the great event looming before them. He was kneading her small shoulders gently by way of reassurance, smiling fondly at her doe eyes and anxious expression.

She turned to the window and the brilliant day it held. She smiled. "Not really. Not *really*. Not as long as I'm with you. As long as we're together..."

"Always. We've always been, we'll always be."

"I know. I know."

He saw her fear plainly. He saw too her looming joy, could envision it changing her, embellishing her features with a new brightness, the kind he hadn't seen there for too long. He smiled broadly. He whispered it: "We're here. Finally, we *made it here*. We're one step from Paradise."

Speaking of it aloud – something which they hadn't done since waking hours before, as if consciously avoiding discussions of the momentousness of the day – now urged excited and relieved laughter from them both.

Together they went to the cabin's long window. The field beyond, cropped low, was exuberantly lush, the yellow Heliconias dotting the landscape glowing like gold in the bright afternoon light. The perimeter was lined with wooden cabins like their own, small and efficiently sparse inside, creating a great enclosed field between themselves. In the centre of the space stood a flagpole, its flag hanging limply in the windless air, though the symbol adorning it remained partially visible: the silver hexagon containing a pair of overlapping gold circles like some enigmatic Venn diagram. In the heat-hazed distance they saw the forest aglow, too: palm trees stirring in the subtle breeze, with occasional monkeys traveling among their verdant reaches like manic acrobats; the bright parrots like fire among the leaves calling from the tropical depths and creating through their wild song the illusion of being transplanted to another world.

It was difficult to believe, he reflected, but true nonetheless: only days before they'd been merely another couple of teenagers living a downtrodden white trash townhouse life in a drab, forgettable little Southwestern Ontario town where few good things happened and badness abounded, where the days dragged one into the next with no end to their monotony and despair in sight. The trees of that former world scraggly and un-pretty, or colossal but still filled only with everyday sparrows and crows. No trees sang as vibrantly in the place they came from. No gold fire burned in the fields they'd known all their lives.

Awed by the might of the island music, humbled by the unbridled wildness and beauty offered up by this un-guessed land floating in the middle of the Pacific Ocean, he was inspired to murmur, dazed-sounding, "It's like a dream. Every minute we're here the sense of it only gets stronger. Here, it's…It's almost like we're already there. You know? It's like we've already found Paradise. What more can there be?"

The thought – the mystery it hinted at – caused him to smile, warm in the sun-filled window. She sighed a luxurious sigh. She squeezed his hand. Watching the bright day, she said, "You know, now that we're here, I...It's like only now, after we got away from them...After we finally got away from him, it's like I realize only now how tired I am. I must have been so tired all the time, but just didn't know it. I feel like since we got here I've finally been catching up on the sleep I missed the past million years."

He smiled sympathetically. He ran a hand across her sun-warm cheek. "Me, too. I was so tired, too. Maybe we were just too busy making up reasons to stay away from the house, and always hiding in all our hideout-places, and trying to not think about everything...Maybe we were scared of getting tired, because if you're awake and ready to run then bad things might not get you..." He could speak freely of these things in this place: the realization filled him with joy.

"Kiss me," she whispered tremulously.

Smiling, he leaned to her.

Sun-warmed lips on lips: it conjured their first kiss. It was an easy and painless recollection in the burning midday, safe with miles and miles and miles from the old world and the wickedness of those days.

Home alone, a brother and sister freed. Best friends from the beginning, warding off the dual attention and neglect of demons hounding their shared home life. Friends crossing an inconsequential boundary to celebrate an escape in one another, all while coloured in late day sunlight slanting in through his bedroom window's shutters while their parents were away on a rare daytrip together. All of the years' worth of restraint let unbound on that special day, as if perhaps the secret burden they shared at last offered them compelling enough reason to forge forward as they both desired, in an effort to leave behind these very secrets through their new union. Lips to lips and arms wound about each other, timidly at first but then more forcefully as the old clock mounted on the wall over the bed continued its staggeringly loud ticking, as if measuring the seconds passing with a more vigorous movement of its hands, as if serving as reminder that they must, as always, make the very most of their rare moments of peace. Entwined in the room's centre and moving eventually into the walk-in closet to close themselves within its safe congested darkness. The musty smell of the closet enclosing them, of leather and cardboard boxes and old clothing. Slipping out of their summer clothes – his faded denim shorts and sky-blue t-shirt, her white and orange summer dress – and once more into one another's sweaty embrace. Even then, in the madness of the moment, they'd both understood it for what it was: their first true step towards the purest happiness they'd known, and could ever know.

They leaned from each other now. Their lingering kiss burned their mouths. The golden-aired cabin made them sleepy. The scent of exotic wildflowers hung heavily on the air. Feeling romantic in the dream-like atmosphere, he reached a hand through the open window and retrieved a bright white lily from its vine crawling across the exterior cabin wall. He curled the lily's stem behind her ear so that the flower rested amid her hair at the side of her head.

Remembering something he'd read long ago he said, "People in ancient times said that lilies were really stars that fell to Earth."

"That's so...That's perfect," she said. She watched him a moment without words, then, "You're the only family I've ever needed," a teardrop appearing in the corner of her eye and rolling down her cheek. She'd been saying maudlin things like this to him since they'd arrived here, flown in with a dozen or so others days before. The island seemed to summon the words from her, as if its elements of sultry climate and burning white-sanded beaches and dense jungle and endless rolling waters and delicious remoteness – a seeming lifetime of distance from the world she'd known – came together like an uncanny spell that allowed her to revel in emotions she'd never been able to fully relinquish herself to.

He held her tightly. He kissed her earlobe. He nuzzled her sun-burning cheek. She sighed and felt it anew: like a wave the surge of happiness, the likes of which she'd known for the first time in their secret stolen bedroom moment years before.

A moment passed. They continued to hold each other, unmoving at first in their place but slowly bending to the lazy but charged rhythm of the day and moving a slow side-to-side dance that creaked the wooden floorboards. "We're here," he whispered in her ear. "We made it." As they danced the memory arrived for them both, like a snippet of dream, hazy and luxurious: the day the path, unexpected, had been revealed to them.

*

A deceiving day for its same-old beginnings: seeking sanctuary in the wilds of fields beyond their townhouse neighbourhood. Wandering among the tall grass and cattails waving in the November wind, shivering in their coats and toques. A chance or fateful encounter on the balding trail cutting a circuitous design through the tangle of woods: a young man, a teenager not much younger than themselves, stopping them where he stood staring with a look of expectation through the ceiling of tree branches into the cloudy sky. Something in the boy's face – a strain in his eyes, maybe, some furtive thing like a shadow seeking to hide a secret knowledge or bleakness but revealing it instead to those accustomed to such shadows – gave them cause to stop and hear him out, to accept what he offered them: a pamphlet from the bag of pamphlets he carried.

They unfolded it, examining the words within while he inexpertly explained its contents, stumbling over his words in his haste, jumbling his meaning and having to start again before skipping along to his next imprecisely-made point. Maybe it was the earnestness with which he spoke, or the desperation in his eyes. Something in the boy they recognized, and sympathized with. Thanking him for the pamphlet, and promising to consider the information it contained, they'd left the boy on the trail, sky-watching earnestly again.

They'd spent the next hour or so sitting along the break wall overlooking the grey river, reading the pamphlet together, again and again.

At some point it became understood between them that the words on its pages made sense, and that the gift of the pamphlet was a special one, and that finally, after all the years and all of the pain, there was suddenly a path opened before them: an escape from the clutches of their shared life.

She'd turned to him, excitement brimming in her hushed voice: "Sirius...I don't...I can't say why exactly, but...but it makes sense. It *feels* right...Doesn't it? *Doesn't* it?"

He turned to his sister. The smile he smiled told her that, as ever, they were caught in this adventure together.

*

His voice came softly, stirring her from her drowsy reveries. "Everyone's arriving now. It's time to go."

She followed his gaze through the window. From everywhere they'd appeared, making the unreality of the moment that much more profound: the lines of people drifting from cabins identical to theirs, from the abutting forest paths, from the white-sanded beach like an immense strip of ivory in the distance, individually and in pairs and in families of three and four and more, and all convening in the great field. They looked like ants, arranged in their neat lines, she thought. Seeing them, her heart beat faster. She smiled, prepared to enter the dream-picture stirring outdoors.

They crossed to the threshold of the open door. The pulse of the forest had risen into the air like a song of celebration. Looking into the bright day – sky cloud-free, blue and pure from east to west – they sensed the stars beyond trembling in the rapture of the moment, and in anticipation of what lied ahead.

A small wooden platform had been erected to one side of the field, flanked by a pair of battered speakers mounted high in steel brackets. A lectern stood in its centre, looking regal despite its rather flimsy construction; its imperial quality stemming from the narrow blue satin curtain draped the length of the podium's front, adorned with the emblem familiar to all those gathered before it: the pair of gold circles filling a large silver-limned hexagon. Resting upon the podium was a small silver microphone which flashed in the sunlight.

A great hush descended upon the people when the man appeared in the distance behind the platform. He emerged from one of the small cabins, crossed the lawn and mounted its steps and moved to a place before the lectern. His white hair belied his ruddy youthful features, his eager blue eyes surveying them all. His smile was broad, benevolent. A moment of palpable anticipation passed as the man cleared his throat into the microphone, testing the reach of his voice across the fields. A brief surge of feedback split the air, and then silence. He looked over the gathered with gentle eyes, smiling eyes, joyous eyes. Michael Boreal had arrived, and in the great hush of his arrival, even the distant parrots and monkeys seemed to have ceased their banter to listen to his words.

The kind-eyed man spoke. "Greetings, brothers and sisters, and thank you for being here with me on this day." His voice was sweet and soft but sure. A yet more profound hush descended upon the fields. Those gathered there – the man's family of four hundred-plus children – hung on his every word, breath, fluctuation of emotion and subtlety of gesture: the creasing of the crow's-feet limning his eyes as he smiled benevolently upon them; the gentle but assured way with which his fingers held the microphone stand, as if he were long accustomed to addressing multitudes through this technological medium, a performer and man of prestige and renown, but without the pomp and arrogance of men in similar roles. Strands of his snow-white hair gusted in the Ocean-salt wind, adding an imperial and noble quality to him.

"Fifteen years ago, nearly to the very day, a vision materialized before me. In the midst of my old life. A life immoral and without law. And then this vision. Giving me purpose. Giving to me a reason to find you, all of you, in time. To find you, and bring all of us together as I have. Here, to this place of wild splendours, unsullied by those who inhabit the places from which we all come. This vision showed me this place. This vision showed me the treasures of this place, treasures beyond its wild beauty, its serenity away from the old, noisy world we've known. Here, on this island, lies the gate, to the better place. Here, today, on this island, is the day that this gate will open – for a brief piece of time only – and allow the chosen and privileged ingress to that place."

Here the man paused, gathering his breath, his strength, as if summoning the courage and faith of his children and disciples listening raptly before him. And,

"Sirius. Twins beautiful and powerful and glowing in the eastern quadrant, like a beacon for the souls of the good, the benevolent, the marked, the privileged. I know not *why* Sirius, but only that Sirius it is. I am but a humble vessel through which a greater voice speaks. I direct you, my beloved and chosen ones, by these unseen means, and it is a voice to which I have listened for fifteen long years, and a voice which has likewise spoken to you. My children. My friends. My family. My *family*."

At this several cries rang out. A portly woman, weeping with joyful abandon, raised her arms skywards, tears streaming from her eyes. Towards the front of the crowd, a middle-aged man, grey-haired and square-chinned and rapturous, likewise lifted his hands high on the steaming air, and proclaimed his love for the father-speaker. "I love you, father!" he cried, weeping, his voice cracking in his ecstasy while his adulation was echoed emphatically by those around him.

The man's new father smiled. He clutched his hand to his breast, showing the man below, and everyone there, that this love was reciprocated. He went on, his voice faltering for the strength of his emotions.

"We each of us wear a mark. It may rest upon the physical shell of some of us, but it most certainly lies in the deepest parts of each of us. It binds us, this mark. Throughout our lives we have loathed it, feared it, wept over its eternal presence haunting us like the most tenacious of ghosts. But it is also that which has brought us together at this end, and this beginning. You all have your reasons for being here today. For exiting your life before and ridding yourselves of its shackles and traveling from afar to arrive here, in this great moment now. Let us leave it behind. All of it. The rage. The pain. The despair. The hatred. The pain. The filth. The vulgarity. The pain. The *pain*. The pain of all kinds and sizes and agonies. The memories of these things. Let us leave those dark places forever to rot in their own cesspool of turmoil and unrest. Because now – finally – everything will be made right. All that is behind us now. We were alone, and are now together, and will have no end, together. Today, everything is okay. Today, the pain dies."

Those gathered in the field echoed their new-father's smile of freedom, relief, ecstasy. They each of them remembered the day not so long past when they had set out on their great odyssey, leaving behind their old life and traveling far from their small corners of the globe so that they could be there in the sunlight of a different place: a middle-aged wife weary of the years of her vindictive husband's relentless attentions; another woman, older and frailer, tired of wearing bruises and burns from the boyfriend with whom she shared her woeful existence; a boy grown into the semblance of a man but hiding merely the boy within the shell, petrified in his place of youth by the ghost of his uncle's secret meetings with him; another man dying inside, too, but his progressive killer the cancer blackening his pancreas and gnawing the life from him each day passing, hoping, this man, to beat his untimely murderer; a former adolescent prostitute grown old and angry and no longer able to live and work in the world and to lay his trust in any of its chameleon-coloured people; a veteran of too many tours whose napalm-fired jungle-dreams have banished sleep and peace from his life; and a brother and sister, thinking back to the day that felt a lifetime ago, when they were children and not the people who now, for the first time, felt like adults, when they'd stood huddled close together at the bus station, tickets clutched in hands, hearts storming inside of them, the air March-dark with rain misting the street and chilling them in their jackets as they embarked on a desperate trek across the world, and then further by far than this meagre opening leg of the journey.

A storm cloud stirred suddenly in Michael Boreal's eyes. Suspicion and mounting fury grew there. Grabbing the microphone from its stand, he stalked the small wooden platform like a hunting animal. His burning eyes scoured the crowd ravenously. The people stirred. His children grew frightened, looking about themselves for the cause of their new-father's unrest. They had never seen the man in such a state. They'd believed they were on the cusp of Paradise, and now this transformation, as if everything they dreamed for was set to fall to ruins. They continued to eye each other. They murmured nervously. When the father-speaker's voice came again all fell right away into a listening silence.

"I sense...I sense a...There is an intruder among us today, my children."

At this a greater anxious murmuring arose. Suspicious eyes flew about. People stepped further apart, setting in disarray the close-knit formation they'd been holding.

"Wait, my children," the man implored the roiling host. "Wait, and let me see...Let me find this intruder among us..." His frantically roving eyes discerned something a moment later. Grown livid, the man gestured towards the front of the group. "There! He is *there!*"

Perhaps it was his being detected by the prescient speaker that caused the man to remove the small camera from where he'd held it unseen within the sleeve of his shirt in a seeming display of admission or surrender. Sunlight flashed angrily from its polished grey skin. His camera-fist swung hesitantly on the steaming air, as if the man was reluctant to cease documenting the father-speaker. A great cry arose, of alarm and fury and indignation. The man did not move. Fear or resignation held him in his place before the stage, traitorous camera held ineffectually in his hand, eyes stunned, awaiting his fate.

This fate was determined by the father-speaker's children. A desperate hand swung from near the man, bringing the camera earthwards. It became lost among a tangle of feet, crushed in the ensuing stampede to seize him. Hands pulled the man to the grass, while others found his throat and squeezed.

Seeing the swarming throngs of his disciples Michael Boreal implored them, "My children, wait! Apprehend this impostor among us worshippers, but harm him not! Leave him his life or else we become as those from the old world from which we escape on this day!"

The people heard their new-father through the clamour of their fury. And when the crowd parted, it was a young man and woman who stepped finally from the prostrate, bloodied, though still living man. These two looked to the blood on their hands, and then to each other. The strange gauze of madness lifted from their eyes as they found one another. They collapsed into each other's arms. A sympathetic murmur arose around them. Gentle hands touched their shoulders, backs, arms, reassuring them of their good intent. Those close to the couple heard their words of lament: "I never meant to hurt him. I don't even know him." "I know, darling. Of course, I know." "I never wanted to be like *him*." "No. You're not. Not ever. Not in any way." "Oh, I never wanted to be like dad." "Never. Not ever. We're free of him. We're free."

The father-speaker's eyes twinkled in the bright air. A tear beaded from each of them, glimmering like jewels as he looked upon his followers. He flew a hand to his breast and held it over his heart. The words from his lips wavered with his great emotion but everyone heard him plainly: "Thank you, my children. Oh, thank you. Now, please, someone, will someone please remove this sorrowful intruder from our midst? Will someone restrain him so that he can't interfere again with our destiny this beautiful afternoon?"

Several of those gathered hurried the dazed man to the shade of a nearby cabin, where they bound his wrists with a stout rope, and fastened these bonds to the sturdy wood of the porch railing. From his place on the porch the man had an uninterrupted view of the clearing.

Michael Boreal looked to his wrist. Sunlight flashed from his silver watch. He checked the position of the sun overhead. He cocked an ear, as if

206

listening to a secret telemetrical voice in the golden air, in the subtle zephyr breeze, among the stirring forest across the fields. And his smile broadened. It grew and became huge and it seeped its way into his eyes, and the father-speaker said in an exultant voice,

"Now: the door lies open. They're coming for us. The moment has arrived, but for a brief sliver of time only. Drink, my children. Drink the energy of a new life, and follow me on our long walk to the better place!"

An immense bird lifted from the trees and arced across the blue sky behind the father-speaker, as if signalling the journey's commencement.

As one, he and his children looked upwards to where the stars frosted behind the clear blue afternoon sky, and tipped the slender silver cylinders they'd been clutching to their lips.

Amanda looked to Dillon beside her: still, brother and sister wept with abandon. They held each other's hands tightly. They were prepared to leave. The world had given them nothing. They'd fought to find each other. A brother and sister bound in the deepest ways. Together, now, in their new family, they were prepared to leave behind the endless blackness they'd known for as long as they'd known each other. He whispered earnestly: "Will you marry me?"

The tears running from her eyes; the smile on her face; the urgency with which she clasped his hands: these things told him her answer.

The sun shone fiercely. Wildlife sang joyously – jubilantly then, as if celebrating the moment, too – from the wilderness to the north, south, and west. In the east, the water shone with a dazzling fire.

Beneath it all, and over it all, and all through the serene fabric of the sun-washed afternoon, a deep energy grew, and roared; shaking the monkeys and parrots from the trees like confetti and filling the air with a rhythm born of a cosmic scale: a song of power, joy, celebration, triumph.

In the years following what came to be known as the Magahatti Massacre speculation abounded as to the various unexplained circumstances surrounding the event. Myriad books documenting the known events which took place on the island of Magahatti in the Pacific Ocean were rushed into publication in the early days following the mass suicide, while a slew of authors returned to examine and reinterpret the subject in the years after. The event continues to enthral many, holding a morbid fascination for some and a point of intense scholarly interest for those working within the disciplines of sociological behaviour and group psychology.

The most popular view of the incident considers eccentric millionaire and Sirius Group founder Michael Boreal to epitomize the supreme cult leader: charismatic and convincing, seemingly benevolent and purportedly prophetic, and owning the necessary monetary capital required to fund and maintain the illusion of the haven he'd created for his devotees. His fifteen year-long crusade of recruiting members for his group and nurturing the farflung ideas which made up the core tenets of the Sirius Group's modus operandi were made possible through both his obsessive devotion to the project as well as the unlimited resources at his disposal. Egocentric and sociopathic, his mastery of group dynamics allowed him to manipulate his followers in the most extreme of ways, fulfilling his religious zealot's mission of mass suicide and promised ascension to the paradisiacal place of his own invention; the fabricated celestial haven for his troubled disciples supposedly having been a location within the binary star Sirius, outside of our own Milky Way galaxy.

Others cast doubt on this popular skeptical perspective of the Magahatti Massacre, positing that the mysterious circumstances surrounding the case of the Sirius Group suggest some authentic basis in the reality perceived by the group itself – most notable among the devotees to this school of thought was Dennis Murray, the sole survivor and witness of the Massacre. It was Murray who, acting in a freelance capacity as reporter to Ontario-based newspaper periodical *The Toronto Sun*, had infiltrated the group but been discovered via inexplicable circumstances during its final moments, and been restrained within sight of the events he would later describe to be both "beyond explanation and beyond belief, but absolutely true" as documented in his best-selling book *Away From Night And Into Light: The Ascension Of The Sirius Group*.

The author's most astounding claims include the arrival from the sky of hundreds of immense silver egg-shaped objects, coinciding with the group's mass ingestion of cyanide; the enigmatic loitering of these objects for several minutes among the throngs of recently deceased suicide victims; and their eventual return into the afternoon sky, leaving behind the bodies of the newly dead.

Dennis Murray committed suicide a little over six months following the publication of his book, likewise by cyanide ingestion, and likewise on the island of Magahatti, in the vicinity of the site of the cult suicide. He left no suicide note, leaving his final thoughts and specific motivations unknown.

A second group inspired by the tenets built and ultimate deeds nurtured by cult leader Michael Boreal is known to exist, with adherents from around the globe. Known as Sirius II, the potential danger (though some argue nature of salvation) posed by this secret society to its members, as well as the danger to those who stand in opposition of its doctrines, remains open to speculation.

TINY BUGLES IN A

DREAM OF GIANTS

"It's a suicide run."

They stood side-by-side in the warm shade beneath the porch stoop, gazing into the dusty sun-bathed yard and the blue-coated men saddling their horses there. The sounds of their preparation drifted to them on the still and expectant morning air: the creaking of leather riding gear, the efficient clack of rifles being examined, the low murmur of uneasy voices.

The advisor's words hung like a mist between the two men. *A suicide run.* He could be so bold with his superior. Old friends could be this way with one another, beyond rules of rank and formality.

You have no idea, the captain thought, remembering his telescopic view from the hills lining the valley only several days before, disbelieving of his scouts' reports until he'd witnessed it with his own eyes; panning among the verdant rolling country, rife with wildflowers like fire in the grasses, and the unexpected wickedness of the enemy. *Satan ruining the summer country,* he'd thought, and spat on the grass in condemnation of the redskins, and then shuddered and rode homewards with the ghost of that Devil licking upon his horse's hooves all the way.

But he said, wishing to keep his dear friend ignorant to the madness living in the world for as long as he was able, "He's the toughest soldier we've got, Albert. What he's been through. Beating odds like no one. Luck and pluck both. We'll see," he said. His thoughts turned to the corporal's bride-to-be, round-hipped and rose-haired and as fiery as the summer burning around them. How hungry she made him. How thirsty. How he wanted to posses her the way he seized and owned all things. As always while swept up in the ecstasy of her the vague feelings of guilt needling his conscience were pushed away. He felt parched, swallowed hard and scowled at the rough desert of his throat. He knew his friend guessed his motivations. He cherished the confidence of his silence, and would repay him as he could in the days ahead.

A bugle's determined voice sounded in the quiet; and then the corporal's strident voice bellowing the order for all to move out; and then the pounding gallop of hooves across the grass as the cavalrymen filed from the yard and into the fields beyond.

"Well. There they go," murmured the advisor in a grim voice, squinting into the new day. "God be with them."

The captain's eyes were hard. "Yes. Yes. There he goes." Without her lover to whom could she turn for comfort but her oldest suitor? There they go. There they go.

Together they watched the troop ride into the horizon. The sun was rising there, making everything bloody and doomed, bloodying the host of blue uniforms, too.

The plains behind them gave way to the gently rolling landscape of hill country. The verdant land around them ran riot with gold and crimson: wildflowers everywhere, making a scenic country worthy of poetry. There shouldn't be blood spilt here, the corporal thought gloomily. In this place where houses should be built, and meals cooked and picnics enjoyed and children shown the beauty of hills in afternoon light. Of course he was thinking of her. His Annabelle with cheeks of fire and eyes just as wild; except when she was surrounded by the orphanage children and the spirit of the youthful girl she'd once been was returned, possessing her to gambol tirelessly with the girls and boys who adored her. She owned his heart, and he was unworthy but happy of owning hers, too.

"Cap'n," a tremulous voice haunted the air. He turned to the soldier who'd rode up alongside him, stirring him from his reverie. His men called him *captain*, a mark of their respect for him, and their belief of his destiny to rise and rise through the ranks. *When you become Captain we'll call you General — that's just how it goes, sir -* This a soldier had declared once, over a simple meal in the fields just prior to a clash with the Pawnee. He'd led them far and wide, after all, and earned this respect, and a loyalty that ran much deeper than this.

The corporal turned to appraise the young man. He was thin, gaunt-faced and anxious in his saddle. As if echoing its fearful owner, the horse beneath the young man whinnied nervously.

"What is it, son?"

"I was just thinkin', sir...You said there was goin' to be a war party, but that it wasn't supposed to be a big one. Out here in the hills somewhere. I was just thinkin'...and I was just wonderin'...How big do you think? How big a war party is it gonna be?"

The corporal betrayed nothing as his stoic gaze surveyed the rolling country before them. His voice he kept level, too, and unperturbed. "I don't know for certain. Reports can be misleading, as we've learned many times over. We'll find out soon enough. Be brave, soldier. We're the best there is at this game. Remember this. Remember this and your rifle at your side."

The young man – a boy really – said nothing, only fell back in their column, his face ashen, eyes distant. His horse snorted nervously still, echoed a moment after by the corporal's own mount. Patting her gently along her sinewy neck, he sought to soothe her with his murmuring voice, "It's okay, girl. It's okay." This calmed the animal somewhat, and it fell back into its steady walk, sunshine lustrous in its lush chestnut coat.

The sunlight made everything mellow. A gentle breeze stirred the flowers, carrying their sweet scents around. The rolling landscape grew more impressive, a sight to behold for the cavalrymen who spent so much of their lives serving in the rugged plains.

The corporal squinted into the undulating distance. Sun Valley lay beyond those hills. Sun Valley, and their enemy – a marauding war party of no more than fifty braves, tribe unknown, that had been harassing farmers along the eastern and western boundaries of the hill country. They had been spied by a troop of reconnaissance men who found them camped in the valley itself – and their mission now was to locate and leave no red-skinned warrior of this party alive. He thought of his darling, of how she felt in his arms. He thought of how she would feel laying beside him in three days' time upon his return from his latest mission. He thought – as he thought from time to time – of the wives and children of the warriors he was to meet in the hills.

And he thought of his darling again, waiting for him at the end of another day of blood and thunder.

*

As if conjured by his drifting thoughts: thunder in the hills.

Horses made nervous snuffling noises. Soldiers murmured, clutching rifles to themselves. Others put telescopes to their eyes and scanned the rolling green slopes. The cavalry division, at the corporal's silent signal, stopped in their tracks. They listened. Still, thunder unabated from the hills to the east, west, and a steadily growing clamour from the north and the south, too. Overhead, the afternoon was blue and cloudless. The sun hung in the west, burning a deceptively somnolent haze over everything.

The corporal placed his telescopic eye out among the hills before them. Wildflower colonies in profusion. Long grass baking in the daylight. Green and green and green land rising upwards and upwards. And a bevy of spooked crows suddenly erupted from the wild grass and into the blue. And rising over the crest of the tallest hill before them, over which lay the valley itself: a long line of heads. The riders soon lined the entire ridge of the slope before them, and topped the hills to the east and west, too. Looking behind a soldier cried out that they were boxed in to the north as well. Scanning the ranks ahead of them, the corporal saw with astonishment that seemingly every tribe of which he'd heard lay gathered there: the war paint and traditional garb of the Comanche, Apache, Sioux, Blackfoot, and Pawnee was convened there, and others whose wardress he'd never before encountered. Many of these were warring tribes, and so the sight of them – united as never before in their history – sent a snaking chill of dread along the corporal's spine. This inconceivable, colossal host – like a storm borne of the most nightmarish of dreams – was soon rolling down the steep incline at a measured gallop, wave upon wave upon wave.

The cavalrymen watched, frozen, transfixed by the sight. Some men swore oaths, looking backwards and forwards and to east and west with wide eyes and bared teeth. Their mounts, sensing calamity, kicked nervously at dandelions. Oh, how wrong the reconnaissance reports had been, thought the men. How could the reports have been so exaggeratedly wrong? The war party of fifty that had been described to the corporal and marked for death was materialized before them as a host the likes of which the corporal and his hardened men never imagined existed in this country, let alone seen with their own eyes, let alone met in combat in odds so staggeringly ill-proportioned. He thought of titanic battles of which he'd heard, stories of myth pitting heroes against insurmountable numbers of foes. He needed to lead his men as such a hero would lead them. He needed to hold his darling in three days' time.

"We stand here!"

He'd made his voice resolute, hard. He shuddered in his knees, in some very deep part within him that had never been touched during all of his many experiences in the field. He leapt from his mount, pulling his rifle from its holster alongside the saddle. The hooves of the closing host sent thunder through the earth and into his feet and through the rest of him, too.

The soldiers dismounted in a flurry. They toppled their supply wagon, taking positions along its expanse and aiming their rifles into the west. The remaining men formed a loose circle facing in each compass direction, with the overturned wagon at its centre – some kneeling in the tall grass, others laying on their bellies, rifles at their shoulders and muzzles pointed towards the slopes. The thought that occupied them: the sheer power and momentum of the oncoming assault, downhill and like a prairie storm to tear through their paltry ranks, their flimsy makeshift fortifications. And they thought of their families waiting in the quiet, thunderless far east.

The rumble of horses' hooves grew. The unnerving banshee din of the warriors swelled. A rainfall preceded the arrival of the great host: arrows darkening the sky and finding homes swishing in the wild grass, striking into the bodies of vulnerable cavalrymen. Cries rang out everywhere, sharp and protracted and agonized.

Over the clamour of the warriors' war song; and through the hammering cacophony of arrowheads slamming into the wood of the wagon; and through the flat meaty sound of the missiles pounding into soldiers; and through the crack of rifle reports and screams of pain all around: a familiar and defiant song of battle.

The corporal looked: the boy was kneeling in the wild grass and flowers, the instrument to his quivering lips, eyes wide and lost, sunlight flashing brilliantly from the brass bugle like a beacon and target for the voracious arrows raining down all around. No arrows found him, though – frail and unprotected though he was, terror-stricken and rooted in his place surrounded by dead and maimed soldiers, he played his song and he played it boldly.

Inspired, the corporal smiled the old grim smile which he forced himself to wear during moments like this. He hefted his rifle through the splintered spokes of the wagon's wooden wheel and fired into the coming fray. He fired and reloaded and fired again. Warriors fell in the grass, toppled from their mounts, blood streaking across their war paint-smeared faces and chests.

The man beside him fell backwards suddenly. The corporal turned to him, his stomach lurching at the sight of the arrow piercing him through an eye, its long slim arm quivering in a violent seizure on the air. The soldier twitched on the grass a moment and became still while the arrow quivered on, as if rejoicing sadistically in the life it had taken.

He turned from the dead man and fired into the seething approaching ranks. "Don't panic! There's as many of us as them! We're exactly even! Keep thinking this! Keep shooting!"

Even as he shouted these words a soldier down the line, guarding the far wagon wheel, collapsed with a quiver jutting from his stomach. The man was his friend, they'd known each other since academy days, when they'd both dreamed of battles as glorious events, and of themselves, one day, as generals and old, dear friends with countless courageous stories over which to reminisce. As he watched helplessly a wanton second arrow, and then a third and fourth, pounded into the man, the first of these finding its mark in his neck with a spurt of blood like a broken spigot, with the remaining missiles making a pattern across his chest. He cried out. He toppled onto his belly, pushing the arrows deeper through his torso. He kicked briefly among the flowers and became still.

A shrieking close at hand awakened the corporal from his daze. He looked and the onrushing warrior's arrival on top of him was imminent. He fired his rifle at close range. The Cree's face exploded in a red soup, the rifle blast knocking him backwards from his horse and into the grass. The animal rushed on, clearing the wagon in a leap and shooting onwards in its battle-terror.

A voice behind him screamed. Despite the danger surrounding them the corporal turned. No, he thought. No. Crouching low he scuttled across the grass and leaned over the stricken soldier: like a grotesque porcupine the bugler boy lay on his stomach with the thicket of arrows pluming from his back and shoulders. Another hung limply from his thigh, an indirect hit reddening his white trousers. A high yelping came from him, reminding the corporal of a coyote's lonely nocturnal call. How he yet lived the corporal couldn't begin to fathom. The boy's bugle lay in the grass beside him, reflecting the sunlight brightly. He consoled the boy as best he could, shouting his words. "Be still, man. Be still and we'll get you out of here and to a hospital. Hang on for me. Let us cross over the river, and rest under the shade of the trees." He pulled his pistol from its holster with a numb hand. Terror came into his heart – he would never hold his Annabelle again. He would never call her wife. He would never make children with her. They would never live together in the house he was to build by himself to satisfy a boyhood dream of following in his father's sure, providing footsteps. At his side the boy spasmed. His cries grew to an agonized mewling din. The corporal shook his head fiercely though he was beyond denial of the task before him. He placed the muzzle of his pistol to the boy's temple. He said evenly: "Sleep." He fired. Distantly the corporal sensed a spiking pain envelop his arm as an arrow found its mark. Vaguely the corporal grew aware of a great shadow – as of a storm cloud rolling across the hills at the wind's behest – falling over what remained of their group huddled about the arrow-riddled wagon. Horses ceased whipping past at high velocities like giant bullets. A chorus of cries erupted around the young corporal then – of a different sort than those mad voices of battle he knew well – but he only held on to the boy, as if seeking to anchor them both in the world of the living as death encroached quickly from everywhere, though it spilled from the boy's shattered skull in a thick red tide that drowned the flowers.

"Oh sweet Lord!"

"Sweet Jesus, they got the Devil on their side!"

"Cap'n, look!"

"Oh God in Heaven help us!"

The corporal, dazed, confused, heart aching at his great imminent loss, uniform soaked through with the boy's blood, turned his eyes skywards.

Perhaps an arrow had found him already and his great journey from the world had occurred. Perhaps the plains tribes were truly in league with evil forces as some white men swore, and summoned demons to aid them in their battles. Blotting out the sunlight, a colossal statue moved. The corporal could do nothing but stare in awe at the giant man towering over him and his quaking men. One hundred feet tall perhaps, or taller than this, the giant's head seemed to scrape the bellies of the scant July clouds. His gargantuan arms were outspread, as if in preparation of smiting them all into oblivion, or perhaps capturing them all for some witch's menagerie of slavery. Glancing to left and right the corporal saw that several more of the statue-men towered over the scene of battle, observing the men like ants beneath their immense gazes.

He'd heard tales of Indian deities said to roam the deep forests of the Great Lakes, giant warriors whom the tribes worshipped and who occasionally manifested themselves in the earthly world to aid in the settling of tribal feuds or to offer sustenance during times when game was scarce. He'd heard how the tribes worshipped them in the same manner of awe and reverence with which they worshipped the natural world about them, the woods and plants and animals, imbuing each with a spiritual sentience. Even now, as he turned his stunned eyes around him, the corporal saw the warriors rapt in their obeisance in the grass, bows and hatchets and spears and rifles discarded about them, thoughts of war suddenly forgotten in the presence of this divine or wicked host materialized in the day. A low murmuring, as if in awed chant or prayer, issued from their ranks while his men stood unmoving, and imbued the scene with an impossible, dream-like sense of calm.

In the queer, time-halted moment, the corporal examined the features of the giant man looming over him: pale-skinned to a nearly albino degree, extremely long-cheeked, hairless and with a great expanse of forehead gleaming in the bright air like an egg, penetrating eyes of a fair emerald and the size of ponds observing them cowering far below. Nothing of the physiognomy spoke of the Natives he'd seen, nor of the whites or the Asians he'd met during his travels in the far East as a boy. The expression worn by the giant was a serene one, and with patient eyes he reached a gargantuan hand to the earth, plucking a discarded rifle from where it lay abandoned before a terror-frozen cavalrymen.

He drew the rifle near to his face, holding it like a toothpick between one immense finger and thumb. Smiling a miles-long melancholy smile he snapped the weapon in half. Its pieces fell harmlessly to the grass, like crumbs from a man's hand.

A sonorous thunder boomed from his mouth, words like the embrace of mountains during a great cataclysm: "Look." He waved a hand towards the milling mélange of Indians. A gentler thunder came then.

"Blue-coats: you would do well to learn from these men. Learn from them, and learn to leave them be. Theirs' is the better way." The colossal smile spread itself wider across the man's face. "Theirs' is the best way, my friends, if we exempt this unfortunate clash as the lesson they seek to impart."

The corporal's thoughts reeled: the giant's words fell in accent-laden Comanche, dense and foreign to any tongue he'd heard, and if not for the great volume of the being's voice might have proven unintelligible. The giants' clothing was alien, too: plain single-piece suits fitting their immense lanky contours like a second skin, a metallic silver-grey in colour which had about it a distinctly resilient appearance. He turned to his throbbing arm, saw with surprise the long arm of the arrow jutting from it. With the help of one of his men, they succeeded in tugging it free of his flesh in an explosion of pain and a gushing of blood onto the grass. The corporal turned his eyes to the giant watching them overhead while his soldiers dressed and bandaged the grisly wound.

As if to emphasize his lesson the giant turned to the overturned supply wagon and brought a colossal foot down upon it. Its wooden frame shattered with a shriek and an immense plume of ammunition dust rose upwards into a great mushroom head like a pall over the men.

In the settling dust, the strange stillness of before seemed yet more pervasive. Then, with a gesture of beckoning to the cavalrymen, the giant said "Come. Come and look with us."

The cavalrymen, quaking in their boots, followed. The atmosphere — as if they walked through the mystifying fabric of the strangest of dreams — thickened, seeping its way into the hearts of each of the men drifting through the wildflowers. They walked uphill in pursuit of the giant men of this dream-haze for many minutes or hours. At last they lined the summit of the high slope, weary, stunned.

The giant's voice thundered: "There."

He waved an immense hand westwards. The corporal and his men followed the gesture. The valley lay spread below them, lush and peaceful, dappled everywhere with gold and crimson flowers like confetti nestled in the grasses after a great celebration. Many tents clung to the grass valley floor, too, their hides stirring in the gentle breeze.

"Easily we could stop your struggles here, as we stopped them on this day. Easily we could do this, through the same senseless means you use to harm each other every day. But instead: go and teach your fellow fighters. Go, and teach them what you know now clearer than you may have known it yesterday. Teach them the wisdom in farming the bountiful land over sullying the days with death."

In the wake of the words the cavalrymen, feeling much like students in the presence of a great and wise teacher, shuddered.

"I can't teach them." The words had fallen from the corporal's mouth. He hadn't believed he'd had the strength to speak to the giant man at all. He looked shocked at the sound of his voice, or at the disheartening admission it held.

The giant man appraised the corporal with a solemn eye. A pensive rumble emanated from his throat. He said, in a much softer voice than he'd spoken in so far, "Yes. Yours is a difficult tribe, it seems. Young in years, and difficult."

They beheld each other solemnly and without words.

His courage bolstered by his initial communication with the being, the corporal spoke again. "Where do you – Do you hail from the deep forests, like the legends of these people say?"

The giant man smiled benevolently. "There are forests where we come from. Great forests the likes of which cannot be found here, though the beauties of this place are plentiful, too."

Then, the giant man said, "We must go now, and leave your story to you for concluding. Our stay here has been an enlightening one. Perhaps we shall return one day, and look and see what you have accomplished, when you are no longer so young." He bowed to the throngs of warriors kneeling attentively among the grass on all sides. "We thank you for your hospitality, and your friendship these many months." Casting his eyes westwards, he added, "Your sun sets here: go now, too, friends, all of you, and share a supper in the valley below. Be together on this night in your lives, and tell each other good stories of peace."

With those words the giant man wended his way gingerly among the Indians and cavalrymen and descended the slope. His companions followed. The corporal watched the path of the giant men and discerned that their progress led them toward a handful of immense silver dishes resting in the base of the valley. The falling sun reflected brilliantly from their shells, mesmerizing his gaze. With the giants' departing steps came a sound of receding thunder among the hills.

The remaining cavalrymen and the innumerable Indians – Comanches and Pawnee and Cree and Sioux and dozens of other tribes of the plains – beheld each other without words. None were needed, of course. After a moment, they too trudged down into the verdant valley, like a single weary tribe returning home from a long and difficult campaign.

A bugle's vibrant song summoned her.

Rushing from the schoolhouse where she'd been giving her students a lesson, arriving on the wooden veranda in the late afternoon's deep crimson light, the smell of gladiolas like an elixir on the balmy air: her heart crashed at the sight of her lover like a Heaven-sent miracle materialized in the balmy near-dusk.

There he was. The battered bugle he held beneath his arm, silenced. His hazel eyes smiled at her. They shone brighter than the afternoon sun hanging overhead. He remained standing in the front yard, waiting for her cordially.

She came to him, running. A dust cloud grew behind her in her haste. Into his arms she spilled, a cry loosing itself from her throat. "Oh, thank the Lord, you're alive! Oh, we'd heard terrible things! Oh, thank you, sweet Lord!" She clung to him. He crushed her, too. Their warmth filled the yard. The schoolchildren, curious, had gathered along the porch and in the dusty yard, watching them silently, sensing the import of their reunion.

She leaned from him, tears beading down her crimson cheeks. She examined with distraught eyes the many soiled bandages encircling his arm, the immense one thickening his thigh.

"Oh, sweet Lord, what happened out there? Are you hurt, darling? Oh, we'd heard horrible things. The captain visited yesterday, and told us. He said the reports were bad, and told of a...of a *slaughter*. A *slaughter*. Oh, thank the Lord you're safe. Oh, you're a miracle right here in my schoolyard."

His smile didn't wane. She drew it from him, kept it glowing on his face with the simple fact of her closeness to him. The smell of her calmed him. The sight of her made him content. To his darling, the corporal said, "Darling, I'm safe, and so we'll be from now on. Let's leave here. Let's begin our life together, far away from the sound of rifles."

A moment of quiet between them as his words seeped their way into her. "Oh, Lee," she cried, tears rising into her eyes anew. "Do you mean it? Oh, Lee, thank you! But why? I'm so happy, don't mistake me, but why your change of heart? You have your career here. Where will we go? And why? Why *now*, I mean?"

"Because, right now, at this very instant more than ever before, I want peace for us."

"Will we manage, though? Can we manage? Money, and…"

"We'll manage, darling," he assured her. "We'll manage – My men, you see. My blue-coats. They're with me, too. I have only to give the order and together we'll leave. You and me, and their families, too. Together, all of us, somewhere, where we'll build anew, a new home, a new town, a new city unlike cities anywhere. We'll ride and we'll ride and we won't stop until we're far from here. And there our family will start anew, in a place of peace like we can never know here."

Her heart hammered. The thought of her and him as a family – hearing the word from him and meaning the two of them together and possibly with children of their own – filled her with a joy she realized in that moment she'd never before known.

"Oh, my darling, Annabelle," he said, his hazel eyes alive with a queer energy she'd never quite seen in him before. "Oh, the things I've seen!" He held her away from him, savouring her apple cheeks and golden hair spilling about her shoulders like fire, and her eyes weeping joyfully. "And oh, but nothing is as wondrous as you! Nothing in this whole strange life!"

She smiled helplessly, bashful and caught up in his great romance and exuberance. She laughed merrily when, with a solemn and theatrical bowing of his head – as if in farewell – he dropped the bugle in the dust at their feet. She wondered, though – even as she laughed at the way he wrapped his arms tightly about her middle and spun her around in a loose lazy circle, making the schoolchildren point and giggle among themselves – yes, she wondered at the tears shining and shining in his eyes of rapture, as if he'd seen God in the hills.

125

225

1983

398

BUT ONE DAY
ALL OF THIS
WILL BE GONE

In a world of despair and disappointment, one must continually rationalize and invent optimistic truths when and where and however one can scrounge them, or risk suffocating beneath the inexorable weight of the everyday. Graspingly and achingly, naively and pathetically, and in the end – if fortune is with you – perhaps even convincingly: this is the way by which we sometimes are able to save ourselves, however tenuously.

This Bill Harliss considers as he reads with weary eyes the crumpled letter in his hands for what feels the millionth time; the individual words grown less meaningful with each subsequent reading but the overarching bleakness of their message more profound than ever beneath the vulgar light filtering through the window, all traffic light blood red and morose street light amber pulsing upwards from the street six floors below, and with perhaps a melancholy influence of the moon's lingering light, too. The rolling pin he clutches in his other hand, its notched wooden expanse glistening fiercely where he'd spent the better part of the past hour scrubbing away with the disinfectant-soaked dish rag, hurting his fingers with the dedication of his efforts. He winces in examination of these haunted items, vision impaired by the gross swelling surrounding his left eye. His tongue probes cautiously along the interior of his battered, bloated bottom lip, tasting the metallic tang of blood, nudging a loosed tooth.

Eventually he tears the paper into many pieces and lets these drift from his fingers, through the ajar window, and out onto the night air. He imagines their descent, twirling and graceful, deceivingly celebratory, like confetti in the pre-dawn gloom. He thinks of the night behind him, and he thinks of the year past, too. He ponders the people he has known, and the stories of their lives and the nature of his intertwinement within them. His is a profoundly melancholic meditation: every memory, every scenario, is entwined with some deeply-embedded thread of misery.

He is weighted down with these ruminations, rooted in his window-vantage chair, sweating in the sultry air, baking beneath the suffocating trench coat wrapped tightly about himself like a cloak. He makes no move to remove the heavy garment nor turn on the rickety-looking fan standing silent sentinel nearby among the detritus of his belongings congesting the room: he is held immobile by his thoughts, and only continues to ponder his life and how he has come to this point, drunk and battered and alone in a cramped, mice-infested, non-air conditioned apartment, with the disparate pieces of his contentedness drifting away into the night, unsalvageable, and a rolling pin the weight of mountains resting across his lap.

He belches, and smells the lingering rot of rum he's exhaled into the room. Several minutes pass and, keeping the rolling pin across his lap, he removes several crumpled papers from his coat pocket, and a pen from another. His hand grows possessed, and attacks the paper with the pen it clutches. Tears well in his eyes, muddying the work of his madly scribbling hand but still he writes and writes, without thought, impassioned, as if it were his heart speaking and urging him to record its Byzantine tale; desperately, frantically, fightingly, as if seeking to arrive at some elusive truth in the unfolding text before him, or at the very least to save himself, however ephemerally, from the weight of the forthcoming day awakening outside.

Father's hands are dirtier and more frightening than nightmares…
But the night can only last so long, and then a new day…

Your grandmother died in a hospital bed…
But you weren't close and shed not a single tear.

Monty, your dearest and most devoted childhood friend, died of a bum heart…
But milk bones were his favourite and you snuck him plenty.

13 always was the number that scared you…
But you were born the day following and were thereby saved by a hair from ill omens.

Your girl's been seen in questionable and mysterious places…
But your first time in bed together remains vivid as photographic evidence.

The day job which you loathe is waiting at the end of a ten-year traffic jam…
But the universe of the car is electric with your most treasured song.

There are some businesses managed by dictators…
But your shift's done in less than ten.

Your husband hits the bottle and then you…
But you once saw a dinner plate-shape hovering like salvation in the clouds.

You watched your peers ditching together, relishing the days…
But hiding inside the library study cubicle wasn't so bad: you read books that took you further away than they could possibly have gone.

She took and she took, making you poorer than the destitute alley dweller…
But there was a time when she gave you fellatio with gusto, and regularly.

The band's '98 release was lackluster by their standards…
But 2000 proved a return to form and a swelling of your proud heart: as a teenager music grew to define you, and gave you what strength you had.

You regret the impulsive juvenile ink in your arm…
But watching movies in the dark allows you to pretend yourself clean…

He shouldered you clear and stared you down afterwards…
But fuck him: you're more intelligent than that cocksucker by far.

You loathe and fear this world of the crude and bellicose…
But who can tell what greater evils the Visigoths saved us from?

The street corners hold whores and the tenements house meth addicts…
But once the world was all jungle, and lizards roamed free of men: a thought to dream to.

The blacks wore fetters and the Jews were cooked in ovens...
But rocket ships promise places above embarrassing histories.

A vulture watches a starving child crawl towards a distant Sudanese food camp...
But we can think of other things.

Rent is looming like thunderheads and student loans weigh mountains...
But pitcher after pitcher brings brief periods of calm.

Turtles live longer than men...
But animals in captivity live statistically shorter lives.

This year's the same as last...
But tomorrow's your day off, who knows what may come?

You only ever cower through the streets of Detroit...
But your racist eyes were sculpted by American news broadcasts over genetic predisposition.

He reminds you when any opportunity arises that he can kick your ass, easy...
But you hate him better than anyone else ever could.

The bus stop-milling high schoolers turn insolent, challenging looks on you, the meek middle-aged loner...
But easy as anything you pretend a bomb into the briefcase in your hand.

Dad disappeared years ago...
But you gave him a birthday present once, when you were little and the two of you were still friends.

They never found the Devil who did it...
But in your dreams he burns every single night.

You saw an arm a hundred metres beyond the pile-up...
But you hadn't eaten breakfast that morning and mostly only water came up.

You never did get to fuck your eighth grade teacher…
But dedication to fantasies has moulded them into near-memory.

You don't talk much these days…
But you used to walk the three hours home from the Mall together.

The world might get to you through inflicting itself onto her…
But you can always seek vengeance on its every malign fold and sick crease.

He's a millionaire and adored by many who know him little…
But you kicked his ass on the playground in seventh grade, a small but great victory you know he remembers.

He had his way and left her a laughing stock at the party…
But he pissed blood for some time thereafter.

The taste of him haunts the back of your mouth…
But the twenty's in your pocket and the sun's setting on a long day beaten at last.

She, the cruel queen to whom you'd stammered ineffectual adoration…
But she's due anytime now and he's well on his way south.

You've fallen behind the pack in most every way…
But if you stay indoors forever, who's to know?

Your friend dared you and you couldn't summon the courage…
But the woman in question died of AIDS not three months past.

You can barely hold a decent barre chord…
But with eyes closed you nightly conquer your bedroom stage.

You still feel somewhat awkward around her…
But at least she doesn't know what you made her do in your head that morning.

The milk's turned into sewage and the cheese has grown a mouldy beard…
But the disability check's in the mail and the liquor store closes at 10:00 tonight.

You'd rather die than work the line tomorrow…
But late night television awaits you at shift's end: something reliable besides the torture of the machines.

The post-work late night talk shows and infomercials have begun to depress you, too…
But you own a book of Frank Frazetta paintings: freedom-vistas opened for you, to roam un-squelched.

The dentist's chair: the terror today as in childhood years of crooked teeth and damaged social life…
But for now a movie theatre, and its safe, flickering-dark embrace.

Through the bedroom wall, you heard dad pounding mom into the headboard at night…
But they hadn't been arguing and so eventually you were able to sleep.

He made you small in front of your friends…
But you might one night find him skunk-drunk and teetering in a lonely alley.

He treated all those women like meat and dirt…
But everyone knows now, and prison treats his kind in kind.

Your living quarters of one room and bath and labouring air conditioner is oppressive with burning summer…
But Winter always returns to murder the arrogant sun.

Your brother went to war and never returned…
But sometimes mystery means hope that closure would kill.

You failed again…
But one day, motherfuckers, one day.

You never did feel at ease there among the suits and the ties…
But she locked the two of you in her office after the Christmas staff party, yes she did.

You've lived another endless and angry day…
But you turned the arrogant trespasser spider into dust beneath your heel.

Dad visited and turned you ten years old again…
But afterwards you beat the cat and felt almighty once more.

You hear her crying next door every night…
But if you had her, you'd worship her like a goddess.

You dread your birthday year round…
But your romantic hope of vampires and fated nocturnal encounters has never diminished.

They fucked up in overtime yet again…
But next year will be their year, and your season, too.

Christmas time is here again…
But they say most other people hate December, too.

Father was the dragon burning momma alive…
But maybe you'd become St. George if you prayed for strength hard enough.

Another one's turned on you…
But tenacity is your virtue if not one of many faults.

There are countless ways to make them all suffer…
But he's only got it in for their mother.

She's been with so many, so many since…
But you loved her truly, and felt like a mythological hero that entire one year.

You understood embarrassingly late that he'd been manipulating you…
But with you gone he has no more puppets to make dance: another man lonelier than you.

Brothers can be cruel that way...
But you filled his meals with secret, spiteful spit for years on end.

The revelation came embarrassingly late: she was a demon...
But you'd lived 18 months of bliss beneath her spell of blindness and delicious devoted slavery.

Two white men mocked a third's skin with words like knives while you said nothing...
But at least you refused to repeat the hateful teachings of your father, ingrained in you like life lessons from an early age.

You emptied your stomach long into the post-party night and morning...
But you'd felt the song in your gut, lingering like a thrumming ghost all through your swooning seasickness.

You're stuck here forever...
But you once saw something strange and fiery arc across the stars, headed upwards: you're a rare witness to something freeing.

As a child you felt misplaced most days after school...
But the first person to learn about father's demonic persona was your first girlfriend, when you were twenty-five, and a man in body if not in courage.

You never thought you'd be like him...
But after the first time in the first motel with the first woman you regretted deeply your faithlessness.

It had been a true summer of pain for you...
But God helped you through it all, as the drunken prophesies of the sun-addled homeless woman drinking mouthwash on the street had foreseen.

The one climbing into the pickup truck is no more than fifteen...
But the driver might die the worst manner of death possible for his impending sin.

Father naming momma a fat whale and beaching her good all over the bathroom floor...
But ancient peoples believed manatees to be mermaids, beautiful and bewitching and eternal.

You recoiled involuntarily as you passed the man of foreign descent on the midnight street...
But no one had noticed. You're still a good person.

Another mall kingdom glittering like a new jewel in the sun...
But somewhere a sapling bends in the breeze.

Never a day devoid of dying armies...
But these things surely must end.

Trees like men and women fall all the time...
But much springs from a single seed.

The anchorman called the scene a nightmare...
But all manner of dreams must finally end.

You wanted her but she went with the enemy...
But you own many books and so have many friends to console you.

The inclement sky reflects your mood again...
But your basement is deep and deep and deep.

Planes are dropping from the sky like flies these days...
But so are meteors, proof of movement beyond the clouds.

The lump inside your scrotum startled you beneath the shower's languorous mist...
But it might be nothing, nothing at all.

You fear the ultrasound's illumination...
But you have a week of ignorance within which to weigh optimistic possibilities.

Hair thinner, eyes dimmer, while newly-arrived cloud fronts fog your brain...
But the average lifespan of males in your family gives you a few more years, still.

True love never found you and now of a sudden you're old...
But nobody has to know and you wear masks well enough.

You took advantage of a drunk girl once, years ago...
But you've nearly convinced yourself that she would have liked it.

Your beloved puppy fell under car wheels late one summer night...
But your friend's father died in a pile-up.

Four decades later and there may still be P.O.W.s caged in Vietnam...
But you can read a less disheartening book of history instead.

A colonel once dreamed of peace between the settlers and the tribes...
But dreams in which conflict is no longer a component of our genetic makeup might one day come true.

The cops harass you and remain blind to teenage whores giving head in alleys...
But now you know to stay away from police like you shun the criminal element, too.

You once caught a man filming you through the bathroom window...
But someone you know was raped behind a gas station one year ago.

The front page tells of a baby found dead in a garbage can...
But some babies grow to stalk and slay women.

The artist you admire and call hero mocked you publicly...
But your memory never was very good, you forget disappointments as easily as victories.

Another child gone missing from the neighbourhood...
But maybe she's only dead.

He's better at everything than you will ever be…
But you could kill him if you really wanted to.

Sleepless nights always prove the deadliest thinking-time…
But you're certain there's a pill perfect for you.

The endangered species black market poaching ring skyrockets daily…
But there's another few thousand families fed.

The man in rags asleep in the bus shelter turns something in your belly…
But you've not fallen quite so far.

The mice in the walls remind you of just where you are today…
But the millions of broken-backed rodents you've trapped make you the king of this shitty downtrodden empire.

You'd let both of them have you in quick succession…
But it's a secret and a secret it will remain.

You deny the beggar's coin-questing hands…
But tell yourself that next time you'll pay for the escape in his bottle.

Your brother maintains that mother was unhappy on the day she died…
But he's been wrong about a great deal of important things.

A child died in the fire…
But you and your friends hadn't thought that anyone could be inside the ramshackle, derelict house.

The streets have cancered, as diseased and perilous as the alleys…
But one might stumble upon unplumbed magic or miraculous science smouldering among trash bins, if fortune is with them.

The dictator led his people through a reign of misery and woe…
But everyone lies wholly alone in their death bed.

His eyes had always unsettled you, alive with malignant fire...
But most disturbed individuals have histories of abuse.

The playground bully ruled your life with an iron fist and demented attention...
But you learned to love his relentless existence when word got out that his father was in jail for molesting children.

A pair of cops getting blowjobs in the alley from a teenage boy...
But you'd needed a catalyst to become the lawgiver absent around you.

Your dreams are haunted by the boy incalculably older than his years...
But through these visions you've been given strength to defy the waking world.

The city is teetering on the brink of ghetto-collapse...
But you'll retire where the lots are made of tall grass, sycamores and wildflowers.

Guilt and guilt and guilt has grown like cancer behind your chest...
But you could have went further with the sixteen-year-old than you did.

Shame owns you...
But heroes could wield worse weapons than kitchen utensils for vanquishing the wicked and cruel.

You wake and find that all hope has been devoured by the new day...
But the dream from which you'd woken had seemed astoundingly real, and in it you'd flown.

True evil lives in men's hearts...
But one day all of this will be gone.

But one day all of this will be gone.

A new beginning...

Bill Harliss, as if stirring from the deepest of slumbers, turns his bloodshot, sleepless eyes from the ink-covered papers to watch the awoken day outside the window. Full dawn startles him: the sun is a bloody warning burning beyond the crooked cityscape of buildings and shingled rooftops in the east. The somnolent cooing of pigeons lining the telephone wires drifts on the air like some strange internal bodily noises of the buildings themselves. Cars squeal, brake, rev and pass by beneath his apartment. A truck's horn barks like a gargantuan sea lion. The stink of exhaust and rubber and awakening humanity drifts to his nostrils and he breathes of it deeply, seeking the truth of it: this is his city, and the life that he has left.

He looks to his threadbare couch on the opposite side of the small room, purchased second-hand long ago, where he sleeps at night: forlorn-looking, unfriendly. The multitude of books bowing the shelves lining the opposite wall own a defeated look, their usual power to bolster his spirits dormant. The brightening light frightens him, crawling along his arms like a malignant presence bent on revealing him in every way for the man he is, small and weak and lonely and living in an immense and cruel world of many. Weak, when he should have been strong. On the threshold of utter defeat, when victory should have been his.

But he'd lived through the night, he reasons, and that is something, something indeed. He places the wooden rolling pin onto the window sill, its immaculately-shined surface flashing brilliantly in the sunlight. His hand, numb, feels the absence of its great weight. His other hand, numb, too, from its frenetic scratching at the papers, rests in his lap, circulation returning into its veins. He removes the papers from his lap, and places them gently, nearly reverentially, upon the floor between crooked towers of books, newspapers, family photo albums. He creaks forth from the skeletal wooden chair a moment later and makes his way to the couch, considers trying to befriend it in his quest for much-needed sleep, and forgetfulness, and delicious escape inside of dreams untainted by knowledge of his everyday.

He realizes immediately the futility of it: he would find no escape in sleep or dreams. He could never find solace in these old places again, for his pain ran too deeply, was too entrenched in the matrix of who he was;

a great melancholy born not only of his own experiences, but a collective sadness felt on behalf of every man and woman and boy and girl he'd ever known or been acquainted with in even the most fleeting manner, every one of whom had shared a role in the aching, lonely, wicked and vengeful world he's come to fear and pity in equal measures, and which he's failed to save from its own fiery iniquity.

Bill Harliss unbuttons and shrugs the trench coat he wears to the apartment floor. The vivid, gay-coloured latex costume lies revealed beneath: embarrassingly garish, he now sees, poppy-red and sunlight-yellow with baby-blue trim, his paunch blatantly bulging the material like a woman nearly due. This, his uniform and message of hope and strength to the city. A failed proclamation, burning his cheeks more deeply than the stifling summer's oven-air could ever. A shamefully gaudy generic symbol, like something culled thoughtlessly from pulp pages and seeking brazenly to be true. He spits onto the floor in self-loathing, grimaces with the pain the gesture awakens in his swollen, blood-encrusted lip. He senses something amiss inside his mouth, spits again, watches entranced as his tooth clatters onto the floorboards like a pristine, blood-rooted jewel.

He turns and hastens across the small room in bold strides that carry him to the window. He removes its tattered screen, drops it carelessly onto the floor. He clambers onto the narrow, pigeon shit-encrusted window ledge, steadying himself with a hand against the rough brick façade of the tenement. The outdoors air is a relief on his skin following the long night confined in the unventilated apartment, despite the oppressive heat. The chemical stink of the city is thicker outdoors. It dizzies him, along with the great height and the blinding sunlight.

He draws himself erect, facing the brightening city – its countless buildings and houses and maze of streets zigzagging into the distance before him and looking especially ramshackle from his lofty vantage – with head held high. He raises a hand sunwards, thinking of feats attainable in dreams, prepared for flight.

Then, though, doubt overcomes him, and he weeps anew. His sun-salute falters, and his hand falls to his side, trembling. Through his tears he blubbers, though he struggles to imbue the words with as much reserve and eloquence as he feels he deserves, if they indeed prove to be his epitaph: "I am your downtrodden dreams. I am your crushed, pissed-on hopes. I am occasional small victories, too. I am joy and heartbreak and contentedness and shame and sadness and fury. I am Everyman. Maybe today is finally my day to find my happiness, and relief from all of this. I'm sorry to all of you whom I've hurt or disappointed in my time among you. I'm sorry I didn't have enough power with which to protect you from the way of things. I've done what I could. And now I will try for you all one more time."

He boldly spikes his hands skywards again. As if answering his salute the sun seems to brighten, intensifying the heat of its kiss into the bright skin of his costume. He edges another inch forward, until the tips of his bright cherry boots hang over the ragged brick lip of the sill. His sunny cape flutters in a sudden surge of wind, beckoned upwards at its behest as if impelling him to follow. Beneath him, six stories far, far below, the hazy city has fully awoken into the new burning day, and begun its great and furious and ravenous clamour.

MAY WE AGAIN LIVE
WITHOUT WALLS

The tribe was prepared to move again. The barren country ahead would be difficult and the threat of predators great, but the promise of bountiful lands beyond beckoned. It had been a difficult season, of drought and sickness and death: this migration was one of necessity.

She turned her head at the pressure in her side: there she was, seeking the security of her mother, as ever. Her little horns seemed to glow in the golden afternoon air. They nuzzled a moment, rubbing their beaked snouts together, before the mother looked once more to the great desolate plain spread before them, rocky and devoid of vegetation but for occasional tufts of sun-desiccated grass and sinewy, inedible weeds. The sun was high in the molten sky. The distant shimmering horizon was fringed with jungle, with crooked mountains rearing far beyond, their summits shrouded in thick mist.

Her mate stepped forward, pointing his stout chipped horns southwards, the signal that the great exodus had begun. She followed, and their children stepped forward, too, excited, anxious, sensing the momentousness of the journey. The others came, too.

Together, they stirred a dust cloud in their wake, as they filled the plain with their numbers. They marched determinedly into the sweltering afternoon, while the sun crawled the length of the sky, from dawning east to dusking west.

Thunder preceded him, his song of old, halting the relentless march of the herd: he appeared soon after, from the trackless forests of the south shimmering like an emerald mirage miles and miles before them; swaying the long-fronded trees with their giant colourful blossoms, quaking the earth with his mighty tread, barring the herd's path as he drew closer on the plain before them: the lord of predators, the terrible King warrior come to eat his fill.

Of course they would fight, for they too were warriors despite their less bloody diet and less violent appetites. For their children they would fight, and likely die. For the air of a new morning they would bring blood into the world.

The King predator loped forward. His steps trembled the earth beneath them. They aligned themselves defensively, shielding the young behind their formidable wall of horns and jagged skull-plates. They waited, conserving their strength for the impending battle, pawing the earth, snorting nervously. They were no longer as strong as they had been at the outset of their trek two days before: one of their elders had fallen earlier that morning, hunger and thirst abetting his fatigue and frailty; and a child too, weak from hunger, limping to his death in the dusty sun-shimmering plain; and all of the rest of them weak too, from the long march and the tenacious heat and the rumbling ache in their bellies.

The warrior drew nearer, nearer, devouring the distance between them beneath his immense clawed tread. His giant mouth leered at them, rimmed in slaver. His tiny eyes gleamed in his huge hunger as he surveyed the ranks gathered before him. His long curved teeth flashed in the bright day. His pace quickened in excited expectation of his meal, conjuring a storm-cloud of dust billowing upwards behind him.

The herd steadied themselves for the violence of his arrival: the wait seemed agonizingly long, yet his progress far too swift. Then, like a storm, he was crashing among them. His massive neck swung downwards and his great jaws snapped closed upon the long arched back of a defender: his anguished cry rang across the plain. The great warrior reared his immense head skywards, bearing a great slab of blood-drenched meat in his jaws.

She felt her child cowering alongside her stout tail. At this small warm contact in the chaos of the battlefield she instinctively lunged forward and upwards even as he spat the meat from his mouth and lunged again among the defenders' ranks. Her great horns found their mark. Deeply they tore through the killer's thick flesh and bit towards his mighty heart far within. He roared a roar that trembled the mountains of the north and felled trees in the nearby southern wilderness, sending up hordes of spooked winged beasts. His tail lashed upon the earth and birthed a whirlwind like a great summer storm. His small child's arms seizured upon the air and his powerful legs seized, too, claws clutching and kicking up immense pieces of grass and earth in his great agony. In the madness of his pain he smote among the defenders with his tail, sending them scattering to one side. He lunged backwards upon his mighty legs but her horns embedded in him pulled him forward again. Falling upon her, the horns sunk yet deeper inside him. His fury and madness grew. He clamped his jaws upon her back and bit deep. Here in the world he was still King and ruler. She cried. Her brothers and sisters came to her aid. A dozen pairs of horns skewered the killer, through muscle-corded thighs and neck, and puncturing his ribcage with a sound like the splintering of rock. Her mate rushed in, his horns – even his stout snout-horn – slamming home to embed themselves in the killer's soft pale belly, the rucked flesh about the horns immediately leaking thick slicks of blood and emitting a hissing like a geyser coughing steam. The killer's writhing tail crushed a defender into the plain. His long clawed foot, spasming, tore another's leg wide in a torrent of blood and bone. A chorus of cries roared in the steaming day.

They held him pinioned between them, while other defenders lunged forward, adding their horns to the attack. The killer ate his fill as he could while dying among the deadly resilient phalanx, by turns roaring in insatiable fury, and keening in an unsettling song of agony.

She felt her child's frantic and frightened nuzzling of her tail. She strained her legs forward, feeling the incremental movement of her horns push deeper into the King warrior even as he champed down upon her unprotected, blood-slicked, ravaged back in one final bid for feasting or vengeance. She roared in pain and fury and determination. They would continue to fight this obstacle to the bounty of the south, holding their horns sunwards in defiance of the great destroyer seeking to impede their march on this day of their migration. Because there ahead lied food for the herd. There lied freedom from the great hunger and sickness of the season past that had decimated their numbers. In the south like a green dream, where they had to believe there lay no mile of desolate soil, no pastures sullied by danger to the herd of tomorrow.

As their family held the mighty and insatiable killer at bay, the vision came to her, making her heart sing, giving her reason to strain forward and forward and drive her horns ever deeper into his thundering, dying heart:

A clutch of eggs gleaming in the sun.

*

He awoke, his heart beating like a gong in him. The pungent smell of exotic flora hung over him until he realized its place in the dream he'd left behind, and then the familiar odour of the bedroom returned: newly-laundered sheets, the lingering scent of his deodorant from the previous evening, and a subtle sterile atmosphere of Febreze hanging over everything. He imagined a buzzing on the air, as of some immense dragonfly, and tensed until he realized the dim shape and sluggish movement of the ceiling fan's long plastic blades spinning languidly above him, the soft electric whirring the only sound disturbing the stillness. He had an erection. He looked and found his wife sleeping beside him. He considered, mechanically, waking her and seeing whether she felt like sex but felt somehow depleted, as if any physical and emotional act was beyond his endurance. He tried to drift into sleep again, to find the thread of his ancient dream but of course he couldn't. With his new hollowness he lay there in his morning bed, contemplating his day waiting before him, watching the sunlight crawling across the bedroom floor with a wary eye.

When his wife woke up not long after, she found him standing at the dawn window with tears in his squinting eyes. "Douglas, what is it?"

"Horns. For sun-stabbing. For putting out this day." His voice was a drugged and melancholy murmur in the brightening room, and she squinted at the outline of him as he touched a faltering hand to his forehead.

"What?" she whispered, confused, unaccountably uneasy. "What did you say, Douglas?"

"I'm unhappy, Ashely," he said, still staring out into the world.

March 21, 2013

I'd do it for the moon.

June 6, 2013

IF I HAD WINGS,
MISTER MOON

Books and movies tell you it's darkly romantic when:

A young woman returns to inhabit the world from an uncertain place, such as a mental institution to which she'd been committed for mysterious reasons over which outsiders can only speculate; or perhaps a girl is claimed from an orphanage but carries with her the great loneliness that filled her days there, a loneliness unknowable by those who come from easier places, such as those who've adopted her and are therefore destined to never fully understand her; or maybe a teenager has left home, vacating a life of dysfunction with parents more immature than the children they raised when, inevitably, she moves directly – almost as if preordained – into a new life as unfulfilling as the one she knew before; or possibly a girl returns from a place whose origins remain wholly unknown to anyone but herself – and perhaps unknowable to those seeking to understand her – with the telltale aftermath signs of that place etched into the hard lines of her face, the distant sheen like film over her eyes, like a shroud enveloping her perpetually and making her somehow different from her peers in some difficult-to-define but indisputable way.

But really, there's no romance in scenarios like these. Really there's only an unsightly reality to them that's more unsettlingly unfathomable than we like to imagine let alone be exposed to ourselves, whether through firsthand experience or even as sick voyeurs of others' miseries making us feel fleetingly better about our own lives; until the inevitable happens (which it always, always does): and then it hits us, tremendously, like a star plummeted from overhead and crashed directly on top of all our certainties and convictions (a metaphor that may seem at first saccharine with romance but that becomes more appropriate as far as certain stories unfold). And then we understand. Then we see it for what it is.

The world as the grotesque and disheartening and mysterious and heartbreakingly lonely orb that it is.

This lesson – or the nascent seeds of it – she taught us, in the summer of our youth, before the girls of our ragtag tribe had yet bloomed into women and long before us gangly acne-cursed boys could be called men.

A teenager like a sad fable, like the most poignant of cautionary tales, like a mysterious celestial fragment fallen from the night sky to smoulder in the summer field where we first found her that weird August night.

We heard her song before we found her.

We followed it across the little rickety bridge suspended over the scummy river that separates the townhouse neighbourhood from the wilderness beyond; through the bramble and cattails and tall grass fringing the river banks on the opposite side; through the maze of willow trees with their weeping foliage hanging down around us like funereal curtains. We spotted a shape in the distance. It was hard to pick her out from the field darkness and wild grass. She was far out and we wondered as we trudged through the dirt towards her how her voice could have carried as far as it had, as clear in the night as if she were much, much closer than she was. It was strange, we commented in hushed voices. Who was she, we wondered, excited but afraid somehow, too.

Details of the girl emerged the closer we came. Her blonde hair looked white in the moonlight. Her skin looked pale but maybe this was only the moonlight colouring her, too. She was very thin in her ratty jeans. Her denim jacket seemed to swallow her. She was very petite, too. Her age was tricky because of her size – she could have been anywhere from a little younger than we were then – tenth graders all of us, except for Andrew, who was a genuine eleventh grade loser and so trapped into hanging around with us, the only group that would take him in – except for her face. Haggard and drawn and dirty and with lost eyes – *crazy* eyes, one of us whispered, and we shut him up for saying it too loud and being so completely thoughtless. It was true, though. No one could deny the unhinged look in her eyes. Like she couldn't take any more of whatever it was that had sent her crying and crying into that night field. I was sympathizing with her, and thinking about parents flipping out and driving you out of the house with their violent voices or hands; a pack of neighbourhood bullies making themselves feel better by kicking the shit out of you five on one behind the strip mall where no hope of rescue existed; a significant other leaving you for someone else, the stinging salt in the wound being that you knew who the conniving asshole in question was, too, but had never suspected, not in a million, million years.

"Hello," I called to her, making my voice soft so as to not frighten her any more than she may have been already.

But she only kept on, as if we weren't there at all, as if a group of strangers stumbling on her crying in the middle of rural nowhere wasn't important enough to draw her from out of the dark spell that had her so completely bewitched. She only kept on with the words she'd been murmuring the whole time – which we'd followed from our townhouse neighbourhood and across the fields – only now we could finally make them out.

"Oh. I. Hate. Them. Oh. I. Hate. Them. Oh. I. Hate. Them. Oh."

We exchanged spooked looks, frightened into speechlessness. But mostly we only watched the girl. Who could look away from something like that? We'd never seen anything like her. I noticed that after a while of watching her: that despite having seen people in distress (my mom when her boyfriends roughed her up, me when I hated everyone in the world and had no one to hang out with, each of my friends at some point and for one reason or another) none of us compared to her. Her misery outdid us all. And the more we looked the more we noticed something truly amiss, and so sad, and so deeply frightening about the picture of her there in the night field.

The blood drops on her hands and thighs were dark in the lunar light. It was hard to look at them once we guessed what they were. Like proof of some savage and awful thing prowling in the night where we prowled, too, oblivious and innocent and carefree, until now. It was like being woken up by a crass elder sibling, shaking you and hollering in your ear and crushing your dream-peace and reminding you that nightmares threatened in the waking world, too. It was like that, but different. I had an older brother who – before he moved out a few years earlier – did just this, and on a regular enough basis that it had made me into a fearful insomniac. But it was different with the girl in the field, and so much more disquieting. As if she was proof that worse existed in the world than malicious brothers, or any other nightmare we knew.

One of our little stunned gang – I think it was Jenny – she asked the girl in her softest voice who she was. What her name was. If there was anyone she wanted us to call for her or anything we could do. But the girl only wept on, repeating those unnerving words. Jenny – really gently again, because Jenny was good with people in bad situations like that, God bless her – put one hand reassuringly on the girl's shoulder and the other hand in her denim jacket pocket. She felt around, and eventually pulled out the girl's wallet. It was made of cloth, and though it was faded and old-looking it had once been a bright patchwork pattern of green and red. I remember thinking of the girl in this way, too: someone who'd once been happy, but no more. We looked through it and found her name printed on a public library card, with her neat looping signature beneath: Sarah Amallo.

We knew what to call her but we ended up saying very little, to the girl, or among ourselves. She kept up her weird catatonic litany the whole time we sat with her. We stayed there until morning, keeping makeshift camp in a circle around her. Maybe we did that unconsciously, as if we wanted to protect her, from someone or something. We huddled close for warmth. We finished our remaining beer. We star-watched. We shadow-watched where the moon's light didn't reach and the tree-line of willows and Black oaks rose up fearsomely on all sides. And all those long A.M. hours the words just hung there with us, like another natural sound of the quiet, dead hours. Like the soughing wind, the crickets, the grass whispering whenever someone shifted a little in their place, the colossal sound of the night breathing all around.

"I. Hate. Them. Oh. I. Hate. Them. Oh. I. Hate. Them. Oh."

The rhythm of it was so strong, so vital-sounding, like it was meant to be spoken the way she spoke it and no other way would do. No lesser amount of fury could do the words justice. No amount less of sadness, either. Her eyes pooled with it, too, an ugly brew of anger and melancholy as unnerving to see there as it was to hear drifting from her without pause. She cried unabated, too, and the moon showed us the silver tears washing her cheeks clean of the dirt powdering them. She looked so small, the crying girl. She looked so frail and wretched and so completely beautiful underneath all the tears and rage and hatred. You could see this in her, this potential buried under her current plight and woe. I was the bookworm of our gang, and liked reading books about people that bad things happened to, but none of those people in the books I'd read looked at all like her, neither the way they were described nor how I saw them. I don't think we'd ever seen something as striking as her. I don't think we ever will, to be honest. To be honest, I don't think that I want to.

There came one anomalous lyric in her song. It came late in the morning hours, and I was the only one of us lucid enough by then to pick it out from her inexorable murmuring voice. It arrived in the deepness of the pre-dawn A.M. while the groggy frogs were taking over from the crickets and sleep tugged at me, too.

"Oh. I. Hate. Them. Oh, Mister Moon, I want to be with you. Oh. I. Hate. Them."

It was a shock of anomaly in the night's rhythm. It woke me instantly. Through bleary, befuddled eyes I looked and found her. She'd paused her rocking in her place. Her eyes were tear-clear, wide and staring upwards with an avid desperation. I followed where she stared out into the north quadrant of the sky. Coinciding with her words, I saw him, too. The name in her song. Her man in the black sky. The moon, gibbous and bright and remote and a far and safe distance away from our scrap of field and whatever ghosts hounded her there.

I looked around our makeshift camp: tent-less and without sleeping bags in the chill air, but my friends all dozed: Andrew alone and curled into himself; Denise and Tony spooning, his jacket draped over them both against the waning summer's cold air; Robert asleep where he sat cross-legged, cradling an empty beer can as if it were a plush toy; Jenny lying on her back near to me, looking peaceful and sexy, her face shrouded in her sweatshirt's hood, her pale bare belly showing; our ragged group of tipsy teenage outcasts breaking curfews in the heart of summer and not caring in the least about repercussions; never even discussing them to begin with. Because some things were much more important to see through to their conclusions. Like certain other ingredients of that morning, this was one we didn't speak of but acted on and experienced together, a mutually understood responsibility to remain with the crying girl.

I stopped watching her during those long hours but the breaking picture of her clung in my thoughts perfectly still. Her song sung me to fitful sleep, too.

"Oh. I. Hate. Them. Oh."

And, after a while – and this was something me and my friends only talked about long after that night was past us, weeks, or maybe it had been months later – after a while we hated them, too, with all of our hearts. Whoever and whatever they were.

The sun woke us.

The crying girl – Sarah Amallo – had gone, to where we never learned. We scanned the surrounding fields and searched the surrounding forest but found nothing. We didn't see her around town during the remainder of the summer, nor during the school months following. There weren't many schools in our small town but we had no idea to which – if any – she belonged. None of us ran into her in a convenience store or pool hall or at the bowling alley where all teenagers wound up on certain listless nights. I was the only one of our gang who frequented the library but I didn't find her there either, though I looked: in the narrow book-lined aisles, among the desks and cubicles to the rear of the building, in the lobby where people waited on the wooden bench beside the water fountain for their rides to arrive and take them home.

But I'm glad to have found her, for those few endless hours between the moon breaking through the clouds and the sun rising and burning everything nocturnal and safe away with a new day. Why I'm not sure. Maybe it made us feel closer to each other, staying with her, as if we were united in some deep, unspoken way as her A.M. protectors. Maybe it only made for a weird and memorable night. Possibly it confirmed something about each of our lives, and the good or bad days we envisioned coming our way.

Because you see: this is the world. This was the lesson we learned that night, as disheartening as it was to digest. This is how it is, the way it works without rhyme, reason, scheme or sanity. Movies depict it one way, romance-flavoured whether dark or light, and books try to map it out, too, and imbue it with relatable drama and poignancy and other callow Hollywood dogmas. But really, the world makes no sense at all.

*

Then, one evening nearly one year to the day of our finding her, I dreamed her.

Mine was a doubly special sighting as it was she who found me in my dream: I found myself sitting on a parking block at the edge of the gravel lot to the rear of our townhouse neighbourhood, looking out into the park before me and the greater wilds of fields and bushes stretching beyond. It was late in the day, nearly dusk, and the falling sun was sending a great shadow crawling across the grass towards where I sat. I heard the crunching of footsteps behind me. I figured it was Jenny, come to meet me, because over the year since the previous summer we'd started going out and the park is where we met every night to make out in the jungle gym, and drink beers we stole from our parents' fridges. I turned, eager to see her. It took me a second to speak, even though I knew who she was right away. It was almost as if I'd been thinking about her right then – or like I'd never really stopped thinking about her for very long at all since that weird August morning – because I recognized her immediately.

She walked directly to me. I was hypnotized by her – the look of her, face clean of dirt, eyes clear of tears – the sight of her at all, like a dream come to life, because in those intervening months I think that maybe we all entertained the idea that we'd dreamed the entirety of that strange morning. In the remaining daylight she looked healthier. Colour reddened her cheeks, the caul of despair was lifted from her eyes, which looked vibrant surveying the park. She stopped behind my parking block and watched the distance without words. Maybe the thing about her that struck me most was how human she looked by daylight, a feature absent from her during our first encounter, subsumed within the great pain – primal-looking and vulgar – that had so evidently consumed her. But now, miraculously: a pretty girl with mellow eyes and casual posture, dressed like most of the girls I knew dressed, simple in blue jeans and runners and plain black t-shirt.

Anxiety overwhelmed me. I knew not what to do or say. I stammered a hello. "Hi. What's up? How's it going?" And then, when she made no answer, I added, "I know you. Well, I remember you..." I didn't know how to put it without conjuring bad memories.

She seemed unperturbed when she said, in a gentler voice than I remembered, "I remember you, too. Thank you."

I didn't know what to say to this, so I returned my attention to the park. After a moment of silence, her voice said from behind me (sounding closer, as if she might have moved a step or two forward), "It's going to be a good night. Cool, after a hot day."

She was right about it. The cooling air was a relief on my bare arms and cheeks after the baking afternoon, most of which I'd spent reading out of doors, as evidenced by the paperback opened across my knee. The humidity had lifted. There would be dew on the grass come morning. I nodded. A silence between us again. It was far from an uncomfortable one. Suddenly feeling queerly at ease, as if I was sharing my time with an old friend, as if our conversation so far was maybe what had brought us closer, I asked easily, "What are you doing tonight?"

Her voice came from closer beside me. I turned and watched her profile where she'd moved and placed one sneakered foot on the parking block on which I was sitting. Her eyes were a little more distant, but peaceful still. "I'm going back. To a good place." And, turning those serene eyes to me, she added, "I've been visiting today. It's good to visit. To remember where you're from. That's something we should never forget." She nodded. It seemed a significant gesture, of finality, or decision. She said, "It's time I got back."

She surveyed the far distance. I knew she was looking to the fields and forests where our gang liked to wander, and smoke, and drink, and have sex, away from our lives at home. I sensed that she was preparing to leave me. Inexplicably, desperation awoke in me. In an effort to keep her with me I said something. I hadn't considered the words. They spilled from me. "I want to go to a good place."

In the wake of them I felt foolish somehow. As if too-young, juvenile and needy while in the presence of someone much older, and much wiser and hardened to the ways of things than I. I was suddenly aware of my heart beating, my breathing in the big stillness, the sun becoming interred in the western horizon. The dream's emotion was spilling into nightmare proportions, immense and insurmountable. I looked to her hesitantly.

She was nodding sagaciously. She stepped over the concrete block and onto the closely-cropped park grass. "You will," she said, eyes still watching the distance.

I watched her walk away. I called out, gravely anxious, the words once again spilling from me without thought, "How do I – Where do I go? How – How can I get there?"

She stopped. She turned. This is what she said. She called it across the lawn to me, in a lilting melody as if it were a song: "You don't really want me to tell you, do you? It would ruin the joy – the huge, huge *joy* – when you find it for yourself."

We watched each other. Suddenly the night had arrived. In the new darkness everything seemed hushed. She seemed even older now, in the new nocturnal light, in the wake of what she'd said. Goddess-old, goddess-wise.

I murmured, quietly, but she heard me, "Will I, though? Find...it?" I was anxious beyond reason. The dream trembled with my fear. I sensed the stars trembling overhead, too, and the earth beneath our feet.

She smiled in her place. She *smiled*. It was a gesture I obviously hadn't seen from her during our strange shared night over one year before, and I suppose it was one I could never until then have envisioned from her either. And her dream-words then have stuck with me. They'll be with me always.

"As sure as the stars are coming back to visit us tonight." And then, softening her voice, as if she was sharing a secret, she finished, "Don't worry, Alex – everything will be okay."

She left me then. That's all we said. That's all she said. It was everything I needed to hear, I think, this second lesson she'd taught me in as many times as I'd encountered her, about the world and the things that might happen in it. Nothing else needed to be said.

I watched her go, though. I made sure to keep her in sight for as long as I could because she looked that good then. Wispy as the night we'd found her and with a curiously buoyant step, walking into the deep August night to a place I hope I'll find someday, too.

I stirred and was momentarily confused because I found myself seated on the same parking block, overlooking the same field, as in my dream. Jenny was there with me, as if materialized from the dream, too, until I realized that I'd merely drifted off while waiting for her, the same paperback opened across my knee. She was looking off into the lunar-drenched distance with pensive eyes. "Who was that? I saw you talking to her when I was walking over." She sounded suspicious, like she thought I shouldn't be talking to someone unless it was her (reality had spilled into my dream in this regard, too, because Jenny and I were in fact seeing each other then, and we met like this in the park each night, too).

I followed the direction of her gaze: the dainty girl drifting across the silver-coloured field. "It's Mrs. Moon," I said, startled at the truth in the words, more words that had come from me without any thought at all, like a snippet of limerick or nursery rhyme or prayer ingrained since childhood.

We looked to each other, wearing bewildered expressions. We looked together to the field again, but there was nothing. There was nowhere for her to have gone in the wide open central space of the park, with the fence marking its western periphery and the wilderness of fields and deep woods ahead. I glanced upwards and found him right away: the moon was with us, gibbous and bright, and a tugging grew up inside me. I realized only when I stood and was following sulky Jenny towards the shadowed jungle gym where we always drank our beer and felt each other up: it was something like longing making its quiet but agonizing noise inside me.

We sat inside the rust-pocked steel skeleton. We nursed the two beers we'd filched from our homes. We talked about school, the year behind us and the frightening final year ahead. We kissed but neither of us got very turned on that night. It was nice, though. It was perfect, really. We stayed the night there in the jungle gym, cuddled together against the cold air. Through the hours of the night and morning, as we grew sleepier and sleepier, our fears of the future became replaced by something else, something good- and relieved-feeling. It took me a while to understand what it was, and when I did I was nearly asleep, watching the moon-coloured field spread open before us: I felt happy for her. I felt so very happy for Sarah Amallo, who had her reasons to hate the world but who'd somehow – whatever her mystery may have been – made good her escape.

Heartened by these thoughts of her courageous feat – and of the promise she'd given me – sleep took me quickly. I relished the luxury of its arrival, because I was very, very tired. And although Jenny and I never were able to recall our dreams that night we were certain when we woke that we'd had them, and that they were peaceful, too.

The sun, we both thought, looked amazing. We didn't often comment on things like that but we did then, so completely taken were we by the warm look of everything, the field and distant woods coloured golden in the dawn. It felt like the day ahead of us was going to last forever, and that we could find anything in its miles and miles and miles that we needed.

*Any Way You Want It
that's the way it will be*

SQUEEZE THE SUN:
STORM DAYS BREW

The clattering explosions of pins across the parquet floor. The soothing slosh and gurgle of the fountain pop machines and deep hum of the refrigerated ice cream display counter. The distant electrical jabber and blipping from the arcade games standing like sentinels overlooking the memories of bygone days etched inside of every nick and scratch and name engraved into the food court tables, the walls, hanging in the musty air and clinging like ghosts in the corners of the bowling alley everywhere.

She was comforted by the old sounds and smells and the intimate touch of the orange overhead lights settling over her, as she was always. Passing by the cafeteria she waved and mouthed a hello to Delores busy even at this early hour Windexing the glass countertop displays. The aroma of the usual fast food breakfast and lunch mélange hung on the air – burgers, fries, hotdogs, chilli, eggs and bacon – and despite the early hour her stomach clamoured for something good and greasy from the menu. Remembering her slight but bothersome paunch and her inattentiveness to her all-but forgotten exercise regimen of months before, she walked on before temptation urged her towards another poor decision.

She slipped through the employees-only door adjacent to the cafeteria and along the narrow hallway beyond. The sodium glow from the overheads lit her way morosely, matching her morning mood. She arrived in the small drab locker room and hung her backpack on its usual peg. She draped her denim jacket over the bag. She wore her uniform underneath – simple khaki shorts and a plain brown collar t-shirt with orange trim, bearing the alley's name and logo sewn over one breast: 'Ultra Bowl'. Tejay sought to shrug off the disheartening morning behind her as she kicked off her runners but felt haggard still. Reaching beneath the bench for her bowling shoes, she sensed his comforting shadow fall over her.

"You beat the storm," the balding man with the belly hanging over his khaki shorts said from where he owned the doorway.

She looked up, smiled wearily but fondly. "Hey, Marty. Slow day, huh? I counted maybe five people, and that's with Delores."

He nodded, returning her tender look. "Yup. The lanes are quieter than usual, that's for sure. Even for a Thursday morning." He watched her don her bowling shoes, and she knew that he was worrying about her, as was his custom. He added, with a furrowing of his brow as if he'd just recalled an earlier, less pressing concern than the quiet, dejected girl tying her shoes before him, "It's probably the weather. The radio's been talking about it all morning. They say it's going to be the biggest storm we've had all summer. They're saying we might get a twister, too, maybe." A faint tinge of excitement marked his words, too, as if the little boy he'd once been peered through the years, adding his voice to the man's.

It was the final week of an unusually inclement August. Rainstorms sullied the seemingly endless heat wave days and nights though never alleviating the record humidity, and only now, towards month's end, had Fall begun to hang in every wind gust and gentler breeze that plucked every leaf from every tree throughout the neighbourhood. She'd felt the hidden electrical tension in the air during her brief walk to work, cutting through the field abutting the townhouses where she still lived with her mother, the way someone her age no longer should; walking along the narrow trail through the scraggly tuft of woods and across the alley's near-empty lot beyond. It was always the time of the year that chilled her most, these days when nostalgia lived in the fabric of everything around her and she was compelled to recall the way she'd once approached the new season: September, made from things like returning to school and meeting new people and dreaming the future days would turn out the way she wanted them to.

A soft scratching sounded in the stillness. It came from within the wall behind her, causing her to cock an ear and trace its progress crawling upwards towards the ceiling. It caused her to consider her few encounters with wildlife already that day: the usually vociferous Doberman pinscher tethered to its small wooden abode in the neighbour's backyard, uncharacteristically meek in the way it mewled in greeting when she'd climbed her own fence, pawing the grass and retreating into its house a moment later; the anxious raccoon that had lumbered across her path in the woods, casting a brief and fearful look her way before thrashing hurriedly into the underbrush; the strident chorus of unseen birds from the branches over her head as if a collective apprehension hung among the animal kingdom in anticipation of the impending inclement weather. She murmured, feeling a queer sensation, as of deja-vu , "Hear that, Marty? I think the squirrel's back from the beginning of the summer. Or else you've got rats again."

He murmured, sounding equally mesmerized by the sound moving invisibly behind the wall, as if it had conjured peculiar ruminations in his own mind, too, "I'll get the bugger, whoever he is."

She finished tying her laces. They sat a moment in the quiet, the electric chatter of the arcade and knocking of pins drifting to them as if from a very, very long ways off.

She saw his stymied expression. She smiled for his benefit. "Thanks, Marty." She stood and moved towards the door, as ready to begin her Thursday shift as she was going to be.

"What for?"

She smiled. "I don't know. For being Marty."

This succeeded in urging laughter – equal parts sheepish and prideful and generally pleased – from the portly man. "I can be him, anytime!"

"Good," she said, slipping past him and into the narrow hallway beyond. She felt him loitering in his place, looking after her with his watery eyes of concern. She liked working for him. She liked knowing she could trust at least one man in her life to think of her in a fatherly way. He made her feel loved, in a gentle and safe and reliable way.

When she reached the end of the hall, she turned and looked over her shoulder. Marty was watching her from the doorway. He smiled warmly, looking goofy and sweet. She raised her thumbs in a gesture meant to indicate that she was okay, that he was okay, that everything was pretty much okay, before slouching on her way looking and feeling anything but content.

She tidied the countertop while Marty exchanged bills for bowling shoes with the customers before him. She smiled at the excited chatter of the two boys rushing ahead of their father to their designated lane.

Something flashed in her peripheral vision. Turning, she followed the fleet grey speck shooting low over the alleys towards the western portion of the building. "Marty," she called. When she drew his attention, she merely pointed upwards without following the direction of the gesture, and said, "Bird."

She watched him instead. She saw his eyes grow concerned, look from her face to her finger and then follow the invisible thread of its direction to search the air of his bowling alley. She knew when he'd found the flyer: his eyes growing wider, briefly startled before settling into the look of wonder she'd felt course through her when she'd seen the sparrow flitting over the lanes, too.

He disappeared into the back room and reappeared a minute afterwards with the bird-catcher in hand. He shuffled from behind the counter, searching the air over the lanes. "When was the last time we had a bird in here?" he asked her or himself or the bowling alley itself. "It's been a while," she admitted, not remembering exactly the last time she'd seen him armed with the plastic catcher.

They wandered out into the alley and looked together. They saw the flash of grey a moment later. The bird flitted low over the lanes and, veering sharply upwards, found a home within a lighting fixture's steel skeleton in the ceiling.

Tejay watched Marty edge forward cautiously, drifting down the centre of a lane. Once directly beneath the bird's nesting place he paused and tentatively reached the long arm of the catcher upwards, its mesh net poised. He paused, though, in mid-air, a torn expression on his face, and then abandoned his efforts. Returning to her side, he said, his breathing laboured from his mild exertion, "I couldn't. His colour's so nice. Grey with some white around his neck. You should have seen him up there. His eyes are so scared, poor little guy. Maybe after the storm's passed I'll open a couple of doors. He'll find his way out."

She nodded encouragingly. She thought in that moment – as she'd thought on many occasions when he'd shown some small bit of his huge compassion – that Marty deserved a great hug, if not from her, then from someone. He'd been divorced for many years, and although she wasn't certain about it she believed she was one of his only friends. She considered her mother alone at home at that moment, without husband and with no desire to suffer a similar man's attentions ever again in her life; knowing also – and with the old tugging sensation in her chest – that she'd likewise never consider sifting through the slew of bad men the world had to offer in order to find the occasional decent partner. She saw Marty's eyes sympathizing with the bird's plight, knowing that he understood its loneliness and fear.

She patted him on the back. "I'll open the door by the cafeteria, Marty. He'll find his way home."

He nodded. He turned to her. The concern in his eyes grew. He lowered his voice, as if sharing with her a secret, and said, "Are you okay, Tejay?"

She smiled for him, shrugged her shoulders, wrinkled her mouth to show that she was, sort of, kind of, not really, but that it could be worse.

He nodded, understanding her in the same way he knew the bird's feelings.

She left him in the lane and padded towards the cafeteria. As she went, she thought she caught – overtop or underneath or wending its way through the clamour of arcade games' electric noise and bowling balls crashing pins to the floor and children's whoops echoing to the ceiling – the bird's song, mellifluous and pretty, and heart-wrenchingly mournful.

The wind brought him. He blew in with the dying season's detritus of crisping leaves, as if he represented the harbinger of the impending storm with which the radio and seemingly everyone out in the world was so preoccupied; as if the years had preserved this tragic element so innate to him.

He stood in the foyer, the automated glass double doors parted and waiting for him to enter this place of his youth. His first step into the alley proper he found her. She'd been polishing bowling balls, grabbing each in turn from their respective slots along the wooden shelves adjacent to the front counter; she was holding one aloft to deposit back into its recess when their eyes met again after ten years apart, she like a magician with her crystal ball in hand, he like another seasonal ingredient gathered before the doors, perhaps summoned inadvertently through her alchemical workings.

They were alike then, she knew, as they'd always been: as teenagers never belonging to the groups of their peers either destined for futures steeped in academic studies or more artistic proclivities. They occupied the lacklustre middle-ground, that terrain of careers on the cusp of tragic inclinations, with one foot planted distinctly in the less-than-grand. Gas-pumpers and minimum wage waitresses, confectionary clerks and donut shop cashiers, bowling alley employees and disappearing men. This despite their being both intelligent and attractive, in their ways – he with his lanky frame lost inside of his perennial tatty jeans and band t-shirt and denim jacket, his strong chin and gentle, disarming eyes; she with her plain mousy brown hair past her shoulders, her soft pale skin and pretty smile too-often hidden beneath her face of worry.

Whenever she sought to identify herself in the greater scheme of the world she always recalled their defining moment together during the years of their being a couple: seated underneath a seldom-used staircase abutting their school's shop hallway, a special spot from where, without fail, the weather captured in the adjacent window was always sunny and sleepy and mellow no matter the day or season; during her spare while he'd been cutting class to be with her, twelfth graders both more than ready and yet wholly unprepared to graduate from those drab halls and into the world waiting, feral, outside; cuddling and whispering their conversation where no eyes or ears would notice them while the occasional hall monitor ghosted past, and this or that similar-minded student who would only nod in friendly greeting and leave them their privacy before wandering the halls in avoidance of some class or bully. He'd turned to her after they'd watched in silence as a herd of cheerleaders galloped past en route to the gymnasium and their practice session, and his words had been perfect: "We're totally the same kind of losers, aren't we?"

They stood facing each other across the room. The electrical jabbering of video games and pinball machines faded. The crack of balls into pins and clattering of the pins onto the floor came from another day, in another time.

She saw it in that time-stilled moment: the way he looked at her – a brief betrayal of his thoughts, fleeting – but unmistakably with his old eyes; as if she looked good to him, pretty or cute or sexy or even still perfect in that rare moment.

He came to her. His walk hadn't changed, still loose and easy as though he rolled along at the behest of wind or was drawn by the desires of those around him to speak with him, have him share their personal space. He stopped before her and she saw that his eyes were unchanged, too, blue and deep, and impenetrable to those who didn't know him. She knew him still, and glimpsed the subtle tremor in his features which revealed his unease.

She knew not where to begin with him after all the time between them. She waited. She shook, too. When he spoke his voice was his voice of old, and it calmed her despite the momentousness in the air.

"I knew I could count on finding you here." Looking to her uniform, he added, "And you work here now. That's perfect." He smiled his smile, and cast a long, appreciative gaze around the alley. Nostalgic like she'd always been, she knew he was suffering doubly while confronting her there in the place they'd so often frequented.

When still she didn't speak, he looked to her and said, "It's been long." They were perhaps the words she'd been most fearful of hearing from him. Confrontational in the way they spoke to everything that they'd once shared and the fact of the great inexplicable gulf of years between them.

To this, she could only resort to familiar and trusted territory, hoping madly to alter the pervasive mood of solemnity and the sense that she must respond to the greater subject he'd begun to unearth. "Want to bowl a game?" She heard the hopefulness cracking her voice and nearly winced in the wake of it. She held the ball aloft, the overhead lights lustrous in its red skin.

If he'd heard her fear he was playing it polite or else felt relieved, too. He looked to the lanes, a fond expression in his face, nodded. "Okay. Sure. It's been a while, but sure. I need shoes."

"You know where to get them."

She watched him wander to the counter. She smiled at Marty's effusive greeting, and how he couldn't hide his anxiety at Jim's presence in his bowling alley and the ways it might be effecting his surrogate daughter. She listened to them talk, easily, cheerily, like the old friends they were reunited unexpectedly after a long time apart.

When he returned, brown shoes in hand, his features looked more relaxed, at ease. Once he'd slipped the shoes on and stood facing her while trying to decide which ball best suited his fingers, he looked just about right.

"Me first?" he asked, hefting a brilliant green ball to his shoulder as if preparing to shot-put it down the lane.

"Sure." She watched him turn and face the pins standing together at the opposite end of the lane; crouch and begin a slow shuffling step forward. Only then did she think to warn him, "Watch out for the bird.

There's a bird in here." And only afterwards, once the ball had left his hand and was speeding a straight course down the length of the lane, did she wonder as to the strangeness of her warning; as if a bird would possibly nest in a place as dangerous as the mouth of a bowling lane where balls and pins met like people destined to fly apart just as suddenly, just as violently.

Marty's ashen face frightened her. His voice was cold with anxiety. "Sorry, guys. The radio's warning for a twister in our area. It sounds like it's gonna happen. I'm sending people home, or they can stay after I lock up."

Tejay grew tense, thinking of her mother and nodding and replacing the half-eaten cheeseburger on her tray. "Do you want me to help?" At the opposite side of the small cafeteria she saw Delores shuffling from table to table, explaining the situation to the few diners in her reedy, anxious voice.

Over his shoulder, Marty called, "I'll announce it over the P.A., but if you could start checking the side exits? Make sure they're locked up tight?"

"Okay. Let me call my mom real quick." She turned to Jim. His eyes unnerved her. Something in them appeared a little amiss, as though their look of concern stemmed from some other, secret thought troubling him. "Wanna come with?"

Their reunion had transpired surprisingly easily, though she'd felt the distinct surreal character of it throughout. They'd bowled a game, and chatted without any real awkwardness during. She'd won, as she'd always beaten him whenever they played here in the past, which was often; and, as he'd always accused her before, he'd decried her efforts as being fraught with cheating. And though she feared sharing her lunch break with him, which wouldn't afford the mild and useful distraction of bowling, it too had passed easily, and their conversation – purposely avoiding touching on difficult subjects – had come as naturally as she'd remembered it always being. They'd spoken of old times but remained within safe reminiscences: their summers spent there in the bowling alley, living off of just such calorie-laden fast food meals as they were eating then; bowling their allowances away and begging Marty to give them free games, which he did from time to time because he'd always liked the two of them spending their time, as he put it, in his home rather than elsewhere where they might get into trouble; haunting the arcade and spending all of their spare change trying to beat their highest scores on *Space Invaders* and *Moon Patrol* and *Frogger* and any other number of games of the time; or loitering in the rear parking lot, kicking at stones and drinking root beers and smoking cigarettes and kissing among the bushes where no one ever ventured except occasional neighbourhood cats answering their inner call to explore the wilderness of the fields beyond.

The pinball game they'd planned on enjoying following their lunch – and which he vowed to best her at, as she knew that he would because he always had and she was awful at it besides – would have to wait until after she'd locked up the alley and helped usher any lingering customers towards their homes.

He nodded slowly, a distant look in his eyes as if he too was reviewing their morning together. Then he stood, slowly, too, as though he was reluctant for them to leave the table they shared, and followed her towards the opposite end of the alley.

They stopped at the counter where Delores let her use the telephone to call her mother. Tejay waited anxiously as the line rang. She was prepared to hang up and try again later when her mother's husky smoker's voice picked up.

"Hello."

"Hey mom, it's me. Are you okay? Have you heard about the weather?"

"Heard about it?" she said, her sarcasm all but drowned beneath her anxiety. "Have you seen the sky?"

"No," Tejay admitted, a lump solidifying in her throat.

"It's like nothing I've ever seen in all my years. Something bad is coming, honey, so you take care and hunker down in the alley, okay? But watch out for bowling balls flying all around, okay? The wind's just vicious out there."

She heard the howling of the wind inside the heating vents overhead, whistling eerily throughout the sparsely-populated alley. She turned to Jim beside her. He was looking towards the doors with distant, inscrutable eyes. In that moment she feared this more than any weather warnings in the radio or prophecies from her mother: not knowing him again, and just like that any smidgen of reliability the day may have held had seeped away, leaving her shaken and uncertain and distrustful.

"Honey? Are you there, baby?"

"Yeah, mom," she murmured, her voice sounding mechanical to her ears. "You, too, mom. Take good care, and lock up, and I'll call you after the storm. Bye."

She replaced the receiver in its cradle and handed the phone over the counter to Delores, who took it with a kind smile meant to convey that she needn't worry because all would turn out well in the end. Tejay thanked her, and walked briskly towards the exit.

She didn't look to Jim walking beside her, but felt an alien, unrecognizable sensation and in this way – heart pounding terribly, thoughts a jumble – decided that he must have turned his new eyes on her.

She pushed the door wide, curious and anxious to see the sky.

"Holy," she breathed. "Look at it."

He slipped past her to stand in the lot. He turned his eyes on her and, without looking to the sky, said, "I have to go."

His words hung like an electrical current in the air. She watched him aghast from the doorway, unprepared for his initiating of their parting after having only just re-entered her life. The solemn timbre of his words chilled her, and she knew the import they held. She could only stammer, "What? Jim... *What?*"

He put his eyes on the cement. She eyed the brewing sky, dark and threatening everywhere. "Jim, the storm's right on top of us. Just come in for now, Jesus –"

Something flitted in her peripheral vision. She turned to look past the thick metal door against which she leaned, towards the edge of the lot. The bushes marking its periphery and the beginning of the wild fields beyond rustled in the wind. She stared, discerned some other movement among the scraggly shrubbery, some shape or shapes gathering there, vaguely animal-like in gait, wholly unsettling.

He followed her gaze, slowly, as if with great reluctance. He said again, "I have to go, Tejay."

Her name in his voice hurt her, like every other aspect of seeing him and hearing him and smelling him again hurt her. She was torn between the sight of his grave features and the forbidding unseen shuffling from the nearby trees.

She murmured, gripping the door edge firmly with her fingers as if preparing to pull it closed with great haste, "What's going on? Do you see something there? I swear I see something there, unless I'm crazy..."

He turned to the stirring trees again. He said, "You do see it, Tejay. Don't be afraid. I'm leaving..." He took a step away from her.

The motion filled her with dread, as if his vacating the relative shelter of the doorway and the bowling alley might prove fatal to him, to her. It also urged her to address the colossal, immovable thing that had lain unspoken between them all that day. "What happened? Where did you go, Jim? *Why* did you go?" In the wake of the words – waiting in the aftermath of the question she'd pondered relentlessly throughout the last decade of her lonely, uncertain life – she trembled, fearing deeply what he might say. It came to her, too, in that surreal moment: their final night together ten years before, etched in her mind as if it had only just passed; only another mellow August night of keeping each other's company, sharing her bed first for sex and then for laying together and listening to records until they drifted and then awoke clothed in moonlight; when, turning to her, his breath thick with beer and sleep, he'd told her that he loved her, before slipping through her window the same as he'd entered hours earlier; framed in the summer night's light with his hand raised in goodbye until the following night when their lazy, comfortable ritual would come to pass again.

She'd wondered at the absence of his afternoon telephone call the following day, called him instead without answer; thus beginning the ensuing ten-year abyss of his enigmatic disappearance, and hers, too, from the life of serene contentment she'd known.

He remained in his new place a little further from the doorway. He watched her with pained eyes. He had to raise his voice over the gusting wind, the racket of nearby branches rattling against each other like the scattering of bones in some violent prophesizing ritual. The mournful timbre in his voice she'd never heard there before, and she shuddered with greater violence as she listened to his answer. "Something happened, Tejay. Years ago, something happened. During that last night. On my walk home. Something I can't describe to you, or you'd think I was nuts, or trying to pull one over on you. There are amazing things out there, Tejay. There are terrible things, too."

She shook her head. She shouted her words, in anger, and in order to be heard over the din of weather. "You can't expect me to...You can't ask me to not ask you what the hell happened that you..." But she only drifted off, too hurt to go on, taking turns eyeing the queer sky and rippling tree-line.

His voice was firm and woeful. "I have to. I have to ask you to not ask me about that. Some things can't be put in words. I just...I had to see you one last time. To just *see* you. And to tell you...Don't wait for me. If you've been waiting at all. I...I have to go now..."

"But Jim...*What*? Ten *years*. What is it? Did it...Were you hurt, or..."

He paused, features struggling as he sought the right words to give her. He said, "I was hurt when I left you." A tear, the first she'd ever seen from him, appeared like a jewel in the corner of his eye and rolled down his cheek.

"Oh, Jim."

The rain began.

Fat drops pattering onto the pavement, signalling the advent of a much greater deluge.

The air was quietly electrified. Thunder and lightning waited and the world held its collective breath. Birds had finished their songs for the day, the voices of children usually heard from over the rooftops of the nearby neighbourhood had been drawn indoors out of the rain and catastrophic atmosphere.

He shouted, plaintively, desperately, as though wishing nothing more than to convince her of the truth in the words, "I would have done anything for you. Anything. I don't want to leave you again but I have to."

With equal desperation filling her voice she cried, "The storm's almost here. The radio's been saying all morning that a tornado's coming. Look at the sky." She paused, and screamed it at him standing mute before her, *"Look at the sky."*

They did. Together they looked: the west glowered with the blackest clouds. Overhead an eerie green sheen peered through the brewing cumulus, like an evil light wending its way into their day from afar. The rain intensified, pelting their arms, upturned faces. Something thrashed among the trees bordering the parking lot. She looked there and discerned something in the green tangles and grass, vague and indefinable and sinister and blooming true fear from the apprehension that had been gnawing tenaciously in her heart. Fleetingly, impossibly, she thought she glimpsed fire there, a strange sputtering flame among the wild grass and trees, defying the deluge and wind; but an instant later the vision had gone.

"I have to lock up now," Tejay cried earnestly, tightening her grip on the steel door. She searched for his eyes but couldn't find them in his face taking turns staring into the sky or watching his feet before him. She settled on examining his down turned features in the growing gloom and uncertain semi-light. Rain lashed downwards forcefully. A crash sounded as a long narrow Black Oak was uprooted and crashed down onto the concrete. She waited a moment longer, breathing laboriously, heart thumping madly, and cried again, "I have to close the door now."

The bushes abutting the building stirred with wind or the behest of something else. She shivered. She looked from him to the trees to the sky to him.

She waited, and felt as though she was beginning another era of waiting for him, much like the one only recently ended.

He kicked at the pavement as if indecisive, sending a white stone clattering dully across the lot and into the small bushes lining the building. He took another step away from her, and then another, keeping his eyes always away from hers, as if he were ashamed, or simply not strong enough to face her.

Then, directly overhead, a peal of thunder loosed itself from the belly of a prodigious black cloud; as if a cue, as if testifying to the tragic import she glimpsed in his grave features, heard brewing in his enigmatic words to her; and he looked up into her eyes waiting for him, still waiting for him after all the long years apart, and they watched each other without words and in this way – slowly, piece by incremental piece – he gave her some of the message for which she waited.

Then, he turned abruptly, and strode determinedly across the lot and into the undulating mass of greenery beyond. As he drew near to the verdant wall its branches appeared to shake more profoundly, as if exhibiting a grotesque excitement at his impending touch. Again she glimpsed the weird profane fire flickering among the underbrush, chilling her. Watching him merge into the foliage, Tejay felt the deepest fear she'd yet known, for him, and her, and for everything else that meant something to her; this, and she felt also a sudden powerful urge for pleasant weather to return – at least this if Jim disappearing once again – so that she could squeeze what she could from the fleeting sun and what warmth it brought into the world.

And she pulled the door closed on the tumult of the day.

He found her in the locker room, pale and lost-looking, like a moth trapped indoors.

"It's passed," he murmured. "The radio says a twister touched down nearby. Houses got wrecked, on the east side so no worries about your mom. But the sky's clearing. Everyone's gone home now. Delores, the customers who waited it out."

When she didn't answer, only nodded disconsolately, Marty ventured, "What happened to Jim?" sounding equally incredulous and relieved that he was no longer haunting her side.

"He went away," she said, her voice coming from the depths of a pit.

"Away? Where away? In the middle of that storm? We're lucky to even be here after that twister hit. Houses got blown down. Where away?"

She kicked off one and then the other of her old bowling shoes. Standing before him in her socks, she said in an awed, uncertain voice, "He took the storm with him. And everything it was bringing. Oh, Marty."

She burst into tears and opened her arms to him, remaining standing awkwardly in her place, waiting for Marty to come to her. He did, without thought. They held each other in the morosely-lit, musty-aired locker room, uncertain about a great many things but knowing only that they had to hold fast in their embrace if the world was to remain at least as tenuously intact as it was then.

Time passed. The lanes were silent. No buzzing or beeping came from the arcade. No scratching sounded in the walls, and the wind was silent in the heating vents over their heads.

From somewhere, music. She cocked an ear, felt Marty turn at the sound, too: the trapped sparrow beginning a new song, putting its vibrant voice into the stillness of the lonely bowling alley for the final time, in the hushed aftermath of the rain and the thunder; as if declaring that it was finally prepared to vacate the prison or safety of its walls; as if heralding the beginning of a new day.

But still he died alone.

LOVE ME, TOO,
BLACK FLOWER

The couple entered the store from the rain.

The employee turned from his place behind the counter at the annoying scraping of the steel door's underside along the threadbare carpeted floor. His initial look of disinterest disappeared when he saw them. The mechanical greeting he offered all customers halted somewhere in his throat. He looked away before they'd had time to make eye contact. He'd taken them in instantly, though, noting the odd juxtaposition of the boy and girl. Their styles mismatched completely. She entirely black-clad from close-cropped jet hair to black stockings and shoes, and equally dark all points between. He dressed neatly in prim khaki pants and demure beige v-neck sweater. She pop culture-vampiric and undeniably sexy, the type of girl the employee remembered well from his high school days, long past. Desired by all but access to their agonizingly alluring made-over bodies restricted solely to those equally pseudo-dark boys adorned likewise with appropriate facial piercings and dog collared throats. The boy he knew from that distant decade of high schooldom, too. He knew him well. He was intimately familiar with his baby fat-round cheeks, his awkward gait shambling through the aisles of the store in the wake of the beautiful girl leading.

The employee followed their progress surreptitiously, feigning interest in the film magazine opened on the counter. There were no other customers in the store. It was late, almost closing-time. The album he'd been playing had finished some time ago and he'd decided to have silence in the store. Outside the rain whipped the window glass. The floorboards creaked with the couple's steps. He could hear their hushed voices clearly. He imagined he could decipher the swishing of the girl's skirt as she breezed among the DVD bins. He eyed the time where it blinked within the debit machine's digital screen. Ten minutes until he could usher these thoughtless late stragglers outdoors into the inclement night and lock the door behind them. Free from customer annoyances, he could count the cash and tally the numbers and make the nightly deposit and set the alarm and finally walk home like he'd been yearning for since six hours ago at the start of his shift.

A female giggle stirred him. He scowled, narrowing his eyes. The playful sound grated on his nerves. He fingered the streamlined curvature of the computer's sides, shaking his head imperceptibly. He closed the magazine, no longer concerned even in feigning interest in it. The girl continued to titter from her place midway through the Horror aisle. He looked to her again, felt foolish and juvenile when his eyes found the girl's bottom and fixed there, seemingly of their own volition. This was okay, he rationalized. This was an acceptable place to rest his eyes. He was alone, with neither fellow employee or customer to discover him in his pathetic voyeurism. She looked good in her black skirt, this he couldn't deny. He didn't really wish to deny the fact, either. He followed her meandering progress through the aisle, observing the movement of her buttocks beneath the skirt. Its material seemed to shimmer, but it may only have been his weary eyes playing him tricks, or else the girl truly owned some dark alchemical faculties that manifested themselves in subtle signs like this.

He turned away in time to avoid a casual glance from the girl's companion as he looked absently about the store. A moment later the two were giggling again and the employee furtively examined the girl once more. She looked exactly as bewitching as she had a moment earlier. Nicer, possibly, in the certain slant of light thrown by the display lamps fastened to the wall directly over the place where she stood, the perfect way her small shoulders lay juxtaposed against the Horror section's large black cardboard header card with its campy-sinister font. Oh, the things he'd do with her if only. Endless nights and delicious days. Paradise in his bed. He'd wanted the girl since ninth grade. The same shapely legs, wrapped in black cotton knee socks. To peel away her layers and spread her open like a gift. Like a black flower opening towards the sun, and he was the sun. He could certainly be the sun for her, he thought. He could warm her if she was cold.

He shook his head in an effort to clear his thoughts. He certainly needed to close. The clock told him he had five minutes remaining until his freedom but he felt desperate so he called out into the store, towards the boy and girl, "Just so you know, we're closing up in a couple of minutes." He felt mildly pleased at the nonchalance with which he'd infused the words. He hadn't been observing the pair. His thoughts hadn't opened her up in a dream-bed and a night that would last forever. His secrets would remain his and his alone.

The boy deigned to respond with only a curt nod in his direction and so deserved any negative thoughts the employee might have for him. The girl had the audacity of smiling graciously at him from across the room, and offering a pleasant, "Okay. Sorry. We're almost done." She tittered, even, towards the employee. Cutely and endearingly. Sickeningly sweet and revolting and yet conjuring a reflexive smile on his helpless lips. He hated her for it. For her black magic abilities to sculpt him in this way, into accepting the incongruous spectacle of her and her mismatching boy. For her black hair and dark mascara and shadowy eyes like pools of mystery he hadn't been able to solve since teenage days. For her dainty legs and small breasts that he yearned to know with his hands and lips.

The employee turned to the register and pretended to fiddle there importantly. He looked to the computer screen and frowned, as if examining some disconcerting problem, a misfiled DVD, a movie unaccounted for. He watched the flickering cursor waiting for him to ring through whatever items his shift's final customers might purchase. He saw her squirming in his bed while he brought her to Heaven. He thought he could imagine her exactly as she'd look in this situation. He knew her behaviour to a tee. He could feel her inclinations and desires and small proclivities towards fetishes which were his own, too. They were identical in this way if only she knew. If only she knew.

Blasphemy rampant in the Drama section then. The boy's sardonic voice accompanying his stabbing finger of accusation. Youthful conceit as he mocked the artwork emblazoned across the poster affixed to the corkboard wall. His offence was met and sanctioned with the girl's affirmation too. "Yeah, what a *fag* movie." Their joint self-assured laughter the vilest affront of all, until the employee witnessed the boy's chubby hand descend to the girl's hip. Wrapping his sausage-fingers there casually, like he was allowed to do, as he likely had done many times before. The luck of those obese digits cupping the girl's round supple parts. The employee searched the boy's eyes carefully while his profile lay revealed briefly in further examination of the disrespected poster. He examined his features, the look of sheer obliviousness resting there everywhere. He wondered if the boy enjoyed a wide variety of movies, or if he only scoffed at the great amount of film knowledge with which he wasn't familiar, as the employee himself had done when he'd been the same age. Old-sounding movies that the boy's parents might like and which he, by default, was required to mock in order to assert his dominion over current trends of cool.

I'm you, you fat boy, the employee thought suddenly, alarmed at the vindictiveness of the thought. He recalled himself wandering morosely-lit high school halls. He remembered lonely spares spent napping in library cubicles or fantasizing about this exact girl whose presence had teased him from across science or history classrooms. He saw himself vividly, pimpled and sausage-armed and destined for loneliness, confiding in a friend of similarly unfortunate physical design during one such forlorn between-class moment of confession: *Man, it would be nice to see girls like those being with guys unlike them. All the breeds stick together, though. Like the rest of the animal kingdom. Athletes and athletes and witches and warlocks and on and on. What if we matched one of those witches perfectly but they'll never know? Maybe we write poems about black magic, too. How does she know me? Maybe I cast spells every night, too.*

Something possessed him then, stirring him from his reveries. He smiled a saccharine smile towards the browsing couple, and inquired, "Find everything you're looking for?" adding, "Good, good," before they'd even really answered him in their mutually polite voices.

Turning his attention to the computer before him he continued his rumination of days past. Yes, the boy in the store had been him a decade and more past. Awkward and un-pretty, stuffed inside of clothes un-cool by fashion standards of the day. Yet this boy differed markedly from his old self for the treasure he wore on his arm. Dark and pretty and delicious. I didn't have her, the employee thought petulantly. What gives you the right? Why are you privileged and allowed to see her naked and do what you like to her? Fuck you, pig-face. You probably don't even understand your luck. You probably believe that you deserve the gift of her. That you have her because you're *irresistible* to her. That you're not the epitome of a current trend for beautiful girls to fuck fat losers who belong in basements running up their parents telephone bills beating off to 1-900 girls in-between reruns of Dr. Who. I doubt you even know that you're the luckiest piglet that ever lived. A ton of porcine good fortune escaped the slaughterhouse to crush a dark flower. See? I write dark poetry, too.

It was one minute to closing-time when the couple drifted to the counter. The employee looked up from the used DVD he was sealing with a strip of Scotch tape, smiled curtly. He rang the boy through, suspecting that the DVD he bought was a gift for the girl. A nice gesture, or a clever tactic to get something from the girl that he might want. Points for the chubby preppy pork-boy, the transparency of courting rituals remained unchanged. "That'll be $11.40," he told the boy, who handed him a credit card. The employee punched in the requisite numbers into the debit pad and thought how he hadn't had a credit card until after he'd graduated from university. They waited in mildly uncomfortable silence while the debit machine whirred its internal workings. The rain tapped persistently at the rectangular picture window running the length of the storefront. It was a cold sound, evoking in its million tiny contacts the greater rage of thunderheads and fingers of lightning illuminating a sky pregnant with clouds. The employee considered the song-less silence in the store and realized then just how much he preferred the song of the rain to guitars or drums. It calmed his nerves and slowed the hammering behind his chest. He felt relieved thinking of the great cleansing of the sidewalks and streets, where trash burned in the sun and where pedestrian traffic milled and spit onto the cement. The machine sputtered its paper receipts a moment later, and the employee risked a glimpse to the girl's lips while the boy signed his receipt. She wore no lipstick, her narrow pink lips almost garish in the way that they stood out among her face of deep-lined mascara lines and bold jet hair. Her lip ring seemed to radiate cold, buried like a hoop of ice within the warmth of her pale, pouting bottom lip.

He chanced to catch her eye. She smiled at him, genuine with warmth as she said, "Too bad you're closing. It's nice and dry in here." The boy chuckled, too, softly. Guilt suddenly overwhelmed the employee. He saw in that instant the couple's innocence, wholly unaware of their criminal behaviour and ridiculous ways. They were kind. Under her stock veneer of darkness, she was only a teenaged girl. Under his fastidiously modish outfit of loserdom he was simply a boy with hormones running amok and using any tactic he might have at his disposal to his advantage. Maybe they deserved each other. They probably did, the employee reasoned, because why wouldn't they? He smiled at the pair, genuinely wistful as he saw them off into the storming night. "Thanks, guys. Have a good night. And stay dry, if you can." He offered an endearing little chuckle, even, to which both the girl and boy responded in kind. They smiled. "Thanks. See you later," her voice pleasant and unaffected. Her vampiric nature sleeping inside of her pretty shell, awaiting the next school dance or house party or mall trip to awaken and impress her peers with its alluring aura. The employee trailed them to the door, locked its heavy lock behind them. He stared after them through the barred windows. He thought, feeling maudlin and foolish even as he did, Goodbye, teenage succubus. Goodbye oblivious boy of good fortune.

A sudden peal of thunder shook the window. A tolling sound that seemed to signal some imminent thing. The employee kept his window vigil a while longer, watching the trails of water pool in rivulets across the glass. Then he stepped away, unable to decipher the meaning hidden in the roar of the night.

He looked and saw her, a small shadow in the misting street. A small miracle, though he tried at first to deny the significance of witnessing her. The rain-soaked sidewalks created mirages to dupe the eye. The streets, smeared with wet amorphous reflections of streetlight and lamplight, were filled with such deceptions. He stared and confirmed her existence. A hammer went off in his temple and knelled behind the wall of his chest. The black-dressed girl leaning halfway into the car curbing the street and the fat boy meeting her midway, too. The girl touching her lips to the pudgy mouth of the doughy pig-boy. Their silhouettes remained connected briefly in their grotesque embrace, framed agonizingly in the rectangle of the car's rear window. The employee slowed his steps and shook. The rain was cold, and the wind, too. It whipped against his too-light Fall jacket and flattened his hair against his skull. He trembled and he considered the probability that it was the chill and wet air causing this reaction in him.

She closed the passenger side door and waved the car off. She watched it grow smaller in the uncertain distance of the street, and a moment after turned into the alley running adjacent to the row of duplexes. He followed as though magnetically impelled, unnoticed. Her steps in her soft black suede shoes made no sound. He made certain to kick a stone clatteringly into the trash bins on one side of the alley. The girl turned but he made certain to watch the puddles at his feet as he walked. He sensed her imminent communication before she'd spoken. A subtly charged second passed and he heard her light voice, "Hey." He looked up, squinting in the rain. She'd stopped walking, though she stood pointed in the same direction she'd been heading in. Looking over her shoulder at him, she wore a smile. Her eyes smiled in recognition, too. "Hey," she repeated, her smile widening. "You're from the movie store. I just saw you." He came close and saw the innocence in her eyes. He saw a paper coffee cup in her hands, evidence of the couple's destination earlier that night. They hadn't visited a cool club or house party, after all. They hadn't flaunted their pleasing aesthetic to similarly-minded peers. They'd left the movie shop and driven to a large chain coffee shop, un-hip by most standards. They'd bought coffee or hot chocolate to help stave off the chill of the evening. They'd sat there a while and sipped their drinks and talked. They might have had a donut, or split a bagel. Maybe they'd necked at the river, except maybe kids don't call it *necking* these days. Maybe he'd touched her and felt her wetness. Maybe he'd gotten to first or second or third base, or maybe he'd even succeeded in landing a home run. He cringed inwardly at his outdated terminology. They would have had time for this in the thirty or forty minutes between their leaving the movie shop while he'd performed his closing duties and the girl's arrival in the rain alley. She could have put the boy in her mouth in that time, or held him quivering and sputtering in her small hand.

The girl squinted in the rain. Steam curled from the torn lip of her cup. Her smile explained how she felt about the weather. What a downpour. A monster storm. The employee spoke to that smile. "Yeah, that's me. I thought I recognized you."

"I left my umbrella in my boyfriend's car," she laughed. "Otherwise I'd cover us up. Do you live here, too?" She pointed down the length of the alley towards the silhouette of the duplexes looming at its end. It was a short stretch between where they stood and the shelter of the long balcony overhang, and the entrance to the building beneath. She sounded mildly incredulous, as if too many coincidences had occurred between them already that night for yet another to exist. The employee watched her a second. He saw a lonely hallway and a teenaged boy drifting there alone. At the far end of the hall lay a door abutting a classroom or gymnasium or schoolyard that he'd never gain access to, no matter how determined his steps. This boy squinted and made out a slim, black-haired figure framed in the door's long rectangular window. The employee watched the rain-drenched girl a while before shaking his head. "No. I don't live there." He added, "But I wish I did," with his hands raised on high, into the rain, a gesture of resignation to his fate of walking in stormy conditions.

He watched her watching him, a queer but amiable expression on her face. He sensed that he liked her, from what little he gathered of her. He sensed the possibility of being truly fond of her if only she let him inside the close circle of her everyday life. He envisioned having coffee with her some day, and sharing good conversation over the telephone and in person, and who could tell what might happen between them in future days of their continuing friendship? They might be very similar. They might enjoy the same interests, and perhaps she wrote poetry like he had when he was her age. And he knew in that instant a few things about her, too. He knew that she hadn't acted out of a youthful need to adhere to the safety of trends: her love for the fat pig-boy was genuine, and incredible in its way. Another miracle in the world. The openness of her eyes told this. Their brave cast, even in the darkness of the alley after midnight. The kisses she gave the boy she reserved for him and him alone. The employee saw her gentle eyes and her pale cheeks like moons and her diaphanous lips and the sexiness of her rain-soaked hair framing it all. And he considered what he might say or do next in their fated shared moment, and understood the two distinct paths opened before him:

It would be easy for him to raise his hand, which had been curled into a fist inside the overlarge sleeve of his jacket from the moment he'd found her in the downpour, and strike her squarely in the teeth. He would shatter her smile with the blow. He would watch her collapse like a garbage bag crammed with garbage. He would see her stunned face staring up at him incredulously, like a deer plowed senseless by an onrushing vehicle and struggling to fathom its immense pain. She would cause waves to undulate in the midst of the puddle where she'd fallen and kicked her small feet reflexively. One of her dark little shoes would have flown from a foot and come to rest among a heap of discarded newspapers. He would turn and see the empty alley yawning behind him. He would look to the windows of the duplexes overhead and each would be dark. He would consider the rooms housing their sleeping people, and he would picture them huddled into their beds and inside of their dreams. He would drag the twitching girl among the nearby trash cans. Once within cover of their plastic bodies he would draw his leg back and kick her everywhere, time and again. He would straddle her and pummel her exquisite face until it became changed, and an altogether different face. He would think about the chubby pig-boy driving home through the storm, hands white-knuckling the steering wheel as he fought the slippery, uncertain streets while he erased her face blow by blow. He would wonder whether this girl and that boy had a system arranged between them, whereby they called one another before turning in for the night. He would wonder about the kinds of things they might say to each other before they hung up the telephone and went to sleep and dream. He would think fleetingly of the store, utterly vacant in that moment but for mice and cockroaches, dimly-illuminated with only a single row of lights on to the rear of the large room. He would think of its aisles, less cluttered the following day maybe than they'd been earlier that night. He would think about the coincidence of encountering the pig-boy in future days, in the store, in a bar, drifting past one another in a crowded mall hallway, and he wondered what his eyes might look like then. He would think about the manner with which he'd greet the boy, sincerely and in good cheer, genuine or affected but jovial-sounding in either case. He would stop hitting her when no more resistance met his efforts. He would listen and hear no breath escape her crushed lips. He would continue to hit her for a while still, to make certain, of something. His fists would make meaty sounds in the alley darkness as they fell. A small tinkling sound might be several of her teeth bouncing along the pavement. His knuckles would burn. The rain would continue its pouring. He would look up into the thickness of its descent. It would appear as if Heaven was opened and giving its sadness to the world. Tears for each lonely night lived by each lonely person in the world. Or else he would consider that maybe someone was simply pissing on him from up high.

He would drag the flaccid body into the mouth of an overturned garbage pail. He would struggle with the task but succeed in filling the receptacle with the girl and setting it upright. He would deposit some stray articles of trash into its mouth, a few handfuls of sodden newspapers, their stories bled away in the rain; a dilapidated cardboard box; a plastic garbage bag filled to bursting and yielding a horrid stench. He would search about the small wet space and find the lid a moment later. He would replace it overtop the garbage pail and the garbage and treasure it held. He would consider how the girl was finally out of the rain and the thunder and in a dry and quieter place. He would think how her presence there transformed the alley that night. A secret flower planted in a filthy pot. The first seed of a future garden. The beginning of an increasingly profound transformation, of squalor to grandeur. He would never see her bloom in her lightless space, and neither would anyone else: she would remain lost among the wilderness sprung up from the unspoiled seed of her. And he the catalyst for this great flourishing of Paradise, a secret gardener of so much wild beauty.

He would then turn and walk from the alley, contented and wholly discontented.

The night might pass in exactly this way, or:

He would say goodnight to the painful beauty of the girl, and bear her kind smile of farewell until a next meeting that, realistically, would never come to pass. The vision of her, rain-drenched and pristine, would haunt him as she wandered away from him while he turned and walked his own way, too. The rain would fall relentlessly, touching him everywhere. He would take solace in the feel of its infinite number of little touches. It would seem a deluge that cleansed sullied things and gave life to those thirsting for drink. It might remake the streets and sidewalks and coming days and nights in a new splendour, or it might not.

Certainly though, the night before him would prove the loneliest, most difficult stretch of darkness he'd ever known. In the downpour as he went he would grow relieved of his uncertainty about where the rain existed and where his tears fell.

They stared at one another in that time-paused moment, breathless, innocent, waiting for the night and its long, long tempest to end.

SONG OF THE
DREAM CATS

They could sense its imminence. It was nearly upon them again, and it was this waiting – those agonizingly prolonged miles of time during which their terror grew to proportions they'd never believed imaginable back in the lives they'd left so far behind they often questioned their reality – it was this agony of waiting for the carnage that was coming for them that parted the fog of the men's terror, and gave them cause to consider what good they'd ever done, or conversely, what evil they must have done to deserve the eternity of such standstill moments.

It was during the electric hour before dawn that the first shell landed in the centre of their ragged line inching its way upwards from the base of the hill outside of La Trang, obliterating several men and igniting the night in fire and cacophony. In the smoke, amid the bloody debris of their companions' strewn limbs, the surviving soldiers cried out in terror; fired panicked rounds from the mouths of their machine guns into the murky green heights of the hill rising over them like some colossal punishment; were cut down by strafing fire from the dark hilltop above; and once again, more vividly than ever, saw the good or evil or fateful choices that had sent them into the green Hell.

It was a little over one month following the pointless slaughter that grew known among the men who survived it as the Battle for Suicide Hill. Captain Denning had stepped outside the dive bar for a smoke while his men – the handful of survivors of the A.M. alpha bravo, who'd followed his retreat back into the jungle gulfs from which they'd crawled in the naive hope of capturing the hill for what they'd been told were strategic purposes – drank and whored their fill inside. The night sweated, the nearby bush hummed with nocturnal life like some immense electrical generator. Shore leave in Pattaya took them away but nowhere near far enough. Denning wondered as he smoked and finished his bottle of tiger piss if even the distance of oceans would keep the ghosts he and his men had come to know so intimately at bay. He wondered whether his wife and son would recognize the man that came home to them if ever he found his way from the eternal country of fear that held him in its bosom.

An uncanny sound in the stillness came to him. Part muffled cry, coupled with a protracted scratching sound, drifted from around the corner of the squat wooden building. He dropped his cigarette in the dirt, placing a hand on his pistol out of habit, unsheathing the dagger from the scabbard at his hip despite the likelihood of the disturbance being a soldier fucking a whore in the lot, or a hungry child picking through the garbage for food scraps. He oozed silently through the sweating shadows in the direction of the disturbance, slinking low to the ground. Squinting in the moonless darkness he discerned movement ahead, partially concealed by a heap of garbage bags, the rancid-smelling overflow from the metal dumpster squatting on the grass like some rusted, stinking idol among the density of foliage encroaching on the small, unkempt lot. He whispered through the grass, closer, closer, his senses tingling, telling him that something was awry, some danger waited for him.

He peered down at the sight, and a queer sense of embarrassment, of empathic shame mixed with the horror he felt in that moment: it was Private Jones kneeling naked in the gravel and broken glass, face dark with cork, clutching the small white kitten's throat in his big hands; it was clear that he'd strangulated the small creature, crushed its windpipe in his powerful grip. His other hand gripped his dagger, its blade red from slitting the animal's scrawny throat, gauging its eyes from its sockets, disembowelling it so that its abdomen gaped open like a hideous blood-puckered mouth. Denning saw the bloody lines making a haphazard geography across Jones' arms and chest too, as if the soldier had sought to map out the maze of some demonic dream in his flesh.

When he sensed Denning's presence he started and, looking up, showed him the tears flooding from his eyes. His voice quavered in the sweaty claustrophobic space of the garbage hills. "I'm sorry, sir. I'm so so so sorry. They were just too beautiful, you know? They were too beautiful to be here with us. You know? I'm sorry. You understand? I'm sorry, sir." He was nodding his head violently, as if attempting to invoke the same gesture from Denning, to birth the same logic and understanding in his superior officer; Denning looked on with stunned eyes, and took in the sight of the others: a dozen or more cats of different sizes and colours — those tenacious roving packs, the scavengers of the poverty-plagued villages and ghetto districts, fighting for sustenance and survival where they could — eviscerated and dismembered and piled high around him in a growing hill; and the dozens of cats still living and tethered by loops of fraying rope to the wooden slats of the fence running adjacent to the dumpster. These captured animals mewled and pawed at the gravel and grass in their terror, understanding the death coming for them in that place of unreasoning slaughter.

The scene stretched itself into the weird eternity such scenes are made of. The soldiers stared at one another, wordless. The jungle hummed around them, its dark voice the great ghost the men would take with them into their lives, however long or short those lives proved to be.

Amid the stink of garbage and death wafted something sweet, the perfume of nocturnal wildflowers or lotus blossoms stirring seductively in the shadows of the nearby jungle. A moment of clarity came over Denning then. His eyes cleared, and his thoughts too. He cocked a thumb over his shoulder in the direction of the bar and the sounds of drunken revelry and music drifting on the steaming air. He nodded curtly and said with authority, "When you're ready, soldier," and left Jones to his duty.

The mournful crying of the cats was the song of lament that would follow him into dreams.

It's the kind of song that holds you. Everyone needs to be held sometimes, by someone or something.

ROARING DREAM
OF THE WEEPING
SPIDER-MEN

The thick air, the tenacious sun penetrating the tree-roof, the noxious mist hanging over the bush: these agonies conspired to weigh on the hearts of the men in their despairing trek through the green gulfs. Through elephant grass taller than themselves, beneath intricate tangles of thick creeping vines and through leech-ridden pools they went, with the spectre of the enemy hanging over all.

This ragtag platoon of weary soldiers, emerging from the dense underbrush, found no respite awaiting them in the small glade: the air here reeked with a potency that stung their nostrils, as they stared with horror upon the great spider web stretched among the trees opposite them, barring their passage into the wilderness beyond. The spectacle of it, like a ghastly mirage in the burning afternoon, halted them, silenced them, awed them.

A voice drifted from somewhere within its congested centre, croaking a single beseeching word: "Help."

Bullets this deep into Laos – when they were still several miles from their objective, and the violence there which was to be their destiny – would ensure their premature death. Mercy wasn't possible in the jungle, they'd grown to understand, when self-preservation might be compromised. And so at the Colonel's silent command the platoon efficiently, wordlessly – and with eyes warily eyeing the stirring foliage encroaching on all sides – passed the string of entwined soldiers; looking away from their distended, infected limbs where the jagged barbwire bit deep into green and purpling and blackened gangrened flesh and the ruined muscle and bone beneath, knotting the men closely together, raw festering skin on raw festering skin where they hung between the trees, disappearing into the greenery on either side like some hideous forewarning of the horror which lay waiting for the platoon beyond. Leaving behind a pair of men – McCall and Harding, their most seasoned veterans – to dispatch what mercy they could with the daggers in their fists.

Times were just dark, and just so strange – Private Sanders knew this, and, like his companions, swallowed his revulsion as he could. He turned his thoughts with great concentration – as he was wont to do during difficult moments such as this – to the baseball games he'd watch every Saturday afternoon once he was returned home, both local neighbourhood games and those broadcast on the television; and of the girls he would chase with his friends, pretty girls who frequented the bowling alley and local bar and other safe places; and of his mother and father and younger brother, all of whom he missed in that moment more than he'd ever cared for their company while he was still home, more so than even several days earlier when he'd yearned to see them during the vicious firefight that saw half of their platoon wiped out, including his friends Jones and Barker, both Kingston boys like himself who'd fallen on either side of him where they'd been holding their line in the bottom of the vine-festooned gulley.

Sanders thought these thoughts of ball games and pretty girls but still the plaintive cries of the several still-living men snared in the meat-web – who, seeing their companions' death by knife, protested as they could – shuddered his heart; still the fetid smell of rotting flesh churned his insides; still the look in the tortured soldiers' faces – relief turned to astonishment turned to terror as the platoon passed the tortured web on their way – clung in the Private's thoughts.

He shook his head in a futile effort to rid his mind of the sight of his fellow soldiers passing him, slinking in the direction of the meat-web with daggers drawn and eyes hard and hardened to the reality of the mercy mission with which their Colonel had burdened them. He shut his eyes to the repeated scything sound – real or imagined – of the soldiers cutting the throats of the weeping spider web-men.

The vivid white blur of a baseball rocketing from a pitcher's uncurling fist; the sharp crack of wood against its speeding leather hide as the batter leans into it; sending it spiking into the July blue overhead, high and high and so high that the crowd, standing in the wooden bleachers – the men with their sons riding their shoulders for better vantage as together they squinted skywards – think that the ball may have been sent out of the park's boundaries entirely, into the clouds far above, disappeared, perhaps never to fall to earth again.

But he only allowed himself these reveries fleetingly, forcing his attention to the song of the forest surrounding them as they slunk ever deeper into its green, vile heart: a wild song, of animals owning the gulfs, and the enemy invisible but imagined all around in every whisper of grass blade and snapping of branch, and the platoon creeping through it, too, with death and death and death on their minds. He'd been trained well, through the months he'd endured in the green, and knew death was the penalty for those whose respect for it wavered.

They marched for hours. They crawled on their bellies when their Colonel gave the command for it, fearing close encounters with hooded monocled cobras and buried landmines, those deadly un-hatched embryos of the war. The sun burned them darker and put sweat in their eyes and made a raw desert bed of their throats and still they edged forward into the wilderness.

Then, a million years into their trek, at a silent signal from their Colonel, the men stopped in the elephant grass, senses alert, hearts hammering so loudly they all believed that the enemy might hear.

They'd reached the summit of a foliage-shrouded ridge. Peering through binoculars the men saw their mission's objective materialized from the steaming ether in the shallow valley spread below them: the village of squat wood and straw huts and simple dirt roads meandering between; its denizens, some drawing wheelbarrows and buggies or tilling the soil of the abutting fields, others patrolling the dirt streets with rifles slung across shoulders and eyes searching the distance guardedly.

The men passed around binoculars. Accepting a pair from the man beside him and putting his telescopic eye into the distant village streets, Sanders saw: a mother and the child she wore on her belly inside a leather pouch slung across her back; behind her, another woman carrying a basket of vegetables in either hand, her straw hat concealing her features; an elderly man and woman seated before their domicile, smoking, their yellow skin pulled taut across their faces by the years and revealing their skeletal design beneath; a trio of women crouched among the edge of the fields, plucking potatoes from the earth with great care, as if handling jewels of incalculable value.

Looking at this scene of valley stillness and peace among the endless miles of the jungle on all sides made belief in the deception easy: perhaps

there was no war at all, and all of their days fighting and killing and dying in the green were simply a mass hallucination or mirage conjured by the relentlessness of heat and sun. Perhaps they'd long ago met their collective demise and stumbled only now on this vision of Heaven: tranquil people tending to some divine strip of earth in a place where bullets never flew and soldiers became merely men again. Maybe the elderly man and woman he saw feeding the chickens in their small wire pen were angels tending to their corner of eternity.

The voice of the Colonel drifted to the soldiers' ears, hushed but hard and strong and uncompromising, dispersing the Private's hopeful reveries: "This is revenge. Everyone dies. Everyone."

Yes, the soldiers answered this order, creeping through the elephant grass with great stealth, with immense patience down the sheer precipice to the valley floor below, with death once more seeded in their thoughts.

"You big boy," the prostitute whispered admiringly as she explored Sanders' erect penis poking from his trousers. Her small ring-adorned fingers stroked the shaft, which he was realistic and sober enough to understand wasn't, in fact, that impressive. Her sharp nails, painted a glossy scarlet which matched her lips, dug into the glans, hardening him further.

He held her little breasts in his hands. He was going to fuck her like his pals were fucking their own girls right then. He could hear some of them – Blair and Windows – making their whores cry in the rooms on either side of his.

He exhaled long and slow as the girl knelt on the dirty floor before him and wrapped her mouth around his erection.

Without his concession the days behind him materialized in his thoughts: a blackness hung like a fog over them but still he saw their endless events through it.

It was only once he'd disembarked from the chopper in the Pattaya airfield, making himself cheer and whoop along with his companions as they'd run together away from the machine raising a dust storm around them; it was only after he'd drank his fill at the bustling bar overlooking the water and taken a whore back to his room; it was only now, as he pulled the girl from the floor and turned her around to fuck her from behind on the narrow mattress, making her squeal; it was only then that he wept for everything he'd seen, and for everything he'd done and those acts of mercy he'd disregarded in order to preserve his life at the cost of ideals he'd been raised to believe were important in life.

He came. He collapsed on the mattress. The hooker draped herself across him. She clung to him, weary from the day of fucking behind her. They slept and sweat together in the oven-aired room. Sanders slept despite his electric thoughts. He was wearier than he'd ever been, and his dreams, of course, roared with the blood and the thunder he'd grown to know so intimately.

Private Sanders awoke in the deep night from just such a red dream. Bathed in sweat he left the moist folds of the bed and the clammy embrace of the girl and went to wet his face in the bathroom sink. Examining his ashen features in the little water-stained mirror he grew alarmed: the feral eyes seemed to belong to another man, until he remembered that he'd become this man somewhere in the endless miles of the wilderness and the endless cries of men he saw die and some whom he'd made die. He stared resolutely at the mirror-man with a great fear consuming him. And then he saw movement behind him.

He wheeled, hand reflexively settling across the hilt of his dagger on his belt, which he'd learned to carry with him everywhere, even on shore leave in whorehouses because the cunning enemy was adept at hiding in the cracks and fissures of the world.

He eyed the web owning the upper corner of the tiny room warily, and its captive moth fluttering there desperately, futilely. It was a large specimen, pale as snow, and it continued to bat and flail about in its sticky prison but to no avail. The web, woven thick and impregnable, held it helpless.

Sanders stepped on the grime-encrusted rim of the toilet bowl and plucked the insect from the web with a gentle hand. Cracking the small window beside the toilet he let it fly from his fingers and into the humid night. He watched it go, erratic and ecstatic in its new freedom, angelic against the dark sky before it disappeared altogether.

He then sat himself on the toilet bowl. He sat like a soldier in the field, silent, unmoving, observing the room's aspects with alert eyes swivelling in his head. He'd been trained to sit like this – invisibly – by the military but more than this by his days in the field itself, which were only ever dangerous places just waiting – as the Colonel was quick to remind them – for their chance to cut down the unwary.

An hour passed, and then another. The heat from the naked light bulb over the sink grew to fill the small room, adding to the weight of the stifling humidity infiltrating the space through the open window. Sweat beaded his forehead but he made no move to wipe it away, having become only another unmoving fixture of the bathroom.

The prostitute awoke during his vigil and, creeping to the bathroom door, whispered to him through the flimsy wood. She asked whether he was okay. She asked whether he'd like to fuck her one more time. He ignored her questions until she grew angry and he heard her curse him in her native language and gather her few belongings before storming from the motel room with a distant slamming of its thin door.

Still he waited. The moon inched across the sky until he could see it from his position on the toilet, owning the eastern quadrant of the little window. It was in this hour, the final quarter of the third hour of his vigil, that the enemy returned to its headquarters:

He eyed the spider with a clinical eye: it was staggeringly immense – baseball mitt-sized – black- and green-furred and with unsettlingly long and nimble-looking legs, a hunter's design. A vivid crimson marking like blood striped its back, raw and scarified. A pair of horn-like protuberances rose from its head, imbuing it with a deadly prehistoric aspect. It had crawled from some place beneath the area of the sink, perhaps squeezing itself forth from the rusty sink hole itself, and traveled fleetly across the sink-top and then in a single darting movement across the peeling wall, leaving a black effluvial trail in its wake.

Finally it scampered into its bed with an ease and assurance which angered Sanders. Your bed, another's prison, the soldier reflected, imagining the thing crawling like some arachnid tunnel-rat through the claustrophobic darkness of miles and miles of shit- and slime-encrusted pipeline running beneath the city, up and up from the blackest foulest nest embedded in the earth's molten bowels.

He watched it carefully as it explored its web, clambering nimbly through its finely-spun centre and into each portion of its periphery, as if seeking a meal or investigating the stench of an intruder clinging to its home. It appeared agitated as it scampered to and fro, in a frenzy of confusion or consternation or fury or all of these emotions while it searched for its missing prey.

Sanders' eyes remained alert. His face didn't budge a muscle, and neither did he stir from his rigidly-held posture of observation. Inwardly, he rejoiced. His heart clamoured, though he willed it to grow calm for fear of its giving his position away to the enemy. Somewhere, beyond this inward celebration, a distant fear gnawed at him, as though he felt a different man encroaching upon the person he was, and begin its usurping of him.

He waited several more minutes. The spider grew calmer in its bed. Perhaps it had fed well in its nocturnal explorations after all. Sanders imagined he could smell the putrid stink of death emanating from the arachnid, though this of course could have been the city's stench drifting in from the outdoors: Pattaya, the city that never slept. He examined the great hunter with a hard eye and thought he could discern blood drops in its thick hackles. He waited several more minutes. The spider grew still in its sticky haunt. A low murmur seemed to emanate from it, as if it droned to itself from the haze of some deep lotus-fuelled dream. The night sweated, clinging to everything.

Sanders stood slowly and silently – like a ghost risen from a grave – knife in his fist.

The night stretched long, and long.

His mother's eyes pleaded. Her voice wavered. Her features seemed especially old, wrinkled with deep fissures that seemed to threaten a sudden calamitous breaking, as if the strain of their farewell would be enough to shatter her into pieces at any moment.

His bags lay about his feet on the hardwood foyer floor. Sunlight fell through the long rectangular windows running alongside the door. His uniform felt tight and unfamiliar and uncomfortable. His heart ran wild with nerves. He felt fear for the first time, distilling his former excitement, swallowing his earlier pride, while doubt gnawed at his heart, too.

But, duty-bound, or so he'd still believed in that pained moment of parting, he only kissed the porcelain-like cracking face before him. It neither shattered nor departed his side: she only waited, tears flowing from her eyes and her lips trembling too hard for words to come anymore.

This was how he left his mother, in sunlight and silence, fear vanquishing her heart and tears washing him away as he passed from her house and into the new and uncertain day waiting for him.

Times were burdened with darkness, and incalculably strange.

And when the Pattaya sun finally rose and burned through the bathroom window, bloodying the room further, Private Sanders, duty-bound, was too enraptured with the work at hand to notice its bloodlight. The music of the dawn songbirds that awoke from their nests among the surrounding tenement rooftops and sagging balconies and streetlights went unheard by him, too, drowned out by the voices of the ghosts with whom he communed: all those lost in the green miles and miles.

And when, hours and hours later still, the soldier woke as if from a long and dark dream and looked about the bathroom, there was no evidence of the enemy to be found at all; but for its blood upon his hands and reddening his knife's edge, and pooling on the bare floor about his feet, its ghost weighing down the tattered web overhead and clinging in his thoughts as if he hadn't done his duty at all.

He hadn't left the fight unscathed, either. One never did, he knew, and felt wise or old thinking this thought. He looked to the deep red circle in his side, fingered gingerly the great gaping wound – raw and serrated – which laid open the glistening muscle of his thigh. He winced, too, at the blood spurting irregularly from a place in his neck where the enemy's fangs had found their target. His vision was blurred, as if he stared through the membranous veil of a caul: the reach of the enemy's venom had been deadlier and more sure than he'd reckoned for.

The soldier closed his wounded eyes. The sky he envisioned, though, offered up no gifts of respite from above. He wondered – with an awakening stabbing inside his chest which he momentarily understood to be hope – whether the wounds he'd suffered in this latest battle of too many would summon angels from the blue as his mother's eyes of farewell feared days like these would; and if so, he wondered what their judgement of him would be, and to which plot of eternity they would escort him.

A lily grows overtop her grave.

The Night is here.

AN ANGELA
NAMED VENGEANCE

"Did you know he brought the apocalypse? It's true. Just like that: the end of the world. It's true, and so is this: I'm bringing it right back to him. I'm going to carry it in my hands and drop it at his door. Tonight he's going to understand what he did. He's not answering his phone but I know where he's at. If you talk to him could you tell him this for me? I'm going to bring it to his door. Tell him to wait for it. It's coming."

The tinny voice inside the receiver implored her: "Miss, calm down. Can you tell me why you've called 911? Is there an emergency? Can you tell me where you are? Are you confused? What's wrong? Miss? Are you still there?"

Angela sought to replace the telephone receiver in its cradle but it fell and battered against the plastic wall of the booth. She watched it swing by its thick steel cord as if mesmerized. The tinny voice exiting the mouthpiece sounded robotic and unnerving. She went to leave the booth but found it difficult to navigate its dual doorway. She barrelled her way through angrily and arrived in the cool nocturnal air, refreshing following the congestion of the booth. Into the silence of the early morning fields to the north and nearby forest to the south, a voice:

"Are you finished?"

She followed the thread of the words. Like a fish on a lure she felt her eyes drawn across the uneven asphalt of the gas station's lot, overrun with weeds rising through the countless cracks; through the alcohol-haze fucking her vision to the immense bulk of the man rooted tree-like at the small lot's periphery. In the moonless dark she could just discern a suggestion of his leering yellow grin and intimate appraisal. Mostly only the immensity of him reared from the shadows, limned in starlight: his swollen belly draped over his belt like a great whale carcass, his thighs like tree trunks, his stout ankles thrusting from his brown leather shoes, his large womanly breasts and shuddering jowls.

She smiled, and nodded, and staggered a wavering line towards the voice.

She'd found him at neither of the three county trash bars she'd visited that night, where she'd looked foolishly for men to wield like knives; this man she'd found, as if preordained, thumbing his way down a little-frequented farm road past 4:00 A.M., a mile or so from her home at the precise moment when she'd resigned herself to a fate of aloneness following her night of flirting with every trucker and biker and farmer she'd come across without a lick of success.

In him she'd found something much more powerful, speaking in terms of weaponry. The distinct sensation filtered through the fog of her inebriation that she'd pulled this one from some deep place, like a figment of childhood nightmare, to fill her current night's life of unabated misery and bitter fury with his sheer size and potential.

She'd pulled the car onto the gravel and watched in the mirror as he lumbered forward. Moving less like a grossly obese man than a great bear, shaking all over, flesh swaying in all directions at once. Clambering in, his weight groaning the vehicle. She'd seen his eyes clearly then: black and narrow and slicing through the dark with their keen intelligence. He was everything she'd wanted to find that night, and much more, too, she realized. Before the man could speak she'd said, "Do you want to come to my house? I'm lonely."

His beady eyes had widened, revealing yellow spots like pustules sunken in the white. Realization seeped into them, and then a devilish exhilaration: maybe he'd understood his own great fortune in that moment, too.

Turning from an examination of the camera on its tripod where it stood before the bed, he murmured in his voice of gravel, "You're a dirty one, aren't you?"

"Yes," she told him from her place seated on the edge of the mattress, unbuttoning her shirt and tossing it to one side. Her bra and pants and underwear followed.

He appraised her from top to bottom.

She saw the saliva bubbles forming in the corners of his mouth. "You like kinky," he grated matter-of-factly, and finished with a confidence and excitement which caused his voice to rise, "I got kinky for you."

He tore the shirt from himself with one great hand, scattering its buttons across the floor. He unzipped himself and let his pants drift like a massive tarpaulin about his feet. He turned around so that his immense ass was level with her eyes. Beneath the tautly-drawn silk of his powder blue underwear she watched the undulating mass first with revulsion and fear, and then with a sickening determination rising up inside her. He peeled the underwear from himself with measured theatricality and his tail lay revealed. It was stout. It was fish-belly pale. It was pimple-covered. Its root was forested with thick greasy pubic curls. It curled and lapped on the air like a thirsty tongue. She saw with equal parts revulsion and titillation that it glistened with a sexual moisture in the dim light. She was revolted. She salivated. She hated her Bobby, who was no longer her Bobby and nor would he nor could he ever be hers again – a god of her own naïve and optimistic invention become an everyday whore and traitor.

She watched the tail stir on the air, mesmerized by the undulating patterns it wove: she hadn't even entertained that such a weapon might exist for her.

"I'm Angela. What's your name?" she asked distantly.

"Well, sometimes they call me Mister Filth, baby. Sometimes they call me the Big Old Big Dick. I'm always the Cheapest Trash Available If A Woman Needs It Bad Enough. I got an eternity of names, sugar-tits. What do you want to call me tonight, honey?"

He licked his swollen, smiling lips.

She told him without thinking about it at all.

"Revenge. You're my Revenge."

He turned about and faced her. His man-breasts swayed at the motion. His nipples had hardened and jutted towards her longingly like long brown bullets. The stink of him wafted from his immense cock and permeated her airspace. She reeled within its pungency. His testicles, bloated and shiny beneath their villous covering of ginger hair, appeared fit to burst. He proceeded to fall onto all fours. He shook himself in a queer, canine-like manner. He rippled everywhere. She examined his stout toes, yellow-nailed and hoof-like. Unlike his gauzy-haired pubis, prodigious back-hair carpeted him from shoulders down to buttocks. His wet tail wove an ever more excited language in the air.

Looking up at her from where his chin nearly grazed her bedroom carpet, he grinned his yellow grin.

His voice was eager, its pitch higher than ever. "*Angela*. In case you want to know the truth. My name's Angela, too. I got teased in school for it, but I'll prove I'm no sissy, honey. See? *See?* We're the same, you and me. We're so lucky to have found each other. A lot can happen on a dark road at night. We're so lucky we found each other."

Bile rose up in the first Angela's stomach. Her senses swooned. Through her revulsion the anger rose, parting it and making clear the path before her. Her nipples hardened. Her stomach turned. Her resilience hardened, too. She slipped a hand between her thighs, testing her wetness. She rose from the edge of the bed and went to the other Angela. He knelt closer to the carpet, draping his fat tongue across her calf. She clambered onto his back, sighed as he straightened himself and she was lifted from the carpet. The other Angela – snorting and bellowing like a great bull – pranced about the small bedroom with the first Angela straddling his bulk.

The first Angela felt a moist touch coil across her bare buttocks. She lifted herself from the other Angela's back, allowing the barbed-tipped tail to slip beneath her. She let herself settle on top of it. The tail explored her. It found her wetness. It slipped inside and settled deep inside her. The first Angela groaned. She cried aloud, louder than she used to permit herself during sex with her former lover of five years cut short. She screamed and howled like the animal without restraint she'd always been hesitant in allowing herself to become.

"Oh, Revenge…you feel *good*…"

The other Angela craned his neck and found the first Angela's eyes rapturously watching him. They locked feral glares and held on, and on, and on.

Bobby, seeing her handwriting on the large envelope he'd discovered tucked inside his mailbox, felt hope seize him. Perhaps Angela had found it in herself to forgive his callous, foolish ways. His apology – heartfelt and written in a flurry of desperation the day before – maybe, just perhaps, had found her heart of hearts and swayed her initial fury with him for his transgression and betrayal. Maybe she'd see him again. Maybe she could – one day – forget all of this.

He tore open the envelope and seated himself on the bed, his heart crashing madly.

He leafed frantically through the dozens of photographs of the hideous fat man fucking his once-girlfriend. Positions she and him had never tried, though he'd wanted to (asked her fervently on many occasions, in fact, but, frustratingly, never been able to cajole her beyond her bashfulness).

He realized then, while examining with revulsion the final photograph of the collection – his girlfriend of a half a decade crushed beneath the blood red-skinned bulk of the grotesque serpent, her mouth filled with its tail as if she were a link in some perverse Ouroboros, her eyes angry and defiant and staring directly into the camera lens with the beast's black forked tongue flicking beneath her eye as if emphasizing her resolve – just how beautiful she was, and had always, always been. Her hard, volcanic stare, utterly lucid as she looked out from the grotesquery, in this way showing that she remained miraculously untouched by the blasphemy crawling on her, but was ruined utterly inside by him and the crime he'd committed upon her.

Bobby replaced the photographs in the envelope and left it on the bed. He sat for several minutes in stunned silence. He thought about the different kinds of evil and wrongfulness living in the cracks of the world and sought to rank himself among them. He stood and crossed the room. He slipped into the bathroom and removed a naked razor blade from an old plastic shaver. He laid down in the bathtub and filled it with his blood.

Somewhere, a woman – broken but remade a queen – knew the truest and mightiest of closures while looking out from her new kingdom.

Christmas without you, mother
the longest dark this world ever knew

Invisible Girl:
I finally see you.

TWO BLUE EGGS
IN A SILVER DREAM

We're here. It's cold. We're warm. We're waiting. We've been waiting days and nights. It's the A.M. sometime. The only light is the moon through the window. Outside everything is white and blue and cold. Here, in the front room of the house that was our father's and mother's, it's cold. We're warm. We have each other. We have the promise in what we await.

We don't have neighbours for miles. It's a secluded area geographically. Black oak forest for miles on all sides. Thick in most places. The nearest road is far away and it's a backroad, little-frequented. This is of course the isolation father preferred. The power went out yesterday morning. The phone line is dead. We're more alone than we've ever been. Thinking of what's coming is made all the sweeter for these things.

Our old family was broken. Father without emotions. Mother his slave. His eyes clouded. Hers too, but differently. His eyes smouldered with fire behind the clouds. Hers with the life kidnapped from them. Stolen by his hands and words and the years of her enslavement to him.

My sister and I slaves, too. Until one week ago. My sister had no father, but a demon. He possessed her when he wanted. I had no father, either (we've always been alike in this way, she and I): he never saw me. Like an invisible sentience - a ghost - watching him in his life. How could a boy haunt his father when his father was the greatest haunter of all? I only ever watched him surreptitiously. From hidden places about the house. From beneath a desk or from within a closet while he sat in his chair or stood in his place, unmoving, overcast eyes watching the air about him or nothing at all. Brief glances from the corners of my eyes when we occupied the same uncomfortable dinner table.

Mother's blood we saw too much of. Dana's, too. My sister and I made our decision years and years ago, as very young children. We only owned the courage to act on it one week before. A lifetime of courage-building given birth one week ago. She'd crawled again from his cave of attentions and into the bed we shared. She'd cried. I held her. Our old ritual again. We were so weary of it. I've never been so tired of a thing. She said this then too: I've never hated something more than him. Father had become a thing of blackness.

We listened while he made mother scream. Her pain that night helped our plan. It was the breath that breathed into us: the courage-seed when we'd never felt it before. It was simple, our plan. It had always been simple, and but waiting for us to enact it. We followed it through like we'd discussed for ten years.

First father, in front of mother so that she could see and rejoice, once, in his fall. Two knives – long-bladed kitchen knives from the wooden block holder – in a simple but frantic series of deep cuts into his neck and chest. He was shocked by the courage we'd shown after years of Dana's enslavement and my unheard/unseen ghostliness. I think it may have been the very first time he saw me. I left my knife in him. It continued to shake in the air when he'd fallen and grown still. Dana kept her knife. It was red from tip to hilt. Her hands were covered with father, too. Mine were, too. To show my courage hadn't left me I took her knife from her and stabbed him for a while longer still. Maybe I wanted to prove to her that the evil was gone.

It had been sometime after midnight. The moonlight was silver in the kitchen where the demon had fallen. Mother was in the corner of the room. Crouched down. She wept. She had insane eyes. More this way than usual, as if part of her usual madness had been augmented by her new joy. She rocked on her heels where she crouched. Soon she was smiling: her joy made visible. Soon after that she was laughing. It was probably the first time we'd heard this from her. It was alien coming from her mouth. She crawled to him then. She examined him a while, smiling.

We gave her this joy, after her long slave-years. We drew up behind her. We made it quick. She was our mother. My knife's blade opened her throat quickly. The fount of her blood jetting told me I'd hit her jugular, as intended. Dana's knife she swept up and around to plunge into her chest. It's point bit into her left breast. She didn't cry out. She only fell over, seemingly dead before the dull sound of her temple cracking on the tiles sounded in the stillness. We cried. We dragged him from beside mother because she deserved a place far from him in her final rest. His red body we threw down the stairs. It rolled and became entangled in itself towards the bottom of the staircase. It rests there still, red and hateful and that much closer to Hell.

Dana and I held hands then. We did this until what had happened was made easier by it. Through our hands we told each other: we've done good. Now it's time for peace. Now the time had arrived to enjoy the peace we'd discovered existed long before but been afraid to embark towards. It was to be a great journey, after all. We laid our knives beside them. We left them, mother in the kitchen and father below, both dead but unfixed but at least dead. Mother free at last. Father dead and dead.

This was our old family.

Our new family promises us a different place: Peace. This is a place, we learned. A destination for those weary of the place into which they're born: peace. True peace without chance of savagery. It's location doesn't matter. The fact of its existence – away from all of this, from broken places and their broken people – is important. Salvation following a black dream of slavery. Peace. The name conjures its meaning in me, even now. I smile, now, where before I could only cry.

The memory of our meeting with our new family is the joy that beats my heart. I hear it crashing in my sister, too. Our joint heart keeps time in this small front room of the house where we sit huddled together before the window. Watching the wee morning sky scratched out by the woods of Black oak. They surround the house, the trees. They box us in, in a way that in the Old Family Time felt like imprisonment but now feels safe, warm. Free from the scrutiny of those who know nothing about our New Family. For those who – like demons and the slaves they've possessed and broken beyond repair – know nothing of peace. For those who know nothing at all about evil.

My sister had made our first call. She'd been all of eight years old. I, younger than her by a little over one year, believed in her powers. I'd concentrated as best I could, and called, too. This we did every night before the demon came to claim her from the room we shared. This we did upon her return, too, weeping and clutching at me. We called each night. We knew to do this, in our hearts. We knew. The moon through the bedroom window was the beacon. We made our voices soft but sure. We called and failed to reach its lunar remoteness. We called and failed to conjure any brightness into the deep night. Only the perpetual moonlight and starlight but no more.

One night – tears not yet dried upon our cheeks – our call was answered.

They came. The moon let them loose, or so it seemed. We went to them, outdoors. We spoke. They told us of Peace beyond the small aching place we knew. We believed for we had no reason to disbelieve. They'd come, after all, answering our call. They explained: the damaged but unbroken may come. The hopeless and destroyed must forever remain bound to the earth. We, though children, were resilient here. Our mother, bearing the brunt of father's savagery on our behalf, was broken by him. Her chance to achieve freedom ruined by him and the things he'd committed upon her and those things he'd made her witness.

We cried beneath their blue light. We understood. Their wisdoms made sense. We'd understood that mother had died long before, and only fought on for us. A hollowed vessel, emptied of what had made her mother long ago through the holes father had opened in her. We cried in their blue warmth. We promised to go with them. We asked if they would wait. They promised that a lifetime here was but a breath in the place from which they'd come. We promised. They echoed with their promise. We explained we would need time. Plans like this need time to hatch. We knew – even then, as children – that the courage required we didn't have. We asked them to wait. Their blue light grew bluer and warmed us in the frosty outdoors air.

We held each other. A brother and sister united by fear and the promise of a blue dream descended from a silver sky. When we opened our eyes they'd gone. Only the light of the night, beautiful but nowhere near as beautiful.

We kissed our hands and blew the kisses moonwards. We returned to our bedroom and when we slept our dreams were the same, and about a very different tomorrow coming.

"My egg is coming."

Her voice startles the silence. Listen to its echo: it calms me. My sister is blessed with an angel's voice.

"I see yours, too."

It's here with me again. The secret beauty of her, unheard by father or mother in the long years. I heard. I've been so blessed. I clutch her hand tighter. She gives me her smile.

We watch now as our eggs descend from the silver air, down between the maze of branches stirring in the yard. Their smooth blue skins gleam in the frost. Their wings move slowly, lazily, but land them gently. It's like a dream. We cry. We cry. We laugh. We laugh. She's opening the door. We're going to go to them now, arms open, to where they've set down in the front yard in a halo of silver celestial dust. It clings everywhere, the dust – in the branches, another skin dusting the snow-covered ground. It will blanket our hair and bank our arms and glimmer on our skin and clothes as we stand in rapture. A first taste of our rebirth.

She's looking back at me from the doorway. She loves me. She says this with her eyes and the tears in them. Her hand she's holding out towards me, waiting.

Our time has arrived. They're waiting. We go now. I must hurry. This long goodbye is finished, finally.

To Peace we go.

We love you, mother, and wish you the deepest rest from your long and terrible dream.

This enigmatic and unsettlingly incriminating cassette recording – the product, professional clinical consensus agrees, of a mentally unsound mind beyond the point of rationality following a prolonged incident of profound abuse and violence – was discovered in the home of Mr. and Mrs. Adam and Agnes Connell in Woodslee, Ontario.

Also found were the bodies of Mr. and Mrs. Connell, dead from a series of stab wounds to the neck and chest. Their children – daughter Dana and son Michael (the alleged narrator of the appended transcribed text) – were nowhere to be found and remain missing.

Neighbours dwelling in the quiet Woodslee hamlet reported no disturbances throughout the week of January 3 – 9, excepting one peculiar detail: Mr. Dan Davison, a retired schoolteacher living on the nearest property abutting the Connell's home on its western side, complained of being awoken in the wee morning hours of the 9th by the repeated flashing of a lightning storm, or 'something like a lightning storm'. Getting out of bed and looking through his window in an easterly direction he witnessed the strange weather phenomena for several minutes before returning to bed: a persistent lightning illuminating the sky and woods, without any accompanying thunder or precipitation. The most anomalous detail of this report lies in the improbability of such weather conditions having occurred at this time of year, a fact corroborated by the meteorological and weather service for the area, which reported freezing though precipitation-free conditions throughout the entirety of the week.

The incident remains unexplained at this time.

Watching the starfish fall
God was caught in the corner of your eye

FAR BENEATH
INCOMPLETE
CONSTELLATIONS

Another bird-dream bloomed:

They were surrounded, he and his lover: trees reminiscent in some respects to the Black oaks he knew so well from childhood, dark-barked and robust; but wildly different, too, and imbued with the awesome capabilities of dream-logic: immeasurably more colossal, these, rearing higher than vision could perceive, their weirdly voluptuous bodies bending impossibly towards them where they stood in the centre of the circular moon-washed glade, stout verdant arms opulent with leaf and fruit the likes of which he'd never seen on any species of oak before. In the unimpeded lunar light her face was clear where she stood at his side: her expression of excitement and joy for their forthcoming journey was a mirror of the emotions rampant in him, too.

Others were gathered there, as well, and though he sensed they were of a friendly and vaguely familiar nature he knew innately that he'd never actually met these individuals – nor anyone like them – before in his life. He strained his dreameyes to find them among the lunar-washed glade but always the surrounding foliage worked with the moonlight to cast deceptive and confusing shadow-speckles over the periphery of the clearing, where they lingered among the purple heather and wild grass, though certain details and attributes emerged: a plume of white flame held in the open hand of a shadow-shrouded figure; his neighbour clutching an immense alabaster jar high on the air before him; another figure holding aloft a lantern in one hand and in the other something that reflected the moonlight in a manner which served to deflect the illumination from the glowing taper within his lantern, keeping him obscured from sight amid this spectral lightshow; and another shadow-swathed individual clutched a long gleaming sword at his side while the figure hovering like a phantom beside him held aloft a white-petaled flower the wan colour of the moon.

Despite these queerly-illumined details it remained only he and his lover who were clearly visible, naked beneath the full moon's splendour for all to examine. Hands – of those convened in the forest reaching from the shadows, as well as the branches' knotted and leaf-swathed fingers reaching into the hollow space of the dell – touched them all over. These embraces he sensed were of a hybrid variety, representing both fond welcome and the bittersweet pang of goodbye, with something like pride communicated to them for his and her achievement: finding one another in the great and treacherous vastness of the world.

Other less savoury touches touched them, too, though: no less tangible for their non-physical aspect, he felt the eyes of the envious burning into his own, resenting them their joy, their good fortune, their imminent escape from these earthly ranks to a better, unsullied place. These disgruntled ones could be discerned as restless shadows moving behind the greater shadow-crowd, skulking among the density of underbrush, their ill-wishing eyes furtively beholding the pair at the centre of the celebration. He saw his lover's hazel eyes follow those furtive skulking shadows with trepidation. He squeezed her hand to assure her of their safety. Turning, she smiled for him, showing him her courage, though fear lingered in her gaze still.

In the distance, a sonorous murmuring, as of a giant grinding his teeth where he dreamed restlessly among the clouds.

The gathered revellers - and those sullen, moody watchers owning jealous eyes – turned together towards the west, eyeing the brooding sky: the lingering echo of thunder cascaded downwards to earth, and then the queer thought struck him that perhaps the clamour might have been some man-wrought instrument or happening of the present age which they all wished to escape: a descending bomb finding its target upon the earth – a sleeping house or speeding vehicle – or an explosion originating on the ground and erupting into the sky like some malefic fire spirit conjured to scorch the stars from their orbits.

He whispered his words into her ear, though all those gathered heard and rejoiced – clapping hands and cheering – in his eager bid for action: "Quickly, my love: we can beat the rain and the thunder! We can!"

She gave him a smile of confirmation. Before she could take his proffered hand, though, the dream darkened, and a murmur of warning stirred among those gathered. Turning, he saw: a rogue among the throng, his umbrage greater than his fellow detractors, had stepped from the moon-shadowed foliage into the glade's centre. He was clad in a ragged, plain earth-coloured tunic and sandals, and wore his hair long and dishevelled. He stood with legs braced wide, barring their path with his feral eyes, his gash of snarling mouth, the long dagger gleaming in his fist.

In a display of chivalry he stepped protectively before his lover, facing their assailant while thunder renewed its grumbling over their heads, beyond the leafy roof. The man, crouching low, slunk towards them with his bright gaze of death and envy.

Suddenly she clasped his hand. The strength in her grip: he marvelled at it, sure and protective. He turned to her: her mouth smiled. Her eyes were fixed on his with determination. Love filled them, and in this knowledge he rejoiced. He understood. He led her, the time for their departure arrived: they ran along the grass between the lines of their loved ones standing sentry on either side; some weeping joyfully, others clapping their hands in cadence to the steps she and he took upon the ground. They ran headlong towards their knife-wielding adversary advancing in defiance of their escape. Cries of encouragement rebounded from the dense thicket enclosing them, shaking acorns from branches even as the thunder boomed again in the west, doing the same, sending squirrels scrambling for their nests in abandonment of their late-day foraging and birds in bevies from theirs.

He felt her grip tighten yet more. Her little fingers growing stronger clutching his own, as if gaining strength through their embrace. Soon it was she who led their manic run. He followed in her wake. His heart bashed a song of joy behind his chest. They conjured a grass storm about them in their haste and vigour. Their collision with the death-dealing knife-wielder was imminent. He felt her pull away and upwards. He closed his eyes. He couldn't help the smile from spreading itself on his face: he felt his feet lifting from the grass. The cold breath across his bare leg was the keen edge of the blade slicing empty air, forever missing its opportunity to feed the old voracious world with his blood.

Goodbye, today: his dream-self thought this, and the relief flooding through him was like ecstasy as they rose up and up and up, like characters of myth ascending into their rightful and destined positions among incomplete constellations awaiting them like a final pair of celestial puzzle pieces. His lover's grip tightened and, with a remarkable strength he found that he'd always suspected her to possess, she drew him upwards to straddle her back. Now, though, he understood her altered nature: no longer petite of shoulder and narrow of waist, the girl was gloriously immense. Reaching for a handhold atop her arched back he realized he was gripping handfuls of silken softness: looking he saw her coat of feathers. Again, he was less startled by the revelation than he might have been, as if he'd known all along the girl's potential for such amazing transformation. Her coat was brilliant, a vivid crimson which seemed to push away the night through which they ascended. A colour of rebellion among the darkness, a fire of celebration racing starwards. He smiled, he laughed, he roared with gleeful abandon while his heart hammered joyously at the awesome spectacle of which he was blessed to be a part.

Looking about him he saw that they didn't fly alone: everywhere sailed the revellers, formerly occupying the forest shadows below and now transformed like she and borne aloft on great wings like hers. Like a fleet of gargantuan living ships they arced with grace towards the stars. Their colours were likewise brilliant: fiery crimsons and icy blues and gleaming emeralds, a veritable rainbow assemblage, the great murder of avian-like beings rising into the heavens. His great joy escalated at the sight. He laughed again. He spread his arms wide, gripping his lover's sides tightly with his bracing legs. This gesture elicited an immediate response from her: a sexual ripple coursing through her silk-soft body which in turn aroused him: a violent pulse awakened in his loins, echoed with the hammering in his temples and a frantic quickening of his heart.

The rushing nocturnal air was glorious on his face. The million stars waiting overhead grew larger as they rose swiftly. He yearned to touch their silver beauty with his hands, to complete the journey and be among them, to know them and be cradled by them after all of the indifference and dissatisfaction he'd known below.

Then: a great stabbing traveled through him, like lightning stretching its electrical fingers into his limbs and extremities. His fingers and toes and penis crackled with it, his vision exploded with it. Slowly he grew aware of the focus of this pain. He stared downwards and found the immense stone arrowhead protruding through his chest, primitively-sculpted with jagged edges, heavy with his blood, ragged with his shredded flesh. He was struck dumb with the surreal sight of it — so simple, so crude an element interrupting his majestic flight — the deadly weapon and the evidence of its passage through his ravaged body. He started at the series of violent thundering thuds: looking, he saw a half dozen arrows embedded in his lover's wings and, even as he watched in horror, another bevy sliced among these. An agonized shriek erupted from the great bird's black hooked beak, a horn's wailing dirge across the mantle of the sky. The chorus of hollow thundering erupting about them he knew to be the other flyers falling victim to the same violence – soon their song of pain rang across the heavens, too.

He understood: assassins among the trees, secluded in aeries upon the earth below, their hateful, envious aim true, succeeding in their simple desire of preventing their escape into hallowed places after their time served upon the earth. His lover the she-bird beat her wings frantically in her immense pain, striving to hold them aloft, though their fate was already sealed.

He reached a hand towards the brilliant pole star pulsing overhead, watched it recede quickly, quickly as they embarked on their violent descent, reclaimed by that most ordinary and savage of worlds. As they fell he felt two new points of pain: along his shoulder blades, a heartbeat-pulsing, a violent ache as of his flesh and bone erupting in the nascent stages of an orgy of transformation, as if trying futilely to birth wings like those of the surrounding host; which might save him and his lover from the earth drawing them inexorably unto itself.

But they only continued their fall, like stars expired and energy-less plummeting towards the nearest rock at hand.

He could feel her watching him with avid eyes where he was seated on the edge of the bed, stubble and fingers and subsiding erection glistening with her wetness. It was this intensity of her attention that had torn him from the pomp and pageantry of his post-coital dreaming: he turned away petulantly, embarrassed, so that his face was pointed towards the tiny window, though he only stared vacantly into the middle distance, dazed from their rabid sex, discomfited from sharing the aftermath silence with her, resentful for her scrutiny pulling him forth from his long and grandiose reverie. Perhaps the familiar vision would have concluded differently this time had she not disturbed it: he considered this idea briefly but knew, of course, that it wouldn't have.

The smell of their sex hung heavy in the air of the tiny room. Her books – both textbooks and the assortment of Japanese language paperback novels which made up the substantially smaller portion of her personal library which she'd brought from overseas – lay heaped about the room in crooked towers of varying sizes like some strange architectural schemata sprouting from the floor everywhere. The room's meagre assortment of furnishings – narrow bed; small wooden desk covered with papers and books and her laptop, open and humming a low murmur; and a single battered bureau that had come with the room – made him depressed. He closed his eyes to the wan sodium light of the single lamp fixture in the centre of the ceiling, and the stained walls, unadorned with pictures or posters or any other decoration which might serve to brighten the dismally austere squalor surrounding him.

From the opposite end of the bed came the soft sound of her stirring amid the nest of moist, crumpled sheets, freeing her small feet from the tangled fabric or wiping his semen from her thighs with an efficient hand.

Her name conjured exotic visions in his mind: Michi Samurakami, like a character of myth escaped from the ancient fairy-lore of her homeland and materialized like a miracle in his world. She was a student whom he'd met while waiting in the interminable line formed before the coffee shop in the student centre one early September morning just prior to the beginning of the academic day. The bustle of young men and women on their way to their classes had surrounded them, creating, conversely, a sort of bubble of closeness within which – in a matter of ten or so minutes – they had introduced themselves, chatted politely about inconsequential subjects, and grown to understand their mutual physical attraction towards one another. This attraction – intense, nearly violent in the way his appraisal of her that first morning immediately conjured vivid images of their copulation – he hadn't questioned, despite the unfamiliarity of his experiencing it towards a girl such as her. The overpowering nature of this attraction he came to realize only much later was, in fact, the same aspect of the girl which he loathed.

They'd left the building together to wander the campus aimlessly for perhaps another thirty minutes before deciding – at his urgent and unsubtle behest – to abandon their morning classes and spend the time together. Perhaps she'd been impressed by his willingness to shun responsibility for her, abandoning his students without much deliberation at all. It was then she'd surprised him by inviting him back to her nearby shabby rooming house room for the first time, in this way bringing full circle a happening which he'd not long ago aspired to as often a possible with as many women (and as many of his students in particular) as possible, and which was evidently for her a wholly new – and therefore exceedingly frightening – experience. He'd felt a certain fear, too, having never been with a non-Caucasian woman and finding, in his unexpected, quickly-flowering attraction to her, that he'd never experienced something as fierce and all-consuming with anyone before in all of his unsatisfying, doomed-to-fracture relationships.

The rustling from beside him on the bed, he knew, was the girl kicking away the bed sheets entirely. Her smell came to him, her subtle perfume like cinnamon, mixed with her sex. The elixir of her stirred his senses. He sensed the beginning of arousal once again.

He considered their first time together: a violent tremor had seized her, running the course of her entire body as he held her in the room, kissing her mouth and neck and shoulders while he unbuttoned her shirt and slipped it from around her. He'd been successful in calming her during these initial embraces, if not his own anxieties, a feat which served to excite him in a way he'd never before then experienced – whispering soothing logic into her ear concerning the fortuitous or preordained circumstances by which they'd met, two people from opposite corners of the world happened to convene in a student centre in a long line of strangers; as well as the acceptable nature of what they were about to do, two lonely people who felt a rare and difficult-to-define connection. These things he whispered to her while admiring her delicate hands and arms with a pair of fingers tracing their curvatures, while wrapping his lips for the first time around each of her dark brown nipples in turn, while drinking in the fragile and unique look of this dainty girl relinquishing herself into his increasingly urgent affections, making her short emphatic cries while he revelled in the success of his casual duplicity.

They'd known each other for approximately one month, and he'd visited her in her home nearly every night in that time; hastening from his classes or abridging his office hours, followed by a reckless drive from the campus to this rooming house and this room in it which she rented for the simple reason that the funds bestowed on her by her family had been nearly exhausted by the high costs of tuition and textbooks, and what remained was enough to pay for nothing more elegant. Never before had he been so driven in something, neither academically nor socially. He'd considered the peculiar notion several days into their relations, while performing cunnilingus on the girl: it was as if he were possessed, by the physical shell of the girl, so incredibly, indefinably attractive to him, as well as by the idea of her representing for him some new, unexplored thing. And, after all this time of their inseparability, it was only of late that the reasons for his overwhelming attraction to – and paradoxical loathing of her – had begun to grow apparent to him.

He started at her voice – timorous, as delicate as the rest of her – disturbing the uneasy silence and his troubling meditations. "Maybe we can go to restaurant somewhere close, and eat dinner now? Are you hungry, Michael? It is almost seven o'clock." The idea of a human voice infiltrating the deep quiet that had settled over the room following their vociferous lovemaking seemed improbable. After what they'd done together it seemed as if every element of the world should be too weary to produce even the smallest of sounds. In the wake of the disturbance he found himself shaken, unable to respond at all.

She'd been speaking to him more and more, a fact which threatened his uncertain peace in no small way. The past week she'd been relentless, in her quiet, timid way, in seeking to cajole him into reciprocating her small wishes and greater desires, this latter of which seen in each of the requests she made that they spend time together outside of their brief and frantic couplings. He mumbled something vague, the very sound of his voice epitomising the fragile armour of excuse-making. This gave him cause to consider the fact that he felt no difficulty in speaking to her while they were having sex; his voice a constant droning murmur while he spoke words he'd always wanted but had never been bold enough to utter with his other sex partners throughout the years.

Her accent, endearingly thick in the first days he'd known her – incredibly sexy still while she spoke to him as he fucked her, encouraging him to continue his own lewd soliloquies – now, in the aftermath of sex, unnerved him; in some ways, even repulsed him; so foreign to the sound of his own voice speaking the language, its timbre and inflection of the words she spoke. He flinched at it, was made discomfited by it, both by its sound as well as for what his reaction said about himself. And yet he felt a distant but growing sense of relief seep its way into him, too: this secret he kept – her, and their relations – belonged to him and no other. Neither his few professional acquaintances nor family knew the girl existed. Few strangers even had seen them together, being that he'd been successful in stifling her wishes that they take their relationship outside of the sex-room and into the social sphere of restaurants, as now, and bars and coffee shops and theatres and groceries and shops. He'd likewise managed to keep to a minimum the evening walks she enjoyed taking, through the abutting park and surrounding streets, unfrequented by much pedestrian traffic, though on the few occasions when he'd relented they'd encountered small groups of students from the nearby university, making him uncomfortable and embarrassed, as if he'd been found out in the midst of some shameful, morally wrongful activity. She'd asked him once, whether he was afraid of trouble arising from his liaison with a student, to which he'd readily assented only to be left stymied with her next simple question: "But we are adults, Michael, who care for each other – there can be nothing wrong in this. Am I right?"

In response to his silence now, her voice came again, plaintive: "Are you hungry, Michael? It is very late now. Maybe we can go to Emerald Tiger. It is my favourite restaurant to eat, and only few minutes' walk from here. I have not eaten dinner yet." He wanted to silence her but lacked the courage or cruelty or strength to do so. Instead, he only shrugged noncommittally and reached for his clothes scattered on the floor at his feet.

The girl was persistent today. "Please. Michael. *Please?* Why you not want have dinner with me? Why you always not do these things with me?"

"What do you mean? I don't know what you mean," he stammered, fumbling with his underwear entangled among the legs of his pants turned inside-out. Anxiety made jelly of his fingers, which he seemed unable to make work quickly or deftly enough.

He momentarily managed to extricate the garments, and was pulling his underwear on when her voice returned, a mournful beseeching in the anxious stillness. "I am hungry, Michael."

Where are the birds: this thought flew into his agitated thoughts, filling him with longing. Snatching his suit jacket from the edge of the bed he stumbled on uncertain legs towards the door, muttering over his shoulder, "I have term papers to mark. A mountain of them. Maybe next time. I'll see you soon. Tomorrow: I'll see you then."

Closing the door behind him, he caught a fleeting glimpse of her within: seated on the bed, naked still, her petite round shoulders and small breasts luring his attention, eyes watching him with an expression of wilful patience, as if her intention was to wait for him in exactly this posture until their next scheduled rendezvous, forsaking any and all commitments she may have to school, to work; using the bait of her nakedness to bring about his return, which she certainly knew to be the most potent means of ensnaring him again.

Then the door was shut, though the image of her burned in his eyes: her nipples like dusky coins, the thick triangle of her moist pubic hair which she unabashedly flaunted, her pouting lips and the ghost of their taste lingering on his own. He stood in the hall for a moment, fighting his growing desire to return to her and fuck her again, but soon enough forced his sluggish steps away and onto the moon-washed street where – despite his lingering arousal, the maddening tingling in his groin and fingertips and toes – he began to feel somehow cleansed.

A shadow darkened his warm yellow lamp-lit work space. Turning he found her owning the doorway to his office, hair newly auburned and eyes as piercing as ever.

"Michael, hard at work. This seems to be the version of you I've been finding of late." Her voice assured like he'd always known it to be.

He leaned back in his chair, squealing its frame. Feeling luxuriously at ease with this woman who'd once intimidated him in so many ways, he said, "Hello, Deborah. What brings you to my dark corner of the hallway?"

He examined her openly, a close perusal of her from top to bottom. He immediately remembered her during sex: the smell of her; her impassioned cries, boisterous but in an unsubtly calculated way, as if she'd decided long ago with some former lover on how best to articulate the physical sensations of having sex in the most suitably sensual way; the way she preferred riding him while only rarely allowing him to be on top of her, clutching his head to her breasts so that he'd suckle them as she came. As commanding in bed as she was out of bed. In recalling her in these ways, a great relish flooded his senses. He found that he was smiling, and judging from the uncertain and mildly vexed expression on Deborah's face, assumed that his enigmatic demeanour unsettled her.

Shrugging off his peculiar reaction to her she entered the office, sullying the room's smell of rich mahogany with her redolent perfume. She ran a finger the length of the bookshelf owning one wall, her words dripping with spurious weariness, "I'm finished teaching for the day, thank God. It's been a long one. I can't wait to get home, and have a long shower, and wash this day from me. And I'm *starving*. I could devour an entire menu whole. Have you eaten?"

He shook his head. He waited, enjoying the discomfited expression which stole over her when he neglected to make the overture she expected and hoped for. When she turned away from him to the book-lined shelf before her he said, "I've got to be somewhere this evening."

She didn't answer, only continued her perusal of the myriad books and academic journals cramming the shelves. Then, "We're not getting any younger, are we, Michael?" She'd said it in a wistful way while turning to examine the framed photograph adorning the wall, several years old, that captured the two of them, side by side with their colleagues in the English department, in attendance at a gala commemorating the retirement of a mutual friend. He understood the undercutting nature of the comment, though, being that she looked exceedingly good for her age (nearly a decade his junior with the looks of a woman younger even than this), aware of the grey in his hair and the crow's feet around his eyes and his increasingly distressing paunch of middle age. But he only smiled ruefully as he denied her. "Sorry, Deborah. I'm busy this evening, and every other this week." He felt a thrill in denying her in so veiled a manner, thinking of his secret life with the wondrous Michi Samurakami, revelling at the visions of this clandestine liaison materializing in his mind while he spoke with his colleague.

"I see." Deborah straightened from where she'd blessed his desk corner with her buttocks. From before the doorway she asked him in a casual voice: "Who is she? A student again? Secretary? Which department have you invaded now?"

He only shrugged and offered her a quizzical expression he was pleased to note irritated her further. He examined her carefully, seeing only Michi Samurakami waiting for him in her bed, naked; different than Deborah in every conceivable way; his. He hadn't felt strong like this since his youth, long, long buried by the years.

"Well, there certainly is *someone*, Michael, for you to deny me." Her outward haughtiness may have been restored, he mused, but certainly her secret pride continued to suffer. He watched her exit the office in a stride certain to attract the interested eyes of faculty and students alike, then returned his attention to the papers drowning his desk, only to see her like a relentless apparition bent on driving him mad with her hauntings:

Michi Samurakami, naked and vibrantly wild in how she bent to his unrestrained will and whim and, in so doing, helped him to achieve what he'd never experienced with anyone else: true, *true* ecstasy. A moment later he returned his attention to the papers spread on the desk before him, and his breath caught inside him.

There, in the centre of the desk, shivering excitedly at his subtle motion: the long brilliant crimson feather.

She was waiting for him in the doorway later that afternoon as he ascended the filthy staircase of threadbare carpet and stained walls, standing partway into the unkempt outer hallway. Her face radiated its customary joy, as misplaced as ever, as if she waited for and expected much more from him than he ever gave her. He smiled curtly, sensing as he did so the inadequate nature of the gesture, its feeble insincerity when greeted by her own genuine exuberance. He came to stand directly before her, wearing a stern look of expectation, in a manner which firmly suggested that they enter the room together. She neither budged nor ceased her disconcerting, inscrutable appraisal of him, leaving him standing there nervously, drinking in her simple smell: soap and cinnamon and the faint underlying odour of her perspiration. It was a maddening odour, different from that of other women he knew – all of whom seemed always steeped in layers of differing cloying perfumes, as evinced only hours earlier by Deborah's malodorous appearance – as all things about Michi Samurakami were different from others. His progress into the room impeded, he was forced to speak to her.

"Should we – Do you want to go inside for a while?" He knew, of course, that she knew his meaning, as she always knew his simple desires too well. He knew, also, of course, that her desires lay elsewhere at that moment.

Still smiling, she said in a voice airy and unperturbed, "Sun is shining today. Can we go for walk somewhere please?" He saw for the first time the bright floral-patterned handbag she wore slung over a shoulder; her bright green sandals and toenails newly painted a matching glistening emerald; her likewise matching green cotton skirt and clean white collar shirt he'd only ever seen her wear at school. She hadn't obeyed his usual wishes to await his arrival clad in nothing but her old bathrobe and pink plush slippers, the teasingly scant outfit which spoke to his innate preference for disrobing her in what he considered her "around-home" or "before-bed" outfits (in his lewd thinking he likened this to the girl being in her natural habitat while he, visiting her, explored and conquered both her and her world).

He feigned a smile, sighed and in the sigh felt all of his great disappointment coalesce into a simple and robust fury directed at her for daring to delay his intentions and expectations with her. As he allowed her to close the door before them, his roiling emotions were overcome with another: and with this tremendous sense of loss filling him and making him nauseous, he could momentarily do nothing but follow her – with bowed posture and reluctant steps – into the sun, feeling quite as if she'd locked them out from the rarest of Paradises.

He wrenched the light shirt from around her shoulders, exposing her soft skin beneath with its abraded designs of fading bruises – encircling her bicep like a purple gauntlet, darkening her forearms, and blood blisters spotting her neck where his feral bite had found and drank of her – evidence of their previous night together; thinking as he did: this is my reward. Here it is. Here it is.

They'd only just returned to her room and already he was manhandling her the way he liked, the way she'd grown accustomed to and accepting of early into their relations. He sought to expunge the agonizingly uncomfortable hour past, and found that this was the only way to do so: wandering the streets of the neighbourhood and idling minutes away in the small park which abutted the building's rear lot. His discomfiture had grown the longer they'd remained in public, with the potential of encountering other early evening walkers who would see him with her, and judge him the way he might likewise judge a man he saw sharing the company of a girl like her. Once, a pair of students, a couple close in age, similarly Aryan with blonde hair and pale creamy skin, wandered past them where they shared a bench beside the narrow cement path which cut from one end of the park to the other. The smiles this young man and his lover had smiled he understood were benign, a well-meant pleasant wordless greeting, and yet it had birthed anger in him, and shame. He'd shrank from Michi Samurakami's gentle touch, become annoyed with the expression of disappointment that fell over her features; as if she was the more responsible of the two of them for this downward spiralling of their time together.

They hadn't spoken for many minutes thereafter, and when they had, it was he uttering a few conciliatory words to her because they'd drawn within sight of the rooming house and he feared her resistance to his desires underneath the pall of their dismal mood.

With a viciousness apparent to him even through his great lust he peeled her sandals off each of her feet by carelessly stepping on her heels with his own shoe-shod feet, scraping her skin and eliciting a startled cry from her. A hard shove between her shoulder blades sent her sprawling across the kitchen countertop. She stood rigid, trembling in anticipation of him, allowing him to unzip her and tear the skirt from her legs. He could smell her excitement and her fear, this new elixir of her clouding out the kitchen around them.

"Fucking stay bent over," he seethed in her ear as she turned towards him, the inexplicable rage overcoming him again. She obeyed, letting him spread her legs further, her little feet clinging to the tacky linoleum while he stepped from his pants and underwear.

He fixed his gaze on her buttocks as he thrust into her, making her shriek. He felt them with his large hands, squeezing them and running his fingers along the cleft between them. He then turned his attentions to her breasts, pinching her nipples savagely and renewing her tortured ecstatic cries. He imagined her in the moment as he'd imagined her every time they'd been together: no girl, she, no student from overseas studying biology in a Canada she sought desperately to understand as she likewise sought to fathom him, too; no girl at all, more exotic a creature entirely, a cobbled-together gestalt beauty of various fantastical minutiae: parts culled from the rich myth of her culture, the wickedness of the folkloric oni sprite merged with the mischievousness of the fox mingled with the magical wisdom of a fairy spirit; overruled by that most ancient and beauteous of deities, the shape-changing avian goddess dwelling within the simple sensual shell of the girl. All of this which he was blessed to posses in every way: a slave to his every whim and will; for him to own and act out desires upon, however dark and perverse and depraved and shameful, however much he would never ever reveal them into the world and to the people he knew who lived unaware of the molten underworld of his mind.

Her cries then as ever were shrill, pained, and carried within them a profoundly alien quality; so utterly alien to the cries of passion he'd elicited from other women, whose sexual language always communicated a pleasure entirely divorced from true, unmitigated release; nearly inhuman, he reasoned, and it was through this logic, as ever, that he allowed himself to fuck her with perfect abandon, to speak the wanton words into her ears that he always did while in no way considering her feelings or what she might think of his most recent transformation from distant, moody man to brutal user of her amazing physical shell. "You... My... Little... Fuck... Animal...You're... Mine... All...Mine... Oh... My... God... What... Are... You... Doing... To... Me..."

It was then, not long after he'd fallen into the rapid cycle of pummelling her madly, that the divine-moment came in more profound a manner than he'd experienced it before, and the door to his ecstasy lay opened: he saw her wings unfurl from two apertures until then invisible atop the smooth curving hills of her shoulder blades; witnessed them bloom violently upwards in a surge of pastel emerald and brilliant crimson feathers which thrashed and fluttered a frantic wind into his face; the wind they made was a hot one, a scorching gale that burned his cheeks and chest like a desert storm, and sent a heated pulse throbbing through his erection. As her cries rose in volume and reciprocal bliss these wings beat a faster windstorm, urging bellowing cries from him, too, and quickening his journey towards his own orgasm like a rebirth into a new, unprecedented cosmology known to only a select and blessed few.

*

He awoke sometime in the bottomless miles of the A.M. He lay rigid, searching for what it was that had disturbed his slumber. He heard it coalesce from the indefinable pulse of the night, drifting into the sex-room through the ajar window beside the bed: music. A songbird's nocturnal hymn blessing the darkness, the moonlight, the stars like winter suspended in the sky. He thought faintly how misplaced the delicate song was among the ghetto of shabby houses and rundown tenements lurching into the street, like cold water seeking to cleanse a wound of irreparable damage and infection run amok.

He smiled within the soothing melody of its sermon to the night, in weird rhythmic harmony with the girl's breathing beside him. A sense of peace stole over him, making him drowsy and luring him into dreams again.

They flew atop the roof of clouds, he the rider, she the great but delicate-boned creature beneath him, around which he clamped his strong legs tightly. Her transformation here complete: no vestige of her former form remained, that shell submerged beneath her new beauty: long-winged, razor-taloned, curved of beak, black-eyed with the moon reflected wetly in each immense and bottomless orb. Her plumage brighter than he'd ever seen it, a vivid crimson that fired the twilight through which they sailed, a beacon drawing the envious eyes of those whom they were leaving crawling far below in their small lives of little worth. Little bits of foliage and other floral debris drifted from his hair and from where they'd gathered among his mount's feathers when they'd burst through the dense forest roof, sailing downwards like confetti celebrating their remarkable ascension.

He spoke, without words, and she, of course, heard him in deep places.

I can live like this for the rest of my life. Like this, I want to live forever.

The mighty beating of her wings stirred a warm and reassuring wind to envelop him: in its embrace his recent troubled thoughts and self-doubts – remote now, barely credible at all – slipped finally away into darkness and freefall.

They grazed the constellations as they arced against the twilight's indigo sky, rising higher, higher.

But: a murmuring among the clouds, like a great voice of danger in the twilight. It grew and grew and then gave birth to a dozen gargantuan steel birds sailing forth from the indigo depths. Machines ugly in shape and brutal in purpose, the murder of bombers of a type he felt he'd seen before somewhere, perhaps in books or in documentaries chronicling one of the World Wars. They were gargantuan, blotting out the promise of the celestial light with a completeness that chilled him. Beneath their great shadow he felt all of his hope and peace crushed. These immense machines in turn birthed their children into the night: lines of bombs hatching from their bellies and arcing towards them on all sides.

Then, a great thunder roared in his dream, swallowing his peace entirely; smiting them down from their lofty ecstasy with its mighty bellowing, two frenzied fuck animals plummeting earthwards within a resounding dirge of agony.

He awoke sweat-bathed and with his heart crashing like thunder. He was delirious from the dream and confused as to his surroundings until the memory of his homebound drive returned, of collapsing into bed without thought, too weary from his time in the sex-room to attempt completing his lesson plans for the following day's lectures. He was gripping his erection. A pulse of excitement thrummed in its glans. He stroked himself, slowly but building gradually into a violent manipulation of the member. He abandoned his efforts when the vision of her that had followed him from his dream – silhouetted against the sky, wingspan prodigious and feathers blood-red – became too vivid, too maddening, making him understand the paltry and insufficient nature of his masturbation.

Throwing an overcoat around himself; snatching his keys from where they hung on a nail beside the door, heedless of his briefcase sent crashing to the floor from the tabletop in his haste, his cache of lecture notes scattering across the tiles; scrambling to his car parked in the driveway; racing through the deserted A.M. streets to the little rooming house on the opposite side of the city; slipping into her room using the key she'd given him as a show of her devotion to their relationship; startling her as he crashed into bed with her and lapped his tongue across her lips, cheeks, neck and, tearing wide her nightshirt, wetting her breasts; moving downwards to her vagina, lavishing his attention there until her dry lips grew moist.

Her cries grew quickly from frightened and alarmed to rapturous. In their clamour he felt himself lifted away.

He woke when dawn limned the window in red. As his sleep-dazed senses sobered he felt her observation of him. He found her watching him from directly beside him, the lower portion of her face hidden within the crook of her bare arm. Her eyes were haunted and unwavering, and unnerved him. Though he couldn't see her mouth her words fell clearly in the great morning quiet.

"I love you, Michael."

He shivered. He felt somehow that he was being tested. That much more depended on his response than merely the girl's satisfaction that her feelings were reciprocated. Uncertain how to reply – confused with conflicting feelings of awakening revulsion and lust towards her naked beside him – he saved himself the only way that seemed possible. He clamped his eyes shut, hoping fervently that whenever he dared to reopen them the vision of her would be gone, only another dream fragment vanished into the ether of the forthcoming day.

It was following his awkward, embarrassingly slapdash lecture to a class of a dozen bemused graduate students that he'd decided to make of her an experiment: Deborah the challenger, disputing the reign of the mysterious Michi Samurakami. She'd found him brooding in his office and he'd relented to her unsubtle proposition – the second in as many days while visiting his office to pass the time with some small talk before her final class for the day – ostensibly a dinner date, which saw them return to his home and make immediately for the bedroom.

356

Of course, she failed to usurp his secret girl's mastery over his waking and dreaming life, despite her meaninglessness to him, despite his emotionless fucking of her. Despite her alluring body, long-legged, big-breasted, full-hipped. This he considered while examining Deborah's long slender calf gripped between his fingers, his erection growing limp inside her. She stared at him curiously, waiting expectantly, looking luxurious with her dark auburn hair billowing freely about her supple shoulders. When he pulled himself from her and moved to sit on the edge of the bed she mistook his silence for shame, and gave him her cruel words in a malicious effort at dealing his pride a killing stroke.

"It's okay, Michael. Don't fret about it too much now: it happens to all men, sometimes." The smile she smiled was spitefully pleased. She relished his would-be indignity.

She only ceased smiling when he said, "But it's you. Deborah: it's *you* that aren't enough for *me*." And he laughed at the expression of defeat and doubt that stole over her.

"You're pathetic." Her voice was a knife cutting through the darkness, though its aim was far from true. He only laughed with greater scorn and triumph. It was his turn to revel in her weakness. He found it felt exhilarating, wrecking her lifelong supremacy over him and all men.

"I'm leaving. Are you driving me or am I walking home all the way across the fucking city?"

"Yes," he told her. "You'll be walking home. You could never fly, Deborah. Not ever."

He rejoiced at her stunned eyes, the revulsion and alarm filling them. He glimpsed something like dread there, too, and he relished having birthed it there. He watched her storm off, high-heels swinging dangerously in a vicious hand, humiliation altering her usual walk, devouring its haughtiness, her assuredness that the woman she'd always known herself to be was a godsend to all men.

Mostly, though, he felt only a great exhilaration at the idea filling him, that he stood at the edge of a mystery whose solution would yield him a fulfillment for which he'd always yearned but – until now – never come close to attaining.

He dressed hurriedly and remembered only when he was driving towards the enigmatic Michi Samurakami that he'd forgotten to lock the door to his house after him. He slowed, but sped onwards a moment after. If all went as he hoped, he would never return to simple rooms like these again.

Another vision like a revelation of the universe's secret potential:

A long line of them winding downwards from among the stars.

The glimpse was brief but delicious: a world un-guessed to most, existing within the fibres of the everyday but known seemingly to him and her alone.

He looked out upon it, squinting in the bright sunlight, for the sun shone perpetually in this place, though occasionally the moon, too, though always with just as much brilliance: a grand colony, a colossal mothernest housing them all:

Seraphs, or the closest thing to them to exist in the universe, or in any imaginable place or place beyond comprehension. Like some undiscovered Mesozoic stop-gap, or an un-guessed future step on the evolutionary plain which would see a marriage between avian and human matrixes to unveil a beautiful hybrid structure and physiognomy; a feather-coat lush and healthy, married to the basic bipedal human form, though its limbs much less cumbersome and unwieldy, boasting a delicacy of bone structure, a buoyancy and aerodynamic grace wholly absent from the former; blessed also with wings and the dream-like capabilities of flight into impossible places: beyond clouds, past stratosphere, and into the furthest places between stars where Heaven or the closest thing to Paradise might lie. Weird-tailed, too, lush with feathers yet serpentine and long, muscular and coiling, as if flaunting some impossible antediluvian trait representing a point at which their evolution diverged yet further from origins begun equally with Archaeopteryx and ancient Stone Age man.

And she among them like a humble and benevolent queen: his little Michi-bird, air-dancing with a grace and aplomb beautiful to behold.

His dream-pulse quickened at the sight of her in her crimson glory, like fire licking the stars. His dream-heart thundered.

Perhaps he loved her after all.

*

"Michael?" from afar, muted as if filtering through a membranous wall separating the realm of deepest, deepest sleep from some far less sacred place.

No.

Revulsion began its measured seeping into him once more as, drawn forth from the dream-place by her voice of concern, he focused on the physical shell of her in the aftermath of their lust: the petite Asian girl with boyish hips and small breasts and slender legs, hair bedraggled, skin coated with a sheath of sweat that glistened in the moon-washed room.

He pulled himself out in time to shoot a residual burst of semen across her small buttocks, found that he possessed enough lingering lust to emit a final jet of ejaculate onto the madly fluttering wings themselves. He watched entranced as they folded in upon themselves, retreating into her flesh in a violence just as quick and startling to behold as their emergence, as if his semen were a murdering acidic agent urging their accelerated demise. He stared at her body while his senses, flooded with the madness of their time together, returned gradually to a more neutral state. The lingering vestiges of his latest dream-immersion faded. The squalid walls and tiles of the apartment returned.

Despite his encroaching lucidity he yet entertained the mad notion that perhaps he'd truly witnessed the physical manifestation of transformation in her a moment ago. Maybe she was beautiful after all, despite the bewitching shell of her that he simultaneously worshipped and abhorred.

Then, in the moon colour and immense stillness, the girl's laboured breathing arrived in his awareness, drawing him fully awake. He realized the lateness of the hour, the frenzy of this most recent possession that had transported him so deeply into the bliss of their sex. In the aftermath of it, while they both dressed themselves by the moonlight, her voice came, small and pathetic with gratitude: "Thank you for eating supper with me yesterday, Michael. Maybe we will do this again sometime."

He winced at the words, and at what they revealed about them both: her achingly saddening manner of settling for whatever scraps of superficial affection he deigned to give her; and his own shameful and selfish and repulsive ways. He looked to her, but quickly away: her smiling lips and eyes, victim of his deception, were difficult to behold with the feral energy of his lust temporarily depleted.

She followed him behind the wall of his closed eyes, though, smiling and smiling as if she were content, and this contentedness, it felt to him, was like a dangerous magnetic force luring his humanity forth from the its buried place within him.

He pulled his shirt over his head, desperate to be away from her unnerving presence. Seeing this, she whispered imploringly, "Michael. Please stay with me tonight. You do not have to go away. You always go away when you are finished with me." There was no accusation in her matter-of-fact voice, though he knew of course that she would be completely just in accusing him. Shaking his head in a futile denial of her claim, he muttered, "I don't know what you mean."

"Yes," she wore on, her voice now carrying a distinctly beseeching – and increasingly annoyed – note. "Yes, Michael. Yes you know my meaning. Please tell me, okay? I want to know from you – why do you like me? You always see me, every day, but you will not talk to me, ever. You come, and you go soon after we are together, and you never say very much to me. Why do you come? What things do you like about me? Do you… I… I need to know from you… Maybe do you…love me?"

A brief arrival of courage or boldness overcame him, despite the tremor of unease he felt at hearing her words. In the softest voice of consolation he could muster, he said, "I don't. I…I don't love this part of you." He gestured a vague yet all-encompassing hand towards her. "This shell - I don't even…*love* it at all. I only love…*using* it. *Devouring* it. I'm sorry, but it's true. But what's inside…What's *inside* you: I'm under its spell." In the wake of this admission a great shame washed over him. Shame, and a kind of stunned resignation, because in that rare moment of honesty with the girl and with himself he'd for the first time allowed his true character to speak its voice. Disappeared was his elaborate and ostentatious world-making, evaporated into the ether of its own opulence.

He dared to look at her, unfiltered through the lens of his myth-making. She was frowning, pouting with a child-like audacity, while despair haunted her eyes. Sensing his appraisal she hid her face from him by engaging in a mock inspection of her bright bag resting on the floor beside her. Her perspiration-glistening body beautiful to behold, her strange eyes riveting, too, and frightening for the emotions they contained, as well as their quiet but unmitigated intelligence: the most exquisitely alien, unknowable animal he'd ever seen.

A moment later she was slipping into her vivid green- and orange-striped underwear while abstractedly watching the sky framed in the little window overlooking the street. Still looking away from him, she said in a nonchalant tone, as if meaning to sound offhand but the tremor in her voice revealing her teetering emotions, "You do not mean that."

He thought of the many people – all strangers – whom he would pass while en route from this girl's rat-infested apartment of squalor, through the city's downtrodden downtown centre where harried-looking businessmen and clerical staff mingled with the homeless and otherwise lost; and finally to his own reasonably upscale apartment on the east side of the city. He considered these nameless individuals, men and women of varying economic status and with differing physiognomies: he didn't hate them, was not repulsed by them: he simply felt nothing for them. A hollowness, as if they could never hope to elicit emotion of any variety from him. He felt, he realized, dead inside.

Except when he flew in the breathtakingly surreal dreams she gave him.

He looked again to the girl where she huddled naked on the floor at his feet, gathering her scattered clothing. Her little bare breasts gleamed in the ugly sodium light. Her little feet, emerald nail polish glossy and bright, were like pretty ivory sculptures. The rolling contour of her upper thigh becoming her buttocks drew his attention. Her small hands clutching her skirt before her small knees were a delicate sculpture of prayer, like a depiction of worship of their copulation. Her pale skin made him hunger for her anew, its smoothness like water to satisfy his insatiable thirst for her. He imagined the smell of her, and the cries she cried each time he visited her and used her as he needed, or else risk his hunger grow when unanswered and inevitable madness overtake him.

He yearned for these aspects of her all over again – and to ascend along the pathway to elsewhere that she provided – but felt nothing more.

He reached a hand to her round small shoulder. Her warmth electrified his cold fingers. He left it there, squeezing subtly. She turned her eyes on him for the first time in many minutes – large, wide, crying, painfully hopeful – and in this way gave herself to him again.

He had her again. Straddling her he made her scream again. He held her ankles while fucking her and shooting his semen into her again. Slipping his erection from her he then crawled over her and inserted it in her mouth. She gagged. He watched her pleading eyes while saliva and semen dribbled from the corners of her mouth. He left her gasping for air on the bare floorboards, pulling his clothes on hurriedly and shambling, half-clothed, towards the door.

Amid her sobbing, cutting-words, slicing through the thick air with their pathetic fiction.

"You…like me. You *like* me."

The words came without thought. "Sometimes I think you might be an angel."

Her response came quickly, and with a certainty and gentleness which shocked him, as if she sought to deliver him a harsh lesson in the softest manner possible. "Maybe there is no such thing, Michael. Maybe you must accept me as who I am."

The words, brimming with a quiet desperation, stung him as he hovered in the doorway. Turning and giving her his profile so that his words could be heard but so their eyes wouldn't meet, he murmured, stunned at the revelation he gave to her as if it was an epiphany to him, too: "I like…I love…I love your body. Every single inch of it. The taste and the touch and the smell of it. If I could, I'd live on it, and inside of it, so I'd never be away from it. But… But that's all you are. A perfect… A perfect shell. A perfect animal. But you're inhuman to me."

This was all the truth he could give her: she, to him, was the world, and though the world in which he lived was rife with the beauty of things to be touched it held no more than this. Beyond the dream of her, there was nothing but flesh. In the wake of this confession that she'd wrung from him the emotion blossomed violently:

He loathed her anew. He told her: "I hate you for this. For what you do to me. I don't want to be seen with you. I don't want a single person in the world to know about the things we do together. And yet I've never wanted something so badly." He was pointing to her. The vulgarity of the gesture became magnified when he realized he pointed to the dark triangle of her crotch. He then gestured angrily about the small room, signifying it, and the greater world of the everyday which it epitomised. "In all the world, of everyone and everything I've ever known, I've never wanted something so much. So much that it *burns*. So much that I want to devour it, eradicate it, because maybe if it's dead and gone forever I can find peace from it."

She watched him unwaveringly through her crying eyes. When she spoke her voice was even and measured. "I know your word for this, Michael. You are...*racist*. This is you. You are *racist* against me. You hate me because you are frightened of what you do not know. And if you are racist against me then there is nothing I can do to change you. *You* must change. *You* must change or you will not find this place you always speak of." Her voice rose then into a pleading timbre which unsettled him. "It is a *beautiful* place, Michael, this place you dream. It is up to you if you wish to make it real place. You must believe me."

He knew in that moment, of course, that she was absolutely correct about him, and his xenophobic heart. He sensed her secret beauty, nearly tangible but always eluding him, when he answered in a whisper, "I love your tribe." A tribe of enigmatic seraphs arced against the sky behind his eyes. The ghostly touch of feathers tickled his spine, was a fluttering breath against his neck. He felt nauseous, delirious in the aftermath of his sexual frenzy and satisfaction. He reeled on his heels, touching a hand to his temple. He heard himself say again, as if from a distance: "I love your tribe, your race. What a magnificent tribe..."

"You need to see...doctor. You are sick." Quiet, subdued, less the whimper he'd half-expected from her than an angry and disappointed resignation. Then, "You made this place...It is only here." Her small hand, hollow-boned and graceful, touched her temple.

He shook his head. He smiled. He laughed. Tears welled into his eyes though he fought futilely to quell them. "No: it's there." And he stabbed his own hand, stout-boned and cumbersome, towards the sky wheeling beyond the water-stained ceiling with its pathetic, weak light bulb. "Somewhere there, but so hard – so *difficult* – to find." A holy place: the words sat in his thoughts like a mountain; and then the conundrum all over again: but can an animal like she, however perfect for him to dominate, come from a place like this?

"I want place like this, too, Michael. But difference is, I want this place right here. With you, and me." She gestured about the room, towards themselves. "Together, we can find this place. But you cannot see it."

He shook his head with a viciousness born of the desperation to deny blasphemous untruths. He spat: "It's only – *only* – there." His hands, both hands, were raised over his head in revelation of the Heaven he knew.

She shook her head now, too, denying her beauty. "You make me like this, but I am only me."

His voice quavered with equal measures ecstasy and terror: "No: you're much more than that. You're everything I've ever wanted. You're like a…you're like a *dream*. A dream for me. I've dreamed of you my whole life…I've never felt comfortable – as at peace – around someone like I am when I'm with you…But saying it – those words –
they sound so banal, so simplistic compared to how you make me feel, what you do to me inside…" He drifted off, confused anew with the conundrum of the girl he loved and loathed. Already he was growing aroused again. Already her breasts and legs and mouth called to him like food to a starving man. He amended his words to her: "When I'm with you I'm at peace. But only when…only when I'm using you…for sex. For…escape from… all of this…" Hearing the audacious vulgarity of the truths he'd revealed, he whispered, "Why do you…want me? Why do you want so much for me to love you, when I say things like this to you?"

The girls' voice was assured: "Because you found me, Michael. You were first – you were only – man to see me. No one else sees me. You were first man to speak to me. You were only man to make love to me. This means something. There is meaning in this. Do you see it, Michael? Do you see meaning?"

Briefly, fleetingly, startlingly, he looked and saw her as he dreamed her:

A headdress of elegant feathers adorned her, spilling its lush crimson assemblage – shot through with a rich chestnut – over her little shoulders; her chest feather-covered, too, the small hillocks of her breasts; her tender eyes revealing her secret name to him: Michi Samurakami his little birdgirl, his secret desire and treasure and gateway to better places.

Tears welled and washed the bird-queen away and when they cleared again only the girl remained, eyes stunned and wary, face bloodless and all-too human.

He gave in to his own desperation and fear when, with guilt stabbing him, he murmured the old refrain: "I'll come again tomorrow." Then, unexpectedly, he wept. He wept from his great guilt, and from his thwarted lust, and he wept especially for the great confusion like a perpetual fog from which he could never emerge, despite always glimpsing a vague tremulous evidence of light and revelation in the uncertain distance.

Perhaps she pitied him his madness. Maybe she was merely as afraid of her own loneliness as he was of his. Her voice was tiny, drifting to him through his sobbing as if from another room, another, much more distant time.

"I should not see you again. My family…if they knew of these things you say, they would forbid me to see you. But I think tomorrow – tomorrow when you come to visit me – tomorrow you will love me. I hope you will… I hope tomorrow you can love me. Because you saw me, Michael. You found me and saw me. And I hope tomorrow you can love me."

He moved towards the door, nearly tripping on his own feet in his haste to be away form her and the enigma of her riddles. Her voice stopped him. Imploringly: "You are right: there is a place. Michael: there *is* a place."

He made the mistake, as he always did, and turned to her. She was standing in the room's centre, naked. Her shock of dark pubic hair slick with his semen and saliva. Her breasts perfect and beckoning. He wanted her. He loathed her. He felt suddenly like crying again, as if the contrasting emotions vying for supremacy within himself were too great and he, caught between them, had no recourse but to give in to his great turmoil and confusion and collapse entirely.

Finally, he left her, without goodbye, easing the door closed like a whisper behind him.

Her weeping, as ever, was the song he would remember most: from behind the door he heard it faintly. He felt it inside, too, as a lingering prickling of guilt behind his chest. At least in this he knew that he possessed some lingering shred of humanity.

*

A final and desperate experimentation: he bought himself a prostitute later that night but even someone like this – nothing more than a physical shell used for fucking by the loneliest of men – offered no gateway for him.

Only the disheartening reality of the woman, wan-skinned and ugly beneath the small motel room's diffused lighting, giving him ineffectual fellatio while he examined her with growing curiosity and disgust, as if she were a rare animal displayed within a zoo's observatory enclosure: her seeming engrossment in the task at hand, the voluble, moist sucking sound, the uninspired, wholly perfunctory groaning she emitted, muted for the shaft filling her mouth; until eventually the woman grew perturbed and removed his shrivelled, flaccid penis from between her lips and eyed him questioningly; and when he offered her no response nor reason for his detachment from her fondling, muttered an indignant-sounding, "It costs the same, man, whatever we did tonight."

Her breath was rank, an obnoxious mixture of morning-breath and alcohol and penis-smell. It wafted up to him like air from a furnace burning garbage, while she fidgeted with her bra, her naked breasts sagging before him like a pair of giant pale marine life forms beached atop her tumid belly. He thought of birds, and how flight was impossible within the suffocating net of this room. He placed a crumpled bill on the night table, and left the woman to slip her giant repugnant breasts back into the cups of her bra.

He was turning to leave but stopped himself, hand on the doorknob. Facing the woman he said, "Wait. Will you... Will you help me understand something?"

The prostitute eyed him in her wary, arrogant way. "I don't know what you mean, man."

He approached her, came to stand directly before her where she sat on the bed's edge. He removed his wallet from his pocket and the robust wad of bills bulging its leather slot. He threw it across her lap. Her expression changed from guarded to stunned to excited to wary again. She said in her voice of practiced bravado, "What do you want to do, man?"

He confessed, "I want...a lot. I want a lot more from you than I've asked for so far, if you have it in you to give. Will you help me? I need for us to try to visit a place, together."

The woman said nothing. To her expression of unease and confusion he made his proposition clear. "The money is yours. Let me do what I need to do."

Fear stole into her eyes. She eyed him cagily. She examined the bills fanned across her lap, traced their edges with her fingers. Resolution usurped the fear in her gaze. She surrendered herself in a voice feigning composure, loud but wavering, true to her role in the many-cogged intricacy of the universe he sought to understand.

"I'm all yours, hon'."

Walking listlessly down the street, he considered the results of his experiments with the whore. How it had proven one fact without doubt: no woman, not even one utterly devoid of personality, nor even owning a name, could elicit escape for him. A desperation seized him, and quickened his steps through the dismal streets, as the magnitude of his conundrum became apparent: how would he ever be able to come to terms with Michi Samurakami, whom he worshipped and abhorred in equal measure? How could their dream-flights be made real, and ensure his escape from his perpetual frustration and dissatisfaction like a cancerous growth stealing his joy each day passing? Would he ever understand her true mystery, beyond the tantalizing and agonizing sense he had that he was halted firmly at the edge of this knowledge?

He flexed his fingers, mired in the woman's residual fluids, crackling within their dried veneer. The pungent stink of her lingered, too, hanging about him like an ominous cloud beneath which he nearly swooned.

He understood then that his Michi-bird – and the dream birthed by her – must die, if he was to survive the madness looming over the world from which he could only escape through dreams.

Merely the sight of the building through the misting rain conjured in his mind the kingdom held impossibly within its walls, and he felt himself growing aroused, and hopeful once again for eternal escape into its fabric.

Turning into the small lot and nestling the car it into its regular slot between the large grey metal dumpster and the Dodge Dart on the other side made him think of him putting his penis in her vagina (she'd grown to haunt the most mundane acts – everywhere he looked he saw her beckoning him). Stepping onto the rain-wet parking lot concrete, his penis hardened, springing from where the waistband of his underwear had held it fast so that its head now pressed with a violent heat into his abdomen. Entering the building all of the sounds from its various occupants – voices speaking, arguing, the tinny electrical jabbering of a television and radio, a dog yipping – merged into a meaningless and insignificant droning which barely registered on his ears at all; while the familiar stale air and uncertain lighting and unsightly stained carpet all worked together to remind him of the girl, and her body, and those parts of her body which he was to devote all of his frenzied attentions to.

Reaching her door at the summit of the creaking staircase, his felt his breathing quicken and a bevy of butterflies become unleashed in his stomach. The failed experiments of the evening behind him were trivial, nearly forgotten beneath the promise of the forthcoming wonder. Nearly delirious with lust for the girl within the room, he paused before her door, eager, tense. Casting a cursory glance about the hall to ensure he was alone, he unzipped his pants, eased his swollen penis into his hand. He stroked himself, squeezing his testicles, too, his nose touching the door wood, the smell of the room beyond wafting to him from beneath the door: the familiar scents but with some indefinable new ingredient mixed there, too. The lingering supper-smells of noodles and chicken fried rice, her subtle scent of cinnamon, the unsavoury smell of the room itself, perennially musty and stuffy with old air; and this new smell, metallic and cold and – beyond these vague aspects – utterly beyond his ability to define.

He continued stroking himself, slowly and gently, rubbed his penis head against the cold door wood while imagining her breasts in his hands, her nipples gripped between his teeth, her wings exploding from her body in a riot of blood and light like proof of the Heaven he'd found in her, but which denied logic every time he imagined the girl while away from her and the madness she awakened in him.

He started: from the opposite side of the door he discerned her low, murmuring voice: "You are right: I am not able to save him. He is not prepared." The words, though he heard and understood them clearly, carried an unmistakeably peculiar aspect, an indefinably unfamiliar intonation, a foreign inflection overriding the Asian accent with which he was so familiar; as if the girl's voice were being translated through the filter of an alien throat unaccustomed to the language it spoke.

He knew not what the words meant, though he assumed they were spoken in relation to him. Something in the statement's inherent sentiment of condemnation seemed appropriate in defining him in relation to her. A fleeting sense of indignation arose in him, but quieted quickly – he was accustomed, after all, to resigning himself to his faults in her eyes.

He recoiled then: another voice, in response to her, neither masculine nor feminine but rich with both sexes, husky yet carrying a subtle soprano timbre, as well as the same indefinably alien aspect as hers, only notably more pronounced: "So few are. It is a wonder madness hasn't devoured this child from his time spent with you."

Jealousy mingled with terror in his heart. Confusion flooded his senses. The girl's universe contained only him. Who was this invader of the divine sex-room? Who dared sully its dirty floorboards and the conduit towards Heaven this tiny but limitless space represented for him? The bronze apartment key was in his fingers and his heart thunder in his chest and his blood a river pounding in his ears as he steeled himself to confront the intruder, to vanquish this defiler in order that his secret existence and the promise of his future peace might be saved.

But when he slipped his key into the worn lock and himself inside the dingy room beyond his eyes rebelled: the small space was crowded with them, its squalor mocked by their strange grandeur, like a far-future alien society's theatrical interpretation of the Roman empire built within a framework and stage neither magnificent nor ambitious enough to contain it. Their numbers seemed to push the flaking walls and ceiling away, to plunge through the trembling floorboards, threatening the collapse of the building, perhaps the entire neighbourhood and city beyond.

He sought to speak but words would not come. Only his mouth agape, eyes spellbound by the vision of them: many were helmeted, heads encased in headgear similar to that which he'd glimpsed – moon-speckled and shrouded in the camouflage of purple heather growing wild – in his dreams. Large, by turns angular and aerodynamic, mechanized and stylized, seemingly utilitarian but remarkably ornamental, as contrasting as every other aspect of them. Their array of arms both entranced and puzzled the eye: a pair of long steel-bladed spears, their pointed tips perforating the water-stained ceiling, were held in the massive silver-gloved fist of the same individual who wielded what appeared to be a rifle filched from a future epoch of conflict, its peculiar hand-grip entwined sensually about his gloved fingers like a living appendage; beside him a figure clutching a curving scimitar catching the moonlight through the window, reflecting also the electric crimson eye radiating forth from the bulky rectangle of metal adorning the left shoulder of another, its purpose as mysterious as the individual's veiled multitude of eyes glimpsed as a piercing array of blue jewels beholding him from beneath the silver steel cap he wore. Another figure, insect-helmeted and gargantuan with steel shoulder-guards like rolling hills, his invisible gaze through the weirdly intricate, tightly-grilled latticework of his helm felt as a resolute and burning touch, clutching in his left hand a large mirror within a frame sculpted from a deep red wood or jasper. A figure crouched before him, head enshrined within a queerly-lit amber globe of glass, holding in one hand a three-thonged whip, while from the wrist of his other hung a silver-golden wreath like a colossal jewelled bracelet. There was a significance to these details of dress and adornment, Michael sensed, though he knew not what it might be.

Their skin gleamed, silver and wondrous and shot through with a powdering of golden dust glimmering in the gloom, as if through a marriage of dust particles from a moon and long-expired sun. The nearly spectral aura which this created hung over them all, those armour-adorned as well as those clothed in what appeared ceremonial robes, long and flowing and rich and patterned with woven exotic symbols like ancient hieroglyphs to his uncomprehending eye. They exuded an imperviousness he admired and envied, knowing he could never possess such rare beauty merged with indomitable strength.

A baroque elegance defined them too, though, seen in their florid headdresses and wild array of pageantry: the long flowing cloaks worn by some, the feather-plumes sprouting from the helms of others and flowing over their shoulders, down the lengths of their backs, the ornate jewel-studded gauntlets encircling their wrists, the great glimmering stones hanging from their necks and reflecting one another's magnificence in rose- and emerald- and violet-coloured glass eyes. Some sported an antique finery, cuirass and breastplate and pteruges overlaid with fine tunics, while others simple robes of an archaic style, inlaid with gold and silver designs, at odds with the strange mechanized nature of certain of their armaments: the pulsing lights organized in a vaguely hexagonal design upon the chest-plate of one; the thick black ridged tubing connecting the rifle-like weapon slung over another's shoulder to the gargantuan smooth-skinned metal cylinder like a silo strapped onto his back, a sturdy receptacle that Michael envisioned might hold the ichor flowing through the being's blood; the mirage-like shimmering orbs hovering about another's head, their purpose as unknowable as the intricate webs of steel cylinders encircling his hands, like great and terrible mechanical arachnids feeding upon his extremities.

He felt in that instant his craven nature, his paltry strength in a universe where such might and beauty and un-guessed mystery existed alongside him. These were warriors, he knew instinctually, of the mightiest order, and scholars, too; theologians, sages whose knowledge and erudition and culture knew no equal anywhere, owning all the wisdom possible to acquire in the infinity beyond the atmosphere of the tiny, tiny Earth. Each of them potentates owning this knowledge, rulers all, governing all those beneath them in an endless spectrum of possibility. He felt his once-vaunted professorly status shrink alongside them, mite-like before their cornucopia of wisdom.

He blinked and their numbers seemed to have swelled, threatening more than ever to tumble the walls of the sex-room, to tear through the weak brick and mortar of the tenement and set the night afire with their otherworldly brilliance. Their ranks stirred now, too, as each shifted in place to focus their attention fully upon his insect's presence intruded into their midst, their uncanny assortment of arms and accouterments and regalia making of them a motley but perfectly conjoined assemblage that entranced his eye and owned his heart in spite of the colossal fear enveloping him while in the presence of ones as awe-inspiringly beautiful as they.

Despite their radically alien quality – this beauty of so startlingly profound a nature that it seemed from moment to moment as he gazed upon them as if it might in fact transcend it and arrive within the equally enthralling realm of the grotesque – despite their possession of so rare and startling a beauty, they were yet familiar to him; yet he became overwhelmed with an uncanny and powerful affection towards them. They appraised him with jewel-like, exquisite eyes of contradiction: neutrally judgemental, equally sympathetic and condemning, hard but munificent. He'd never looked into eyes like those, utterly inscrutable, but then he realized that he had, every day since he'd first met her waiting in an endless, unmoving line of unremarkable people so much less fortunate than he.

And she among them now, on bended knee upon the groaning floorboards as if in obeisance before them though her splendour surpassed theirs: his Michi-bird. Now, though, her beauty lay exhibited in the most profound way: her sleek limbs soft of feather, the pair of silver-dusted wings, arched and radiating a consummate power, unfolded fully from her back like the sails of some great galleon of the future. And her eyes: oh, the familiar ache filling those mournful black orbs as she beheld him stumbled into the midst of their gathering like a new speck of dirt tracked onto a gleaming golden floor, like a flea leapt blasphemously upon the pristine rostrum owned by an angel army convened in their secret stronghold.

He knew not how long he stared, enthralled and speechless before their beauty. Bathed in their appraisal, a vista of scenes materialized in his mind's eye, and himself at the centre of each:

He was a child of twelve years, squatting at a keyhole and marvelling at the scene within the room beyond, in which his father and mother stood naked in room's centre, the fingers of his right hand lost amid the thick black hair of her groin while she leaned her head back and groaned with a pleasure he yearned to know. It was the rarest kind of moment for him to have witnessed: his mother would be alone forevermore only months later, never to remarry after the sudden death of her husband, housebound and unhappy until her own death from cancer three decades later.

The vision vanished and was replaced with another: waking in his bed when he'd still been in University. Running a hand across the naked girl asleep beside him, remembering her promise of devotion made during sex only hours earlier. She loved him, and was prepared to marry him once they'd graduated at semester's end. He was the man with whom she wanted to make her life. He'd believed that he loved her, too, yet knew in that moment of observing her asleep, serene, vulnerable, delicate, that she deserved a man who reciprocated these feelings in as complete a way as she'd given herself up to him. Ending their relationship of two years – while seated across from one another on his bed with the dawn sun reddening the walls – had been difficult. She'd wept through the soliloquy he gave her, in which he bended the truth so that she'd feel loved while taking the brunt of the blame for the way things had turned out for them. He wasn't ready. He needed space, and time to learn what it was that he wanted. Her name had been Sylvia. It was three more years before she was finally married, to the man she'd once overlooked – a fellow student and mutual acquaintance – so that she could be with him.

Sylvia's ashen face of distress disappeared, replaced with much more recent history: he was straddling Michi Samurakami in her human form, penis filling her mouth while he filled her with his semen. Her groaning, pained but blissful as she rejoiced in this love he gave her, seemed to fill his ears, the room, the world more brightly-lit beyond the darkness of his dissatisfaction and flowering obsessions.

This sex-room moment disappeared and a fragment of dream-scene materialized in its stead, an amalgam of the place of Paradise to which she'd taken him time and again, though only ever ephemerally: astride the girl in the glory of her final transformation, winged and mighty soaring against the beckoning constellations.

Finally, this vision too was evaporated into the ether, leaving the incredible reality of the creaking room and the magnificent assemblage gathered within it, silent as they beheld him.

He turned his eyes to the girl with her entourage surrounding her. He winced beneath their light. Tears streamed from his eyes. He remembered his fruitless attempts to replicate with others the ecstasy which only Michi Samurakami could provide him. The memory of the infidelities bloomed a great guilt in him, and his failure a deep shame. He confessed to her, tears upon his cheeks: "She had no wings. The whore had no wings, and I looked deep. Oh, my Michi-bird, I looked so *deeply* for them but, in the end, there was only you. I should have known. I should have known." His hands he held high on the air for the host's judgement, blood- and semen- and feces-encrusted.

She gazed upon him with a great pity in her obsidian eyes. The entourage surrounding her surveyed him, too, though their appraisal was a colder one, detached and scientific, as if he were no more to them than a curious animal locked within its vivarium for observation. It chilled him while her eyes burned him. A scalding touch he knew well, though never in so potent and concentrated a degree, as if through entering the sex-room on this most vital of nights he'd unwittingly stumbled into a portal leading to the very face of the sun.

He sensed the message within it all, some immense truth partially exposed. He sought to fathom it. He felt himself exploring along its periphery. He wept, in his confusion. Still, he failed to understand it.

Through it all, her new-voice cutting tremulously through the great clamour like a thread needled through armour:

"I cannot save you, Michael. You are not ready. You have come closer than anyone else here but still you are not ready. I hope that what knowledge you may have gleaned has not hurt you so much that you cannot find some joy in the life you will live."

He heard the sorrow filling her words. Her eyes bewitched him, more slanted than he remembered them and more bottomless and wild, too, more cherub-like her face, more pronounced the colossal wings flowering from her shoulders as if filled with a gale's wind.

He looked from her to his erection gripped in his fist and to her again. There was logic in the gesture, he sensed, though at that moment even it lay beyond his comprehension. Acting instinctually he began to masturbate. Struggling to waken the hot fire to jet from him and into the world where it could exist alongside the host convened before him. He stroked himself with growing ferocity. Pain seared from his loins. His member and testicles ached with it. The beauty of the host filled him. Her splendour owned him. He sensed but couldn't catch the elusive thing flitting through his reeling consciousness: a thought, some idea, a path long and long and winding and winding but worth the walking for the blindingly bright but unseen destination waiting at its end; a path nearly-formed but made invisible by the lust boiling between his thighs and threatening to set him afire, a shell of molten blood and flaming flesh.

Then a violently divine light erupted silently into his eyes. It silenced his volcanic thoughts. It quietened the world around him even as he understood the futility of adding his semen into it. Blinded, he felt himself descending floorwards, and then he felt no more.

When his eyes cleared from his dreamless slumber he was first and foremost uncertain about time: how many seconds or minutes or hours or more may have passed. The light was gone, another dream-scene vanished. Looking to his shrivelled flaccid penis dangling from his open pants he found that he'd ejaculated onto himself. Judging from the extent of the dark, soiled fabric it had been a prodigious amount of semen, and noting the thickness of its consistency he knew he'd come recently. It was only then, after understanding his post-ejaculatory state, that he examined his surroundings:

The room he didn't recognize, though he felt a certain familiarity with its spare design, a kind of affinity for its bedraggled, shoddy appearance. Alarmed, he scrambled to his feet, making for the door. There, though, he halted, heart smashing, breathing pent-up, held by the sudden compulsion to remain in the room. To examine more closely the dirty bare walls, the ceiling with its water-stains in the shapes of continents never before mapped, and the spartan furnishings of ancient bureau, small work desk, and bed; to the bedside he crept and looked long into its dishevelled folds, its sodden sheets and chaotic blankets, its un-laundered pillows and cloying smell of sweat and sex and cinnamon wafting to him.

For a moment he'd stood on buckling legs, seeking to orient himself. Fear of amnesia evaporated when he remembered the route home, and soon enough he found his way there, weary, frightened and confused as he toppled into his bed, desperate for sleep to come and take away his great uncertainty.

In the days that followed he grew to engage in a peculiar ritual:

Every night, long past midnight, he would drive to the rooming house, and let himself in with the matching key he'd discovered in his pocket. This wee hour because he'd relished the kinky notion of finding and surprising a possibly new tenant with his arrival and – insofar as his fantasy unfolded – seducing her (it was always a woman who roomed in the fantasy) to his every desire. But every time he slipped his key into the well-worn copper keyhole and entered he found the room as barren as when he'd first awoken in it. In fact, no other tenant ever roomed there, despite the commonplace murmur of voices from behind the other closed doors of the little decrepit building. Never a window yellow with lamplight when he watched furtively from the street below. Only the meagre furnishings of bureau and dresser and bed – never made, the bed, but remaining always and forever in the dishevelled state he'd first found it, as if it were a sculpture meant to represent some human trait or quality – these permanent fixtures of the room. He went to the window at some point during every visit, seeking clean air to clear his spinning thoughts, and there he saw, and was surprised to find them there, as if the discovery was a new one every time:

Upon the floorboards below the window, a variety of feathers which stirred mockingly at his approach. Each night their colour grew more faded, and their lushness more threadbare and balding until nothing remained of their original uncannily vivid crimson and emerald and indigo and golden and silver hues, only a hoary, lifeless and ragged gathering stirring idly, like ancient cobwebs, at his approach. He would stare at them. He cried for them. He yearned to witness the flight they'd once been capable of, while wondering at the nebulous sorrow the thought birthed in him.

Turning to the sky framed in the window, and seeing its clear expanse of stars beyond the trees, he shook his head in futile denial of the great loneliness that awoke in him, and could do nothing, of course, but weep and weep more.

A new era had begun for him the night of his inexplicable awakening in the dingy room. It was a period he grew incrementally thankful for each day passing, for the world which had seemingly opened for him then.

This he considered while the girl – a slim student fresh from Africa whom he'd found in the school pub, poring over notes for a first year English class, her accent deliciously thick – kissed him fiercely. His lips bruised hers. His teeth bit her neck. His strong hands crushed her tiny breasts, first overtop the orange cotton shirt she wore and a moment later through her bra and then along bare flesh when he yanked the undergarment down so that each breast spilled from its little cup.

The epiphany had arrived in him that he now possessed the wicked power of greedy deceit as he never had before: and so he'd approached her, and impressed her with his academic credentials and flattered her with his avid interest in her physically, as well as those subjects she chose to bring up in their hour-long conversation before he'd succeeded in luring her, tipsy from the pitcher they'd shared, to his home.

She pulled away, keeping her fingers encircling his erection so that he would know she still meant to allow him to have her. His eyes cleared momentarily of their lustful frenzy. "What is it?" he gasped, fingers still pinching her hard sharp nipples.

"Will you tell me again? Tell me again: do you like my body?"

He was nodding. He was smiling. "Oh yes I do," he was saying over and over again as he twisted her erect nipples to make her cry, and then pulled her skirt to fall about her ankles. He didn't heed her plaintive requests their entire ten minutes together – he was engrossed in owning her. At some point while fucking her he chanced to look out the window and became mesmerized by the first stars awakened and hanging like something sacred in the tapestry of the western sky. Something in them unsettled him and he returned his attention to the girl beneath him. She felt right. She felt perfect in the sex-moment, much like the other women he'd been with in the past several months had felt while he'd fucked them, too; after the tedious game of wooing them, during which his secret anxieties and self-consciousness troubled him, and he questioned the things he said and the way he perceived himself in relation to others. She – this exquisite, strange, and unknowable girl of foreign descent – was the polished faceless slate of delicious mystery he needed most in the world to make himself feel secure.

In her ecstasy she spoke with abandon, thoughtless and impassioned. "Oh, I love you, Michael. So much, I love you."

His words came without thought: "I love you, too. Oh yes."

A peculiar thought arrived in his mind then: *I once knew your sister* - he thought this as he raised her buttocks a degree higher while continuing to fuck her. In another time, in another world: *I knew your sister.* Her cries grew more shrill and pained as he fucked her. He cocked an ear, listening intently past her voice – he thought he'd perceived a violent wind outside, the panicked cries of birds – but heard nothing.

He pulled his penis from her a moment later, startled at its limpness. Desperation seized him, and he turned the girl about to sit on the edge of the bed. Kneeling before her he urged her to lay back, legs spread. Placing his head between her thighs, he slipped his tongue into her vagina. Closing his eyes he found the path opened to him again, after too long being denied entrance: a portal, through this girl, to the only Paradise he'd ever known, evanescent, but wholly renewable with her and any other woman he could convince to love him.

The gentlest of touches, feather-light and teasing, grazed his naked shoulder as he pleasured her, and traced a delicate design the length of his back in its descent towards the floor. He shivered, but maintained the slow, circular-moving rhythm he'd established unabated. If this was all the Paradise he was ever to know, he would keep it, and revel in it, and grow dizzy with transient joy while engrossed in it.

The new dream was always a brief journey but it had grown to hound him relentlessly, always recurring in the very same way:

Waking from slumber he was startled to see: a million points of light frosting a cold glow in the endless blackness. Dazed by the sight of the naked starscape stretching infinitely, humbled and frightened by it, he lay there a moment seeking to understand his situation, seeking familiar designs among the trembling lights.

When no constellations coalesced from the million light-points a great terror consumed him. He scrambled to his feet to discover himself located on a small rough-hewn rock, approximately as wide in all directions as his bedroom. He reasoned that it was an asteroid, or meteor or some such cosmic detritus drifting through the space miles. And he, like a wildly misplaced flea, was unaccountably trapped upon it.

He shook everywhere at the realization of his hopeless plight: he was blessed or cursed with an atmosphere of life-preserving oxygen and gravity holding him rooted to the rock. He had this gift-curse of a sustaining atmosphere upon the spheroid, but nothing else. He crept with trepidation to the edge of the rock in various places. Peering carefully over its ragged lip his stomach reeled:

Nothing. Nothing and nothing and nothing.

He crawled back to the centre of the rock, and there he sat in a heap, and wept. Never before, in waking or dreaming life, had he felt so profound a sense of abandonment. Some time later – he couldn't be certain exactly how long for time felt queerly protracted, surreal, a false idea beneath the weight of the naked stars – a trickle and a splash reached his ears. He turned at the miraculous sound, and was amazed to see a small pool of milky water several feet from him which he'd inexplicably failed to notice upon his initial examination of his surroundings.

He scuttled to it, feeling the cold breath of the universe licking at him every inch of the crawl, blighting the foolish shred of hope sputtering in him at the discovery.

The pond surface was stirring subtly, as if some invisible hand had recently disturbed it. He eyed it wondrously, warily. He stared and he stared and at some point in his beholding of it he understood that it was not water at all, but a prodigious amount of semen gathered in this crater upon this drifting rock upon which he was imprisoned. Revulsion came over him at the epiphany, and soon a kind of horror stole into him, too. Then, he discerned something beneath the semenline: a dark amorphous shape resting in one place, as if floating, or mired in the viscous liquid like an ancient creature preserved in prehistoric amber.

The desperate hope reawakened in him at this possible clue to his quandary. He reached a hesitant hand beneath the gently undulating pond surface. The semen was hot, a freshly-spilt ejaculate filling the hole. He watched as a series of reluctant ripples widened from where he'd plunged his arm into the thick mire of it. Tears came to him then, though he knew not why. They washed the semen away and made his efforts difficult, but momentarily his eyes cleared and he saw that the semen-pond was still once more.

Searching about he closed his fingers around the dark object embedded within. He withdrew his hand and stared: between his sticky, dripping fingers he clutched a bluebird. It was like any bluebird he'd seen back home, which called from the Black oaks in his yard or visited the wooden birdfeeder he kept below his bedroom window. Its tiny body was black with wetness, heavy and sodden. Its white crest was sullied a filthy grey, too. It was dead, of course, and radiated an intense cold as if he gripped an immense ice cube, despite the hot bed from which he'd withdrawn it.

He wept anew. He could do nothing more nor less. The cold breath of infinity surrounding him lapped at him like a black ocean eroding a stone, chilling him deeply. His tears took the vision of the bird away and – despite the certainty of doom overhanging him like a pall – his dream-self felt an infinitesimal relief at this small mercy.

Upon waking from the dream, while the young woman dozed naked and spent in his bed beside him, the great loneliness assailed him anew. And with it, another bludgeoning thing swept over him, too, as it did in the aftermath of sex with the woman – and every other person he'd lured into relations with him throughout the past months – every time: the certainty that he'd lost some very profound and meaningful thing, beyond the transient intimacy of the last body he'd devoured in his bed, far beyond anything so mundane as the everyday pains and pleasures and satisfactions he knew.

Wrapped in the cloying, suffocating fabric of this certainty he crawled from beneath the single sodden bed sheet. He looked for the girl's feather upon the hardwood floorboards – frantically, desperately he scrabbled about, searching with a nausea churning his belly which was his escalating fear and regret growing like an epiphany in his heart – but found nothing as ever, only their soiled underwear and the deceiving moonlight drenching the room like a dream he could never fully fathom.

Nurse Sweetness, thank you.

MOTHERLIGHT
GO TO SLEEP

The creek smelled green. The air was idyllic August, deep with humidity and unmistakeably summer. A long Wednesday was behind him. Work at the hardware store until mid-afternoon and deliveries throughout the county until near-dusk, the rattling of the load from his pick-up truck's bed lingering in his ears long after he'd rolled into his gravel driveway and silenced the chugging engine. A quick breakfast-for-dinner of bacon and eggs and potato wedges, washed down with a glass of warm milk, and here he was again, in his usual place owning the old rusty lawn chair with its acrylic peeling away in long tatters from the seat bottom. He felt peace settle upon him. He sat looking over the great field which was his property, abutting his backyard lawn with the farmer's fields of wheat and corn stretching still in the distance beyond. He felt a little bit like a king in his tatty throne, awaiting his disciples from far and wide.

The old acoustic guitar rested across his lap. He'd retrieved it from where he'd left it the evening before, leaning beside the back screen door in the safety of the enclosed porch. He now tuned its strings with a gentle hand. The sound of the tuning process – the ringing of harmonics and the pinging of strings turning and altering pitch – sounded in the quiet. The rich mahogany odour of the instrument and the metallic smell of its old strings came to him. He was careful to keep the strings clean, and scrubbed his hands liberally before picking the instrument up. This familiar arrival of notes – along with the bloody fire of the sun plunging into the west and firing the Black oak tree-line of the horizon, and the sleepy buzzing of the crickets awakening for an evening of music – signalled that the time had arrived.

He played. He strummed with his practiced fingers, using no pick. He finished the chord progression and repeated its cycle, again and again and again. The notes rang on the air, and drifted across the field before him. He imagined them traveling in widening invisible waves, like the concentric rings invisible within a tree, rustling the flaking wheat stalks and soughing the corn rows and stirring sparrows from their nests in the distant oaks. He directed his song to the fields. He sang in his softest voice, only a lyric-less murmur at first, in order to fortify his vocal cords. Their subtle raspy quality inflected even this melodic murmuring with a rough melancholy.

He played and he played. He settled more comfortably into his creaking lawn chair. The pieces of the ritual had begun to fit, like interlocking pieces of a puzzle constructed only to be torn down each night, only to be reconstructed and disrupted again and again on subsequent evenings. His fret-hand fingers grew comfortable, too, finding the old familiar places dancing along the well-worn strings. His picking hand fluttered over the sound-hole like a hummingbird hovering before the flower it was preparing to kiss. His breathing grew peaceful. His heart retreated from its mad clattering of earlier into a serene drumming. His day of work, and dealing with people, with their trivial problems and complaints and banal small talk, fell away behind him. His eyes anticipated the light of her; his nose the comforting scent of her haunting the green darkness with her frosty perfume of gardenias revelling in moonlight; his ears the elegant song of her whispering through the night in answer to his own paltry music.

The arrivals began soon thereafter. In ones, in pairs, sometimes threes and fours, while occasionally more came together. A mangy, long-furred dog sauntered through the field first, eyeing him with its mournful, milky eyes as it settled onto its haunches in studied examination of him. It cocked a drooping ear at his playing, fixated with his hands over the instrument. A moment later he saw a ripple in the wild grass and, following its progress, saw a pair of jet-black cats emerge from the foliage nearby and rest themselves on the grass, near to the dog, who remained seemingly oblivious to their arrival.

He admired their beauty, the sleekness of their coats. He was grateful for their attention. Even as he thought these thankful thoughts a soft clamour rose from the field and he knew even before it waddled forth from the grass that a raccoon was arriving. When at last it appeared its small dark eyes were already beholding him through its black mask. It came to rest directly alongside the cats, who remained unperturbed. A muskrat came next, and several more cats – tawny- and sable- and white-furred – and then another muskrat and a variety of dogs. A cow lumbered from the west, its rust-flecked neck-bell thunking dully. Horses, three of them, cantered in from the wheat in the west, too, and snuffled only briefly in the grass before halting to examine him in his tattered throne with their large black eyes. Birds made their landings among them, too, sparrows and bluebirds and several crows making black fans with their spread wings as they settled upon perches along the branches of a nearby oak.

His audience swelled. The dusk deepened. The great hulking thing arrived then, as if stepping from the musty pages of an ancient fairy tale to thrash through the wheat in the west and through the corn nearby until it had found its regular place towards the rear of the throng. He knew not what the thing was, only that it was immense, long-limbed and burly and fur-coated like some primeval Sasquatch; and that it, like the other animals, was a reliable member of his nightly audience. He knew also that it owned lost, lost eyes. These eyes watched him now as they did every night, rabidly, small melancholy orbs the colour of the moon set within its massive face of fur and shadows.

He'd never questioned the miracle of their convening with him, nor the power of his spellsong over them all. He'd only ever questioned what it was about the happening that caused him to never question it. But then, he saw the world differently today than he once had. He viewed it askance, questioning the nature of those things which lived in its sunlight and those things dwelling under its moonlight and those things inhabiting the fringes and fissures of both, unseen by most but lurking there besides. Yes, he believed in the existence of these things, when once there had been a time he hadn't.

His strumming grew more assured. His singing-murmuring rose in volume a little, strengthening. His voice yearned for words. He felt them rising from within him, from the deep place in which they slept through the days, until the nights came and he let them out. The moon frosted away the scant handkerchief of cumulus obscuring it, silvering the fields with its unmitigated snowy light.

She arrived last, as always, beneath this moonlight and starlight. She'd always been one for being fashionably late. She was set in her ways. *I'm not one for change*: she'd whispered this in his ear while they'd lay curled together on the grass at the creek's edge at a time when he was young enough that such embraces were still allowed, were still wanted. They were luxuriously sleepy with her dinner filling their bellies, drowsy with the cricketsong surrounding them like a gentle electricity pulsing from the grass and distant fields. A boy knew no greater comfort than his mother coddling him while the night held them both in this way, too.

There she was now, as always, and, as always, they bowed before her splendour: the pair of foxes and the geese and the muskrat and the cats and dogs and raccoons and beavers and owls and bluebirds and sparrows, parting like a sea before divinity. She hung among them, the blue light of her pulsing a melancholy glow that fired his fingers playing across the strings, helping him hold fast the chords, and imbuing his words with a fierceness of expression he never was able to achieve without her presence there guiding him into these difficult places.

Finally, he released it from within the pit of him: his voice found its melody, and the melody its lyric, and settled into its old mournful croon, imbuing the words drifting on the dark air with their meaning:

> *Momma, the world is bright and kind*
> *You are all I have ever known*
> *Then in a great darkness a man was born*
> *And inside a night he brought it to me, too*
> *Momma, I cannot jump away*
> *Momma, this dark is spun too tight*
> *O you, you are the one I hate*
> *O you, you are the one I hate*

This verse he sang and sang and sang, the words exiting his mouth in a repeated mournful cycle. Throughout the song he watched only her melancholy light hovering over the field darkness, pushing that darkness away with ease, brightening and brightening like fire stoked and excited by a subtle gusting breeze, the addition of further wood to fuel its appetite. The gathered animals beheld her, too, held transfixed by the quiet beauty of her.

But his voice eventually grew hoarse as the minutes and minutes passed, as the moon crawled across the sky. And as his voice became more raspy, less fluid and sweet, so too did her light begin its waning. From its brilliant blue – nearly silver – incandescence it dimmed and dimmed, until only a cold-looking flame hung on the air, shrunken completely from its original pregnant, breathtaking spectacle.

A final chord struck, a final wavering vocal melody tapering into silence, and the glowing orb of her drifting westwards across the fields to vanish into the ether a moment after, even as the echo of the song faded, too.

The song was finished for this night. His vigil concluded. He watched them growing slowly restless before him, as if waking from the deepest of dreams. A moment passed and they began their withdrawal from the plot of field: in pairs and threes, the cats slinking into the shadows, and the raccoons lumbering on their way, and the horses wandering off towards the horizon where a farmer's yard awaited them; the birds lifting from the grass and from the branches of nearby trees to sail away into the darkness in weirdly hushed flights.

He lingered a while, savouring the stillness of the night asleep. Relishing the memory of her light, of the way it had brightened during his performance, the way it had pulsed with an eagerness and a joy towards its climax. He frowned at the thought of its leave-taking, too, of course, drifting without sound across the field, low overtop the seafloor of wild grass and wildflowers and, further in the west, brightening the wheat and corn fields with her sad glow until expiring in the far distance.

He stood with an ache in his knees and fingers. Clasping the guitar's neck tightly near its headstock, he drifted across the lawn and into his sleepy house, shoulders slumped, eyes weary but destined to watch the stars through his bedroom window throughout the early hours, sleepless and pensive and full with the old, old ache that was the nemesis of his dreams.

Towards dawn only did he catch some slumber and, though brief, it was long enough to carry with it the old sliver of dream, fleeting but never ephemeral enough. She flowed through it, of course, drowning his dream-heart as she owned his waking heart and thoughts.

The dreamstory was the retelling of the true tale: it was years and years ago. He a child, wakeful and alert in his bed, listening with drumming heart to the booming steps like thunder on the hardwood floor of the hallway outside his bedroom door. His vision of the world grown blighted in the instant of the door swinging wide on screaming hinges that presaged his own wailing cry.

The final dream-scene before he woke, echoing once again the childhood scream that had never stopped plaguing his sleeping or waking world: the vision of his father filling the doorway, eyes invaded with an otherness that had never existed there before, detached, cold, ravenous in some indefinably epic way; his father but not his father, familiar but remade with these new eyes and the blood painting his hands hanging like death at his sides.

This the last he was ever to see of his mother: her blood drenching the shadowman's hands from where he'd dipped them deep in the pool of her in search of her pure, pure heart.

A new dusk was settling. Sun-fire burning the tree-line, the early moon pallid and full overhead. Refreshed from supper following another long work day behind him, he owned his rickety throne overlooking the fields. He waited with the patience he'd perfected over the course of the springs and summers and falls and winters. His guitar lay nestled atop his thigh, tuned and waiting for his fingers.

They arrived one by one, some in pairs. All of the usual animal watchers and a few he thought might have come for the first time – a small dusty-looking poodle, its once-white fur sullied and grey; a garter snake which slithered in from the field and curled itself upon a spot of grass, resting its head atop its coiled body and beholding him with its black eyes; and a strange crimson bird that fluttered down to land at the border between his yard and the true beginning of the field.

The great and weird hulking thing lumbered through the corn, leaving the book of fairy tales from which it had climbed opened somewhere in the darkness. Its steps rumbled the night, its legs swished the crops like the sound of rain slicing against the tree-line. It gathered its gargantuan limbs together and sat upon the grass to the rear of the throng. He discerned its bashful eyes, small and moon-white, watching him raptly.

Her light materialized soon after, drifting in from the western fields.

She appeared as ever after the great host of them. They bowed before her. The night grew silent and still. Their snufflings and snortings and chirpings subsided. She prettied the moonlight and softened his already mellow thoughts into a deeper calm. She breathed awe into the night, and into him, and within the heart of every other animal observing her wondrously then, too.

He played. He hummed. He sang. His heart, as ever, ached at the sight of her light. He sang and the night was quiet but for his mournful voice, and the old words he'd given to her on so many, many vigils.

> *Momma, the world is bright and kind*
> *You are all I have ever known*
> *Then in a great darkness a man was born*
> *And inside a night he brought it to me, too*
> *Momma, I cannot jump away*
> *Momma, this dark is spun too tight*
> *O you, you are the one I hate*
> *O you, you are the one I hate*

He played and played and the moon crept from one end of the sky to the opposite.

He watched her and only her. Her light soothed him. Her light ached him, too, as always. With it touching his retinas with its soft glow he felt a luxurious sleepiness encroach upon him, like a great invisible blanket covering him and warding off the nip of the late-summer night air. Then: her light wavered. His fingers nearly forgot their chord change. Her light brightened. His heart calmed. His fingers grew confident once more. Her light dimmed towards the climax of the song, and remained this same diseased un-brightness until the final chord had been struck, its final ghost-notes ringing off into the shadows like raindrops slipping from a sluice and into the night.

The crowd sensed the anomaly, too. They were discomfited by it, made restless beneath its dying beauty. He considered beginning anew, striking the chords with a more savage hand, entertaining the notion that perhaps such renewed vigour and passion might revivify her light. But something in him halted his hand: a sense of finality to that evening's recital, as if his voice and the ears of his audience could bear no more melancholic song; or as though her faltering light could bear it no more either.

And so he sat silently, watching the creatures make off into the night, towards their nests and burrows and dens and warrens or onto their nocturnal hunting trails and whatever adventure was their fate in those wee hours. When the last of them had gone – his strange Sasquatch-like disciple, with its great shoulders slumped and doleful eyes watching the ground, as if it too sensed the conclusion of their strange shared story – he remained in his chair, relishing the great stillness, the pale moonlight enveloping the countryside spread before him while her light faded like a dying ember in the far distance.

He was startled by the fact of her suddenly there with him in the gloaming: a woman, wearing a faded brown and orange plaid shirt, simple blue jeans, and old blue runners. He'd sensed her presence watching him from the southwest side of the yard, and found her there with an anxious hammering in his chest.

"Hello. I'm sorry to startle you." Her voice soft, apologetic, soothing in the quiet. "I heard your song. I heard you singing. I hear it every night, from my window across the field. I don't know how – it's far from here – but I hear it perfectly." She gestured eastwards across the uneven crops. He followed the direction of her gaze and found the tiny house with its lit-up windows marking the horizon, small with distance like a treasure chest silhouetted against the lunar light. "It's very pretty. It's very sad."

He looked to the guitar in his hands, as if seeking to glean from it some direction on how best to respond to her. He was prepared to utter something noncommittal before wishing her goodnight and retreating into his house. Unexpectedly, in a delayed appraisal recollected in his mind's eye while he stared helplessly at the instrument's scarred wooden skin, he saw her beauty which had somehow eluded him when he'd first found her scrutinizing him: eyes so kind; figure so shapely; brown hair so long and youthful-looking; smile so timid, so benign.

His mother would have liked this woman, and her kind eyes.

He turned to her with new eyes. He smiled. It felt strange. His mouth un-practiced. "Thank you." His voice an ethereal presence floating between them.

She smiled, too. She watched him a moment. She urged their conversation along gently, making him feel comfortable, and comforted, as if she knew innately that this was the best way for their conversation to proceed. They talked of the late season, its lingering humidity, the suggestion of Autumn cooling the evening air; of the great quiet and stillness of the county.

They fell into an untroubled pause. Into it she said, "You're not from the county, though. Not originally. I can see the city in your face."

He nodded. Her knowledge of him somehow didn't surprise him. He smiled for her. There it was again, this unfamiliar-feeling smile. "You're right. You can see it there." He was thinking of mirrors, and what they revealed to him every day: the wounded boy looking out from within the time-weathered man.

When he looked to her she was scrutinizing his eyes. He knew she saw it there, too: the nature of his memories; and also his peace here, with her, in this place of whispering grasses and trickling creeks and star-frosted skies and inexplicable happenings like all the purity in the world contained in a single burning miracle. She too was an ingredient in all this now.

Seeing whatever it was she saw in him, she said, "Who needs it? The city, I mean." She cast her eyes about them. He did, too: true nightfall had descended, past midnight when even the subtle but perceptible lingering glow of the sun no longer haunted the western horizon. The fields were silver with lunar light. The electric voice of cricketsong haunted the distance. It was cool and refreshing and like a new world following the heat and brightness of the day behind.

Her voice was the delicate presence floating on the air again. "I have a big vegetable garden. More potatoes and tomatoes and carrots than I know what to do with. I haven't had a guest in too long. I'd love it if you joined me for supper tomorrow."

He examined her face. Its openness was there still. There was no limit to the unexpected things to be found in the depths and miles of the night. His smile grew – the longer it remained, the less strange it felt upon his face.

He was left alone with the nocturnal sounds of his trusted friends the crickets violining in the grasses, taking up the music of the night until the sun rose to redden the new day. For now, moonlight silvered everything. Its blue cast was melancholy and beautiful. He turned his eyes over his property, and the fields reaching far beyond it, empty of her beautiful light floating like a message from a place far away. He gave the moon darkness his final words before retiring into his little house and the first night of sleep and dreams he'd had for a very long time.

"I'm sorry. The song is over. But it's yours. Always and always and always, the song is yours. Goodnight, momma. Sleep well. Dreams of peace to you, forever."

He leaned the battered guitar against the base of the lone Black oak owning the eastern corner of his lawn before crossing his yard and slipping inside his house, and putting out its lights.

Later, in the trackless miles of that wee morning his dreams were haunted by the ghost-plucking of the instrument's ancient strings, like a voice – soothing, gentle – that he'd always, always known.

Robert, I hear you
Robert, I love you
The blood and the thunder
an echo of the gods
still calling from young Summer
1933

I can hear the Ocean.
No, you can't.

Shells
and empty shells

PROTEUS IN
THE MOUNTAIN

Alan checked his watch, squinting as the sun's reflection in the glass stabbed into his eyes. Midday, the heat already oppressive. He was weary. His trousers and shirt were sodden with sweat at this relatively early hour of the day, before the sun had reached its zenith overhead. He felt the clinging of the cotton shirt along his back like some grotesque layer of skin in the process of molting. He removed his pith helmet and wiped his brow with the back of a dirty hand, beating dust from the hat against a knee. A pungent scent of sweat drifted to his nostrils.

Beside him, his companion groaned, conveying his own fatigue, and a deeper malady, too. "I'm aching everywhere, Alan. It feels like lightning in my joints. The fever's worse than ever. I can't stop the shaking. I'm so cold. I'd rather the heat than this Godforsaken fever."

A grimace worried Alan's face. He looked fretfully at Marion's haggard features, his bloodshot eyes and dusty sun-bronzed limbs. They'd both been inoculated against infection, malarial and otherwise, before their expedition had set out from Zanzibar in early winter, but it appeared that they'd encountered some new vile strain in their travels. More resilient strains of the virus cropped up from time to time, he well knew, each deadlier than its predecessor. His companion must have been assailed by just such a poison, somewhere in the trackless jungles they'd left behind. He took a moment to consider the morass of swampy, miasmic bog-land through which they'd travelled, where gaseous emissions rode the air like malevolent spirits, that treacherous terrain where snakes hid like stout vines draped among the grass, and chestnut-sized spiders slept the burning days away in their massive and intricate webs; those unmapped regions of wilderness where gargantuan mosquito queens filled the ears with their furiously buzzing tumult and succeeded time and again in drawing blood no matter how determined the companions' efforts to remain unmolested.

"After today, my friend," Alan assured his comrade, squeezing his shoulder. "We'll rest after today, Marion. We'll climb Tombanik today and if all goes well — and there's no reason to believe that it won't — we'll descend by morning, and rest in town for a few days before heading home. We're done on this continent after this. One final slog onwards, and then we're done. Okay?"

It had to be. Marion nodded his assent because what else could he do: they'd been traveling for nearly six months without any respite and this, amazingly, almost incomprehensibly, was the final leg of their journey. Perhaps they'd yet find clues to the myth's tangible existence among the precarious granite cliffs and gulches ahead. Who knew: perhaps parting a bush's fronds would reveal it to them, the treasure nestled like a jewel in the lushness of the bush's heart. They had to look, he reasoned, because what if? Because how could they return home without having explored every one of the plethora of potential sites of this vast and mysterious continent the way they'd planned so meticulously in the months before their safari had set out? Could they leave one village unvisited and believe without any nagging doubt or suspicion that the elusive treasure hadn't lain waiting there, as it may have lain in wait since before the time Europeans had first scampered like children through this dark country, eager and greedy?

The worrisome notion haunted them both, of course, that perhaps they'd overlooked it weeks or months back, among the many villages rumored to have born witness to its beauty. Perhaps some tribal chief had hidden the jewel in the wilderness where no rapacious Englishman dared look, among his kingdom's verdant infinity of spear grass like the sharp green ramparts of some long-lost jungle stronghold of the ancient apes; perhaps submerging it in some stagnant leech-ridden pool or wadi shrouded beneath the perennial curtains of mist that hung like a pall over the swamps.

Yet still it may lie before them — this infinitesimal hope was reason enough to venture onwards: this the faltering man of science still living inside of Marion's bent and aching frame reminded him, despite constant pain and weariness and his waning optimism like a weight filling him more each day passing. This, and the wish to not disappoint his companion, so much more devoted to the science of their quest than he was those days, though the realist in him knew that they would likely return from their

400

perilous climb at some point fairly late in the morning, bone-weary and disheartened, wrecked with disappointment.

Alan offered Marion his hand, and hauled him to his feet. Together they trudged onwards.

The two explorers circumvented the final signs of human habitation before the boundary of the true wilderness began, the small rondavel jutting into the road like some squat wooden mushroom cap overlooking their path. Its thatched roof was in tatters, storm-battered and home to several birds-nests dotting the skeletal framework. The structure's sides were splintered, the boughs swollen with the gathered moisture of humidity and seasonal rainstorms. More of civilization's decaying, tottering presence in the wilderness, Marion mused, with the jungle's emerald fingers encroaching on all sides in bold reclamation of its territory. They sidestepped the skeletal remains of the dead man curled like a baby in the path just beyond the dwelling, what remained of his entrails spilling from him into the dust. They held their breath through the ecstatic atmosphere of buzzing flies summoned by the eviscerated corpse, the victim, most likely, of a lion attack. They said nothing about him and gave him no further examination – they'd learned quickly to dismiss the suffering of the human beings they encountered during their months of travel through those lands. It represented only another lure for the riffraff of jungle vermin, perhaps a vulture descending from the midsummer blue like some hideous skeletal hand of doom to claim ownership of the body with its raucous cries while pecking away at the flesh; or maybe a party of wandering cannibals lusting blasphemously for human meat to bring back to their tribesmen.

The scientists ascended the narrow trail that wound between the walls of granite before them. Overhead, the cliffs rose on and on, closing in on them as they climbed. Without the other members of their party, Marion – his fever causing him to shake violently and making his vision blurrier than it had been the evening prior – felt small and exposed in the enormity of the precipices looming about them, and utterly frightened. Superstitions abounded in those parts: his research and personal experience made him expert in this, and so he understood well the trepidations of their native guides and bearers who'd refused to climb the forbidding chain of hills and mountains about them. The region was shunned by local denizens, who feared the ominous rumbling of the earth and the peaks which spit smoke all day long; where unholy things were rumoured to roam among the towering spires of stone and where inexplicable shapes were said to move in the clouds and frighten predatory birds from their nocturnal hunts.

Alan grunted, a raspy sound deep in his throat that Marion knew was an indication of his companion's mounting anxiety. They scanned the precipices stretching over their heads, but perceived nothing anomalous among the grey rock and surrounding greenery. The mystery of what lay beyond, as ever, beckoned them. The look in Alan's eyes, Marion saw, was resolute. *This one final exploration, and then home.* Marion, wiping his feverish brow and swallowing down the bitter acidic phlegm gathered in the back of his mouth, followed his companion, eyeing the thin trail before them determinedly.

They stepped through the crack in the cliff walls. It felt as though they were passing from the outermost periphery of the village and into some far-removed place, crossing an invisible yet distinct barrier between the merely exotic and the utterly unknown. They climbed higher, sweating profusely in the dank, heavy air, their breathing laboured. As they ascended it felt as though the world they'd inhabited fell away completely.

Like the explorers who'd visited those lands before them, Marion's and Alan's safari had been inspired by excitement and knowledge; both ingredients embodied in the geological artifact they sought with such eagerness. They'd travelled far together, and explored many places: Zanzibar and Kenya and Buganda and Karagwe and Cameroon and so many other regions. It haunted their dreams in the same way that it lingered in their wakeful thoughts, making of them children as much as men of science. A nebulous rumor, an enduring myth, and cause for adventurers' hearts the world over to thump excitedly despite the widespread cynicism concerning the object's existence. Theirs had certainly pounded in tandem upon receiving the Royal Geographic Society's approval of their proposed expedition, arriving in the mail in the simple form of a stamped letter of acceptance and signed release-of-grant-funds form.

During the most difficult parts of their journey, Marion had often recalled his friend's high-spirited voice of romance. Like a lantern's light it had shone reassuringly in the deepest, densest quagmire of miasmic swamp country, burning away the rainforest gloom while the other members of their increasingly dispiriting undertaking carried on with stoic faces, the local bearers lugging their packs of provisions and supplies through the wilderness, short stout spears and revolvers always close to hand for fear of brushes with tigers or unfriendly tribesmen ranging from afar. He'd brought this encouraging voice to mind often while nursing swollen ankles and pocked, insect-ravaged skin, while wiping mud and slime and peeling leeches like ugly black tongues from his boots and calves and thighs, while crouching beneath beetles-festooned vines stirring like primordial evil in the dark heart of the wilderness through which they'd dared to trespass, a pair of foolish white mice in a land owned by black panthers and other more formidable hunters than themselves.

But it was a single word that encompassed the object of the explorers' devotion and all of its scientific and historical significance, continually conjured in their minds and often uttered like prayer in some stretch of dismal wilderness: *Bukara.*

Marion recalled his companion's soliloquy, impassioned, compelling, infectious in the sumptuousness of the office quarters in his vast Westshire countryside home, old maps surrounding them everywhere like further enticement for them to take the Society's grant funds like a dare and plunge headlong into the unknown.

"Marion, listen: Listen: *Listen:*" Alan's voice had been hushed and urgent, eyes manic and youthful despite their frame of crow's feet. "It's rumored to have survived the ages. The *ages*, Marion. It's a chapter in myth. It's supposed to have survived volcanic cataclysm and inter-tribal wars. It's located somewhere in the heart of the continent, they say. In the heart of *Africa*. Bukara, the god who fell from the sky to be worshipped in the dark heart of the continent."

In the end, the names were what had convinced Marion. The romantic colouring of them. The perilous quality inhabiting their syllables. *Zanzibar* and he'd thought of pirates and storm-tossed sea voyages along jungle coastlines where old shipwrecks lay crippled on the rocks like symbolic auguries of the dangers awaiting the unwary. *Unyamwezi* and strange creatures and alien flora flitted into his mind's eye, alongside images of old tattered maps like those surrounding him and his dear friend, time-weathered and marked in their farthest blue-tinged sea corners with ominous and tantalizing warnings of '*Here Be Monsters*'. *Tunisia* and he'd seen heat mirages shimmering among dune seas where legions of spear-bristling warriors marched, like an immense throng of terracotta statues baking in the sun.

Bukara: and he'd seen a vision of mystery as his manic imagination produced it, culled from fragmentary bits of scholarly text and other portions borrowed from books of myth, embellished with his undying child's-eye for wondrous subject matter. He saw, among the promise of flash-bulb fame and their names printed in historical texts for years to come, the simplicity of the great stone egg, the hulking primordial pagan idol paying ode to the skies and the mysteries they held. The oldest example of deity worship recorded, as much legend as historical fact, and a precise and meticulously-constructed vision of romance and wonder in his mind's eye.

He'd clapped Alan on the shoulder to him to show him that his mind had been made up. They'd embraced. They'd toasted wine long into the morning among the dusty, creased maps and prodigious array of scientific journals, many of which held their own articles on various subjects. They'd passed the grant form between them many times until it too resembled one of the ancient maps, lovingly wrinkled and dog-eared. Two doctors of science, throwing their voices into the lofty expanses of the lavishly-furnished office as they allowed the youths residing obstinately within their aging frames to emerge and bask in the grandeur of the unknown awaiting them. The blood-rush of leaping into adventure as if they were still young enough to live inside of penny magazine swashbuckling features – this kept them wakeful and ebullient long after dawn had seeped its golden glow into the room, signalling the arrival of a new day awaiting their courage.

"Look. There's death nearby."

Marion followed his companion's finger stabbing the sky. A trio of bony slashes wheeled against the blue, feral in their circling pattern: vultures haunting the cliffs, displaying their great patience for the onset of death, stretching their long wings until the time arrived when they could descend and feast unimpeded.

"We should be careful," Alan's voice drifted back to where Marion trailed him in the dust, limping and lethargic. "In case of predators. Mountain cats, perhaps."

Marion un-slung his rifle from across his chest, levelled its barrel before him with tremulous arms. The sun hung lower in the sky now, a pulsing bloody bead washing the mountains in fire. His skin felt this way, too, fiery and tumid. He veered from the path, leaning against the cliff wall for support while he vomited yellow water and maize curds among the wild grass spikes.

Alan, waiting in the path ahead, called to him in a cold voice, "Do you want to turn back? We can turn back." His eyes looked dangerous in the burning light, anxious and excitable.

"No," came Marion's raspy reply, as he wiped spittle from his chin and blinked the salty moisture from his eyes. He heard the judgement waiting in his companion's words, and in his misery couldn't help resenting him for it.

A moment later and they were ascending the trail once more, their progress as determined as was possible given their circumstances. Marion discerned, filtering through the bewildering haze of fever and tremors shaking his body, his companion's voice. "The Empire is proud of you, my friend. *I'm* proud of you."

Marion struggled along, his rifle held limply in his fists, its barrel occasionally dipping to graze the granite floor with a metallic scratching. Distantly, the lapping sound of the Ocean came to him, a muted clamour drifting on the torrid air as if from a dream. Mostly he felt only the hungry eyes of the doom birds overhead, watching his faltering frame with rabid interest.

They'd landed in Zanzibar nearly six months past and had to fight to retain the romance in their hearts. It had floundered, despite the staunchest efforts and reciprocal reassurances to keep their spirits buoyant. They traveled and they searched, and their colossal hope and quixotic purpose in that realm of exotic fauna and peoples continued to falter and, ultimately, drifted heavy as iron fetters to the bottom of the ocean. They'd done extensive research of the geographic and cultural landscape beforehand, of course, but nothing could have prepared them for the reality of planting their feet onto the soil of this far-away land. To actually see with their own eyes its true heart: its wildness, its hardness, bereft of the homely things that they'd always known and whose luxuries had served to soften their fortitude. An untamable world where tigers slinked through jungle thickets and roared like thunder in the night, shuddering the companions in their tents or in the bamboo-and-earth sleeping quarters offered them by friendly Native peoples they encountered throughout the endless months. A place of ineffably rabid disease devouring the populations of village after village after tottering village in these years following the Colonial scramble for Africa. A proliferation of pitiable hovels marking the landscape through which they slogged, prostitution and death rampant like so many other infections rooted in the very fabric of the land. Everywhere they'd roamed these sights abounded to stifle their idealistic dreams of grandeur: corpses bobbing in rank pools in every corner of every village, the antediluvian savagery of senselessly violent youths fighting each other with rocks and clubs and fists in the dusty streets; the seemingly plan-less mazes of the streets themselves, impossible to navigate for the traveling foreigner and teeming with fearful cul-de-sacs and ominous gangs of adolescents following their progress with keen, cunning eyes; ramshackle abodes rearing from the mud on all sides where denizens would convene and pig together in grossly uncivilized fashion, earning the Britons' scornful, all-encompassing title of *Zanzibarbarians*.

But, impelled by the dual spirits of discovery and adventure, the men had struggled onwards, questioning from time to time whether their innate biases and intrinsic refinement held too strong a foothold, perhaps, when delivering judgment upon their exotic surroundings. Or perhaps they simply couldn't equate the nearly pandemic devastation of death from disease and violence and implacable climate to any sort of beauty as they construed it.

As they climbed a grey rain began.

Motes of all sizes drifted down about them, clinging to their sweat-moist arms and cheeks and necks. A small sizzling sounded at Alan's ear and he dabbed the charcoal fleck of volcanic ash into silence, startled. They were drawing closer to the summit, where the mountain breathed fire and smoke.

406

Marion looked about them, the falling ashes reminding him of grey moths fluttering forlornly to their deaths. He shuddered, repressing the sudden urge to try and dissuade his partner from plunging forward. To implore Alan that they might wish to reconsider this final, forbidding leg of their incredible journey. Perhaps they didn't belong where such queer precipitation fell after all. Possibly this perverse snowfall represented an augury for them to return home to things they understood, to abscond with greatest haste from this wicked land of hellish climate and grumbling mountains whose ancient voice even the Natives feared.

He'd long ago heard of the mysterious Ash People, sometimes referred to as the Grey People, those dwellers among the charcoal rains and precarious mountain crag paths. Legend, fragments of Native mythology spoken of in whispers among some villages as a means of ascribing meaning to the strange precipitations, to the ever-grumbling earth which caused fruit to drop from the trees and the elderly to topple in the road like wheat beneath the scything hand; describing a strange tribe who tended to the mountain in some ages-old, mystical and symbiotic but unknowable way. Perhaps their time in these lands had birthed in him some sliver of superstitious dread, too, Marion reflected, or else awakened it from some long-hibernating sleep within him.

The sound of surf was louder now, a perpetual crashing of waves against rocks. Brine lingered in the air, and although the late afternoon sun scorched the companions' skin, the oppressive weight of humidity had been lifted, allowing their breathing to come easier. Alan scanned the sky but found no sign of the predator birds. They'd probably descended and were now feasting in a raucous din on some dead or moribund prey along some cliff edge or plateau escarpment or in the bowels of some nearby arroyo.

They trudged onwards. The air cooled yet more, and a brisk breeze emerged from between the rock walls and relieved the sweat from their faces, arms. Stiff grass grew in ragged tufts lining the trail, and occasional skeleton-bushes yielded small, shrivelled berries containing thimblefuls of rare sweet juice which the companions savoured.

Then, very suddenly, they ascended a lip of jagged lichen-bearded granite and arrived upon a flat shelf of rock that represented a final place of rest before the upraised rim of the volcano itself, smouldering fitfully

beyond. Upon this miniature plateau the companions stood, breathless, amazed into stock-still silence while they gazed on the sight spread before them.

People milled there, many of them, dark-skinned, stone-skinned. Some turned to the wanderers with alert eyes, fretful, while others looked upon them briefly and then turned their gazes away, untroubled. Their clothing made the scene initially deceptive, being the common attire of Native sparseness that they'd grown accustomed to - breech-clouts of tan-coloured hide, beaded jewelry adorning necks and long sculpted wooden piercings in nostrils and earlobes. The Englishmen stared, entranced. It seemed to Marion in that queerly protracted instant as if perhaps time operated differently in this lofty place where the sky spit ashes and the perennial murmur in one's ears was the voice of the great Ocean far, far below in union with the grumbling mountain itself.

It was then that Alan, whose vision wasn't marred by violent fever as was his companion's, became conscious of the anomalous nature of the menagerie gathered upon the plateau: a man standing nearby beheld them with pensive eyes, his lanky frame unremarkable but for his magnificently distended ankle like the colossal foot of a giant rooting him upon the grass; the bulbous foot of another man, like some hideous, thick-skinned airship, protruded from beneath the fringe of his worn tan pants. A woman like a queer statue watched them warily, her hands like immense grey stones hanging heavily at her sides, slumping her small shoulders with their great weight. A small child stood at her side, his small dark eyes lost in the midst of his gargantuan skull.

Alan shuddered against his will, butterflies fluttering nervous dances inside his stomach.

Marion squinted and through stinging, watery eyes, saw, too. He involuntarily drew a hand across his mouth, a small startled sound escaping his dry, cracked lips as he clutched at his companion's arm. A man shuffled forward along the escarpment, dragging a swollen leg like a sap-engorged tree trunk through the grass, a goliath's hand raised high in greeting. His features were grossly misshapen, as if sculpted from wax, his lips curled towards the left side of his face into a peculiar puckering shape. A massive tumor swelled the skin of his brow like a cliff ledge overhanging his smoky eyes, deeply set within the strangely bowed expanse of his skull. A grimace wrinkled the man's features as he edged closer to the travelers. A thick, brightly-dyed crimson scarf that looked like garland was wrapped about his neck, its fringed ends stirring in the breeze. With his other, much more ordinary hand he clutched a small bundle swathed in a brown blanket to his frail chest. Once near to the explorers, he greeted them in Swahili, in a voice coarse yet gentle. "Hello. What do you want here? Have you lost your way?" He scrutinized them, and before they could provide an answer ventured in a somber tone, "Do you believe you have stumbled into some strange, dark dream on this mountain? Your eyes say so, strangers."

They could only continue to stare silently, feeling wholly disquieted and exposed. Alan tried for words but faltered beneath the scrutiny of the man's piercing dusky eyes, observing the trespassers in their great discomfiture. He'd read the scarce scientific and medical journals available which detailed the origins of conditions such as the one they seemingly witnessed in such profusion before them, but had never thought he would be effected so acutely by actual firsthand observation of its manifestation. Something stirred among the blankets in the man's arms: seeing the child struggling towards the daylight, Alan considered what he'd read of teratogenic conditions such as Non-filarial elephantiasis: the infant was small and shrivelled and ancient-looking, with immensely swollen arms and one gargantuan foot jutting from its tatty blanket, its wizened head like some symbolic mask of death staring impassively from where the man cradled its strange body to his bosom. "Non-filarial elephantiasis is thought to be caused by persistent contact with volcanic ash," Alan murmured, sounding to Marion as if he were lecturing in his famously aggravating academic manner. He'd likewise read the selfsame articles on the subject as his companion, but something in the bizarre alien physiognomy betrayed a different origin than this. He felt his scientific curiosity in that moment utterly engulfed by sheer youthful wonder at the spectacle before them, held captivated by the scene, and murmured in a voice distant with wonder and revulsion as he sought to solve the puzzle of the alien baby, "Unlike elephantiasis, Proteus syndrome is named for the shape-shifting god of Greek myth. It affects tissue other than nerves. It is a sporadic rather than familially transmitted disorder. As it stands, many people still mistakenly refer to this condition as elephantiasis." He sensed his companion turn to him, felt his stunned appraisal, before returning to examining the child and the old man.

A collective cry startled them from their bedazzled reveries, joyous, free and exultant.

Alan and Marion turned, and they saw:

A dozen little elephant-like creatures filing from a wide cave mouth on the opposite side of the plateau to frolic on the sun-bathed grass: swollen and pendulous-skinned children chasing one another, while other unearthly boys and girls rested their huge limbs in the shade thrown by the rearing precipice. Several others loitered with their elders beneath a patch of skeletal trees near the cliff's edge, their ragged headdresses of sun-bleached leaves rustling like lettuce in the gusting breeze.

The garland-wearer's voice returned, softer then, and reflective, narrating the scene before them, offering explanation. "Many come to us as orphans. One day a mother delivers one, fearing the appearance of her child like a baby hippo. Another day a father climbs the lonesome path with a strange bundle in his arms, and there is loathing and shame in his eyes, as if he has committed some wrongful deed. Once a woman walked up from below, leading a boy of fifteen years by the hand. His face was different from hers, large and like the rolling sea, and with a small hill upon his forehead which was to one day blossom into a long and beautiful horn. She did not know what had happened to her child, who had changed in his tenth year, from boy to some other creature." The man drew his great brows together into a scowl that swept the rocky floor before them. "Sometimes the children find us on their own, when they are old enough to despise the ways of men. I think…I hope that we here are as a dream to these children. Here, where they may suddenly dance freely in the skin in which they were born or into which they've grown!"

The scientists in that moment truly felt like explorers, temporarily forgetting their science and simply basking in the discovery. Listening to the man's soliloquy was like hearing a voice belonging to myth – in rapture, they allowed his words to wash over them like water, storybook-like and enchanting.

"A miracle came to pass here, many years ago. I was very young but I remember the commotion well. A boy, named Alohandro, had leapt into the Ocean from this very plateau. He had grown fins, you see, and I, one of the few elders still alive today, can attest to its perfect shape. Two fins growing from the boy's spine, long and slender, and webbing filled the spaces between his toes, too. A long tail sprouted from his buttocks as well, dark and sleek and fine, like the tails owned by manta rays. It was on a bright blue day much like today that the boy decided that he would try to swim. So that he might give strength to the grumbling god in the mountain, you see, who was grumbling and spitting smoke a great deal during those days as he tried to free himself from the prison of the mountain. This noise and fire spread much fear and unrest among the tribes in the below-world, but we here knew a different story, and only celebrated the great grumbling. There are some people who believe we give our prayers to the skies, for our people often look upwards to watch the stars and the clouds, but really they are for the Ocean, into which all goodness returns." Here the old man paused to toss his arms outwards from his body in an all-encompassing gesture to the water sparkling into the horizon. "He jumped, the wondrous boy Alohandro. He swam. He made circles below like a fish. The water foamed all around him. We waved our hands goodbye to this beautiful child, and he was gone." The man smiled solemnly in the wake of his impassioned oration. The garland about his neck whispered a secret sound. He murmured, distantly, eyes searching the blue-green shimmering of the Ocean. "That fish swims out there still, in the Deeps. Waiting."

"Waiting?" Alan murmured, eyes rabid again.

The old man's smile broadened. "For the great god, Bukara, to rise from the deep red sea of Tombanik, from the deep fiery place He has rested for thousands of years since He fell from the sky, grazing the clouds before drowning in the restless red waters."

A chuckle fell from his twisted mouth as he beheld the bewildered explorers. "I see how you look on me, friends. I see your eyes that do not believe what they see. But I ask you to think of the world: is it not a changing place?"

Then the garland-wearer was waving his arms towards the children playing on the plateau in a great gesture of summons. His tongue clicked and the youthful throng moved towards them, groups of adults shuffling nearer in their wake, too, eyes cautious and probing.

The misplaced Englishmen looked to each other, stunned. Their eyes watered in the bright salty air. The sun was sunk beyond the crooked mountain horizon but its bloody light lingered, colouring everything in a fiery radiance. The children gathered around them, curious, their hands touching the new arrivals' clothing, the packs slung across their backs, their hands dangling at their sides, grimy and quavering anxiously on the air. The dreamlike quality of the moment suffused them. They felt detached from themselves, curiously disembodied as though the fantastic scene was transpiring without them in its midst, as if they were a pair of birds watching the spectacle from some distant aerial vantage.

Through the fog of incredulity hanging over him, Alan felt a pulling on his arm. He looked: her left eye sparkled like the water while her other lay submerged beneath the overhanging precipice of her immensely distended brow. Her teeth flashed pristinely as she coaxed him from his place and onto the sward. The girl, he realized, was swathed in the bright crimson clothing of a large kite, like some royal personage. He left Marion trailing behind, struggling to discern the goings-on about him in his ill, blurry-eyed state. He smiled as he watched Alan conveyed off by the ebullient child, awash suddenly with gratitude. He wished to thank him then, for climbing with him that day, for toiling through the harsh travels behind them so that in the end he might see the miracle revealed to them on this mountain of myth.

The little girl huffed as she scurried along, her breathing laboured with her nose squashed inside of her labyrinthine face. She had something to show him, it appeared. She led him to where the cliff fell away completely to the Ocean far below.

He looked and he saw, though a moment elapsed before he allowed himself to trust his eyes and what they beheld. Laid upon an immense white rock like a crude altar erected to hold its magnificence: a man-sized sculpture of stone, garnished with wan chalk designs faded by the elements, regal-looking presiding over the Ocean iridescent in the distance, resting before the kite-wrapped Queen who held the explorer's fingers in her massive malformed hand. His senses reeled as he sought to absorb the magnificence of it.

Of course it was the idol of Bukara, un-hatched from the folds of myth and time, resplendent in the honesty and austerity of its beauty resting there in the sun. Because where else would they have found it, he thought dreamily. What other place on Earth could it rest more pristinely than there atop that volcanic precipice, among this wondrous guardian clan of strange, un-guessed people? He'd waited a very long time for this sight to come to him, or him to it. There it was. There it was. He dared to place a hand against its surface, worn smooth by the high altitude raging of winds like the breathing of gods upon its ages-old face.

"It's a masterpiece, truly," Alan dared to utter aloud, and Marion's small gasp several feet beyond informed him that he'd perceived it now, as well. "A masterpiece," he repeated, awed by the grip that the sculpture had on the surrounding land, this relic of an age lost to the mists of time. The haphazard chalk design covering the egg's ancient skin seemed to portray a countenance of sorts, bearded and with bright eyes, with a peculiar quincunx of symbols patterned into the visage's forehead. It represented a language the explorer didn't recognize, but whose fluid pictorial beauty struck him deeply.

The girl held a chalk nub in her giant fingers. He watched as she dabbed with seeming abandon at the rock, embellishing those areas where precipitation had worn away since last she'd worked her artistry on its smooth face. He saw the child's beauty. It was everywhere that he looked, in the by turns jubilant and fastidious attack of her chalk-strokes, embodying the eagerness of all children as her elephantine hand moved in precise and grand whorls and zigzags over the stone.

Very suddenly he felt the rapacious man of science seep its way into him, displacing his wonder while witnessing this most astonishing of artifacts, this corporeal proof of what had for countless years been regarded as legend but which he now knew with conviction to be a historical link to an ancient, ancient past and its people's mythologies concerning the skies and the wonders they held; representing as well the most venerated of stations for himself and his companion in the pantheon of great scientists and discoverers.

Marion watched him warily, concern in his eyes, for while he already felt the final and irrevocable death of his once great ambition inside of him he knew his old friend well, and saw clearly the dangerous gleam in his gaze as he looked beyond the stone egg, beyond this mountain, beyond this sacred sliver of time they shared overlooking the great Indian Ocean. Watching the girl embellishing the stone idol, he understood in that moment that his own quest was concluded. "My time to swim is close," the girl said then.

As if on cue, the wind plucked her cape-kite from her, and it slipped with a watery rustle from her small round shoulders and onto the grass. She was naked beneath and it was then they saw her sail: a caudal appendage growing from her spine and stretching tautly into the cool air. It was a dusky grey-brown, like her skin, the cartilage glowing warm and red where it narrowed along its extremities, limned in sunlight. They marveled at its aerodynamic appearance, sharp and sleek, and designed to cut water at a good clip, leaving dolphins as stragglers in the deep blue, coveting her beauty – a little seahorse drifting in the deeps, leaving the vast Ocean more mysterious in her wake.

They beheld her in wordless wonder. Marion felt faint from the great altitude, from the perennial smell of sulfur in the air. Something fluttered in his eyelash, and he blinked away a snowflake of ash.

A rumble grew beneath their feet, spreading its sonorous voice upwards into their ankles and up through their calves. It trembled inside their bellies, rocked them to and fro where they stood. They looked dazedly about themselves, to the volcano rim and immensity of sky. It sounded to their ears like the somnolent muttering of some gargantuan being inhabiting a hidden stronghold within the mountain. Deep and booming, a primordial echo that created an impression of having existed in this place long before man or tiger stalked its surrounding trails.

The giant shuddered one final sleepy shudder, and fell silent.

"You feel Big Tomas deep inside your bones, too?" inquired the garland-wearer, his tumor-laden face smiling among its hills and hills.

"Is that what you call it?" Alan asked.

"*Him*, yes. This is indeed our name for *him*. Tombanik, we named him long ago, long before my time, even, and that is certainly a very long time indeed. *Tommy*, the little ones call him. He is talking in his sleep a great deal these days, a grumbling language of pain, for the god he swallowed those many years ago fights and fights to free Himself from his fiery prison. We believe that He will be breaking free soon. This is what He says, when we press our ears upon the earth and hear His secret messages spoken to us through the Earth, underneath the painful grumblings of Tombanik." He paused and peered closely at the Englishmen, and finished. "Whenever Tomas grumbles in his sleep, a swimmer jumps. This is the way it has been, always. For long ago, Tomas – being of the earth, and greedy – opened his mouth wide and swallowed the sky's great gift to us before that gift could touch the water, which was His destination. One day the great egg-gift will escape the greedy and hungry mouth of Big Tombanik and meet with us in the sea, you understand, and then we will all be together, in the Perfect Place. One day the Great Egg will leave Tombanik's fiery stomach and fly from the stone mouth that swallowed Him so long ago. And we will be waiting for Him on that day, to take us to this place."

Alan gestured to the granite egg before them. "The egg…*Bukara*…it's…*he's* beautiful…"

The old man chuckled. "No, friend, this is not Bukara. You look upon a child's vision of Him, yes, but not Bukara Himself!"

The old man saw the confusion in the Englishmen's eyes. He said, "Come," and taking the girl's giant hand in his giant hand limped along a narrow trail leading up the precipice to the rim of the volcano's mouth. They followed, climbing and climbing, the smoke and ash thick in the air.

The travelers gathered alongside the man and followed the crooked line of his gesturing finger. They looked over the vertiginous precipice and into the volcano's granite mouth, down and down through its blackened, sheer throat and into its fiery heart far below. There, floating like a great jewel in the lake of restless lava, lay an immense object, nearly three-quarters the circumference of the volcano itself, perfectly smooth and rounded, its virgin skin a gleaming silver that dazzled the eye. Like a gargantuan steel egg, a large portion of it protruded from the molten stratum, miraculously unmarred by the violent volcanic bed in which it lay embedded. Clearly distinguishable, even among the chaos of smoke and ash, was the arcane quincunx of symbols engraved into its brilliant skin, identical to the crude chalk drawing on the stone idol.

"My God, what is it?" Alan murmured.

But he knew, even before the old man told them in his wise voice: "Bukara, the great God who fell from the heavens, whispering secret messages in his great sleep, gathering his strength so that he may fly from his fiery prison and into the Ocean where the angry fire of this world will be put out forever, and we His humble children and servants will be waiting for Him so that together, all of us together, we will rise from the Ocean and leave this place, and go to a better place."

Here the garland-wearer pointed back across the escarpment.

The kite-queen stood there, bold and regal in the gusting wind threatening to sweep her up and away from the ledge and into the hugeness of the empty-air void beyond. Her arms were extended to her sides, revealing the webbing of skin stretched taut between arms and ribcage, while her long tail curled on the air. Like a ballerina the child stood poised, frozen in her dangerous aerie like a small caramel idol.

The girl leapt, toppling like a diver from the lip of the ledge and into the air.

Alan gasped. Marion recoiled a step. A great whoop erupted from those gathered on the plateau below them, joyous, exuberant. Children and adults alike held their arms skywards in supplication or celebration. Beyond the cliff edge, Alan saw the bright flashing of sunfire all over the Ocean's face.

The wind gusted, carrying the clamour of celebratory voices skywards. Beneath their feet, the mountain rumbled.

"Protean," Marion murmured, trying to give meaning to the things they'd witnessed that day. "It's like the story of Proteus, of the sea. And these people are waiting for him to come. They're his… They're his *children*. They're *changing* so that they can meet him… properly."

Drums sounded from somewhere, a hand-pounding tympani heartbeat that Alan and Marion felt in their bellies, in their chests, in deeper places than these, awakening them a little from their stupor of awe.

The garland-wearer said, sounding as if he were reciting a prayer, "When Tombanik grumbles, and when Bukara whispers to us in His sleep, a tribesman swims. This is the way. One day we will all be together in the Deeps. We are waiting for His Return, you understand? It rains here every day. Grey rain, black rain. Ash rain that is like a penance we must pay for the sins of the world we have left behind us. And one day soon coming Bukara will return and drowned will be the great fire of hungry Tombanik. And Bukara, He will lead us to Peace. It has been a long wait. But up here," and he spread his strange limbs upon the air in summation of the Ocean glimmering like a dream and the sky wheeling overhead, "Up here to wait is an easy matter, for the world is better up here. We are closer to the sky here, and to the stars and the gods who live upon them and in the spaces between them, and this is a good place for the children to be. Here, they wait for a good tomorrow, better than any the world below could ever give to them."

Marion considered the rest of the world, with its downtrodden peoples existing within the splendour of great gleaming cities. He considered Zanzibar and Cameroon and Somaliland and the myriad other nations through which they'd traveled and that had ceded to Colonial hands; and Marion gaped more and more at the purity of the scene before them, and the sage advice it represented like a parable for those wise enough to decipher its meaning. While the Somaliland of the earth was turning to dust and blood each day passing, he thought, this heavenly African colony escaped this fate every day. Here, on this mountain like an island unto itself, like another place in time.

He looked to the people milling on the grass and found that he was happy for them. The mountain dwellers, the sky people waiting through days of fire and ash for a chance at the sea, where a new evolutionary mechanism blossomed within the alien shells of the children.

The garland-wearer said, "Will you join us, friends? Will you join us on our long journey away? Perhaps this is why you have landed here today among our tribe. Perhaps you are meant to fly away too, to a new land? Perhaps change lies within the shells of you both too, and your true beauty will bloom one day soon coming?" A boy of no more than ten years appeared at his side – naked from the waist down, his many-tentacled lower half writhed languidly upon the grass. He coiled an appendage lovingly around the old man's ankle and watched the explorers with a tranquil gaze.

The friends turned to each other. Alan murmured, voice cold and clinical and removed utterly from the surreal nature of the moment, "Which is it, I wonder? It could be elephantiasis, perhaps? Or as you said, some offshoot of Proteus Syndrome, though not as sporadic, of course? It could be either. It could be some amalgam of each, or it could be something else entirely. It could be the fault of the mountain – who knows what prolonged exposure to volcanic dust might do? Its effects on the tissues of those living within a certain geographic radius might be profound."

Marion considered his companion's words. The theories he sought to put forth were wholly misplaced in the moment. Fatigued, somnolent, weary of pondering scientific verities, and with a pang of something like sorrow in his heart, he said, "I think it might be Proteus grumbling about the wickedness in the world, my friend."

They watched the milling tribe. Alan murmured, "Incredible. And nobody knows about them. An entire colony of them on this mountain." The thought returned to him like an old dream remembered, and he considered the look of his name in countless scientific journals, emblazoned across book jackets in a variety of pressings and editions and languages. "We'll be known the world over, my friend." Alan placed a hand on his friend's shoulder as they observed the tribe before them.

418

A great shame stole over Marion, who saw the wondrousness before them. Journals and books seemed incalculably remote, an uncertain and vile fiction. Fragments from another life, another place. The world would go on without them. He wondered at the absence of the old academic's spark in him, felt hollowness even as he murmured, defining the moment for them as he saw it. "I'm happy that we came. I'm happy to have seen. That's enough. That's far more than enough. Yes. This discovery is discovery enough." He knew his friend well, and considered the demon of selfishness which had always possessed him more violently than it had ever succeeded in owning him, and a fear began its gnawing inside him, a fear for the preservation of the secret peace and quiet splendour of this remote and unknown Paradise.

He said: "Thank you, my dear friend, for this great journey." And he lifted the rifle in his trembling hands and fired a bullet into his companion's skull. Alan crumpled to the ground. The echo of the report rose skywards, spooking a trio of vultures from some nearby nest and sending them beating furiously towards the sinking sun. Marion stared at the ruin of Alan's shattered head and brain spread across the grass, and wept.

The old man watched the Englishman with a curiously penetrating gaze, saying nothing. Behind him, the tribe stood watching in solemn silence, too.

Minutes passed. Two tribesman – a horned man and another with patches of gleaming silver-scaled skin and a long twisted beard of tentacles – came and gathered the corpse. Lifting it wordlessly between them, they walked to the cliff's edge and threw it without ceremony to the water far below. Marion turned away and looked across the plateau: the pendulous-skinned children had turned away as well, to run and leap and limp onto the sward. A boy held aloft a gargantuan fist like a mountain of stone from which sprouted a bright crimson string. The explorer followed its path into the sky and saw the bright diamond against the blue: kite-flying once again from the mountain top, like a message of peace struggling away from the smouldering mountain and towards the heavens.

The ground tremored then. The mountain rumbled. A god murmured in his sleep. The children went on in their play, as ecstatic as before the quake had arrived and stirred birds from their nests. Cheered by the tremor, of course, comforted by its all-encompassing presence and the promise it held for them. Marion remembered being like them – boundless in vigor, enthused for the many mysteries of the world.

Marion walked towards the narrow, winding mountain path which led down to another, infinitely more mundane world. He arrived at the fissure in the cliff's summit and the winding trail beyond. Turning, he waved to the garland-wearer and the others. The old man nodded, and a silent communication was passed between him and the Englishman. A look of understanding. A look of peace.

Behind the gathered tribe the water sparkled blindingly as the day's final sunlight scorched the horizon. The scene conjured yet more tears into his eyes. It was a breathtaking picture. The explorer would take it with him, always. The ground continued its somnolent rumbling, communicating a divine message from afar which trembled his bones, his heart. He heard the children's voices in their play, free and free and free. He saw their extraordinary bodies and their faces like remarkable alien sculptures. He saw their fins and tails and wondrous webbed hands and feet. He thought of the Ocean, and its abundance of miraculous creatures. A hippocampus swam through his reveries, towing a chariot of jewels-encrusted gold as it leapt from the water towards the clouds and a place of destiny among the constellations. This picture soothed his weary thoughts, and breathed strength into his battered body. He saw the children's avid eyes drinking in the fiery watery scene, too.

He turned and walked on, letting them keep the Ocean, and the sky, and the secret bridge spanning the gulf between the two.

The choice is mine.

DISCIPLES OF
THE FIRE GOD

The man on fire emerged from among the festive lights-studded, garland-choked pine trees and strode towards the middle of the downtown ice rink, looking like a weird living effigy.

He went unnoticed until he was among the skaters making their slow idiotic circuit around the oval rink. Shrill screams rang out. Skaters tumbled to the ice in ones and pairs in their panicked bid for escape. The fire-man made his way slowly into the centre of the ice, where he fell to his knees and burned to death while the skaters looked on in mute horror.

The couple were enjoying their dessert pie slices in the late-night downtown diner. She tried his cherry cheesecake and he her apple crumble. They'd had a good night: a few drinks at a nearby dive bar followed by sex at his apartment and now the dessert they'd forgotten about between leaving the bar and heading the few blocks to his place.

The few other patrons looked just as drowsy as they felt. A quartet of elderly men, each of them bald or balding, sat huddled over their table like a monkish cabal. The old T.V. set flickered down at the couple from the top of their booth, the re-aired hockey game from earlier in the night playing inside its screen fuzzy and indistinct.

"Mm, so good," she said through a mouthful of cheesecake.

"I know, yours too," he agreed, offering a thumbs up.

They finished their desserts. Their T.V. winked off. They frowned at the anomalous little occurrence, and polished off their colas. They sat in comfortable silence for a while, letting their desserts settle. Outside the snowfall continued.

Then:

"We deserve this," he murmured.

"What?" she said, looking from the drink menu she'd been absently perusing. "What are you talking about?"

"I'm sorry, darling," he told her, watching her strangely and standing suddenly from the table. "You know I love you. You know I'll always think of you in the new kingdom."

She watched him with wide incredulous eyes, waiting for the punch-line to her boyfriend's latest quirky antic, wondering how he had the energy after the long night of drinking and lovemaking behind them. She smiled, shaking her head at his eccentric sense of humour as, leaving his coat behind, he made his way to the door. She watched his progress out onto the sidewalk, frowning as he held his arms upwards in what looked like a grand gesture of supplication towards the snowing sky.

She screamed when he burst into flame.

Through her tears, and the great horror that consumed her heart and stole any words she might have had in that unfathomable moment, the only thought she had was that the fire seemed too immense, much too gargantuan a column of flame to have sprung from her lover. And the way it licked skywards and skywards appalled her, the way it shuddered and sputtered and seizured like something alive, so very alive and ecstatic.

Further down the street were a group of gawking bystanders, a group of friends stumbling their way homewards after last call and held spellbound by the spectacle; as she watched, one of them burst into a great pillar of fire.

The Tower of the Elephant:
my heart flies there too.

Their kisses were tainted
Black thoughts were the Summer storms behind their eyes

COME ON, NIGHT!

It stormed briefly but memorably at midnight on October 25, 1932. Bobby Erwin, who never had been a good sleeper, happened to be outdoors doing one of the things he was very good at: night-fighting. Not fighting another boxer or fighter during the night – he was finally finished with all of that, after a good and long and hard-fought run – but fighting, as ever, *with* the night.

He crouched low, edging gracefully from side to side like a cobra while eyeing the shadows encroaching onto his front yard from the dark fields beyond, and then struck upwards with a quick and vicious uppercut. He grunted with the force of the punch. He spat into the dust in wrath, for his opponent had parried yet again. He squinted, seeking the elusive form with whom he fought but, as ever, found it difficult to follow in its fleet movements, feeling only the heat of its mocking breath along his neck. He moved his feet again, seeking the chink in the night's armour which he might exploit – he knew this chink existed, for all mortal combatants had theirs – breathing through a snarl of clenched teeth and a reddening vision of the world as the bloodlust in him grew and grew.

"Hold still, damn you…"

His girl – before she'd left him – and his mother – before she'd been taken away from him by Death – and his father – whom he'd never known but for the lone picture of him that he owned and which he as a child spoke to before bed every night – these were the only people with whom he shared the nature of his ongoing battle.

Nobody else believed him, of course, and he understood why, had understood this even as a much younger man. His mother had always smiled patiently and patted his head (even as an adult she'd done this) and remarked about his vivid imagination; his girl at first laughed at his strangeness and eventually grew distant from him and his weird and unsettling notions; his father listened but, well, he was merely a photograph that Bobby Erwin realized early on could neither listen nor care about his struggles (though he never ceased describing them to it, dog-earring its corners from countless sleepless nights spent whispering his woeful tales to the faded taciturn black-and-white face).

So, on this chilly Autumn midnight, Bobby Erwin fought his customary fight, dancing in the gravel and conjuring a pale dust cloud like a phantom hanging about him as he whirled one way and then another, ducking low and letting loose relentless flurries of left and right hooks like a machine.

And, as it happened to pass on that night, a storm befell him while in the midst of his feinting low in the gravel and punching hard at the air.

It rained, hard, and it rained a rain of human eyes.

Seeing the nature of this precipitation, Bobby Erwin was naturally overcome with revulsion and terror. He shook his head violently to shatter the dream-vision, if such it was, but the mad nature of the spectacle remained. Seized by the primitive superstition of the barbarian (with whom he'd always felt a powerful connection), he floundered beneath the horrific rainfall. Eyeballs collided with his head and face and arms raised ineffectually seeking to protect himself, a monstrous spongy touch the likes of which he'd never imagined could be bestowed by the sky.

Despite his terror he was seized by an instinctual urge to preserve something of the spectacle, and so he scrambled madly to gather what he could of the slimy, slippery, spongy orbs – a double armful cupped to his massive chest – and dashed into the garage, guts churning and skin crawling and thoughts travelling back – against his will – to another night of darkness he remembered all too well.

Once within the dry, musty safety of the garage he laid down his uncanny cargo onto the bare concrete floor. He watched the eyeballs slowly dissolve into a mass of milky grey and pink mucus that both mesmerized and appalled him.

He thought of past deeds returning as ghosts to hound his mortal life. Again, he felt the saltiness of tears rising to smear his vision and struggled to hold them at bay.

432

He fought the punching bag for a long tough hour. Removing his sodden t-shirt he stepped to the battered rubber bag suspended from the ceiling. He fought bare-handed, reddening and purpling his scarred knuckles. His old leather gloves, hanging from a rusty nail on the garage wall, seemed to watch hungrily. As he fought, as always, he was brought back to the days of his youth.

He was the Basher and he bashed his opponents severely every match he ever fought. He didn't always win, but made certain that the pugilists whom he met would remember the fight for the rest of their lives.

He began and ended his career in secrecy and obscurity. Warehouse fights no one knew about but for the other fighters and the handful of teenagers who were willing to spend their nickels and dimes to behold the blood of the spectacle; bare-knuckled brawls in the cold-aired arena of the ice trucks' cargo holds where the vehicles were parked behind the old skating rink. Earning a name and reputation, luring growing numbers of fans of his fisticuffs until management came calling. Graduating then to local cards held in gymnasiums and rented halls, and some tours throughout surrounding towns, too, wherein belts were won and lost, and teeth lost and blood spilled. He'd killed an opponent once, though accidentally: a big Texan who fought dirty and had caught him with a knee to the crotch during first round, nearly setting him up for a knockout until, early second round, the Basher had caught him off guard and landed a heavy one to the man's temple, sending him to the mat for good and for good.

Full-circle then, a slow descent from the squared circle to fist-fights in garbage-teeming alleys and abandoned factory yards. He had white hair by then, and was thinner than he'd ever been – even when, chestnut-haired and wiry, he'd begun his long career – but still he never let a fight go easy. There was always more of their blood spattering the walls, and more of their teeth scattered on the floor than his. There was no reason to give up the perpetual fight entirely, despite time wearing on his bones and muscles, devouring his former cat-like speed and preternatural endurance: it was all he'd ever known.

Then: a sparring practice with the old punching bag after midnight in preparation for a big oil rigger who was new in town and looking for easy money and a reputation among the roughnecks (he'd seen him fight that very night and, though he knew he could beat him, knew too from the senseless state of his opponent that the man could bludgeon a skull good). So Bobby Erwin had bloodied his knuckles with the bag and felt no sting of pain either, so enraptured was he with the forthcoming fight and the bag he punished with such tenacious fury, as if it sought to best him in the same way men sought to steal his pride and reputation and dignity.

And the clamour of thunder erupted outside as the first rainfall of Autumn began to touch the earth in a million smacking pelts. The chance flickering of the single bare bulb lighting the garage space wanly; the chance striking of a crooked finger of lightning into an electrical tower somewhere in the county and subsequently extinguishing its light altogether, plunging the room into the purest blackness of deepest night; and the chance arrival, in that very instant – as if fated by a cruel deity overseeing the moment – of a person into the garage. Unheard by him amid the thunder outside and the thunder deafening him from the inside, the old bloodlust that awakened whenever a man called him out and the contest loomed like a challenge of the man he sought to be. And, sensing this human presence upon him he'd wheeled instinctively and reached out viciously into the darkness with a fist like a sledgehammer.

The blow, he learned a moment – a mere moment! – afterwards in the awful clarity offered by the return of light in the garage, had caught her directly in her left eye. He'd knelt to her side, cupping her small head in his immense bloody hands. The bird-like frailty of her, such a diminutive woman, struck him. He thought for a moment that he'd killed her there and then, but then felt her breath on his fingers, erratic but warm. He watched in terror as her eye socket, with its surrounding shattered and misshapen orbital bone, emptied itself of the blue jewel it had held, a viscous white syrup running down her cheek and into his trembling palm.

He'd accidentally blinded the only woman he'd truly loved, and who'd loved him back just as profoundly: his mother.

"Oh momma, I'm so sorry. I'm so sorry, momma."

Her lingering fortitude would prove a deception, and she died two nights later, upon her bed, after drifting in and out of consciousness for hours on end, the trauma of the injury she'd suffered too severe from which to recover.

It was the only time in his life that Bobby Erwin wept.

*

He woke as if from the deepest of slumbers and the most bottomless of dreams. He sat up, found that he was laying on the cold concrete floor of the garage. He looked habitually to the place where the punching bag hung and found that it was gone – only the simple brass fixture in which it had been fitted remained attached in the ceiling. He found the bag several feet away from him, battered across the floor by the fury of his fists minutes or hours before.

He shook his head. He rubbed at his eyes. He felt strange. The taste of iron filled his mouth, as if he'd taken a good one square in the teeth. He spit. Crimson muddied the saliva. He shook his head. He remembered: the darkness again, and a deluge he would never forget. Fury seized him.

He sprang to his feet and plunged from the musty room and into the night. He knew not the time, but saw that the moon had traveled a good ways across the sky.

His words were a new thunder in the night.

"Hey, Night! Hey, you rotten bastard! Come on down here and let's be fair about this! Come on down here and gimme one more fight! I been waiting how many years now! You owe me! I owe *you*! Come on, Night! Show yourself! Come *on*!"

In the distance, a deep murmuring among the clouds, as if giants wrestled in the mountains of the north. It grew, this great clamour. It seemed to make words, to call Bobby Erwin's name like an answer to his challenge. Thunder, a colossal din rumbling inside the earth as it fell from the sky, too.

Then, inclement weather erupted once again. Teeth, of all shapes and sizes and discolorations, fell from the sky. They pelted his bare arms, struck the crown of his head and stung his cheeks and bit his broad shoulders. A heavier blow crashed against his shoulder and, turning, he caught a glimpse of the human skull – split with a chasm-like crack from temple to crown – roll into the shadows.

He remained standing in the gravel, bearing the onslaught of bones. He eyed the darkness on all sides. He roared to that darkness. "Come on! Where are you, bastard?! Where are you, Night?! I feel you! Come on out! It's you and me, one last time! I loved her, you bastard! I was her guardian, you Devil! Come on out and show yourself to me!"

He snorted, bull-like and savage, smelling the air for sweat and blood. He cocked a cauliflowered ear. A crunching from behind him. Footsteps approaching along the narrow gravel path leading in from the miles and miles and miles of dark fields.

Bobby Erwin squinted into the dense shadows.

The Basher grinned the gap-toothed grin that had sunk the hopes of his opponents in his golden days owning rings and ice trucks and back alleys and other arenas everywhere.

"There you are. Finally, after all the years, you got the guts to answer me."

And he curled his fingers into hard fists of granite.

And he thought: *This battle's for you, momma.*

The Basher set his feet wide apart in the gravel. He raised his square block-fists before him. He bared his teeth and felt his heart – the old notched hammer that was yet to let him down – crashing inside him at this, his final chance to right what he could of the wrongful world.

Thousands of chariots were destroyed, then deep silence descended on the sea. The winds began to blow and the earth grew bright. It was a terrible sight to see. The corpses of the fallen were mutilated by the terrible heat so that they no longer looked like human beings.

- from the Mahabharata

Hate, but hate good.

BLACK LASH
OF LUCIFER

Black Lash Of Lucifer

To have never known?
Or to have been bound in Paradise
until savage Sunday saw the golden embrace cut?

Of course we would take the same paths of pain
if given the choice again, and again, and again...
This is who we are.

We're everywhere in this lotus dream
These tangled streets are heavy with us,
honeycombing the slumped buildings, too
We need and fear the same havens
while drawing light inside of mirrors
But it's everywhere,
the Black Lash of Lucifer:
our loneliness

- The Deathray Bradburys

I like my pies in the skies.

HEAVEN A MILLION
HEXES AWAY

The small diner had been infiltrated by the humidity of the outdoors. The few customers seated at the tables looked immobilized by it, slumped over their coffee cups and dessert plates. Even the flies were heavy with it, sagging in their listless patterns drifting through the sweltering air, like airships weighted down with oppressive cargoes. From the near distance, overtop the low wheeze of the diner's wobbly, ineffectual ceiling fan, the traffic of the 401 came like a continuous somnolent murmuring voice.

The teenager slouched at the corner table ignored the menu opened before her. Instead, she eyed the sole man occupying the bar, as she'd been observing him since settling down at her table only several minutes earlier. He would stand out no matter where he was, she thought, but especially so in the drowsy diner, with its handful of quiet patrons, mostly elderly men and women wearing summer clothes of khaki shorts, pastel-coloured short-sleeve shirts, and sandals. Most of these would be county regulars, she figured, with the occasional traveler like herself, those people passing through this town en route to some outlying city or other and merely taking a brief break from the road with a coffee and doughnut. The man at the bar fell unmistakeably into this latter category, she knew. His blue jeans were filthy, stained a yellowish brown as if from many weeks' accumulation of dirt and sweat. His plain white button-down shirt was similarly dirty, and his brown boots dusty and scuffed. His tangled, unwashed hair shone with grease, and his profile when he peered about the room was scraggly with days' worth of stubble. These aspects of the stranger, and some indefinable otherness, told her that he was no county dweller.

The waitress shuffled towards her from where she'd finished jotting down a woman's order at a nearby table. "You ready to order, sweetie?" She had a smoker's voice, raspy and masculine. Her small rectangular nametag read 'Floe'. The girl marvelled at the clichéd sitcom-ready perfection of the name in matching a middle-aged waitress with a conspicuous limp, employed in a dump of a diner off the highway, the lines in her face and surrounding her eyes seemingly less a product of her age than of the hard experiences she'd had in her life. A sudden image came to her, in which she saw herself in thirty or forty years looking much the same as this woman, haggard and limping through her own sad diner-life, her own memories bending her towards the tiles.

"I can't decide," she said with an apologetic smile, more than a little unsettled by the vision.

Floe smiled benevolently. "Take your time, hon. I ain't in no rush." She watched the woman hobble through the narrow aisle formed by the compactly positioned tables and through the swinging door into the kitchen. She found her thoughts lingering on her, pondering the nature of her limp, and whether this too had its origin in some difficult experience of her past; an abusive husband or boyfriend, an accident from which she'd never fully recovered her former un-laboured walk.

She found the man at the counter again. She wondered what aspect of him it was that drew her attention so forcefully, beyond his conspicuous clothing and dishevelled, road-worn appearance. He had a riveting, frightening quality about him, she decided: brooding eyes flitting guardedly about the room at any minute disturbance, a woman standing from her leftovers with a squeaking of her chair across the linoleum before heading to the restroom, a new patron arriving with a squealing of the screen door's hinges and a tinkling of the door chimes; his posture, hunched but unlike the sagging denizens of the diner – whereas they appeared merely as victims of the day's tenacious heat and humidity he had a dually wary and vulture-like, predatory aspect to him, as if he were prepared to pounce on any who chanced or dared to come too near him.

Maybe it was this alien quality in the man that compelled her to approach him, eliciting the peculiar hope in her that, of all the other more ordinary people in the diner and in the world at large, he might be able – maybe even willing, if he likewise related to her own deviancy – to help her. Perhaps he felt as misplaced there among those outwardly normal patrons as she felt. Furtively, so as not to draw the attention of the other customers, she slid from her chair with a quiet groaning from its faux-leather seat and, grabbing her knapsack from where she'd placed it out of sight beneath the table, glided through the aisle. She slipped onto the stool next to the man at the counter and removed a menu from its place between the condiment rack and napkin dispenser.

446

She perfunctorily scanned its items and prices and list of daily specials, her heart hammering. His smell came to her: a potent brew of heat, and oil, and sweat, all the combined odours of travel of countless miles. Manly, unpleasant but not entirely so, and the longer she remained within its atmosphere the more profound became the unexpected feeling of exhilaration it awoke in her. This man wasn't like the men she'd known in her life: where her father was soft and malleable and grotesque and the boys in her school loud and foolish, this stranger was hard-edged and resilient and handsome, quiet and seeming to hide some secret knowledge that, for whatever reason, she felt a desperate need to know, too.

She wasn't sure whether the man had seen her when she'd entered the diner, though she suspected that he had – she sensed that he was wary of every happening within the small room. She thought frantically of something to say, growing increasingly discomfited by the silence between them. Catching a glimpse of Floe in the kitchen through the small circular porthole-like window set into the door she settled on, "I think everybody should wear name tags all the time. Like the kind they wear here. That way you wouldn't have to introduce yourself ever." When the man said nothing, indeed appeared as though he hadn't even registered the sound of her voice disturbing his meditations, she gave a nervous laugh and added, in a slightly louder voice, "I hate introducing myself to people."

Risking a peek at the man she saw that he still only stared into the air, looking quite as though he was thinking of very distant things, oblivious to her and her mouse-like voice. She returned her attention to the menu in her hands, feeling foolish in failing to elicit any reaction – let alone actual conversation – from him. A renewed sense of dread crept over her, too, as the awkwardness of the situation she'd placed herself in came home to her. Seeing Floe emerging from the kitchen she scanned the menu hurriedly. Needing to be as frugal as possible while satisfying her rumbling belly, she marked the laminated page with her finger – the dessert menu was reasonably priced, and she loved apple pie – and looked for the waitress. She'd moved into the middle of the room, though, and was wiping down an empty table with a spotted rag. The girl was watching her intently, waiting to catch her eye – willing her to return and take her order – when his voice startled her.

"That's one of the dumbest things I heard in some time."

She turned to him, a queer thrill pulsing through her at the realization that she'd succeeded in urging words from the man. He'd turned his attention to the beer bottle sweating in his hand, eying it with the same intensity with which he'd stared into the air. She felt frantic, and at a loss as to how to respond, and only stammered, "Pardon? Sorry, what did you say?"

Still gazing at the bottle, he said in a measured tone, "I ain't keen on introducing myself neither, but to think the good answer is for everybody to wear a name tag – that's plain dumb." He drank some beer and then replaced his perspiring bottle on the countertop with soundless efficiency.

"Why?" She was insulted by his words and had intended to sound assertive, demanding, maybe even a little interrogative, but a disappointingly whining timbre infused her voice, pleading and frail in the quiet.

"You're young, so maybe you never learned this yet: it ain't never wise to tell people who you are if you don't got to. That can lead to troubling times." She found the man's voice, though discomfiting in how he spoke to her, somehow soothing. Deep and smooth, the way she'd always believed men were supposed to sound, like the voices of the old crooners she'd discovered while pilfering her mother's record collection years ago, the Del Shannons and Dave Clarks and Frank Sinatras of the world.

She ruminated on his words for a moment and found that they made sense to her. "Yeah, I guess so. Yeah. That sounds about right to me, now that I think about it." The fact that she'd agreed with him without any real reluctance made her feel an unexpected sense of maturity. Maybe asking this man for help wouldn't be as difficult as she'd imagined it would be. Perhaps he would understand and sympathize with her plight now that she'd acquiesced to his wisdoms. Perhaps he'd see the dust in her clothes and the unwashed sheen of her hair and feel a kindred affection towards her. Deciding that plunging in was better than timidly hinting at the subject, she said in as nonchalant a voice as she could muster, "I don't have any money. Well, I have a little, but not enough to get where I'm going. I've been hitchhiking, but the going's slow, and I've got to be there by tomorrow."

The man took his time drinking his beer. When he set the bottle down again and spoke, his voice was unconcerned. "That's a Hell of a problem you got yourself."

She eyed him resolutely though her breathing quickened with anxiety. Desperation seized her as she continued. "I've got to get there really bad. To where I'm going. The thirty bucks I have left won't get me there."

"No," he said, noncommittally. "That don't get nobody nowhere."

Seeing no reason to abandon her efforts, and with the added incentive of exploring beyond the weird barrier of the mysterious man, she wore on. "I've got to get there really bad. It's…*important* that I get there. I'll… I can do anything for you that you want, if you help me out…"

She hadn't meant to go so far. She'd vowed to never go so far again with anyone, and yet here she was in the great aftermath hush of giving herself up like an offering to this grim stranger.

She stopped short, seeing Floe limping towards them. Perhaps the waitress saw the shock and fear in her face, or else she merely sensed something amiss between the teenage girl and the silent ominous man – she'd probably had years of experience observing and assessing customers in her diner, after all – Floe hastened towards them. In a quiet, urgent voice directed to the girl, she said, "Is everything alright? You okay, hon?"

She nodded and gave Floe as encouraging a smile as she could manage. "Yeah. Fine."

The woman smiled sympathetically. "You made up your mind yet?" She looked to the menu opened in front of the girl, her pencil poised over the little notepad she held.

"Yeah. The apple pie sounds great. And a coffee. Black."

Floe eyed her lingeringly before offering an approving nod and replacing the pencil behind her ear without having written down the order. "Good choice on the pie. It's my favourite." She eyed the man warily and then limped into the kitchen, leaving them in silence again. In an effort to quell the awkwardness – and hoping desperately to somehow nullify her propositioning of herself by changing the subject – the girl said, "Diners always have the best desserts. Pies and other pastries and stuff. Way better than in the city."

She scratched the Formica countertop with a dirty fingernail, thinking distantly how Tomboy-like she'd become throughout the past few days of travel; hitchhiking along dusty roads and sleeping in the woods like she had the past two nights were erasing the girl she'd been and replacing her with this oddly genderless person who smelled boy-like but retained her girlish walk and predisposition to throw herself at men the way she'd long ago learned helped her get what she wanted.

A nearly inaudible groan of leather disturbed the stillness as the man swivelled on his stool to look at her. She felt his scrutiny as a near burning sensation, like intense sunlight on her skin. This feeling intensified the longer he observed her, and she felt herself blushing beneath his appraisal. His deep smooth voice came quietly, "You're a pretty little girl. It's true. Real pretty. And stupider than that by a long shot."

She said nothing. She knew not what to say. Suddenly the prospect of waiting for her apple pie and coffee, let alone finishing them, seemed an impossible task when confronted with the stranger's judgement of her. Deciding to ignore her ignoble overture to the man and remain dedicated to her efforts of securing a ride, she ventured, "Where are you headed? I just need a lift as far as you're going, and that's all. Every mile helps."

This time he answered without delay, his tone irritated. "How come you're so smart and know I'm going someplace? How do you know I don't live in this county and I'm just out for a quick beer on a hot day before heading back to my farm to milk my cows and feed my chickens?"

"I don't know," she admitted in a resolute voice, feeling more than a little bold when she added, "I don't know how I know it but I do. You're not from here."

He turned from her and finished his beer before responding. "You're right about it: I ain't from around here. I'm from a long ways off, and I'm running even further than that. I'd best be getting on my way soon, then."

Something in this caused her breath to catch. Her heart fluttered. She was succeeding in breaking the man's stony silences time and again. Maybe she'd learn his story, if she acted quickly enough. Suddenly this story seemed incredibly important for her to know, more so even than securing a ride with the man. Maybe the knowledge would somehow prove to be the key in escaping this place with him. Words escaped her now with great urgency. "What are you running from?"

She was disheartened to see the man give a dismissive shake of the head and sneer, "Looks like I should be running from you and your jabbering, little girl."

"I'm only wondering. I just… I'm curious, that's all. What is it? That you're running from, I mean."

"You're asking, but you don't want the answer I got."

"I do. No, I do."

He turned to her. She recoiled from his grim, bloodshot eyes. He spoke slowly, enunciating his syllables with great care. "The Devil. Or some cocksucker like Him."

She made her voice sound as casual as she could despite being both nonplussed and completely unnerved by his forbidding answer. "Oh, okay. You – Is he… I mean, did you get a good head start on…him? Whoever he is?"

He gave a sardonic-looking smile. "I told you who He is, and He's always close. He's licking my heels even now. And yours, too, little girl. You can feel Him, right?"

The man's self-assured tone angered her when he spoke of her own fate. She braved his brewing eyes and muttered sullenly, "No I can't. No he's not *close*. And stop calling me that. I'm not a *little girl*."

He was nodding solemnly. "Trust me, little girl. He's an angry God and he's coming for you like he's coming for me and every other sad fucker there is."

Fury bloomed from her mounting desperation. "One minute you're talking about the Devil and now you're telling me about God like He's hunting people like –"

"One and the same, little girl. They're one and the same bastard. We all got different faces and different stories, but the same bastard is after us. That great taker who does nothing else besides taking. Loneliness hunts us all. You got that part right."

Loneliness hunts us all.

She shuddered visibly, as if some great fear that had slept dormant deep inside her was awakened at the words.

She watched him. His words had bludgeoned all thoughts from her head. Only despair remained, now owning her completely. She felt her lower lip begin to tremble, and hated the man for bringing her to this: she hadn't cried in days, and had vowed to never do so again. Monday night had been an exception: the man who'd picked her up and taken her a few miles east down the 401 before pulling into the wooded cul-de-sac where she could make good on her end of their bargain: he'd given her good reason to despair of people. And here she was now, broken by a stranger whose hatred and mistrust of the world seemed miraculously to rival her own; the same man who denied her a simple ride from one Godforsaken roadside diner to the only place that might save her.

She wept. She felt his eyes on her. She muttered in a surly voice, "I just need a ride."

He laughed a cruel laugh, dismissive and callous. The man wasn't moved by her tears, in this way showing that he was impervious to the type of emotional manipulation that she'd learned long ago as a means of swaying people to her will.

They shared silence, the girl wiping at her eyes, the man unmoving beside her. When he spoke his voice was just as hard as before: "You don't want no ride from this bastard, little girl."

An uncertain hope sputtered into life inside her. Resigned to her display of weakness, she turned to him and through her tears said in a quiet, imploring voice, "Yes, I do. I *do*. I just need to go as far as you can take me, and I'll find my way from there. That's all. Every mile helps."

It felt almost as though he waited for her tears to clear from her eyes so that she might see him unfiltered by her despondency. Then, watching her in his wolfish, wary way, he said, "I killed people."

A vision materialized in her mind: this man crowning the summit of a hill of dead men. These corpses were bloodied and raw, torn and scratched everywhere, and the look in his eyes was more feral than any he'd shown her yet. She felt numbed by the vision. With it in her eyes she made her voice even and said, "People? You mean…more than one person?"

"Where you come from don't *people* mean more than one person?"

She watched him avidly, though she wished to escape inside the safety of the menu before her. Where was Floe? Maybe she could quell the fear rising in her, and take her from this unexpected language. But she only ventured, in a whisper, "How come? I mean, why did you do it?"

The man didn't answer her, turning to look over his shoulder, perhaps to examine the sky through the grimy window, or to will another patron to put their eyes far away from the two of them at the counter, immersed in their frightening talk. She was curious about the way he scrutinized the outdoors or the patrons, though, with narrowed, wild eyes, as if searching for some very particular thing among them. She realized it reminded her a little of the way her father looked when he used to show her animals formed from the cumulus: standing in the centre of their backyard in the long hour's stretch before suppertime, shielding their eyes from the brightness, his finger pointing out a family of gazelles gambolling in the blue, and just as often the cloud-predator beginning to form nearby to skulk after and disperse them, and chase down its prey somewhere in the vastness.

The man stirred her from her reveries: "I killed the man who stole something what was mine. I cut his throat wide open. Hung him up in his bathroom, from the shower pole, with his spraying veins and intestines wrapped around his throat. I sliced his privates away, too, and flushed those to Hell down the toilet. And that was gonna be the end of it. A good end, too. Just, and good. One I could feel good about. Then, though, his family came after me, see? Brothers – he had five brothers, the biggest family of bastards I ever heard about – and what must have been every friend each of them brothers had. I lost my count after about a hundred or so. But there was more than that. So I killed them. I had to. It was them were gonna get me, or I was gonna kill them instead, and live. And I was gonna live." Then, with a subtle imploration, he added, "But I didn't do none of them with no hate in me. Not a one drop. My hatred I gave it all to the one. The one that done stole my good joy."

She trembled. A chill defied the languorous heat of the day and snaked from the base of her spine upwards to clasp her shoulders. She saw this man, grim and kingly, owning his bloody mountain once again, like a traveler come through time from a barbaric era long past to cut the air of the present-day with his vicious tongue and the red stories it told. Her voice came as a whisper once more: "What did the one brother steal from you?"

"I ain't gonna tell you big answers like that, little girl. Truth is, I don't believe you got the right to be asking me big questions like that neither."

"I'm sorry." She was mildly surprised at the guilt she felt for pushing him, for being so inquisitive about his private affairs.

He startled her: "Fair trade, then: what's got you running, little girl?" She was unsettled by the way he turned to her then, eyes seemingly relishing her discomfiture. This was a conversation and confrontation for which she couldn't be prepared.

"I'd rather not say, if it's all the same to you."

His eyes grew livid as he turned fully upon his stool to examine her directly. "What you mean you'd rather not say? I just told you my goddamn life story, in full bloody colour. I asked you a question: where you going, and why you going there?"

She looked for Floe, but found herself alone. Why did the world insist on her honouring bargains she regretted immediately upon making? She admitted as much as she dared. "I'm running away from home."

"Where's home?" He spoke quickly now, with genuine interest or else a perverse glee in witnessing the great discomfiture he aroused in her.

"The city." She didn't say which city, which seemed somehow appropriate. The man didn't ask her to specify. She pictured the burning day outside, the tree-line shimmering in the heat-haze beyond the edge of the parking lot, and yearned to be moving eastward again. Eastward: the direction of her hope. When he said nothing the thought occurred to her and she added, "It's better out here. Where the trees are." Seeing a plump bluebell light upon the counter near her elbow, she added, "When I was hitchhiking yesterday, waiting for a ride on the side of a road, I saw a beaver. I'd never seen one before. He was huge. His fur was a dark brown. He had big black eyes. And a big tail like a pancake. He came out from the tall grass growing inside a ditch, and looked around for a second, and then went back into the bushes. He saw me for a second, though, and kind of looked at me for a second. And it was so nice, you know? There was nothing scheming in his eyes when he did it. He just looked and I looked and it was nice and quiet. And then he was gone. I caught a ride a little while later." The woman who'd picked her up had been pleasant: chubby in the middle and round-faced, too, with a gentle voice and only a very gentle admonition concerning a girl her age hitching out in the county. Who knows who might pick you up in the middle of nowhere and take you to who knows where?

She sensed his lingering stare. She looked to him, saw his scrutiny was as avid as that with which he watched the air, a bottle of beer. He pressed her, though she thought the hard edge had left his voice: "Where you going and why you going?"

She answered him. There was no reason not to, really, and with the realization she felt something inside her fall away. "My daddy did things to me. That's the why part of it."

He watched her. His expression remained unchanged. He looked away and put his eyes into the nebulous near-distance again.

She decided to answer his other question. There was no reason not to. "So I'm going far away. To this place. I heard about it in a pamphlet. A guy was handing them out at the county fair last summer. I was there with a friend. We both got one. We laughed about it. She threw hers away, but I kept mine. I laughed about it, too, but I never thought it was funny. I was just pretending. It talks about a place, far away from here."

"You're hitching your way there? Ain't there a bus or train goes there?"

"I don't have the money for a bus. I saved as much as I could, but I don't have that much. But anyways, that's just the first part of the trip…"

"You're talking in riddles, little girl. What's this first part business? What's the second part? You hitching cross-country or something? What's the name of the town you're trying for?"

"It's not that kind of a place. It's… Maybe some people would think it's silly, or crazy, but it's…out *there*."

He followed her gesture, ceilingwards – skywards – with a curious expression. "What are you saying?"

She shrugged, began toying with a napkin she'd pulled from the dispenser without thought.

"No, come on," he said. "Tell me. You got my curiosity."

A queer peace came over her. The diner felt quieter then than earlier. The afternoon seemed time-paused, as though each of its ingredients – patrons, flies, sunlight – had ceased their movements, while only she and the stranger stirred within the strange bubble of their hushed conversation. She opened her mouth, and her story came. "The pamphlet says…The pamphlet says there's going to be… There's going to be a saucer coming. For everybody who knows about it, and believes that it's coming. It's going to travel to this far-away place –" she raised her eyebrows towards the ceiling again – "and…save everybody. Everybody who needs to go away on it. But first we all have to meet at the first place, tomorrow, at dusk. We meet there, and drink a special potion, and then the spirit part of each of us will be able to board the saucer. That's where I have to go, and when I have to be there by. Or I'll miss it." Her heart clutched at the thought even as she added: "I can't miss it."

The man didn't speak for a minute. When next he spoke his voice was different somehow, though she couldn't say exactly how. "You *got* to go there?"

"Yeah. I have to go."

"On a… on a saucer? What's that exactly? Does that mean like a flying ship or something? A pie in the sky? Like from magazine-stories and such?"

She nodded, watching the ketchup bottle in its slot within the condiment rack. Its encrusted mouth made her vaguely nauseous, reminding her of congealed blood. She absently tore off a corner of the napkin, crumpled it in her fingers.

"You believe stories like those?"

"I believe this one."

Floe came, maybe a little late or perhaps right on time, bearing her slice of pie and steaming cup of coffee. Placing it before her she smiled her kindly smile and said, "Sorry about the wait. I had to brew a fresh pot. Enjoy, hon." She limped back into the kitchen.

The girl sipped her coffee. It burned her mouth. She didn't mind. It woke her from the strange torpor that had besieged her senses. She said hesitantly, "If you don't mind me asking –"

"I mind you asking. Why don't you shut up already. Your pie's getting cold."

"I didn't get it warmed up," she said petulantly, annoyed by the man's sweeping mood swings, especially abrasive following their queerly tranquil shared moment.

He stared at her aghast. "Are you bat-shit nuts, little girl? You ain't got your pie warmed up? You telling me that's a cold pie right there?"

She looked to the dessert. "Yeah. I don't ever eat it warmed up. It's better cold."

He eyed her warily, and then the pie on her plate with the same guarded expression. Shrugging with what she thought to be far too much theatricality he said with something like resignation, "This world's filled with weirdness, through and through. Through and through." Shaking his head, he said, "But then I guess that's just the way, ain't it? I guess that's what makes it go round and round in the ways it does, this weird world. Or else it would be another place, and not this place, right?"

This made sense. She nodded. He nodded now, too. She looked to her plate and found that her appetite was immense. The pie was gone in a moment. Her stomach made funny gurgling noises that, days before, would have embarrassed her in the presence of strangers. Now, though, she didn't care. She washed down the pie with the coffee, relishing its heat, the energy with which she envisioned it filling her body, waking her senses for the trek remaining before her.

She somehow wasn't expecting him to talk much after that. He surprised her. "I got a friend kind of like a brother. A friend the kind you stop making when you're grown up. He'll help keep me buried good and away from anyone looking for me for what I done. Unless he don't hide me, for whatever reason. People change, I know it. But if he ain't changed since years ago, well, I'll be staying in this place I'm heading to. That's where I'm headed, see. East from here. Nice and quiet and green everywhere."

"It sounds like a really nice place."

He said nothing, only nodded.

They sat in the silence, he watching the air, she polishing off the pie crumbs on her plate. A fly buzzed its tiny din somewhere around them, and then disappeared into another part of the diner.

She pushed her plate away and stooped to search in her handbag. A moment later she produced something and placed it before the man on the countertop. He examined it initially without touching it. Realizing what it was, though, he picked it up. He eyed the picture adorning the pamphlet's cover page with his rabid eye: a strange, vaguely hexagonal symbol, looking simultaneously archaic with its solid, hard edges and ornate design, and futuristic with its silver-tinted colouring. A stylized representation of a disc occupied the symbol's central point, looking crest-like and regal. She eyed the picture, too: as always all of her hope came awake at the familiar sight of it. She pictured herself reading the words the pamphlet contained, with as ferocious an eye as the man examined it now: in bed at home, tears drying on her cheeks as the symbol conjured hope in her heart from the great desolate space yawning inside her; or while wandering the old neighbourhood streets, alone as always with her dark thoughts, looking at the symbol on the cover page beneath open skies and then to the sky itself with a new hope in her; and during the past several days especially, sneaking peeks at it when no cars glimmered in the western highway horizon, pausing in her afternoon walk in the shoulder of the road to gain a quick fix of energy from the looking; and laying curled among the grass of the off-highway wooded lot after the man had left her there, the taste of him still haunting her mouth and making her stomach queasy despite her having spit and spit and spit into the grass running amok with vibrant wildflowers. Anything to make her destination on time. Any small or great sacrifice to crawl another mile or another inch into the east waiting for her.

He opened the pamphlet and looked through it.

She closed her eyes, imagining the words it held, memorized long, long ago.

It was strange hearing his husky, hushed voice reading from it, utterly engrossed:

Join us as brother or sister, and leave all that behind which burdens your joy.

We, the People of Sai-Markesses, await you with open arms and hearts. We are ever present to help all who trust in us and call upon us in their time of direst need. Be with us, and you shall have joy, delight, and comfort. Join us, and we will be a new Family, and we will leave our collective heartache behind upon this scarred Earth, on our great journey into the Heart of the Twins of Sirius, and beyond.

Never again need you live a day with your old pain. Leave it behind, forevermore.

The bloody sun sets, but our Morning Star rises…

She half-expected some derisive comment, mockery of the words he'd read and which he knew she believed in. But he said nothing.

She murmured, eyes still closed, "The address is there at the bottom of that page. And the date and time they're leaving. That's tomorrow, at dusk. It's a couple towns east of here. I have to get there. They've been planning it for years and years. It talks all about it in there. I have to get there."

The man closed the pamphlet with an efficient hand, placed it before him on the countertop and stared again at the cover image. A moment passed, and he slid the pamphlet across the counter to her. She quickly placed it in her bag, and then sat silently awaiting the next thing he might say to her.

Together they watched as a plump bluebell appeared from the ether and settled atop the napkin dispenser. He addressed it: "You a good creature. You got no meanness in you."

She admired the insect in a way she never would have before hearing the man's weird wisdom concerning it. Before, flies were just annoying bugs attracted to shit or nauseating roadkill putrefying in the sun. Now, though, she appreciated the insect's glimmering multi-faceted eyes, the light reflecting from its green-tinted body as if it were wearing a miniature coat of steel; its tiny tacky legs holding it securely in place atop the dispenser, its two front legs rubbing together as if it shared its afternoon prayer with them. She'd begun appreciating the natural world around her more and more during the past few days, and hearing the man say to the fly what he'd said validated something for her. He was right: it was a beautiful creature, pure and jewel-like.

The insect took flight, disappearing into the air over their heads, another little miracle overlooked by the other diner patrons.

Around them the diner continued to drowse in its own sleepiness; the fan wheezed; a woman coughed; a spoon tinkled inside of a coffee cup; the midday sunlight pouring in through the front window crawled its way deeper into the diner, bringing with it the indefinable sound of shadow being devoured by light.

"How come you asked me, instead of asking Floe?"

She raised an eyebrow. He'd noticed the waitress's nametag, too. Of course, he would have, being as vigilant as he was, but still it reassured her a little, though she couldn't say exactly what of. She admitted, "I don't know. She seems nice. And she probably would've tried to help, but…but sometimes nice people aren't nice for real anyways…. I just… I guess I just knew to ask you."

She turned and watched him full-on. Her heart raced. He was nodding, eying the air. He held his wallet, its brown leather worn, in a brawny hand. He removed a handful of dirty bills from it and placed them on the counter between their plates. He stood from his stool without a sound, casting his cautious gaze over the room one final time. She watched him walk through the aisle with the silent, sure, measured stride she'd somehow known he possessed, through the door, and into the afternoon. The golden light limned him, swallowed him, making her think a little bit of representations of angels that she'd seen in books, a little bit of the avenged man of her vision standing astride a mountain of the guilty and necessary dead.

She gathered herself, tying the drawstring of her bag closed. Floe came shuffling from the kitchen. Her milky eyes were concerned. Her breathing sounded laboured, as if she'd shuffled too fast for her own good. She said, "Is everything okay, hon'? You all set?" She eyed the money on the counter suspiciously, and then the diner's doorway, from which tinkled the door chimes signalling the man's departure.

"Yeah, that's for both of us." The girl pointed to the money on the counter.

Floe watched her carefully. Her eyes narrowed with her concern for the girl. "You *sure* you're alright, hon? You *sure* about it?"

She smiled for the woman, and found it an easier feat to achieve now than it had been earlier. "It's okay, Floe. Really. Thanks for the pie. It was the best thing I've eaten in years." It felt good calling her by her name. She hoped Floe liked it, too. She slung her bag over her shoulder and turned to go.

From behind her, Floe said, "Bye, darling. Good luck to you."

The waitress and the girl looked at each other in the sleepy stillness. An old man seated approximately midway between them had turned to eavesdrop on their exchange. The girl looked to him and, amused by the child-like audacity with which he continued to scrutinize them, told him, "You take it easy, grandpa. If you move too fast on a steamer like today it might kill you dead in your tracks."

The man frowned, but continued to watch her. Floe chuckled a wry chuckle, seemingly put at ease by the words. The girl smiled at her, turned and followed the stranger into the sunlight.

She found him owning the centre of the small gravel parking lot, watching the sky through squinting eyes. She sidled alongside him without words. They sky-watched a while together in the great baking quiet while the cicadas buzzed like electricity from the trees fringing the lot.

A dense gathering of perfectly white clouds took up the eastern quadrant of the sky. They hung completely motionless in the windless afternoon, looking quite like they'd been painted against the azure backdrop of the sky.

"My dad, he used to show me animals in the clouds. He used to say there were animals living in the sky everywhere, if we look hard enough to find them." She discerned an immense bison sky-walking, then another and another, and several smaller specimens: bison-children. Soon enough she had the entire herd spotted in the blue. She scanned the cloud-depths for any sign of preying lion and with some relief found none.

His voice was surprisingly gentle. "Your daddy said that? About animals in the clouds?"

"Yeah. Before he turned bad, he used to say that."

"Your daddy sounds like he was a smart man, once. Before the badness came."

She said nothing.

"What was your other question?"

She turned to him. "I don't… What do you mean?"

"You were gonna ask me something else but I never let you."

She looked away, eyes in the sun-washed gravel before her. "It's nothing. I was just being stupid, and nosy. It's not my business."

"No it ain't, but I'm telling you to ask. It's okay by me."

"Did you… Was she one of the people you killed? Because of her pain?"

She was certain that the man knew she meant his wife. She'd never loved a person so much that she could hurt others in their name, but she believed there were people in the world who would, and something – the blood in his story, maybe, or the sorrow and war in his eyes – told her that the stranger was one of them.

He turned to her, a queer blend of emotions on his face: shock, fear, shame, and, finally, something a little like relief. He said, "Naw. I thought about it, I admit it, but no. I could never. I want her to be without no misery more than anything, but I could never bring myself to give her peace that way. Maybe I'm weak for it, but it was easier to just put that bastard in the ground. Some might say what I done was wrong. Maybe so. But I'm just a man. So I'm thinking it's okay for me to be wrong in things I do, from time to time. I'm…I'm going to miss her, though." He sighed, as if unburdened of some heavy thing that for too long had weighed on him.

She nodded. It was somehow the answer she'd expected. Maybe it was the same answer she would have given, if she'd lived the stranger's life. Feeling hardened, and courageous, she said, "I'm ready to go." In the wake of the admission she understood its truth, and something inside her, old and heavy and deeply entrenched, began its crumbling.

But the man had something to talk about still. "One night, though, before I got strong enough to do what I done, I got real weak. Weak like I never been weak. I done something I'll be ashamed of for a good long time." She turned and was startled by the sight of him, sleeves of his white shirt rolled to his elbows, his wrists and forearms criss-crossed with grotesque scars like pale molten tongues licking at the unblemished skin surrounding them. Among them, ruined by them, she was able to discern an insignia: a bird, encased within the hard edges of a military crest of some sort, a tattoo decades old, faded with time. He explained, "Because the thought of living in this world while she had to live in it, too, after everything that done happened to her – that was the hardest thought I ever tackled. This was loneliness like I never knew could exist. It came close to breaking me. But the weird thing about it all is this," and here he looked into the girl's eyes closely, with an earnestness that unnerved her, as if he needed her to hear this if no other part of his story, and to understand it unequivocally, "I made sure to make the cuts deep and deep, so there wasn't no mistake about where I was headed. I made sure they did the job they was intended to do, bleeding hard, and fast, and me I held the razor blade like a sword in my cutting hand. I made those cuts like a warrior but…but I never died from them. I bled like a fountain shooting from both my wrists and my vision turned black as midnight and I swam down and down into that deep red, but when I woke I wasn't in no Heaven or no Hell or no place in-between unless that place is this right here right now. Maybe God wanted me to stick around a while longer still. Maybe He understands righteous vengeance. Maybe He understands it's a necessary goodness or evil for us, when the hurt and the evil in the world get to be too heavy and the only way you got left is the warrior's way. There's a message in these cuts and in my heart still beating. I'm going to understand it, one day."

Looking to the sky again he said, "Life she drops hexes on us, all different kinds. There's hexes falling on people all over this weird world every day." He said this in his peaceful-voice, and finished after a moment's meditative pause: "Some hexes they can't be fought, though. Only lived through. Marching one step and then another until your march is done. And then you run which way feels right, hoping for peace after all the long shit days and warrior-years is done with you. Or maybe all this is just too big for me to understand right now."

She didn't know what to say. It made sense, so she said nothing. This seemed the right thing to do. A deep kind of stillness settled between them, over them. The humid day burned, the sunlight baked them like clay statues. Turning westwards, the man murmured, "We best be gone from here. He's coming. It never takes Him long. He's found us again."

She looked. Squinting, shading her eyes with a hand she searched the shimmering horizon, the Black oaks and bushes on either side of the tarmac driveway, with the concrete highway beyond like a black snake coiling into the distance. Then, in the highway's haze-blurred centre, walking a measured gait that would take him straight to where they stood baking in the heat, she saw her father, eyes filled with the badness that had sent her there.

Us. *He's found* us *again.* Those had been the man's words.

"I see Him," she said, feeling calm, and sleepy, in the fierce light.

The man turned and put his eyes eastwards again. She followed him and looked there, too.

"Looks to me like we're headed in the same direction, girl."

"Yeah. It sounds like we're going to the same place."

He walked with his quick step to the Trans-Am parked at the lot's periphery. Its skin was filthy, weathered-looking like he was. She scuttled in pursuit. They climbed in. He woke the car's engine. It roared. It shook her in its grip. The longer it roared the more it felt to her as if she was being held by a strong and good force, to be trusted. She relinquished herself to it. He eased them from the lot and down the gravel drive onto the eastbound highway. He accelerated the vehicle rapidly. They rocketed along the smooth black track. She watched the passenger-side mirror and saw the diner, coloured golden in the sunlight, fall away behind them. Apparitions they left in their wake, too, stirring tenaciously in the haze and dust.

Neither of them spoke but the girl was certain the man was as grateful as she for the eastern sky before them: overrun with cumulus, iron-grey in parts but predominantly a pristine white; formidable and brewing overtop the horizon with a million faces and stories in which to live, before the inevitable winds came that would scatter them like a herd before a hunter.

GARDEN THE SKY,
JIMMY

Where did the Essex women go?
Summoned like the tides by the moon
But where did those county women go?
Lost like a whisper in the waving wheat
But people ask "Where did the pretty girls go?"
Away like smoke on a midnight wind
But where and where did the Essex Fifteen go?
Like bonfires they finally were put out

Why did the Essex women go?

They say no one knows why
they let Jimmy put them in the sky

The song drifted through the open car windows, crackling and fuzzy. The familiar chords bolstered something in them, the sweeping melody, bittersweet and aching, made them feel brave to be able to endure it. Behind them, far, far behind them, lay the unlighted strip of 6th Concession long after midnight, devoid of traffic but for occasional county rabbits and raccoons crossing from one field to another on their A.M. foragings. Before them rose the wall of Black oaks and willow trees and the shadows they held between them, quivering and forbidding and thick as oil. The sward before the trees was marked with headstones, fifteen in all, each wreathed with memorial flowers of differing species in varying stages of life or outright decay. Everywhere among them the wild grass stirred with colonies of the incongruous white lilies, that great enigma of the county, like restless moths preparing for flight into the dark air.

Johnny, unnerved by the momentousness of the night and sensing its effects on his wife, absently stirred the gravel of the cul-de-sac with his toe while attempting to distract her with all manner of small talk: "September's in the air tonight. On our way back we should grab some coffees and warm up. Coffee would be good right about now, huh?" "I wonder how many deer live in these woods? I seen a whole herd here once." "The moon's so huge and low in the sky – I bet I could grab it with a good rope toss." "The sky's clear everywhere, but the forecast called for rain. I'm sure we'll get rain. We always do, this time of year." But on this night Monica only smiled distractedly, or laughed falsely, or nodded wordlessly, all while dragging anxiously on the cigarette clenched between her lips and keeping vigil over the woods with distant eyes. Beyond the small plot of headstone-studded grass, the Essex woods stretched deep and deep, and deeper still on anniversary nights haunted through all of their A.M. miles.

The song's pained, crooning bridge troubled the dark air, its thousandth playing that night, while they shared the cigarette in silence.

And where did your great thief go?
Where's Jimmy Wood this lonely night?
No one knows, no one knows,
Maybe Jimmy burns in the sky now, too
Maybe Jimmy isn't the thief at all

She held the cigarette to Johnny, who took it from her wordlessly, feeling defeated at his repeated ineffectual attempts to change the melancholy mood hanging over them. He felt it coming, had sensed the unavoidable build-up of her thoughts since arriving at the site nearly thirty minutes earlier, much like every time they came there, but of course different now.

"I feel her tonight, Johnny. Tonight more than usual, I really *feel* her out here. I…I miss her so bad."

She hadn't meant to talk about her out loud, not yet. They'd only chugged their way through a single Keith's between them and she wasn't anywhere near fortified enough to discuss tragic subjects. She hated herself for the frailty she'd allowed to get the better of her. Of all nights to be weak: she was pathetic. Of all nights to give in to the weight of the world's ways: she was disgracing their mourning ritual. What good mother could commit such a crime?

Johnny, seeing the emotions seizing her, declared, "I know, sweets. I know you do. I miss her, too. But she's at peace. I know it. Kathy's at peace." His voice faltered, though, as always when he sought to be optimistic in the face of the hungry world when that world had its sights trained on his fractured family. He hoped his hand on her shoulder was reassuring, if only a little. He hoped his meagre words were some small comfort. He knew, though, how difficult a task reassuring her would be, on this night especially, while they were hounded more tenaciously than ever by that ubiquitous haunter of their life:

Katherine, their only child, sweet and shy and taciturn, straight-A high school student in her graduating year with promising future cut short, and one of the unnamed women in the song playing on the chill air. They watched the woods and the sky and, as always when visiting the site, saw their daughter's long straw hair blowing among the weeping arms of the willow trees; glimpsed the playful glimmer of her eyes watching them in the low-hanging orange pumpkin-moon in the west before evanescing like some uncanny celestial mirage; heard her unmistakable laughter muted and floating on the wind, up from the earth and drifting starwards like the fulfillment of the song's prophecy.

Their ritual was one they clung to devoutly: making as though they still had their youth every Saturday night, after Monica's shift at the diner was finished and Johnny had picked her up in his beloved Trans-Am, taken out of the garage solely for these wee hour weekend excursions when the minivan just wouldn't do, unable to tear up the lonesome back roads with as much power as his old teenage dream-machine; buying cigarettes and sometimes some beer and driving out to the end of 6th Concession to spend time with the headstones and trees and moon and moths and lilies and great overwhelming stillness. Once there, it always seemed a little like Kathie was there with them, too, even when she wasn't a part of their conversation. Maybe this was because once convened in the familiar place, graveyard-hushed and redolent with flora, the songs of crickets pulsing from the fields all around and the music Johnny and Monica brought with them playing there, too, nostalgia overcame them and they remembered a little of what it had felt like to be young and courageous and reckless; though frightened, too, of the burden they'd once faced together: a baby, and the trial it would prove to be for a young couple with little life experience and even less money between them. Katherine lived between their words to each other, in the same way they could feel her dancing out between the oaks and willows; a comforting presence there with them, and sometimes they were able to drive home in the wee morning when dawn fired the eastern horizon feeling content about their latest vigil, as if their time with the deer and raccoons and nightbirds possibly brought some solace to the ghost of her in the same way it comforted Monica and Johnny. Occasionally during certain of their vigils it even began to seem to them that they'd known their daughter, though of course by morning the tenacious enigma of Katherine was returned to dishearten them all over again and they were forced to accept it as they were able: they'd stopped knowing their girl during her teenage years, when the child they'd raised had transformed into the strange being who spoke to them little and preferred solitude to their company.

This night was an anniversary night, though, so Katherine's presence there with them was too strong to pretend away as merely the eerie sounds of wildlife crunching through the brittle carpet of fallen leaves out among the trees, or the persistent seasonal wind rustling their clothes: ten years to the day of the great abduction and disappearance, a night for troubled spirits to convene with the troubled mothers and fathers left behind to brood in the emptier world.

The event had captured the imaginations of many and crept into pop culture consciousness in innumerable ways, ensuring that the ghost of it was never far away from their thoughts, no matter the presence of other catastrophes or occasional joys in their lives at any given time: a feature-length Canadian-produced film entitled *The Essex Fifteen* had been made in the early years following which chronicled the event, all shot on location throughout the county, as well as many documentaries; several novels had been written inspired to different degrees by the tragedy, the most popular of which – *Stars Fall Up* by Martha McNiff – remaining on top sellers lists for many months; numerous popular songs by a variety of groups of different genres were written, as well, lending the story an air of old dark folk balladry in the tradition of the enduring Stagger Lee mythos. One such song had become a controversial cult classic, and the chosen musical accompaniment for Monica's and Johnny's weekly vigil, though they kept this fact to themselves: written and recorded by underground cult rock band the Deathray Bradburys, and entitled "Peace-Star For The Lost Sixteen", the song seemed an attempt to simultaneously mourn the fifteen victims as well as to empathize with the perpetrator of the crime, James Adam William Wood.

Wood, a resident of nearby Windsor, confessed to the abduction and murder of the fifteen women in a letter sent to authorities in the days following, citing a motive of divine inspiration for the crime which was interpreted by and large as an indication of his insanity. Wood claimed to have convinced the unsuspecting party of fifteen women – members of a summer leisure expedition investigating the appearance in the county of the white lily, a flower species remarkable to that geographic region – to accompany him on a "great journey". Wood went on to explain that he'd been shown this particular group of people in a repeated series of vivid dreams which served to guide his actions. The greater purpose of his crime, he stated, was to transport the women to a 'better place'. His chosen method of murder was forced ingestion of cyanide, though Wood's letter suggested his victims had acted of their own free will. He used the same method to commit suicide. The sixteen bodies were found several days following the arrival of Wood's letter as a result of a massive county-wide search, in a small grove several miles east of the abduction site, in the heart of the woods. The bodies of the women had been arranged in a circle, with Wood at its centre.

Appropriately enough, the Deathray Bradburys themselves gained their cult status and infamy due to their own mysterious disappearance, along with hundreds of their wildly devout fans, as part of a planned cult-like exodus which took place in the summer of 2000. No member of the disappeared has ever been located. The song in question remained a somewhat obscure one, having only been released in very limited edition as a rare 7-inch single, which Johnny had long ago taped onto cassette for play on his car's deck as a pivotal ingredient in their weekly ceremony. Wood's meandering and disjointed confessional letter was made public in the months following, destined to become infamous.

"I saw them first in dreams. Dream after dream after dream, and so I knew they were meant to come with me on the great journey away. All of this was like the ancient myth come true: the white lily was a star fallen to Earth. This is how ancient, wiser peoples explained the lily's exquisite and fragile beauty. The women's expedition for the starflower became my mission of

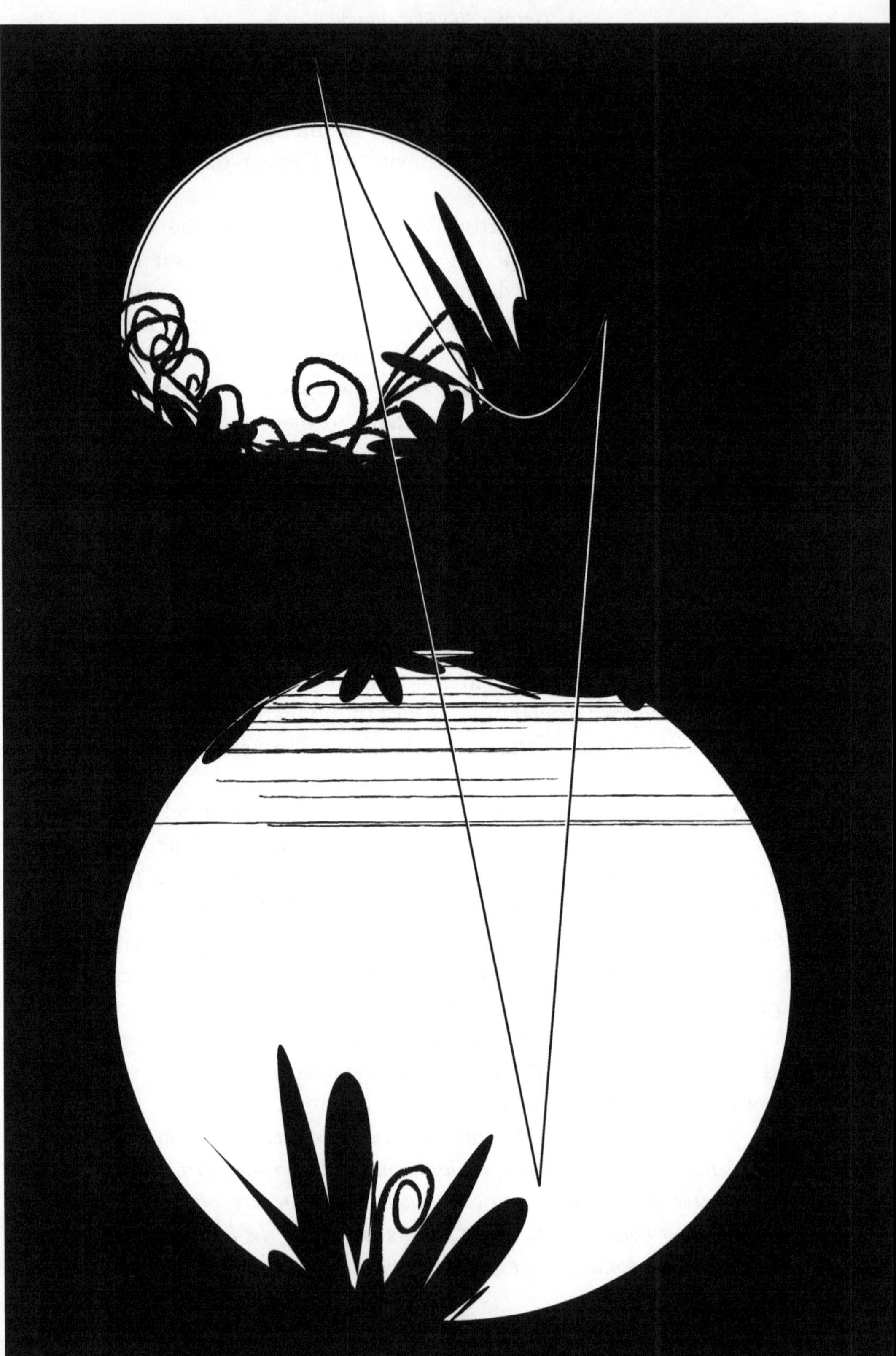

salvation. Their salvation, and so I gave it to them. I welcomed them with a smile and embrace that afternoon in the woods, and I explained my dreams to them, and they understood the goodness of this vision. They were too beautiful. A world like ours shouldn't be allowed such beauty. I had to put that beauty to sleep. So this is what I did. Put it to sleep. I put every one of them to sleep. But now...now they dream. Now they're always dreaming. I dreamed of them, and now I've given them dreams forever.

"*I'm lucky,*" Jim Wood had concluded, in a statement brimming with undisguised wonder. "*I'm such a lucky, lucky man, to have had time upon this Earth in the company of such beauty. They deserved to be in a better place than any offered here. I freed them, you must understand: they were prisoners here. Their beauty was imprisoned here upon this ruined savage Earth. Monsters abound here. Like ancient maps with warnings etched over the great seas and oceans: 'here swim Monsters.' Maps and atlases today should be this truthful. They're in a better place now, away from all of that. They're in a better place and I take my joy in knowing I put them there. In the sky, upon a heavenly point of light pure and unscarred, where only the righteous and innocent of heart may live. As part of my reward for delivering them into the light, I go now, too, to be with them, forever.*"

This had been Jim Wood's bizarre and unsettling confession, immortalized in every news medium, and with time growing to serve also as some sort of secret and bittersweet hope and epitaph for all those mourning the great loss. Fifteen women of different backgrounds and ages, united solely by their great misfortune in having taken part in a fateful summer outing investigating the rareness of the white lily in their county: Delores Audrey; Samantha Jensen; Maria Reedmere; Jennifer Dowdy; Tejay Lawes; Natasha Sabian; Dana Radinsky; Jennifer Carl; Hillary Rogers; Estelle Babbich; Corrin Jones; Erica Flair; Claudia Weiss; Harmony Matheson; and Katherine DeSweet.

They were honoured with fifteen headstones arranged upon the site of the abduction. The surrounding woods, nameless until then, had been christened in the years following as well, given a name approved by local county citizens, constabulary and mayor as a fitting designation for a plot of land eternally rich with tragic history: Lily Wood, named for the mysterious spectral flower colonies which began their unprecedented flourishing upon the memorial site and surrounding area in the aftermath of the incident, as if a secret hand had planted their seeds there by way of honouring the deceased.

Listen in your heart and hear his words ring true:
the Essex Fifteen are in a better place,
a kinder place after all
The Essex Fifteen are burning good, Jim
Left their ghosts behind to haunt Lily Wood
We're headed lightwards, too
to meet the quiet county's girls
On your peace-star we'll gather again
to pick starflowers every day

The song or the chill August air or the ghosts of the night caused Johnny to shudder. A tiny brown frog leapt suddenly from the grass to a place before him in the gravel. It remained there only an instant before ricocheting like a skipped stone into the rushes growing opposite. He whistled after it and murmured, "Safe travels, brother."

Monica followed the creature, too, and, watching the grass undulating in the gusting breeze, said, "Badness is out there, isn't it?"

He made his voice sure, strong, to boost her fragile whisper. "It is, darling. It is." Together they would face this knowledge, then as they'd faced it for ten endless years.

"But it's not all bad."

"For sure it ain't, sweets. For sure it ain't." He clutched her hand to remind her of the goodness they made between them.

The forest before them stirred its skeletal limbs, a rustling-rattling clamour like cadavers stirring fitfully in their tombs. The wind picked up, adding menace to the night at large.

"Let's be careful," she said with determination, as if they hadn't lived by this creed for the past ten years: "Let's stick together, and we'll be careful out there."

He nodded. "That's a good plan, sweets. The best I ever heard."

They were plunged into darkness: the car's headlights had expired without warning, as if the night itself had gathered its windy breath and blown the light out in denial of the courage they were seeking to birth between them. Their eyes sought to adjust to the new blackness but clouds had blown over the stars, making the task formidable.

"It's so dark." Monica heard the fear in her voice but felt no embarrassment now: fear drowned out smaller emotions like this.

Johnny continued to squeeze her hand resolutely. His voice sought to make her brave: "It's dark, but not for long." He made a fist of his other hand and hammered it upon the car hood. His usually deft touch – alchemical, Monica had always claimed, greaser-cool he'd always quipped, back in the days of his youth, when his hair had been fuller and friends knew him as *Johnny* rather than *John* – summoned no magical light. He was no longer young and magicianly and able to awaken light from sleeping machines. Something in him panged at the realization. He tried again, and again, but still they remained in the lightless woods, abandoned even by the moon hiding behind the clouds.

They waited. Their breathing and the night's wove together intimately. The chords of the song, so familiar, and the reverb-drenched vocals, so very, very familiar, crackled the car speakers and comforted them in the cold darkness.

A rain began, as forecasted, but different. They felt it touching them everywhere, heard its gentle pattering among the trees, onto the vehicle. It took them a moment to fathom the anomalous nature of the countless touches. Looking, they saw the gift given up by the sky: their white petals were like velvet, their lush green tendrils clung between their fingers as they held their hands aloft, as if seeking to root themselves to their skin. Johnny and Monica continued to hold one another, bewitched in the lily-rain.

Then, the twin light beams of the headlights were with them again – brilliant, blinding – as though the arrival of the flower-host had wrested away the night's dominion over things and returned reliability to the world. They stared around them:

The windswept forest loomed overhead: oaks tall and gnarled-fingered, willows long-haired and weeping their foliage grasswards in the frenzied wind, shadow-plagued and menacing all; and everywhere in the rustling wall of foliage hung the lilies, moon-pale and agitated, speaking secret messages in unison with the whispering leaves in which they were nestled, like quivering stars caught in the most turbulent of night skies; everywhere they looked the flowers filled the heavens, their mass presence casting a wavering ghostly radiance over the woods, the fields, the lonely road winding into the sleeping county.

They stared skywards in awed silence.

"Help me," she said in a hushed voice, extricating her fingers from his and hurrying out onto the sward. He followed, a peculiar excitement growing up in him.

Together they lifted the immense white stone from its place embedded in the earth and staggered with it between them among the headstones. There they placed it onto the grass, she holding it upright while he dug up the earth at its base with his hands, never questioning her reasoning in the dreamlike moment. Soon, he'd succeeded in hollowing out a shallow fissure into which they lowered the stone like a cenotaph. They stood back and admired it amid the rain of lilies, torrential now, a resounding percussion among the trees, along the car roof and hood.

A soft whirring sounded from the car then, as the cassette reached the end of its forty-five minute playing time, the song concluding its millionth playing that night. The sudden silence was profound. In it, Monica and Johnny felt a great unease settle over them, quashing the slowly growing exhilaration that erecting the cenotaph had conjured.

"Flip the tape over," she said.

He did, knocking his head on the window frame in his haste. He leaned from the car a moment later just as the familiar opening chords rang onto the air anew. The car's headlights pushed back the dark as they could, and Monica and Johnny suddenly felt an unexpected liberation from the night's former indomitable bleakness: morning was coming, and who knew what goodness might come with the light?

The lilies continued to come down. In the inexplicable celestial-born snowfall, they maintained their mourning vigil, though on this night it began to feel a little like a celebration, while the song's chorus haunted the air again, as it was meant to do.

Jim Wood and the captive women
All Sixteen of them finally freed
Take care of them, Jimmy
Take care of our lilies
Garden the sky, Jimmy
Brighten the night
Tend to the night, Jimmy
tonight and every night

Monica and Johnny added their own poetry into the night then, too:

"I believe him, darling. Finally, after all these years, I believe him."

The wonder and the certainty in her voice lifted something from him. He felt his youth again, his old strength. Maybe he finally understood their daughter, after all the long hard years.

"I believe Jimmy, too, sweets... *I believe, too!*"

They held each other without words, tears in their eyes, the music and starfall touching them everywhere.

Now we're strong.
Ghosts fear us.

Their music is not ours.

It took this many long hard years too.
If only we'd known
what Roads lied ahead

And after the Maze: Home.

SONGS FOR THE LOST

In an outer rim galaxy of frontier violence and sin, a legend is whispered, making the rounds of the dusty worlds and spaceports. It tells the tale of a temple in a cave in a town in a valley in a planet just as dusty and dangerous as any, but with something special and impossible and nearly unfathomable growing in abundance at its core, for those lucky or worthy enough to find it.

Peace.

I:

Lasso the Sun

"Trying to talk sense to her was like trying to teach your peter to piss up a rope, son."

The boy heard his father's words as they stared out across the sun-bathed plain. He thought of his mother, and fought the tears that threatened to well into his eyes. He focused his vision on the vastness of the plain before them, its sharp granite outcroppings like bizarre sculptures formed by the wind, its occasional wisp of skeleton-tree stark against the earth – to the south a flock of earthen bison shooting over the ground! To the north a gigantic valley serpent reared from the plain! But his game of old didn't entertain him that hot morning. This day he could only ache bitterly and wince at the stinging in his eyes, the dust and tears itching and scratching and making him wish the world wasn't so mean.

They stood in silence. The father spit into the dirt. The boy saw, and spit, too, like his father. Together they continued to watch the scene burning before them. In the distance, the boy saw a circling shape, slow, lazy its progress, a scratch against the crimson sky. It looked a little bit beautiful, too, the way it dipped and made long arcs in aerial show like some gargantuan majestic bird, but of course the boy would never dare say this to his father. For fear of his father's hard hands curling into fists and finding his cheeks and arms, adding to his collection of bruises. For fear of sounding like some kind of a traitor, to his mother's memory, to his father still alive and like a statue beside him, hard and quiet. He was only eager to point out the flying speck's presence to his father, proof that his eyes were sharper than they'd been the day before, and much keener than they'd been one week before that. But his father spoke up first, "There's one, son. Ruining the sunrise with its wicked shape." And he spat into the dirt again, and added, with venom, "I *hate* them. Those Varkoom scum. Blood-skinned cocksuckers. *We* hate them, don't we, son?"

The boy nodded, focusing his squinting eyes on the black shape making arcs in the stifling air. Focusing what hate he had on that single mote in the sky, sagging his shoulders with the effort, feeling small and weak in the act.

The father watched the arcing shape in the air a mile away, with scowling features and aching grey eyes. He recalled the clouds on the day his wife left him forever, their heavy grey look overhead as he regretted for the first time his terrible ways towards her every day that they'd lived together. Every long day of her serving triple duties of toiling in the fields and tending to his needs and of course raising their son, dutifully, admirably, honourably. A strong woman, to have borne his ways for so long, and the equally wicked ways of life in the Colonies.

"But still," murmured the father, "She was a great woman, your mother. And strong. Fiery like this picture burning out there. Piss and vinegar and tough as nails through and through." His voice grew unsteady as he finished. "Your mother, son, she…she was like this here sunlight, when you put it all together and look at it long and hard. Sunlight, bright and fiery."

And he gestured with his good hand, his left hand, which still owned all of its fingers; and the boy nodded, thinking of his mother wearing her own bruises like badges around her sad eyes and lips.

"Yup. Like fire," said the boy, thinking he might impress his wise father with the conviction he put into his words.

"But don't forget, son," the father said wistfully, shrinking his son a little more in the shoulders, deflating his chest where he'd tried to swell it out like a rooster owning the chicken coop. "It's also the colour of blood that we're looking at. And always remember it, son. *Always* remember the colour of blood."

The boy heard, and together they nodded their heads in the shimmering air. They stared into the bloody sky until the father raised the battered silver stick in his hands, awkward work since his left hand had been mauled in the attack weeks past, along with his knee; sighted along its ancient telescopic lens and searched through a film of scratches and nicks the air one mile in the distance. A moment of panning the instrument from east to west and west back to east, and then the magnified flare in the crimson, like a deeper spot of fire against the blistering sky.

The boy tensed when he sensed his father become taut beside him. He wanted to raise his hands and plug his ears with his fingers, but wished to appear tough, hardy, ready for anything. Unafraid of loud noises like men are unafraid of such things. Still, he jerked against his will when the loud report cracked from the old gun, knocking his father back a half-step with its force, clapping his ears like two invisible hands smashing down on either side of his head.

Through watering eyes, father and son surveyed the sky in the west, saw the black speck dropping like a stone through the air.

Satisfied, the father cleared his throat, spit once more into the dust. "Got him. Got the cocksucker like he deserved it." And he paused with the Old World rifle slung over his shoulder, still smoking its grey wisp of smoke from its nose, and he turned his eyes downwards on his son, and said, "*We* got him."

The boy looked to his father's ruined right hand extended toward him, missing three of its stout fingers, making him look crab-like and alien. He felt proud as he took it in his own smaller hand, pumping it up and down vigorously as though it didn't feel grotesque, nodding his head in unison with the motion. His father's skin was boiling, a burning touch gathering all the fire of the morning sun in its leathery landscape and transmitting it to him through the binding gesture of their handshake.

They took a moment to look at the farm spread out before them, forlorn and quiet with its machines shut down, its animals set to pasture, never to return again. The whirring ceased in the old moisture sheds. The air filters silenced and baking in the light. The electrified fence surrounding the property on all sides and above, too, in order to prevent attack from the sky, silenced from its regular quiet buzzing. The sparse grass unmoving in the oven air, the twittering of triceedas from the dry corn husks bordering their property on the east and west sounding somehow nervous, frenzied in their calls.

The father said, "There is a place." And it was all that he said.

And, wordlessly, they stepped into the space bubble resting like a gleaming silver egg in the weeds and dust along the periphery of the yard, prepared to leave memories of blood and fighting forever, and find Paradise.

Black Charm, Black Hex

Harry Dalmar felt the coarse bite of the hangman's noose sink into his throat through the thin fabric of the black hood, circling his oxygen and constricting its progress. He imagined his throat as a shrinking pin-hole through which the final moments of his life were fast bleeding. The courtyard air was still, boiling, and the murmurs of the rabble grew as the moment neared its grisly climax. His hands were being bound with the same coarseness of rope, he felt its biting touch as the executioner fiddled there roughly. Harry Dalmar wore the hood of the dead man, and in the darkness of its shroud, saw her like a mirage amid his despair:

Hair red like her lips like the wild roses that grew along the river bank behind her father's plantation home. Lily-pale skin and her body's beautiful shape, long and strong and sleeker than a canyon cat in its prime.

Something buffeted him then, a hard collision across his back and shoulders that staggered him severely, buckling his knees where he rocked unsteadily in place atop the trap-door set into the creaking wooden platform. And then the touch of oil upon his neck-skin stirring him from his reveries. The furtive touch of movement slithering on the outside of the sack he wore over his head. The jarring screams from below, as the witnesses to his death reeled with the sudden sight of some horror; and his executioners, too, and the priests and his enemies standing attentive all around, all crying out in fear and revulsion, and the knocking of their boots upon the wood of the death-platform as they scrambled madly to distance themselves from him. The heavy sound of falling objects striking about him, a loud pattering in the dirt and the deep hollow knocking from the rickety floorboards around him. Uncoiling himself quickly from the frail grasp of the half-knotted ropes. Tearing the hood from his head, and marvelling at the necklace he wore — the black snake, its skin slick leather and its eyes obsidian and deadly. Its forked tongue darting into the boiling air and quivering something inside of him.

Frozen with terror, he stared about himself and watched the rain of snakes. Specimens of varying lengths, infant snakes like long dark worms, and adult serpents like immense coiling whips arcing downwards from the sky. All were the same deep black colour as the serpent he wore tremblingly about his neck and shoulders. He stumbled back a step, aghast at the sight of the purple-faced priest near to him with his new black collar of slippery flesh, thrashing about wildly, his shoes clattering frantically along the wooden floor while the snake squeezed his life from him. Harry Dalmar looked into the chaos of the street below and turned away when he saw the massive serpent strike its fangs into the face of the woman around which it wound its powerful body. Her shrieking clamour followed him as he wove through the men crowding the execution platform, as he stumbled on quivering legs down the squealing wooden steps and into the street. A dust-storm billowed upwards from the commotion of fleeing and struggling people, putting dust in his eyes and slowing his progress. Around him, the horrific rainfall continued unabated, the deep sound of the serpents striking the earth reminding Harry Dalmar of some dark drum dirge signalling ominous things. Their numbers seemed to cast a shroud over the daylight, or perhaps it was only the dust billowing around him that caused this darkness.

He fled amid terrified and pleading cries to Heaven and bullets and heat rays singing through the boiling air. The serpent clung tenaciously to him, and with it flickering its hisses in his ears he scrambled through the filthy alleys of the town, crying fearfully every step of his terrible journey. He wept and groaned miserably, until he came across the lone honji tethered to the rear of the dive tavern, an ancient pre-Frontier Era tune drifting languidly through the ajar window.

He road his sturdy little mount to death in the Black Santiago steppes bordering the town, and then he ran his boots to tatters among the cacti and horned Lecki lizards beyond, and then he crawled until his knees bled into the dust and attracted giant grass spiders with the sticky taste of iron. Throughout his entire long trek he'd worn his serpent like a grotesque ornament about his neck, like a black charm or hex, and when he discovered that it hung less tenaciously against his flesh, and with the first tinge of an icy touch, he finally let it slide from him and into the dirt. He stared at it, shaken and awed once more, and when he saw what it told him he remembered an old legend he'd heard whispered in space bars and cattle yards countless times since the days of his youth.

As though possessed by some tenaciously clinging mad demon spirit, the serpent's body was stretched in two distinctly opposing directions: its tail still quivering in its dying throes and pointing into the sun-dropping northwest, while its black-eyed bullet-head trembled due northeast; its thick leather body cracked sharply midway through its rotund bulk, creating a horrid base of grotesquely bunched, cracked and flaking skin and scales, marking a distinct 'V' in the dust, a single gruesome letter trembling terribly in the heat haze like an oracle.

And he thought of his own hand scribbling this same symbol into wood with a rock in his fist long ago, along with his reckless friends of youth and easier times, the only smattering of writing he'd ever learned how to set down.

V.

V, for Valley. V for the Valley of Green.

The silent planet too far from the sun to grow any lush greenery and forests but defying science and logic in every way, or so the tales said. Amisam, with its deep green valley and impossible supply of contentment. Paradise, in the wildness of the Big Black's nethermost reaches. Impossible and amazing. Like a dream warm and beautiful in the icy reaches between stars. Like a legend or myth, for young and old. Whispered hopefully after a father's harsh beating left his son petulant and resentful of the world in his bedroom; or muttered like a prayer to the setting sun during a weary man's recollection of less difficult days. Before the Great Expansion brought war and hunger to the New Worlds, and to so many of the Frontiersmen who were supposed to have been revelling in their promised glory long, long ago.

And Harry Dalmar blinked sweat from his eyes and watched the salty beads drop down onto the serpent blistering in the weeds. And he stared and stared until the snake became a crumbling mound of skin husk and scales. And gathering these remains to himself, because this suddenly seemed the right thing to do, he draped them over his shoulders once more, where they clung despite their limp, ruined state, as if with some lingering shred of life. And then he crawled several miles more into the bloody setting sun, into the back roads and alleys of some unnamed small mining town in the far west. Into the dark reaches of a dusty market square, hidden in shadows where lawmen were too afraid to look. It was here that he strangled a merchantman with the silky kerchief he'd worn, directly beneath his stall's filthy striped canopy, and then emptied the man's pockets for their gold coins, and his small tin box of eclectic multi-world coins, too, kept in the safety and shade beneath his tables all day long, away from the eyes of furtive cutpurses and murderers like himself.

Harry Dalmar thought about very important things as he choked the man's life from his slumping body. He thought about how he wanted judgment for his wicked ways. He wanted answers for why he was allowed to live and walk among men being as cold and unfeeling as he was. He wanted to know just who or what he was, Devil or awful man of unforgivable sins, or whether these things in the end were one and the same. He wanted to shed his snakeskin hide and reveal his heart to someone who might understand him, and explain him to himself so that he might see what he was all about, and whether he existed for any reason other than to be hurtful and wear snakes like witchy charms around his neck. He wanted to rest his aching heart and tired thoughts the way he'd needed to for far too many years, but never been allowed by the ways of the universe.

And Harry Dalmar bought himself a junk ship that couldn't get the best pilot on any world to any place at all, and with hope hammering and smashing inside his chest like he'd never ever felt it there before, he rocketed out of that lawless dust-bowl town and into an evening sky filled with a billion stars. And among them all, he searched with a frantic eye until he found the brightest-glowing, and this was the same one that whispered to him across the gulfs of blackness. And towards this glowing emerald speck he steered himself inside of his rickety ship, and sailed off quickly, straight as an arrow and just as surely.

Blood Skin

The Varkoom were rowdy, all fire-skin and canyon-dust and arcane primeval rituals.

Untamed and primitive, a race of savage warriors who devoured their children and set fire to the land. The atrocities they committed upon humans and their children were the stuff of hushed campfire tales, to scamper children off to bed when mothers and fathers wished to be rid of their naggings and complaints. The Varkoom were archaic and stupid and the deadliest obstacle the Colonizers had met in their sweeping expansion throughout the Rim, obstinate and determined to not bend to the will and wise ways of their superior man.

These things men called them.

The Varkoom were in fact the only strong race of the Fringe, resilient and proud. Rebels in the face of the pioneering poison spreading across the worlds: Man, and his hunger for expansion, his penchant for slaughter where slaughter furthered his selfish goals.

These thoughts Helma-Rar pondered as he held the shrieking human baby in his enormous hands. The creature's skin against his own both repulsed and attracted him – its wan hue, so fragile-looking, soft. He thought the thing might simply burn up inside of his red-skinned grasp. But the infant wailed on and on relentlessly, chilling him somehow, a nervous racket that unnerved him the longer it went on. He'd eaten them before, the human children abducted from Colony towns during skirmishes. It was a taste that had only ever sickened him, bringing to mind aftermath battlefields of corpses burning in the sun, rotting in their atmospheres of ecstatically-buzzing flies and twitching maggots.

He turned at his comrade's roar beside him where he owned the attention of their fellow warriors gathered in the grassy compound. "The would-be Colonizers brand us wicked, while acting out their own wicked deeds upon us. They feed our young and old alike into the mouths of their ovens on the Extermination Worlds, and preach against our sinful ways of wishing peace between all." Here the Varkoom soldier raised a human infant high into the air, carelessly, violently, as if it were a sack of feed. "Then let us fall in place among the honourable white raiders, and feast as they feast."

And the Varkoom soldier brought the mewling infant to his mouth, placed it between his immense jaws, and champed down viciously.

An awful crunching sounded throughout the compound outside of the barracks, accompanied by a piercing shriek from the child and a celebratory roar of his comrades that shook the earth. It was in the wake of this terrible song of blood and vengeance that Helma-Rar thought, very unexpectedly in that moment, of a place he'd heard tell of long, long ago. The young whispered of it, and the elderly cackled of it, too, while only occasionally those of the in-between ages acknowledged the mystery or legend. Amid the screams of babies being murdered and the exultant roars of his brothers-in-arms, the gentle touch of the name fell upon his ears like a gift of softness in the war field.

Hamisamrah, and the caves of peace.

In that moment, of blood and death, Helma-Rar wished like he'd never wished before in his many many years, for the chance to rest his weary bones in this place. The only place where true peace could be found, if the fables were true. The caves and caverns like a great metropolis beneath the green valley, tended by an ancient and peaceful people much like his own, secluded and safe in their impregnable retreat. For unnamed dangers barred the path to Hamisamrah's warm heart, littering the world above with the skeletal remains of those unworthy who sought egress into this wondrous sanctuary.

It was the potency of the suddenly-arrived need to discover this truth that urged Helma-Rar to do what he did that fateful day, guiding his hands as he set the infant down in its steel tub; tearing free his weapon from its scabbard at his hip with a quick whisper of steel slicing leather.

Turning upon his brothers and with his gruesome gun letting fire. And his six brothers falling dead before they even realized the great betrayal, in vivid pools of blood and bone drenching the grass of the compound where the shells had exploded their cargoes of steel spikes, splitting skulls and chests and abdomens wide.

Without thinking, he scooped the screaming infant from its steel tub, and with one giant hand deposited it inside the warmth and shelter of his belly-pouch. And with a sound like the popping of springs and groaning of tarpaulin, Helma-Rar spread his long powerful wings from where they were tucked along the length of his back, and he drifted upwards like a bloody beacon into the star-filled sky.

Sun on the Run

In the instant of the Big Death, she'd given up all that her father's preaching had committed her to over the years.

Just like that, in the unreality of that moment of blood and bullets, and she'd forsaken her beliefs like snakeskin shed and discarded in the dust of a derelict town where only ghosts roamed. Like the sun put out, and from then onwards a life living in shadows and uncertainty.

Darla was the heaviest little girl in the universe. Her father had told her this as if it was something to be proud of, to stick up in the face of anyone who might use the same words but in a way that would try to make her feel very small and weak. Like a bug in the dirt, easy to be crushed into dust under a tough man's boot-heels. She kept her thoughts to herself, like secrets, especially those that concerned her embarrassed feelings about the way she looked. She only shared her secrets with one friend, and it was the only friend she'd ever made in her life: Lucky Lecki, her tiny and old Lecki lizard that she'd saved from the steel jaws of a canyon cat trap where he'd wandered by accident and got his tail snagged. She'd cried as she pried open the rusty steel trap-teeth, and the little emerald Lecki wriggled and spasmed in silent pain in the grass. She'd taken him home hidden inside the pocket of her apron, and when she plucked him out in her bedroom less than one hour later, it was the first magical thing she'd ever seen in her life: her Lecky had sprouted a new tail, healthy and nimble as he flicked the air with it cheerfully. "You're my good luck charm, Lucky," she'd whispered to the creature, and helped nurse it back to health with a steady supply of live field flies and baby grass spiders appropriated while her father and mother were looking elsewhere.

There wasn't very much lucky about the Death Day, though, not really, not for anyone except maybe her, and for her only a very little bit. None of those big eager men had expected her to be packing something more than her rolls of skin and giant sagging breasts beneath her faded print dress, like an enormous flag wrapped around her immenseness. The Old World shotgun fitted like a secret toothpick between her folds, under her big sweeping dress, it was a surprise when it snuck out in her pudgy fists and shot up the little room and all of the dirty-thinking men getting in line to take their turns with her like they'd probably taken turns with her momma and sisters in the other rooms. Those dirty filthy pioneers, revolting like her father had always predicted they would, if the innocent killings got to be too many and the people sick of it all. Killing and raping the wrong side of the war, this is what conflict will achieve in the end, he'd predicted and been right about it all, as she eventually saw with her own terrified eyes.

Big Darla loved the red look of the men's faces when she set off that big ruckus. Like a bunch of Varkoom taking over the faces of those ugly dirty men, red everywhere, and wasn't that just perfect, wasn't that just *right*. And she only cried about it a long time afterwards, once she'd escaped from the room and the town and the planet aboard the little single-pilot ship she barely squeezed herself into. Only when she was already among the stars, and they twinkled on every side and she felt how utterly alone she was in the universe – only then did she finally let herself behave like a little girl.

Big Darla looked at the red and brown smeared all over her fat hands. She saw the dirt under her nails, and caked on her big body where her dress had been torn during all the fighting and shooting and running away. She remembered finding her momma and little sisters, big Windy as big as she was, and tiny Maria, only a little girl and with such pretty eyes like two green-watered ponds – all dead with bullets cracking their heads, their dresses gone and thrown around the room, unholy and awful. Leaning in close to baby Maria, Darla had heard it, clear as day – the tiniest of voices, whisper-quiet and frail but unmistakable the impossible words it spoke – "In the Valley in the Cave, we'll be together again, sister."

Babies didn't talk, Big Darla knew, and she took it as the final sign from a God that had otherwise abandoned her to the awful and cold embrace of the universe. At least Lucky Lecki hadn't left her, she reasoned while considering the icy ways of every world in the universe – he'd remain her truest friend, until the end. Amid the stars, Big Darla cried and let go of God, but not before vowing to seek Him out if He existed at all. Because she had some questions that only He could answer for her. He might have forsaken her forever, as though all the warmth of the sun had gone away and left her feeling cold and alone, but she aimed to find Him so that she could get to the bottom of some very big things. And with all the sadness and rage she'd felt throughout her life burning her up inside, Big Darla, feeling very tiny and hugely guilty, guided her ship towards the brightest star in the field before her – a green and green star pulsing in the dark miles – and flew and flew and flew.

II:

Lost in the Crossroads

The man and his son left their silver bubble nestled among a small grove of trees which bordered the great desert. Looking over his shoulder, the boy marvelled at the heat waves shimmering the distant horizon line, magically. He waited to see whether a castle or fort would appear there, but soon he grew tired and turned his eyes back to the path he and his father followed. It was in that instant he realized that the oasis lay before them and not behind.

His father had shouldered through the overhanging arms of tree-branches, holding them aside for his son to see: in the distance, a valley, its sides steeped in the most lush of green grasses, dipping down and down, with a promise of deep forests at its mist-shrouded bottom, and all the mysteries and answers they might hold in their leafy reaches. A strange animal scampered into the greenery at the commotion, its silvery fur dappled in sunlight filtering through the treetops. The boy risked a bit of childish excitement, and asked his father, "The caves, papa? The caves are down in there someplace, huh?"

The man laid his ruined hand on the boy's shoulder, firmly, warmly, murmured, "Hush now, boy. We got some walking ahead of us still."

The boy nodded and walked onwards, silently exhilarated with the new smell on the air: like perfume, something sweet and exotic which he'd never smelled before, and then he noticed the pretty pale flowers dotting the path everywhere. He breathed deeply of their scent, heavy and juicy, and different too from any of the wildflowers he'd smelled back home. A small flash of crimson blurred the air, coming to rest on the fragile branch of a sapling sprouting from the earth near to him. He looked, marvelling at the wondrous creature, bird-like, yet nearly completely globular in shape, its butterfly-like wings spread open on the warm air like a pretty scarlet fan. It fluttered off a moment later, another whizzing bulbous blur of red, and the boy watched amazed as it disappeared among the branches over their heads.

A worry-thought wrinkled his brow for a moment, and he asked his father, "Papa, what about our silver egg? We left it behind, at the edge of the desert."

The man shook his head, muttering, "We're done with that egg, son. Hopefully, we're finished with all of that from now on."

And they walked on, silently, along the slowly dipping trail.

It seemed for a moment as though the old ways had returned to haunt the father and his son.

The scene of the gigantic Varkoom towering over the obese girl in the glade like some immense bloody obscenity chilled them both. An instant later and he saw the pale-skinned baby nestled in the crook of the thing's arm, and ice stabbed at his heart. Tearing free the gun from where it lay slung over his shoulder, the man hollered for the woman to take cover.

The girl and the Varkoom started at the commotion, she instinctively raising her hands on the air and the creature stooping into a threatening posture, fingers rolled into square fists, legs spread wide in battle-ready stance. Its wings opened like vegetable chutes in some sort of incredibly accelerated growth spurt, whipping the long grass with their wind gust, bobbing the fruit in the branches of the trees about them. The man's finger tensed on the trigger of his weapon as the girl's frantic cries broke through into his awareness, halting him only barely.

"No! Don't shoot! Please, stop! We're friends!"

The incongruous sight of the Varkoom passing the tiny infant to the woman, one-handed, gently, daintily, puzzled him. The man ceased sighting along the tip of the gun, but didn't lower it from its place trained on the Varkoom. His ears heard and his mind reeled as he processed what the girl had said, matching her strange words to the incredible scene of her standing fearlessly alongside the horrid creature, arms thrown up in its defence. It shivered him all over his body, and when at last he found his voice, he croaked, "What place is this, where girls walk with Varkoom on their arm?"

The Varkoom stood to its full height, grazing the branches with the top of its fiery-plumed head. Its eyes smouldered, but its voice was gentle when it murmured, "I've a feeling that you know what kind of place this is. We are here for much the same reason, I gather."

She'd followed the song of baby's burbling, she explained, and found them curled together at the base of a tree, the infant and her strange guardian. She implored the man and his son to believe her words, that the Varkoom was gentle and kind, to just look into his eyes and they'd see for themselves.

The man's expression remained ashen and strained as he tried with great difficulty to suppress the hatred trembling his body while he looked at the red-skinned monster before him. He looked into its crimson eyes and saw his wife's face of terror being ripped from him forever. He saw the thing's massive wings and fists like square blocks of molten rock, and imagined his wife being flown into Hell and touched all over by the hands of demons.

He simmered and trembled, but managed, "Okay, Darla. Okay… You…You're with this Varkoom, and we're all here for the same reason. I'll give you that, and so I won't do right now what I know should be done, on God's own will." And his knuckles twitched white along the stalk of his rifle. And he raised his wild eyes to Helma-Rar, and whispered hoarsely, "But I want you to know something, Varkoom. I want you to know that I won't ever trust you. I know what you are, and I've got my eye on you. I'll always be watching you close, and I'm waiting for the chance to kill you good, demon."

And he turned and drifted away from them, stopping to peer over his shoulder at his son; a small, wide-eyed owl, more curious than fearful, distractedly stroking the gregarious Lecky Lizard in his palms and staring with unabashed awe at the Varkoom warrior towering over him like a scarlet mountain.

And the man's anger was swept away by the deluge of sorrow which then gripped him, putting tears in his eyes, and he could only turn away from the blasphemous sight and hide among the bushes and flowers with his huge shame and grief.

Big Darla's voice was soft as she observed, "She's adorable. Just so gorgeous. I had a little sister once."

Helma-Rar looked up at her words, sensing the sorrow filling them up and making them significant. He only grunted, and turned back to the pink infant he cradled in his lap, her eyes serene blue jewels as she drifted in his embrace.

"Don't worry, I'm sure he'll come around," she added, meaning the angry man, and she gave the boy a gentle look where he sat close to them, entranced by the alien warrior in the grass.

The Varkoom said simply, "I could kill you all, very easily. Right at this moment. Eat you and have my supper. Sharpen my teeth with your bones, like so many of you think we do. But I like this grass more than thoughts like those." He stirred a wildflower with a gigantic hand, and then he added, almost as an afterthought, "I am Varkoom, in blood. I am Varkoom in spirit. I've come to be set free, from all that I've seen my brothers do." He cocked his head at the small gurgling sound falling from the infant's moist mouth, said, "What is her name, I wonder?"

Big Darla smiled at him, blushing because of her secret thoughts: how she would make a good girl for the warrior in the grass, a big girl like herself. A girl of rolling hills to his hard mountain range physique. She said, "Her name can be whatever you want it to be. She's starting over here."

Helma-Rar wrinkled his brow in thought. Soon, he murmured, "Pomma." And when he saw Big Darla's eyes smile at the sound, he revealed, "In Varkoom, this means 'soft'. Because she is so soft." And he stroked the child's round cheek with a huge callused thumb, marvelling at her texture.

The boy barely heard Helma-Rar's words, only continued to stare, awed, at his massive limbs, shining in the bright light. Corded heavily, his arms were red tree trunks rooted to a body of prodigious mass, rippled all over with muscles like steel springs beneath his skin. Sitting in the grass, stooped and with sunken shoulders, he was still much taller than his father, who was a big man among most men and the tallest of their family. The boy eyed the Varkoom's enormous tusks with awe and fear, the bright bones like ivory glistening where they protruded from his immense mouth. His single tuft of red hair drifted in the breeze, a crimson plume like a banner of war in the valley grass.

Because it sounded like the right thing to say just then, the boy said, in a small voice, "I don't know nothing about you Varkoom."

And Helma-Rar answered, "No one knows, but the Varkoom."

The boy noted Helma-Rar's sad eyes, but said no more for fear of angering his father once again, who he knew might be able to overhear where he sat cleaning his rifle several feet away. The boy's eyes continued to be drawn, however, to the strange trinket, carved from steel, which dangled from the massive creature's hip and made little tapping noises whenever he moved any which way. A carven image, of a Varkoom, it seemed, vivid crimson in colour, and shiny and glittering in the sunlight. Only its shape was less sleek, less taut and wiry and immense and dangerous than all the Varkoom the boy had seen in pictures, as well as this one sitting beside him in the tall grass. A baby Varkoom. A child alien conqueror, although something about those words put together in such a way sounded strange and not right to the boy.

Helma-Rar saw where he looked, and only said, "It was a gift from my mother. She is dead now."

The boy looked into the grass, mulling this over and twirling an emerald grass blade between his fingers; pretending it was a magical pen and that he scripted secret invisible words on the air, which were really his secret thoughts that only the truly good-at-heart would be able to decipher. But no one said anything about the things he wrote, and he reasoned that it might only have been because he'd been to school for a few years and probably nobody else among their party had done that.

But the Varkoom watched the progress of his air-writing, and seemed to understand. His livid eyes softened, and he cupped a huge hand over the boy's, gently, briefly, before returning to fiddling among the tiny flowers stirring in the breeze. And when a gentle dusk breeze blew through the branches, he unfurled his mighty wings and curled himself beneath their canopy, like a living tent to shelter the softness of his adopted child through the coming night.

*

Helma-Rar saw his mother, on the final night before he'd embarked on his quest, during his brief visit to her house. Her skin like fire and eyes like water, sad and mercurial and unseeing, her thick fingers clutching in her death-grip his last letter to her, in which he'd confessed to her his war-time sins: he'd partaken of the human flesh-feast, too, and eaten babies with his warrior-brother brethren, even though his eyes had welled with tears as he'd told her, recalling the tiny creatures' high shrieking screams as his tusks had ripped and crunched into their flailing little forms. And even though he cried his reasons into his dead mother's manifest folds, quoting his own letter-words, yet he wept the night through and through afterwards: "I saw them, mother, I saw the grown humans spearing our children in the villages and way-stations. I saw them slaughter our little ones so easily. I understood my comrades' thoughts, to eat through their ranks, too. But still the taste was awful, so very awful in my mouth..."

He'd found her that night, only hours following his treason and subsequent departure from the lines. His mother's gigantic form toppled over among her newest diorama, a piece cobbled together from the thin, tough branches of talji saplings and totra roots; their sinuous fingers coiled about one another tightly, expertly combining to create the semblance of her very own humble little home, her place of haven and sanctuary from the insanities living outside its walls; complete with tiny replicas of both her and her son, sculpted expertly and with her patient hand from the difficult material of bosool weed, twisty and unreliable. Her life-colour faded, her skin pale and pink and her body lifeless. A pool of her bright blood surrounding her, from the place in her skull where she'd shot herself with the spear-gun. The long spear incongruous in her serene home, spiking her clean through, grey and ugly and savage where it entered her head on one side and stabbed through terribly on the other, red and sticky with brain- and bone-gore.

A peaceful woman, unable to bear the scene playing in her head and over and over like a nightmare snippet of film — her son the executioner. Her son the soulless. Her boy like a human being raiding and raping and reaving and eating the young as if they were morsels in the changing galaxy's new food chain hierarchy.

Helma-Rar, writer of murderous letters, who killed his own mother with the evil deeds he'd committed and foolishly documented as if in some weak hope for forgiveness.

Helma-Rar plucked the noisy human fruit from the branches over his head, easily, holding it aloft for the others to see.

The lanky man with weeks-stubbled cheeks and wild eyes, brandishing futilely the small Old World pistol in his fist, the weapon's nose twisted upwards grotesquely where the Varkoom's fingers had wrenched and pinched the steel like paper. He squirmed in silence a moment, until Helma-Rar deposited him roughly on the grass and held him beneath his volcanic gaze. Firelight played over the man's frantic features, sent shimmers along his strange scaled hands. Peering closer, the group saw that these were gloves of a sort, and when the man snarled at them it was Big Darla who tried to calm him before violence erupted.

"We won't hurt you," she said, pudgy hands raised high in the air. "We all just met each other today, too. Maybe you're here for the same reason we're here, stranger."

The man's eyes grew less livid at this last, his demeanour more relaxed as he allowed himself to settle in his place before the fire. He breathed heavily and shook dirt and grass bits from his filthy clothes. He was nodding his head, and when he found his voice, it was low, husky. "I crashed my ship a few miles back, in the desert. I been wandering all day and night. I – I heard you a while back, and snuck up, in case you was…dangerous." He offered the group a wan attempt at a smile, looking eerie and gruesome in the fire glow. "But maybe…maybe this place isn't so dangerous, huh? At least not the…the place I'm looking for."

He saw the solemn look in the strangers' faces, only now allowing himself to ponder the bizarre rag-tag look of the group. Something in their silence, in their sad yet hard eyes and slumped shoulders, told him that he'd met up with fellow searchers. He muttered, "I'm Harry Dalmar. And I'm so damn tired. Maybe can I grab a couple of those fruits you got there, to quiet my belly?"

*

Harry Dalmar settled himself near to the man, maybe because he was the most silent of the group, much like himself, or perhaps because he looked to be the loneliest of them all. Harry Dalmar was just laying down on the grass and getting set to close his weary eyes on the moonlight, though, when the man's voice chilled him from the darkness.

"You got the skin of the snake around your fists, brother. I don't know if I can trust the look of you." The old man's gun hung motionless in his hands on the silvery-blue air. Moonlight glinted from it in blinding flashes. His eyes watched Harry Dalmar's eyes, though, and not his hands sheathed in snakeskin. Something burned there that he recognized. Some awful thing. Some lost burning thing that kept his own eyes trained there and nowhere else. He murmured, "What'd you do, Snake-Man? What happened to you? Why are you here? You're among fellow lookers now. You can tell. Why are you here?"

Harry Dalmar, very close to the flickering fire, felt utterly cold.

Harry Dalmar saw sweet Jane Smithsa the way he used to look at her for hours every night back in the old world: rope loops wound tight around her wrists and ankles where she lay naked and beautiful and terrified in the attic room of his little shack hidden away in the gulley, spread-eagled across the bed like some kind of present for him and no other man in the universe, eyes only for the silver gun always itching Harry's finger while he circled her slowly, naked and sweaty and frightened, too, at the awful things the universe allowed him to do if he wanted.

Her lips blood red, her skin like virgin-white lilies.

"I done bad things."

And it was all that Harry Dalmar said, and the tears that beaded from his eyes gave him away for certain, he thought. And with suns of shame burning in his cheeks he turned his face towards the rustling green roof overhead, and tried to breathe, and tried to sleep, and tried fruitlessly to shut out the old pictures playing behind his eyes, relentlessly, relentlessly.

Harry Dalmar's silence chilled the man deeply. Something inside of it spoke to him. He curled into himself before the wheeling embers of the fire, numbed with cold, and barely stirred when the heat touched the bare skin of his old, scarred hands. His eyes clouded over, and in the flames, he saw things as they were, as they could never be undone.

His fist crashing against her chin, sending her tumbling into the stall with the baby honji. Descending on her and letting loose with words and his fists, too, always his patented dual attack on the only woman he'd ever loved. A booted foot found her side, and another her belly, bowling her over while he pummelled her head and neck relentlessly. His words grunted, curses in the cramped wooden arms of the stall while the frightened honji kicked anxiously at the hay, unable to break away from the commotion because of the tether holding it helplessly in its place.

"My woman won't make me small in front of my son, not ever again. That won't happen again, will it? This land is ours, just like the government companies say it is. I won't go on defending myself from you like I got to from those goddamned Varkoom raiders every day."

Delivering punches until his arms had grown numb. Lashing a discarded loop of rope around her wrists and securing it alongside the honji's tether where it was fastened to the bracket in the wall. Leaving her bleeding and weeping in the straw with the flustered animal still pawing at the earth.

The last time the man had touched his wife before the dawn attack.

And then he was blinking sleep from his eyes, staggering outdoors with his old rifle in his hands to the song of alarm sirens wailing. Watching the sickening sight with a hollow, sinking feeling filling him up everywhere: the flailing arms of his wife as she was carried away by the wing-borne Varkoom horde, through the rend in the overhead roof of mesh cage fence; the doors of the barn across the yard thrown wide where the raiders had pilfered the building of its supplies of animals and feed and imprisoned woman.

His own knee bleeding and spiking suddenly with pain as the shells exploded in the dirt about him, shrapnel finding his flesh and crippling him into immobility. His left hand mangled, fingers lost in the dust and chaos. He dragged himself futilely in the dirt, spreading blood and bone bits into the earth where the spikes had severed his limb clean through; screaming his voice hoarse as his woman disappeared into the rising sun in the hands of the savages that men feared more than any other demon in the universe.

"There she goes. Oh sweet Lord, there goes my sunlight…"

And he weeping into the dust, and cowering into the small embrace of his trembling son, the loneliest creatures in the universe at that awful morning moment.

Into the nocturnal silence, broken only by the crackling of fire and the electric whirring of crepuscular insects, Big Darla whispered to Harry Dalmar, or to the man and his boy, or to the Varkoom. "I killed someone, too. A long time ago, it seems. The…It's a tough place, this shit universe. Any world, any place. They're tough places. Right?"

Harry Dalmar nodded, and wiped surreptitiously at his closed eyes with a dirty finger.

"Tough," Big Darla muttered. "Tough. Tough." And she muttered it again and again and again, as though she was trying very hard to convince herself of something.

She'd only ever felt pity for the young Varkoom, slaves in chains dredging in the fields in the name of the Colonialists. Working to abet man's goal of stealing from them all of their worlds, with all of their lands, these outer rim backyard worlds which should only have been left alone, in peace.

She'd only started to spill the beans about her father's plantation to the town boy because he'd been so pretty. His blonde hair with its curls. His green eyes like summer grass. How could she have known that her big blabbermouthing would get him and all his cronies up in arms? How could she have foreseen that his rescue operation would turn out so altogether different from its original plan?

She shouldn't have told about the mistreatment of the little red ones, poked and prodded with electric lances in the fields if they slacked off in their work. She never should have said that those young kiddie Varkoom got their wings clipped nice and early, while only in their thirtieth or fortieth year so her father wouldn't have to worry about fly-aways every long work day, a lot harder to handle than grounded children, even with the security cage surrounding the property. She shouldn't have leaked about how when they got to be too old, and the muscles started bulging in their backs and along their arms and legs, that this was when the farmers and plantation hands would take the pretty blood-red children to the furnaces and throw them in like wood into a fireplace.

Big Darla shouldn't have but she did. Because of a boy's lovely eyes and hair, and because he talked to her for a long time, and he didn't seem to mind her tree trunk arms and legs, and the hills of her many bellies and the fat cheeks squashing her features so ugly. She'd do anything in the universe to turn back time and undo her bad deed of snipping the security cage wires with the pair of big shears the way her pretty-eyed boy had instructed her, just to help out his group's small rescue mission. Get those poor kids and get out, and good riddance to slavery on the New Worlds. One two three, mission complete – easy as making pie, or even eating it.

But Big Darla never even guessed that what happened could have happened. That the rescue would turn into a slaughter of her whole family, and all the hired hands, and her fathers' house and property all burned down around her ears, while her sisters and momma got touched by all the bad men disguised as pretty and nice boys with good reasons for sneaking onto Colonial farms in the deep dark night.

If only she'd been smarter. If only she'd been less ugly and weak, and then she never would have thrown her darling sisters into such an easy and evil trap.

If only God hadn't left her, when she'd needed His guidance most.

The group lay about the fire, tired from their long journeys, and drifted. And they each of them wondered what meaning they might find in this place like a dream or myth from their youths, among the grass and mountains and strange and beautiful flowers and fauna. And the thought chanced to flit through each of their minds, too, that perhaps they'd already discovered something very important and vital, by finding each other, and the distant, forlorn looks in their eyes which they all recognized.

The old man dreamed, and in his dream he saw certain of the same pictures as his son saw in his own dreams, only neither would tell the other and so they would never learn how similar their deepest wishes really were.

A green valley.

Lush and verdant.

Birdsong in the trees instead of bullet symphonies.

Life everywhere instead of death gathering clouds of flies on the corpse-littered ground.

His wife held his crab-hand, and she smiled, and she wore no bruises to blemish her sweet rugged features.

Flowers and trees and all their guns discarded on the grass, useless and un-needed in this new place of wonders where violence was a fable of some dark and far-away past.

Harry Dalmar dreamed…

The girl in his arms held him back.

She wore a smile, red-lipped.

She forgave him, and squeezed his hand in hers.

Together, they strolled among flowers, beneath a canopy of trees.

Together, they sang along with the birds.

Together, with the girl on his arm, Harry Dalmar felt un-alone, and loved…

The boy dreamed, too, and he watched them from above, from his sky-vantage because in this dream he owned wings which sailed him high and far, amid clouds and birds.

Below, far far below, his mother and father waved upwards at him. They were smiling and beckoning him to join them. He declined with a playful laugh, and urged them to join him with his cloud friends.

He watched them sprout their own wings, and lift from the lush grass and come to him through the still, bright air…

Big Darla dreamed of Little Maria.

In her dream she cradled the child to her immense bosom, cooing like a pigeon into her ear. Soothing, comforting her words and gibberish non-words alike, reassuring the child that they were headed through the forest of flowers and fruit and secret magic, and towards the rest of their family waiting safe and happy at the end of the path.

In the dream, Big Darla could sense her sister's ease, her tiny gurgling noises of comfort as her older sister held her closely, tightly, protectively, just in case, just in case…

Helma-Rar dreamed…

His wings took him into the emerald reaches.

The air tasted delicious, moist and watery.

Below, lakes and rivers nestled among the green landscape of trees and rolling hills like sparkling flashes of light.

Beside him sailed a ship. Her wings gigantic, elegant, his mother was wrinkled and beautiful and vividly crimson, the most gargantuan ship owning the sky at that and any other time.

He stretched his long wings and revelled in the sensation. No Colonial sniper threatened him in his high-air flying. He slipped his spear-gun from its holster and let it fall earthwards. He watched its slow descent as it turned over and over, headed for the sparkling blue of a sun-blazing lake. He unveiled the pink baby inside of his belly-pouch and transferred it, mid-air, into the waiting embrace of his mother.

Together, he and his mother watched the weapon fall, and when it was lost in the shimmering distance they turned to examine the tiny baby with her soft eyes. And Helma-Rar felt something in his chest lighten, tear away from him and drift off into greenness like an old thought or memory…

When they awoke, a path had appeared.

A narrow, balding trail leading off through the overhanging trees to the east. Beyond them the morning light shone brilliantly, enticingly. They exchanged sleep-blurred glances, struck anew with the awe of this place. They scrambled to their feet, wiping the sleep from their eyes, and looked, incredulous.

A wooden sign that hadn't been there in the night stood amid the tall grass and colourful nodding flowers as well, its message carved deeply into its fabric in a patient looping scrawl.

They stared at the sign together, the young boy helping them all with the longer words, because the boy had his first few years of schooling done, unlike most people he ran into.

"We the sufferers have gathered here. We the once-broken, convened in this valley haven long ago, and here we shall remain, until the end of times arrives and sets us free of our bad memories. Welcome, or, perhaps, be gone…"

They stood in awe a while. The world about them was still, only the distant whirring of insects in the trees, the grass. A wind gusted, stirring their clothes and the branches surrounding them.

They looked down the sun-stippled forest path, and saw their ghosts, waiting.

"My God," murmured the father. "It's true. It's all true."

They saw them through the trees, down in the valley beyond: hanging like peculiar hazy cumulus low over the sloping plane: thousands of spectral lights, ephemeral and shimmering among the tall-grass and sparse trees and tumbleweeds drifting like gigantic spiders over the valley floor; intangible orbs and eddies and halos of light whose languid movements floating over the grass and among the flowers carried a melancholic deliberation, an indisputable sentience.

The path upon which they stood was verdant on either side, and canopied overhead with entwined tree branches. They felt safe beneath this shelter, where no eye might find them, judge them.

"We got to think," said the man, shielding his far-roving eyes with his crab-hand. "About exactly what we're going to do now. We got a lot of thinking ahead of us."

"You know what the stories say," murmured Harry Dalmar quietly. "This road isn't for everyone. Not many make the walk. Just look at the place. A dead sea over there."

They followed his squinting eyes and saw the graveyard plane to the west: bones burning in the shimmering heat, the calcified remains of countless wanderers making a rolling landscape upon the earth, baking in the early morning sunlight. The unworthy or the unprepared. The weak or the too-strong. Among the bonescape, riddling its white-grey surface, sunlight glinted dully from countless implements of violence: rifles new and old, pistols and daggers and sabres and spear-guns, like an exhibit chronicling a history of inter-species relations in the universe.

Harry Dalmar laid a tentative step forward along the path, but Big Darla stopped him with a hand on his elbow. He recoiled at her touch, the unfamiliar warm feel of it on his skin, so foreign this kind of intimacy. His eyes found hers, and he noticed suddenly how pretty she was, beneath her fleshy cheeks and many hills of chins. Maybe he could love her, too.

Her whisper was emphatic, frightened. "Let's not make a mistake now. Let's not become skeletons today, okay?" And she un-slung her rifle, and tossed it from her into the fringe of the skeleton-field, adding to its collection of silenced weaponry.

Harry Dalmar eyed her nervously, shaking his head a little. "I don't know, lady. I don't think so," taking another step in the direction of the valley, and then another and another. "I don't know if I feel right about going down there without no…"

Something roared.

They became still in their places, frozen bodies and numbed minds. Nothing stirred in the forest, only the deep roar that they felt seeping upwards from the earth itself, and from the air and trees, too, it seemed. And a moment later the sound had ceased.

Eventually, they all breathed again, casting shivering glances to the skeleton-field on one side, and then longer looks along the canopied path before them and the openness of the alley shimmering beyond.

Harry Dalmar had stumbled back several steps, throwing his weapon away from him like an accursed thing when the deep roar had begun. Now that it had ceased, its absence left the forest around them in a huge and deep silence. He stammered apologetically, "I don't want no trouble from this place. I don't want to bring anything at all like that here. You were right, Darla. That was a warning…like we got to watch what we do here in this place. It's not…This isn't the Colonies. Or the spaceports and slum towns, and Extermination Worlds. This…This place isn't those places."

They nodded at Harry Dalmar's wise words, silently.

Helma-Rar slipped his gun from its sheath. The group watched in awe the strength in the Varkoom's arm as he hurled it skyward, to join the ancient graveyard of weapons and bones, far, far out on the plain. The boy's eyes twinkled in admiration. He liked how this Varkoom was different from the ones he'd always heard people tell about. This one carried human babies in his belly and threw his weapon away because peace was better than shooting up the quiet morning and daytime. He liked this Varkoom alright.

They felt it beneath their feet.

They felt it course through their bodies, rattling them deeply. A distant tremor, rising quickly and quickly in volume. The roar returned, only so much louder. Filled with fury, indignation. A bellow from within the earth beneath their feet. A warning or reprimand. The voice of the world on which they stood making itself known, explaining some little part of itself to these new searchers.

They turned, and saw the man with his Old World shotgun, sunlight glinting from its long stalk where he levelled it at Helma-Rar's bright red chest. The man's eyes sighting along the sleek barrel unwaveringly. Hatred burning there lividly. His lips a tightly-drawn line stabbing across his unshaven face, grimacing with his disdain.

"I got you, Varkoom," his words whispered, low and heatedly. "I got you dead on, cocksucker." His finger tightened on the trigger, and he whispered, "You took the sun, demon. You took the sun from me, and now…." He trailed off, his eyes burning.

Helma-Rar stood rigidly in place, stooping to lay the baby he'd been cradling onto the grass beside him, out of harm's way. Then he stood once more to his full height, chest thrust forward, head grazing the tree branches, eyes watching the man's, grimly, proudly.

The grass beneath them shook. Fruits dropped from the trees over their heads, pelting them like a heavy rain. Birds scattered frantically, their anxious cries adding to the chaos. The warning in the planet was a cacophony. The new searchers toppled like pins in its throes, but for the man with the gun, and the Varkoom. It deafened them, put tears in their eyes as they awaited their unfathomable end.

And the man lowered the shotgun, and hurled it up and away from himself and into the graveyard field.

The earth trembled a while longer, an uneasy grumbling, a fading thunder, and then was no more. Birds sang again, nervously. Insects buzzed like electricity. The searchers looked about themselves in awe. Big Darla's Lucky Lecki lizard poked his tiny bullet-head from the pocket of her dusty coat, and blinked his revolving eyes in the sunlight.

"We got a long way to walk still," said the father to his son, and to the Varkoom, and to the others, his ruined hand gesturing down the balding trail and the valley beyond. "We got time to get to know each other ahead of us, I'm guessing. We got time to get to know each other real well. The good stuff and the bad, and how come each of us is here today." He looked to the Varkoom, noting how it once again cradled the human child so gently to its massive breast, so lovingly. He laid a hand, his good hand, with all of its fingers, on his son's shoulder, and squeezed, clumsily yet warmly, winning him a confused smile from the boy.

They stood in stunned silence, puzzle pieces baking in the air, confused as to how to arrange themselves for answers, perhaps only dimly aware that their tenuous union may have been clue enough. A fat girl, a rapist, a winged demon or angel, and a father and son, all with aching thoughts and breaking hearts, stepping into the path together. Stirring dust and ghosts. Bathed in the blood of the sun-emerging sky of dawn. Steeling themselves to drift among spirits, the mysterious valley's and their own, toward their dreams of peace while around their ears sang the songs of their pasts. Making their way, slowly, surely, towards truth or revelation, towards peace or lush trees convened like a living roof over Paradise, or maybe these things were one and the same.

All fled, all done, so finally lift us on the pyre
The feast is over, and the lamps expire
The heavy red pages all have dried
and here is left a book…

Alexander Zelenyj is the author of the short fiction collection, *Experiments At 3 Billion A.M.*, published by Eibonvale Press, and the novel, *Black Sunshine*, published by Fourth Horseman Press. *Songs For The Lost* is his third book. He lives in Windsor, Ontario, Canada, and sings songs of joy and woe in equal measure. His online home can be found at www.alexanderzelenyj.com.